One Last Dance

ALSO BY MARDO WILLIAMS

BIOGRAPHY/MEMOIR
Maude (1883–1993): She Grew Up with the Country
(Cloth)

CHILDREN'S STORYBOOK
Great-Grandpa Fussy and the Little Puckerdoodles
(Illustrated by Yukiko Mishima)

ONE LAST DANCE

It's Never Too Late to Fall in Love

A NOVEL

by Mardo Williams

with his daughters,
Kay and Jerri Williams

CALLIOPE PRESS
New York

This is a work of fiction. Names, characters, places, and incidents are either the product of the authors' imaginations or are used fictitiously, and any resemblance to actual persons living or dead, business establishments, events, or locales is entirely coincidental.

Published by Calliope Press. For information, contact Calliope Press, Post Office Box 2408, New York, NY 10108-2408; phone (212) 564-5068; fax (212) 563-7859; credit card orders 1-800-431-1579.

For information about special discounts for bulk purchases, contact Calliope Press.

   Library of Congress Cataloging-in-Publication Data
Williams, Mardo.
   One last dance : a novel / by Mardo Williams with Kay and Jerri Williams.—1st ed.
   p. cm.
   ISBN-13: 978-0-9649241-4-7 (alk. paper)
   ISBN-10: 0-9649241-4-5 (alk. paper)
   1. Older people—Fiction. I. Williams, Kay, 1933- II. Williams, Jerri, 1938- III. Title.

PS3573.I44995054 2005
813'.54—dc22

                                                          2005042014

www.CalliopePress.com

Printed in the United States on acid free paper

9 8 7 6 5 4 3 2 1

First Edition

Interior Design by C. Linda Dingler

CONTENTS

Book IV - The Hospital

Book V - Family Business

Book VI - The Accident

Book VII - Other Arrangements

FOREWORD

When our dad, Mardo Williams, was 92, he sat down at his computer and began his first novel. How hard could it be? He'd been a writer for over seventy years, first as a journalist, then as a teller of tales. He was writing *One Last Dance*, he said, to inspire old folks not to sit in a corner and wait for life to happen, but to go full speed at life, and yes, even have a love affair.

At the time he was a widower, living with a "significant other," a woman he'd become reacquainted with while touring with *Maude (1883-1993): She Grew Up with the Country*, his biography/memoir about his mother, written by him at 88 and published by Calliope Press in 1996. The way Dad tells it, "Ann invaded my home on the pretext that I autograph her copy of *Maude*. We talked of past experiences at *The Columbus Dispatch*, where we'd both worked. Then she threw her arms around me and suggested we share the lonely moments of our lives together!" For parts of two years they shared living quarters, expenses, and chores, saw movies, and even went to dances when, as Dad once laughed, she wasn't "too weak to hold me up."

Dad wrote much of this novel between media engagements, book signings, and hospitalizations. He more than believed in the book. He was consumed by it. He kept plugging away at it despite hip replacement and sinus surgeries, congestive heart failure, and pneumonia that wouldn't go away. He had a great deal he wanted to say about the landscape of aging, and what it means to be in your nineties with the body failing and the mind and spirit still wanting it all. And he wanted to say it as humorously as possible. Blind from macular degeneration, he was forced to dictate the last chapters of the first draft.

The three of us planned to work together on the second draft, our now sightless Dad revising as we read aloud to him, chapter by chapter.

For some time, he'd mulled over how the book should end, upbeat or down or in between. He decided he wanted a positive ending and was going to dictate it to us when we three next met. He insisted we finish the book if he couldn't. We promised. Dad died two weeks before we were to start revisions. He was 95.

The two main characters were 100% there. We fleshed out a few others. We completed the ending using his notes. If we reached an impasse, we reread his manuscript and found the clues we needed to continue. Dad's presence was palpable. He was our guide and our inspiration. This is his story, the way he wanted to tell it.

"There's no such thing as being too old," Dad once told an interviewer. "Life is for living, no matter what our age or condition. If we can sing, we should sing. If we can write, we should write. We should always be in search of a new experience, always be ready to commit ourselves to a new interest."

He lived this philosophy right up to the day of his death, February 3, 2001.

His daughters,

Kay Williams
Jerri Williams Lawrence

ACKNOWLEDGMENTS

We thank the writers group, Al Ashforth, P. M. Carlson, Stacy Kaplan, Robert Knightly, Kathleen Treat, and Theasa Tuohy, for their invaluable support and insightful suggestions each step of the way. Our editor at Calliope Press, Eileen Wyman, has been instrumental in shaping the book, offering unstinting encouragement and perceptive comments.

We are grateful to Fred Lawrence, Mara Stark, and Joanna Wolper for their astute and penetrating observations on the completed manuscript, and to Barbara Brett for her wisdom and encouragement throughout the process.

Thanks to Dr. Mack Lipkin, Professor of Medicine at New York University School of Medicine, founder of the American Academy on Physician and Patient, and a pioneer in the field of the doctor/patient relationship, for information on teaching the medical interview.

While the book is fiction, Dad drew inspiration from our late mother Geneva and from friends and relatives who impressed him with their vitality for life and sense of humor about growing old: Fern Smith, Doris Barnhart, the late Erma Bowman, the late Jackie Ballinger, and the late Austin Williams.

Special thanks go to Ann Davis who shared living quarters with Dad (at his Florida home and her Columbus home) as he wrote portions of the first draft of this novel. And we pay tribute to the late Opal Welch of the Westerville Retirement Center, who shared meals, walks, and companionship with Dad during his stay there.

BOOK I

GETTING TOGETHER

1

A Violent Encounter

At first Morgan saw only movement; colorless shapes milling about. They turned into people.

A woman using a walker labored his way. Her eyes were anxious, her ankles so swollen that her legs looked like thick poles. A pinch-faced gentleman leaned on a counter behind which a receptionist sat. "Where's my wife?" he asked petulantly. Two women, slumped side by side on the couch like two rag dolls, stared forlornly into space.

Morgan took his handkerchief from his pocket and patted his forehead. *What am I doing here? I'm too young for this.* He whirled around in a panic and dashed back through the double doors, heading for the sunshine.

At the same time a woman in a yellow dress hurried up the walkway. The two strangers collided.

Morgan's spectacles were knocked askew. The large white box the woman held so carefully in front of her flipped and was crushed against her chest. She stumbled and almost fell. When he grabbed her by the arm to steady her, she pulled away, clutching at the box as it slowly slid down the front of her, opening as it went, leaving blobs of white and red icing on her bright yellow dress. "Oh, no," she wailed. "Look what you've done." Chunks of white cake with red and yellow roses smeared the sidewalk leading up to the entrance.

Her face turned pink. She called out to a passerby, "He's ruined the cake for Effie's party."

Morgan, still stunned by the collision, took off his glasses and tried to bend the earpiece back in shape. It snapped. He stuffed it in his pocket and held his glasses on with one hand as he looked down at his pant leg, streaked with icing.

She gave him a scorching glance. "If you hadn't jerked my arm . . ." Tears welled in her eyes. "Now we have no cake for Effie's party."

"Let me pay you for the cake." Flustered, he drew out his wallet, cracked it open, and held out a twenty-dollar bill.

She ignored the bill in his outstretched hand. Her gray-blonde curls bounced as she rummaged furiously in the purse hanging from her shoulder.

She's pretty high strung, he thought. Feeling like a fool, he put away the money. His glasses felt lopsided on his face. He took them off and jammed them in his pocket with the broken earpiece.

"You've also ruined my dress," she snapped, whipping a handkerchief from her bag and scrubbing at grease stains on her shoulder.

"You nearly broke my glasses," Morgan spluttered. "And this is my new suit." She had a spot of icing on her cheek. He resisted the urge to reach over and brush it away.

Half the cake was still in the box and the message was almost intact: *appy 100th Birth*. "Some of this may be salvageable," Morgan grunted, feeling more and more embarrassed as he became aware that people on their way in and out of the center were stopping to gawk.

He heard a passerby say, "Looks like just another domestic argument." A man plunked himself down on a nearby bench to watch. "Poor devil," he said to a lady beside him. "She's trying to get rid of him. She'll visit him here once a week and someone else will do the dirty work."

"That's unfair," the lady broke in. "You think women are to blame for everything wrong in this world."

Did they think he was here for their entertainment? "Why don't you folks go on home?" he flared. "This is just between me and"—he groped for a word—"the broad." He stooped, jiggling the cake box to shift the broken pieces toward the middle. With some smoothing-over of the icing to connect the chunks, there'd be a perfectly healthy-looking half a cake.

Just then she bent to rub the icing off her skirt. Her shoulder bag slid down her arm, knocking him on the side of the head.

He looked up in surprise as a cascade of cosmetics, credit cards, a checkbook, hairpins, papers, and assorted trinkets rained down on him and scattered across the walk.

The woman muttered, "If you'd been looking where you were going, none of this would have happened."

"Drama queen," he mumbled to himself.

He helped her gather up the items, thinking the quicker they were collected, the faster he could be on his way.

His hand accidentally brushed hers and their heads nearly touched. They were eye-to-eye.

Her cheeks were flushed, he noticed, her blue eyes blazing. She was a damn good-looking woman.

She stood, snapped her purse shut, and hurried toward the parking lot.

Face flaming, Morgan gathered up the residue of cake and icing from the walk and dumped the box in the trash, a clear indication to himself at least that he remained a gentleman under stress. His eyeglasses were broken, his hands were sticky, and his pants and shoes had frosting on them.

Now what? *What the hell*, he told himself, *you're here. You don't want to be a burden to your friends.* He had to admit that sometimes in the night he woke up in terror, knowing that old age would eventually get him. It was the beast in the corner, waiting to dig its claws in him and sink its teeth into his neck.

On that beautiful July day in Columbus, Ohio, the birds were singing, the flowers were in bloom. As if he were facing the firing squad, Morgan squared his shoulders and walked into Whispering Pines Retirement Center and Nursing Home for the second time that afternoon. "I have an appointment. I'm a little late." The receptionist's eyes were merry behind her glasses. Had she heard the commotion and peeked out the door?

His face felt hot. He hoped he wasn't blushing. Had she seen him come in and hightail it out of the place once he saw the lethargic crowd? If he'd stuck to his guns, he'd be on a tour of the center now and would have missed that awful fight.

The receptionist lifted the phone and dialed. "Mr. Morgan is here for his appointment." She looked up at him, nodding. "She'll see you in five minutes."

He asked her where the restroom was. He'd clean up first.

❦

Dixie fled to her car, gunned the motor, and drove from the parking lot onto the street, tires squealing. She slowed after seeing a patrol car parked a short distance away and forced herself to proceed more calmly.

That splendid cake, with the magnificent red and yellow roses—Effie's favorite colors. She'd never be able to find another cake that lovely on such short notice.

Her heart was pounding. That man was obnoxious, overbearing, and insulting. He'd almost knocked her down. He'd ruined her dress, destroyed the beautiful cake, and threw money at her as if she were a beggar! Then he had the gall to call her names.

She increased speed on the open road and found herself watching in the rearview mirror for flashing lights that would warn her of a patrolman in pursuit.

She reached for the cell phone and speed-dialed a number. She needed to talk this over with Vera, her closest friend. Sympathetic Vera.

The phone was ringing when she glanced at the car in front of her and saw the bumper sticker, YOU COULD DRIVE BETTER WITH THAT PHONE UP YOUR ASS. That teed her off again and she pulled out into the left lane, almost hit a car, and darted around the vehicle with the offending slogan, waving the phone at the woman driver. Dixie gave her the finger and watched for signs of road rage. When the woman just grinned, Dixie sped on.

"Hello, hello, is anyone there?" Dixie heard Vera's gravelly voice ask through the receiver.

"Hi, it's me," Dixie said breathlessly, jamming the phone against her ear.

"You sound awful. What happened?" Vera asked.

"I bumped into a man, literally."

"In the car? Is he hurt? Are you okay?"

"No, yes. I mean, not in the car. On foot. And now I'm late for Effie's party. And I'm in charge. I'll tell you about it later. What are you doing at four? If you're not busy, I'll bring by a six-pack and some chips."

"It's a date," Vera said.

At the bakery, Dixie picked up three small cakes to replace the destroyed sheet cake meant for fifty people. The clerk squirted a couple of flowers on each and wrote a quick *Happy 100*. Dixie felt like crying. The cake for Effie had been specially designed for her: ornate, dignified, and old-fashioned. Effie didn't have much to look forward to, confined to a wheelchair the way she was. But she did look forward to her birthday parties. And 100 was a very special birthday!

Dixie rushed back to the retirement center. With the three cakes stacked under her chin, she carefully entered the front door. She glanced furtively around to make sure that dreadful man wasn't lurking in the hallways.

Flushed and apologetic, she swept into Effie's birthday celebration only thirty minutes late. Multicolored balloons floated gaily throughout the party room, crowded with Effie's friends, most of them residents of the center.

Coffee was perking in the urn. Dixie was thankful she'd decorated and started preparations before heading out to pick up the cake, the first cake, that is.

She lined up the three small cake boxes beside the paper plates, opening each lid, feeling fresh disappointment at the sight of these second-rate substitutes.

Effie wheeled herself over to look and clapped her hands. "Scrumptious!"

"You should have seen the one that got away," Dixie began, but didn't want to get all worked up again. "Effie, you look gorgeous! Who did your hair?" She gave her a hug and kissed her on the cheek.

"You look pretty gorgeous yourself, Dixie. Full of pep and ginger. Wish you could pass along some of it to me."

Dixie laughed. She liked being with Effie. She always made her feel like a spring chicken. Well, she was a spring chicken compared to Effie. Only 79. And a young 79, at that!

⊙✝⊙

"I'm Bryce Morgan, but everyone calls me Morgan." He shook hands with Mrs. Fontana, activities director of Whispering Pines, a matronly lady with a pale, square face and very black hair. Now that he'd calmed down, he took a second look around him. The place seemed bright and airy, with comfortable overstuffed furniture grouped around a fireplace, a kind of simulated cozy living room.

"We light a fire in winter," Mrs. Fontana said, smiling. "People sit around and visit after a meal."

Morgan nodded. A woman and a man sat at opposite ends of the makeshift living room. The woman fidgeted endlessly with the ruffles on her blouse. The man dozed, his mouth slightly open. With each breath, his upper set of teeth moved in and out between his lips.

Mrs. Fontana pointed to her left. "There's the dining room. People have moved in here from other retirement villages just because of our wonderful meals." She beamed. "We're also known for our friendliness."

Mrs. Fontana turned to her right, with a gesture toward Morgan to follow. They passed four women playing bridge with oversize playing cards. One woman was hooked up to oxygen. Another had her neck in a brace. In a nearby chair, a woman with bright red lipstick and painted nails called out, "Hello, Mrs. Fontana," her curious eyes fastening on Morgan.

The activities director waved, speaking softly to Morgan, "The women far outnumber the men. You'll be very popular here."

A shrunken couple, gray-faced, each with a cane, stood by the elevator, holding hands, smiling a greeting.

Morgan and Mrs. Fontana rode up silently with them in the elevator. At the second floor, Morgan held the door while the couple laboriously inched their way out into the hall. *What am I doing here?* he asked himself again. He had no real ailments, just a touch of arthritis and asthma, kept in check by his inhalers. Okay, so he was 89, but everyone told him he seemed at least ten years younger.

"This is independent living," Mrs. Fontana said as they exited at the third floor. "Are you interested in something unfurnished or furnished?"

Feeling glummer and glummer, he followed her down a hallway. "I have furniture."

She unlocked a door. "Our one bedroom." He stepped into the apartment. It smelled shut up and dusty, and it was smaller than where he lived now. The drapes and carpeting were drab. The kitchen was just a sink, cupboards, and a small refrigerator. Not that he did much cooking. Mrs. Fontana seemed to be waiting for his comment. "Umm hmm," he grunted. Dismal, he wanted to say. Well, furniture would make a difference.

"If you like, you can bring in a microwave," Mrs. Fontana offered. "We allow them only in independent living." She shrugged apologetically. "We don't want a fire."

They left the model apartment and walked down another hallway.

This place is a maze, he thought. He wondered how many residents got lost trying to find their apartments.

"Now we're in the assisted living wing." Mrs. Fontana waved to a woman who sat on a gaily flowered couch, wheelchair beside her. She was missing her leg from the knee down. She massaged her stump, the prosthesis resting on the floor.

Mrs. Fontana whispered to Morgan, "Game soul." Then she turned into yet another hallway.

Morgan trudged bleakly behind. He scarcely believed his ears when the sounds of music and laughter drifted his way.

"Our party room," Mrs. Fontana said. "They're having a birthday celebration for our oldest resident, Effie Cartwright. She's 100 today."

This was more like it, Morgan thought, as he peered through the open door. Balloons rose and dipped festively in the room. He recognized the music, "In the Mood." Beyond a group of people laughing and talking, he saw a familiar bright yellow dress. Seated beside an old lady in a wheelchair, helping her open gifts, was the gray-blonde woman who'd hit him with her purse. She glanced up in the middle of a smile. Their eyes met. Morgan touched his forehead, as if tipping his hat.

Her smile faded. She pointedly ignored his greeting.

"Oh, you know Dixie?" Mrs. Fontana asked.

So her name is Dixie. "Does she live here?" he asked.

The activities director shook her head. "She works for us part-time. Helps with the newsletter, bingo, the parties, reads to a few residents who are blind. They love her!"

"I see." So she could be lovable if she tried.

"Would you like to fill out an application?" Mrs. Fontana asked when they were back in her office.

"I'm not sure," he sighed. "I have an apartment with a lease."

"Do you live alone?"

He nodded.

"Independent living would be the same as having your own apartment."

He tried to smile but his face felt frozen.

She added, "Then when the next stage of your life arrives, you'll move down the hall into assisted living. We even have a convalescent center. If you break a hip or whatever," her red lips parted, showing very white teeth, "you'll return to us, your home, for rehab and skilled nursing care. The beauty of it is you'll already be acquainted with everyone."

Except for those who've died, he thought, and the new batch who've filed into this elephant burial ground.

She moved some papers around on her desk. "Why don't you come back for a meal? Our food is delicious."

"Maybe I will." He shook her hand and left her office. He had a lot to think about. Luckily, there was time. He sank down on the couch in front of the fireplace, his head spinning.

A heavy woman lumbered his way. She collapsed beside him. "You're new," she said, slightly out of breath.

"I was just visiting a friend," he lied.

She leaned toward him. "I'm pretty good today. Except from my waist down. Hips and knees are bad. Nothing wrong with my head. A month ago I gave the supervisor a list of things missing. She said I was getting confused, that her girls didn't steal. She thinks it's me, putting things away and forgetting where." Frowning, she gave her head a quick shake.

Morgan nodded warily, sorry he'd lingered.

"I've had girls working for me for twenty years and no one can make me believe if they see something they want, they won't take it—thinking she's old and don't know what she has." Her voice drifted off.

Morgan stood.

She held him with her eyes. "One who works here now used to work for me when I lived at home. Since I've been making such a fuss over all my stuff that's missing, I've found three things hidden around my apartment that I missed from home after she quit working for me. She'd put them back."

Morgan waved good-bye.

"Nice talking to you," she called as he walked away.

He was sweating profusely. He wiped his face with his handkerchief and loosened his tie. His chest felt tight. As soon as he was out the front door, he drew his Albuterol inhaler out of his suit pocket and took a deep puff. He'd follow up at home with a puff of Azmacort. The air was humid today, full of allergens.

ॐ

Dixie and Morgan each savored the drama of their violent encounter and each told friends a slightly different version of how they met.

"She broke my glasses and ruined my new suit," Morgan laughed over the phone to his good friend Nate. "I managed to keep both of us from falling to the concrete. We could have saved the cake—half of it anyway. When I suggested that, she slugged me with her purse." He added, "She might be attractive under other circumstances."

Dixie wasn't so kind. "He was rude and boorish," she told her friend Vera when she met with her at four.

"What did he do that was so bad?" Vera asked, opening a can of German beer for each.

Dixie enumerated. "He ran into me so hard I almost fell. He destroyed Effie's cake. Look at my dress! It has to be dry-cleaned. He had the nerve to throw money at me. My purse was torn from my shoulder. Everything fell out. It was a mess. And then he had the gall to stop by Effie's party!"

"You're kidding. He crashed the party?"

"Not exactly. But he stood outside the room and waved at me!"

"He actually had the nerve?" Vera giggled.

"I hope I never see that oaf again." Dixie shook her head. "Why should anyone, unless he's demented, live in a retirement center anyway? He looked perfectly healthy."

"Maybe he didn't live there, but was just visiting."

Dixie took a long sip of beer.

"Was he good looking?" Vera asked with a sly smile.

Dixie frowned. "I didn't notice, I was so upset."

Vera's eyes twinkled behind her tortoise-shell glasses. "I have a feeling it was probably as much your fault as it was his. Maybe you could sort of straighten things out with him. You know, if he's cute."

"Are you serious?" Dixie exploded. "He left no doubt he considered me a royal pain. Of course, he could do no wrong. It was all my fault." After a few moments, she sighed, "Anyway, I've almost given up hope after that last fiasco with that—playboy."

Vera chortled. "You mean the guy who said he'd like to move in with you but he'd be gone maybe three or four nights a week?" Vera lit a cigarette and inhaled deeply.

"You think he's married?" Dixie asked.

"Find out."

"I don't know even know his name. I don't even want to know his name. Stop smiling," Dixie told her friend. She finished her beer just as Vera's husband Paul breezed in from the golf course.

That night, Dixie performed her bedtime ritual. First, she took her pill, that important, not-to-be forgotten pill, and said silent thanks for the gift of another precious day. She cold-creamed her face, wiped it off with a tissue, and then used cleansing lotion. It left her face feeling tight and shiny. She peered into the bathroom mirror. She looked darn good, considering all that life had doled out to her. She slipped on her nightgown. In bed, she brooded, deciding she'd make no effort to seek this man out. She'd let things develop as they would.

2

Mixed Messages

The next week, as Dixie went about her duties at the retirement center, she kept an eye out for that rude man, relieved not to see him again, but disappointed too. On Friday, she spotted him entering the dining area. That lout wouldn't be bad looking, she decided, if he'd get rid of that scowl.

She busied herself at the residents' bulletin board for forty-five minutes, arranging the notices and posting social events for the week. Out of the corner of her eye, she saw his tall figure exit the dining room and head toward her. She was careful to look the other way.

"Why, hello there," he said, as if he'd just noticed her.

Dixie turned to face him. She studied him seriously.

"That was a helluva way to start a relationship!" He had a cocky smile on his face.

Relationship. What nerve! What did he think she was? Some kind of tart? Without a word, she turned and headed out the front door of the center. She wouldn't give him the satisfaction of a reply here, in full view of staff and residents.

He was right behind her. He followed her into the parking lot. She had no choice but to climb in her car, which she did, and pretend to be about to start it but, of course, her keys were in her purse, back in the activities office.

He tapped on the car window.

She sighed, rolling it down. "Yes?"

"Give me a chance?" he pleaded.

"Well . . ." she began, waiting to see if he'd apologize and admit everything was as much his fault as hers.

He gave her a friendly chuckle. "I'm sorry for the way I acted."

He'd been crude, obnoxious, and called her names.

"And I'm sorry I called you a broad." He grinned crookedly. "My only excuse is, you rudely interrupted my thoughts while I was pondering an important question. Should I continue living alone or give up and enter a retirement center?"

"I see you were able to fix your glasses," she said coolly.

"How's your dress?" he grimaced.

"It's at the cleaner's."

"I hope it isn't ruined," he said.

"Me too. It's my favorite dress." She leaned over to rifle through the glove compartment, pretending to search for something. Maybe he'd get the point and leave.

He stuck his hand through the open window. "I'm Morgan."

What else could she do? "Dixie Valentine." She shook his hand. "Morgan what?"

"Morgan," he replied, looking down at her with a teasing grin.

"Morgan Morgan? Sounds like a pseudonym." He was probably getting a crimp in his back, bending down that way to talk through the window. But she'd feel like a fool getting out of the car now when she was supposed to be driving away.

"Aubrey Bryce Morgan," he chuckled. "My mother read it in a book and liked it. Friends call me Morgan. I hope you will too."

"You're thinking of moving into the center?" She was melting but trying not to show it. He was almost handsome when he smiled.

"I came by for a meal. I've heard so much about their delicious food." He rolled his eyes.

"Well, Morgan," Dixie smiled, relenting, "I have to tell you. The kitchen here is a work in progress."

"Aha!" Morgan exclaimed. "Spoken like a connoisseur of fine dining! And a point on which we agree! A definite sign we should get together soon."

She looked at him closely, inspecting the laugh lines around his mouth. He had full lips, heavy-lidded eyes, and a slightly hooked nose that gave him a patrician look. Pink scalp showed through his thinning hair, combed down flat today, probably held in place with hair gel.

"Look, let me give you a call," he persisted.

"I'm in the book," she said lightly.

"I'll look for it," he replied, adopting her same careless tone, and then he turned away.

She watched him walk to his automobile. He moved at a brisk pace, his shoulders held high.

She waited until he drove off, then sheepishly climbed out of her car. She rushed back to the center, took the elevator to the second floor, and burst into the activities room. "Sorry," she mouthed to Beth, who'd already doled out root beer floats to the assembled residents.

"Don't worry about it." Beth waved her hand.

Dixie scurried around the room, distributing bingo cards.

At three-thirty, she hurried home. The rest of the day she listened for the telephone, willing it to ring. You're behaving like a teenager, she told herself. For all you know, he might be married. He said he lived alone, a voice in her head replied.

 ❦

That night Morgan had dinner with Nate Radebaugh, his good friend of thirty years.

"How was your free lunch today?" Nate asked.

"The food was terrible." Morgan hungrily attacked his omelet. "I ate with two other inmates. One was an engineer who'd supervised oil pipeline installations in the Middle East. The other had taught at OSU. Both were World War II vets, men with interesting tales to tell. Instead, they talked about the weather, and went on to 'supervise' the installation of a new roof across the street. 'Well, we got the house under shelter before the rain came,' observed one. Then," Morgan chuckled, breaking apart his roll and buttering it, "they turned their attention to a nuthatch that walked the window ledge. It stopped every few inches to peck on the pane and look inside. 'I'll bet that's the bird Billie has been feeding,' said the engineer. 'Billie?' asked the other. 'You know Billie. She's the nurse who sometimes walks the grounds with a small bird either on her arm or diving at her in search of seed in her hand.' They didn't say another word until dessert, when they asked for seconds on ice cream and cake."

Nate shrugged and gave a short laugh. "So? To each his own."

"They have stories to tell," Morgan replied indignantly. "Instead, they're spectators, looking on at life outside the window, and eating too much junk." He nibbled at a french fry and let it drop to his plate when he saw Nate's pointed grin.

Nate asked, "What's the plan?"

"I have four months to decide. I'll either renew my apartment lease or check into the old-folks home."

The two ate silently for a few minutes.

"I had another run-in with that wild woman. You know, the one who bumped into me and broke my glasses."

"Oh?" Nate said.

Morgan laughed. "The last time she hit me with her purse. This time, she ran away."

"No kidding?" Nate's eyes lit up.

"First she pretended she didn't see me. When I said hello, she dashed out to the parking lot and tried to hide in her car. I followed her, and at least got the chance to introduce myself and apologize. She seemed to expect an apology. If I decide to move into the center, I don't want to be meeting her every day and be subjected to that icy stare."

Nate grinned. "Why don't you take her out and get acquainted? It's time you found someone who'd give you some tender loving care."

"Tender loving care! Are you nuts?" Morgan exploded. He didn't want to admit to his friend he'd broached the subject of a date already. Her response had been less than enthusiastic. "Torture would be more like it! She has a terrible temper."

"So do you." Nate laughed. "She could make life interesting."

After they finished dinner, Nate drove Morgan to his apartment. "This woman you met—what's her name?" Nate asked.

"Dixie Valentine."

"Call her up. Who knows? Maybe Dixie Valentine is worth some effort."

"Yeah, yeah." Morgan opened the car door. "I'm almost 90. How long have I got?"

"No one knows how long anyone's got," Nate replied gloomily, "at any age."

Morgan knew Nate was thinking about his wife, Irene, only 61, dead from cancer, gone only a few months. He envied his friend his happy marriage. Morgan had been divorced for—what was it now? God, almost forty years.

As Morgan exited the car, he mused, "I hear if you can get through 90, you have a good chance of making 100." He thought of the old woman in her wheelchair at the birthday party. Would he want to make 100, stuck in a wheelchair in the assisted living section of Whispering Pines?

⚛

Three days later, Morgan picked up an application packet for admission to Whispering Pines. He stood by the reception desk, thumbing through the thick sheaf of papers to find the list of costs. In addition to his room and board, he noted that assistance, when he reached that decrepit stage, would cost him by the piece: eight dollars for helping him with his bath, four dollars for wheeling him down to lunch. He supposed there'd be a charge for giving him an enema if he needed it. He searched but couldn't find that service listed.

On his way to his car, he saw Dixie, clicking up the walkway in her heels, cool and elegant in a blue dress and matching hat. Suddenly elated, he waved.

"Why didn't you call?" she demanded. "Are you one of those men who always let the woman take the initiative?"

"I didn't want you to think I had nothing else to do," he teased. She looked stunning in that hat of hers, wide-brimmed, navy blue with a wide white band covered with blue polka dots. He could smell her perfume. "Are you hungry?" he asked.

"Starving."

"How about the pancake place?"

"It's too hot for pancakes," she said. "Let's go to the Village Inn."

"The Village Inn?" She had expensive tastes.

She gave him a huge smile. "Whatever you suggest."

"The Copper Skillet," he said emphatically.

She sighed dubiously. "How about Bottilini's?"

It was too hot for pasta, he was about to say. But he agreed, so as not to seem mule-headed.

They walked toward the parking lot, debating over who would drive whose car. Morgan won that round. He soon regretted his victory. His ancient four-door sedan smoked and rattled all the way to the restaurant.

"How old is your car?" she asked.

"Twenty-one," he replied. "Old enough to drink—a quart of oil every three days." He'd made up his mind not to invest in another car until he knew for sure what he'd be doing.

Everyone at the restaurant knew Dixie—the man behind the cash register, the waiters, even a few patrons seated at nearby tables.

"You're a popular gal," Morgan said, pleased. He winced when he picked up the menu and saw the prices.

"I'll have the chicken parmigiana," Dixie said. "Try it. It's out of this world."

"Okay." He noticed it was the least expensive item on the menu that wasn't pasta. "How about some wine?" What the hell. After all, this was a celebration! He had a date.

She shook her head. "I have to go back to work."

Over lunch, to impress her, he told her he was a graduate of Columbia University in accounting.

"When was that?" she asked.

Morgan pretended he didn't hear her question, worried she'd think him too old. "Despite the fancy degree, I started out as a teller," he said quickly, "moved to Chicago where my career took off, then transferred back here as a bank officer. Not bad for a kid whose dad was a janitor."

"Chicago. I love that town," she said. "Why on earth did you leave?"

"Long story." He could have kicked himself for mentioning Chicago. He'd never been back since his ignominious departure, decades ago. And he never would go back. "Let's hear about you."

"I'm a farmer's daughter, a graduate of secretarial school." She gave him a wry smile. "In those days, it was considered a waste of money to send a girl to college."

Morgan nodded.

"After the war, I was able to land a glamorous job as an executive secretary in a big advertising firm."

After the war meant World War II. Morgan guessed her to be about ten years younger than he was. A ten-year age difference is a lot, he mused, at the beginning and at the end of life.

"In my job I heard plenty of juicy secrets about prominent people here in town." Her blue eyes sparkled.

"Not about me, I hope," he blurted out, trying to sound flirtatious.

She raised an eyebrow.

He felt his face getting red, but continued anyway, "I used to be quite a man about town." He sawed at his chicken. Those days were long over. He remembered vividly what his last girlfriend, Miranda, had said about him eight years ago. All blow and no show.

As they talked further, they found out they both knew a few of the same people, like Barry, Dixie's former boss at the ad agency. He'd been in the Kiwanis Club with Morgan.

"Small world," Dixie said. She glanced at her watch and gasped, "Oh, dear, I'd better get back."

He wanted to pay for lunch, even though it would put a crimp in his budget, but she insisted, "We'll go dutch." She picked up the check. "It's not the forties! Maybe I'll let you pay next time."

Next time! He felt a rush of pleasure. He hadn't lost his touch after all.

On the way back to the center, Morgan's car died at the stoplight. The motor kept running but it wouldn't budge, no matter what gear he put it into. "I think it's the transmission," he said. "I've been having trouble with it." They were a mile from Whispering Pines.

"I'm going to be late for work," Dixie fumed.

A kind motorist pushed them over to the side of the road. "Calm down," Morgan said as Dixie fidgeted. "I'll call Triple A."

"You insisted we take this . . ." Dixie mumbled something that sounded like *junk heap*. "You knew all along it had transmission problems." She sighed and rolled her eyes. "We should have taken my car!"

"Well, we should have gone to the pancake place." He carefully kept his voice even. "We'd not only be back at the center by now, we'd have had better food."

Dixie put her hand to her chest in mock surprise. Was she laughing at him? He sprang out of the car, slammed the door, and walked stiffly across the street. He knocked at the door of a private home and was given permission to use their telephone.

When he returned, the two sat in silence. He rolled down his window. "Stuffy," he mumbled.

"For once, we agree," she said, rolling down her window.

Morgan worked hard to keep from smiling.

After his car had been hooked up to the tow truck, the two squeezed into the front seat of the cab beside the driver. Dixie giggled. "What's so funny?" Morgan asked.

"I just hope someone's looking out the window when we drive up to the center and I get out of this contraption."

Morgan grunted out a laugh. He had to admit this was a more interesting day than he'd had in a long time, sitting shoulder-to-shoulder and thigh-to-thigh with this good-looking woman.

"I'm sorry," he began, as she climbed out of the tow truck. He always seemed to be apologizing to her.

"Next time we'll have pancakes," she said, waving good-bye over her shoulder.

Inside the center, as Dixie made the popcorn and set up the game boards, she made small talk with the residents who were fussy about starting late. Her mind was going a mile a minute. If he really had been a banker, why did he drive that old car? And why did he leave Chicago? And what did that funny look on his face mean when he said he hoped she hadn't heard any scandal about him? Maybe, just maybe, she'd give Barry at the ad agency a call about Aubrey Bryce Morgan.

☙❧

The wind tore through Tony's hair and slammed against his face. Must be almost six g's. Rocket to Mars! He cracked the beer on the seat beside him, gulped down a long swallow, then clamped the can between his legs. He sped down Lake Shore Drive, Springsteen's "Born to Run" blaring, screaming, throbbing in his ears. He zigzagged, switching lanes, passed the navy pier, then slid off onto East Jackson. He beat time on the steering wheel with his hands. There was a looker, a cutie pie, on the corner in very short shorts. He honked and turned to admire her legs.

Cripes! He almost got creamed. He didn't see that stop sign. Better watch it. He had an open can of beer. He needed another day in court like a hole in the head.

He forced himself to slow down. The sun was just coming up. He'd hit the skyway. Sprung from his cage! Yeah, man! Escape to New York City.

He hit the gas. He shot past the Sears Tower, over the Chicago River. Jeez, a siren behind him. Red light flashing. He cleared the bridge, screeched around the corner, careening down a one-way street the wrong way. Did he ditch the cop? No. He was coming up fast behind him. He made a quick right, then left. Now there were two cop cars after him. He felt like someone in a TV car-chase show. He turned the corner again. Dead end up ahead. He was back at the river. He was going around in circles. He was losing control. Next thing he knew the car was wrapped around a street light. He tasted blood. His lip was bleeding.

A cop was in his face, framed in the open window. "Get out!" he barked. "Hands on the hood." He drew his gun. "What you trying to prove?"

"I like to drive when I get stressed out." His head hurt. He must have hit his head.

"What's your name?" asked the other cop.

"Tony."

"We got a report on this plate. Stolen car."

Peckerhead! He'd turned him in!

3

The Inspection

That night after work Dixie drew up a plan. First she'd call Barry, her former boss, at home. She put it off as long as she could. At nine o'clock she dialed the number, her palms perspiring. It rang and rang. Thank God he wasn't there. When he said hello she wanted to hang up, but forced herself to say, "Hi, it's Dixie."

"Dixie! What a surprise! How you been, sweetheart?"

"Good!" she squeaked brightly. "I'm working part-time now at Whispering Pines Retirement Center."

"Lucky them," he drawled.

Same old Barry, good-hearted, full of BS. She relaxed. "We need readers for our sight-impaired residents. Someone to read them the newspapers, their correspondence, write letters . . ." She was hurrying. She forced herself to slow down. "You think Kiwanis might be interested in helping out?"

"I'll find out. I'll bring it up at the next meeting."

"Great!" Get on with it, Dixie, she told herself.

"What else is new?"

She chattered on about the center, the church, her bridge club, hardly listening to what she was saying, sensing his perplexity. They hadn't been in touch since she retired years ago. She took a deep breath. "One other thing. Do you remember someone by the name of"—she pretended to be reading it—"let's see, Aubrey Bryce Morgan? He used to be in Kiwanis, I believe."

"Doesn't ring a bell," he answered.

"He said he knew you." She was disappointed.

"Give me more to go on."

"I think he was an officer at one of the banks in town. Transferred here from Chicago."

"Yeah, yeah. It's coming back to me now—Bryce Morgan, liked to be called Morgan. That's right, he was a banker."

Her spirits perked up.

"Chicago, I don't know about," Barry continued. "He and I were on a couple of fund-raising committees together. This was a few years ago. Seemed like a decent sort."

"Any scuttlebutt, gossip? I mean," she stammered, "he just started seeing a friend of mine."

"Ahhh," Barry said, sounding amused.

"I owe her a favor," she said defensively.

"Look, I'll sniff around. See what I can find out. What's your friend's name? I'll call her."

Damn that Barry! "I'll relay the message," Dixie replied breezily, determined not to let on that she knew he'd guessed the "friend" was her. When Dixie hung up the phone, she felt galvanized. Step One, set in motion. Now on to Step Two: invite Morgan to her home.

⚬✤⚬

Morgan showered and washed his hair. Still in his underwear, he shaved carefully, patted on aftershave, and slicked down his thinning hair. He carefully inspected his best suit. Traces of cake icing still clung to one pant leg. He scrubbed it off with a damp washcloth.

He'd been surprised to get Dixie's phone call last night asking him to brunch today. He'd been hesitant to call her, afraid she might be sore at him for losing his temper on the way home from Bottilini's Friday. If it had bothered her, she hadn't let on. He felt wary too. She seemed to be pushing things. He laughed to himself. She'd been determined they go to the pancake house today. He supposed she wanted to rub it in, since he'd made such a big deal out of their not going there last Friday.

After he dressed, he hung up clothes that had collected in a pile on the floor and cleared dirty dishes off the kitchen table and put them in the sink, keeping an eye out the front window for her car. He didn't want to ask her into his apartment. It was a mess. Dusty furniture. Dirty carpet.

As soon as he saw her red car pull up at the curb, he quickly headed out the front door.

She met him on the walkway, a pained smile on her face. "I came straight here from church. Can I use the john?"

"Of course," he said, graciously, he hoped.

Once she was inside the apartment, he noted that her eyes flicked over the rooms, taking in the newspapers strewn about, the trash—cartons from TV dinners mostly—overflowing the wastebaskets, the crumbs on the coffee table beside his favorite chair, the lint on the carpet. "Lacks the appropriate female touch," he grinned, as he showed her to the bathroom.

"Why not try the appropriate male touch!" she said briskly as she swept into the bathroom and closed the door.

Had he put the lid down? Had he cleaned his whiskers out of the sink? Was his dirty underwear in full view in the bathroom clothes hamper?

He heard her clothes rustle behind the door. He felt as if he were eavesdropping. He went over to the kitchen sink and rinsed dirty dishes so he wouldn't hear her pee.

When she came out of the bathroom and saw him scrubbing away, she smiled her approval. "Better late than never!"

He smiled back sheepishly, stacked the dishes and dried his hands on the dish towel, checking to see if she noticed its grimy condition.

She caught his eye and grinned, a dimple showing in her left cheek.

"Well, you're dressed up!" he said. She wore a green suit that complemented her slim figure.

"So are you."

As he followed her down the flagstone walk, he realized what was different about her today: her hair. It wasn't the usual wavy gray-blonde, but light brown, with a perky youthful-looking cut.

As he climbed into the passenger side, he groaned to himself. These compact foreign cars. Not enough leg room. He'd always believed that Americans should buy American cars, not boost the economy of overseas businesses. When he knew her better he would explain this to her. "Nice car," he said. He guessed it to be about five years old.

"Great mileage," she answered. "If you move your seat back, you'll be more comfortable." She started the engine.

He pushed his seat back and stretched out his legs. "What did you do to your hair?"

"Do you like it?" She took her eyes off the road to look at him. "I thought it would set off my green suit."

"It's different," he said. It made her look younger.

She fluffed it with one hand. "It's a wig," she laughed. "What do you think?"

Now he could see the hair had a stiff and artificially shiny look. He liked her real hair better. He searched for something positive to say. "It does go well with your suit."

A phone rang. Oh, yeah, there it was, in a holder attached to the dashboard.

She held the cell phone to her ear, driving with her left hand. "Vera. Hi! Yes," she said. "Yes," she repeated several times, her eyes shifting Morgan's way.

He waved his hand to motion she should keep her eyes on the road.

"See you then. Bye." Dixie turned to Morgan. "My best friend, Vera. We've been friends forever." She prattled on about Vera.

She's nervous, he realized, that's why she's talking so much. But he didn't want to know this much about Vera. And the way her eyes kept darting from him to the road and back to him was driving him nuts. He breathed a sigh of relief when they finally arrived at the restaurant.

The waitress greeted them and took their order.

"Thanks, Adele," Dixie said as the waitress walked away.

"You know her?" Morgan asked.

Dixie shook her head. "I read her name tag."

Adele was extremely solicitous throughout the meal and once asked Morgan, "Would your wife like another cup of coffee?"

Dixie offered quickly, "We're just good friends." At the same time, Morgan said, "She's not my wife."

They both laughed.

"Bread and butter," Dixie said. "Give me your hand."

Morgan took her hand. Her skin was soft as butter.

"No, like this." She linked her little finger around his. "We both have to make a wish." She closed her eyes, her lips moving silently.

What the heck. He'd wish for more days like this!

Dixie released his little finger and opened her eyes. "To make it come true, we can't tell each other what we wished," she said solemnly.

He nodded, just as serious. He'd play along.

They ate their pancakes and eggs, Dixie exclaiming throughout how much she liked the restaurant's brand of maple syrup.

"So, what's happening with your car?" she asked when they'd finished eating.

"They'll be able to patch up the transmission, they say. It's like throwing money down a rat hole."

"You ought to consider a compact car, like mine."

"I can't stand those little cars," he blurted out. "Anyway, if I buy, I'll be patriotic and buy American!"

Her head reared back. "Are you suggesting I'm anti-American?"

"No, no. It's just that it's a proven fact," he blustered, trying to steer the conversation in a safer direction, "that the larger cars are safer, more comfortable, and easier to handle . . ."

She cut him off. "The imports are more reliable and the big cars are gas guzzlers."

He made his voice ingratiating. "I only wanted to say that larger cars are easier to handle in bad weather."

She smiled demurely. "I bought my car used with over 80,000 miles on it and it's still going strong."

She was slippery, not responding to his comments and just plowing ahead with her own agenda to prove that foreign cars were better. Well, two could play that game! "I repeat, it's patriotic to support the national economy."

"Well, if you look in the door panel of my *foreign* car, you'll see it was assembled in the United States of America," she said, her voice triumphant.

"Okay," he grinned. She liked—no—needed to have the last word. He shrugged. "I like the Buick, the way it rides."

"Well," she said, squeezing his hand, "you have every right to."

He wondered what she used to make her skin so soft.

Just then Adele came with the check. Morgan grabbed it and gruffly said, "I'm paying for both of us today."

"Come back now," the waitress chirped, as they got up to leave.

"We certainly will, Adele," Dixie answered, "and we'll ask for you."

Morgan smiled and nodded.

When Morgan paid the bill, he bought Dixie a jug of maple syrup. It cost more than if he'd picked up a bottle at the grocery, but he felt the occasion demanded it. We're good friends, she'd told the waitress. He felt a glow.

As Dixie backed the car out of the lot, she asked, "Would you like to come home with me?"

"Okay," he said, not sure what she had in mind but eager to find out.

Dixie slowed the car when they passed a playground. "Look, the children are out playing today," she said excitedly. "Little League. I stop sometimes and watch. There's a darling little boy . . . he's not here all the time." She took her hand off the wheel and pointed. "There he is, the one with the baggy uniform and the big ears."

She really liked kids. "You have kids?" he asked.

"No," she said. Her voice sounded muffled. Were those tears in her eyes? He must have been mistaken because when she turned to look at him, her eyes were clear and she wore a big smile on her face. "I'd just like to take that little boy home in a shopping bag," she said.

⚛

Dixie slowed down at a splendid two-story pink stucco house situated on what looked to be a half-acre corner lot. They coasted up the driveway, bordered on both sides by neat rows of multicolored flowers. A leafy elm shaded one side of the large lawn. The grass was thick and green. Shrubs and flowers bloomed in front of the cement porch, which held a swing. "Why, it's almost a palace," Morgan told her. This place must be worth a half million dollars at least, he estimated. "It's a very pleasant neighborhood."

"Yes," she smiled. "Can you give me a hand?" She opened the trunk of her car and handed him two reams of stationery. She picked up a couple boxes of envelopes and a large packet of printed labels. "Church mailing," she said.

A little dog met them at the door, dancing ecstatically as the two entered the hallway. "Hi, Jiggs." She put her packages on a marble tabletop and swept Jiggs up into her arms. "He's a Lhasa apso and has been my male companion for the last thirteen years. We love each other."

"Pretty frisky for an old man," Morgan said. Jiggs would be 91 in dog years, two years older than Morgan. The little dog's rust-colored fur held a tinge of blonde and was faded with age at his ears, eyes, and belly.

Dixie nuzzled Jiggs, then slid him to the floor. He scampered away, looking like a dust mop without a handle.

Morgan set down his two reams of stationery beside Dixie's envelopes and followed her into the spacious living room which spread out from the front entry. He sat in one of the matching barrel chairs.

"Would you like some iced tea?" she asked.

"Wonderful!" While she was in the kitchen, he looked around. Light green drapes with sheer white curtains hung at the windows. Darker green wall-to-wall carpeting, still showing the vacuum-cleaner tracks, complemented the drapes and wall fixtures. Light ivory walls added a touch of brightness.

When Dixie returned with the iced tea, he looked at her with a new appreciation of her abilities and taste.

She served him, handing him a coaster.

She probably thought he was such a slob he might set the sweating glass down on the walnut tabletop and ruin it. "Sorry about the mess in my apartment," he made a face. "You know how it is, when you live alone as long as I have."

"How long is that?" she asked, sitting on the sofa. Jiggs looked up at her mournfully until she invited him into her lap. He jumped up and licked her face.

Morgan took a sip of iced tea. "Delicious." He didn't want her to know he'd been without a wife for almost forty years. Sure, there'd been plenty of girlfriends in between, but it wasn't the same. Besides, he didn't want to give away his age. He didn't want to scare her off.

She persisted. "How long have you been alone?"

"Almost eight years." Not exactly a lie. His last girlfriend hadn't actually lived with him, but she'd slept over from time to time.

"Your wife, did she die?"

He hesitated, shook his head. At least he didn't think she was dead. "We're divorced. How about you?"

"My husband Alfred died twenty-seven years ago." She rose, pushing Jiggs gently off her lap, crossed to an end table and retrieved a photo from the clutter of photos sitting there. She handed it to Morgan. "He worked for the gas company, in charge of warehouses and shops."

Morgan examined the picture of the smiling man. "Nice looking."

"A jewel," she said mechanically, her eyes distant.

"Lucky you," he answered.

She gave a mocking laugh, took the photo from him, and returned it to its spot. When she sat down again, she seemed almost sad.

He wondered what the story was.

He felt something warm and wet on his ankle. "Why, hello, there." Jiggs stopped licking and stared up at him, waiting for an invitation into his lap.

"Jiggs likes you." Dixie smiled. "He's usually very standoffish."

Morgan reached over and patted him on the head, hoping that was enough to keep Jiggs grounded and his suit free of dog hair. "So you're a busy gal. You work for Whispering Pines and the church too?"

She nodded. "I work at the senior center four hours a day, five days a week. But I find I really spend more time there than that," she complained good-naturedly, "reading to residents who've lost their sight, taking those without cars to the supermarket, helping with special activities. Some months it's hard to fit in my church duties too."

"Just like to keep busy, huh?" he asked. Maybe she needed the extra income. Heating and upkeep on this home must be out of sight.

She gave a noncommittal grunt. "I enjoy the residents. So many have no one who takes an interest in them. And at the church . . ."

He half-listened as she spoke of her responsibilities connected with the bimonthly mailings of the church newsletter. He tried to see into the dining room from where he sat.

"Why don't we take a tour?" she asked.

He followed her into the dining room, which occupied the back corner of the house. It was at least fourteen by twenty feet and furnished with an elegant china cabinet that extended across one wall, a gleaming corner cupboard, and a massive walnut table with twelve matching chairs.

"Beautiful." One shelf of the corner cupboard was crowded with pigs of all sizes, shapes, and colors. Another shelf held an assortment of dolls and pincushions with old-fashioned hatpins. A third shelf contained a variety of ancient Bibles. "You're a collector," he said.

She nodded proudly.

He felt edgy. He wasn't sure why she'd invited him here. Maybe she wanted to impress him with this home on which she'd lavished so much care. Maybe she wanted something else. Could he rise to the occasion? Damn it, he would try!

They passed through an archway into the kitchen, a well-planned area with a counter and room for even a small dinner party for two or three couples. He envisioned himself coming over here for meals. He hoped she was a good cook. "Do you entertain a lot?"

"No more dinner parties," she laughed. "Just intimate friends." She patted him on the shoulder.

Intimate friends? Did that mean what he thought it meant?

Off the kitchen was a half bathroom and a laundry room with washer and dryer, and then a small den or family room with an entrance to the two-car garage. The fireplace, stocked with birch wood at one side and little hickory logs at the other, gave the room a comfortable, lived-in look. "Do you use the fireplace?" he asked.

"It's just for show," she said. "Too dirty."

Through the sliding-glass door, he glimpsed the backyard, surrounded by a rail fence. Like the front, the grass was green and thick from being watered properly. Well-trimmed shrubs and flowers bordered the patio and the back of the house. Two hummingbirds sipped from a feeder hanging from a maple tree. "Do you do the yard work?" he asked.

"I do what I can," she said. She opened the sliding-glass door and Jiggs bounded out into the yard, yapping happily. The hummingbirds flew away.

"This is a lot of house for one person," Morgan said, as they left the family room and walked through the hallway to the stairs. "How many bedrooms?" he asked. Just as he thought she was going to show him the upstairs bedrooms, and he was deciding he would try to kiss her up there, the doorbell rang. Then someone rapped on the door and pushed it open. "Anybody home?"

Morgan jumped guiltily.

"Why, hello." The lanky woman with long stringy hair looked from Morgan to Dixie and gave a meaningful glance up the stairs. Morgan felt she could read his mind and knew what his intentions had been. She strode toward him holding out her hand. He shook it.

"Vera, what a nice surprise!" Dixie said. Morgan could have sworn Dixie was blushing. "This is Morgan. Morgan, Vera."

She was tall, almost as tall as he was, and wore slacks and horn-rimmed glasses. "Nice to meet you." Morgan forced a smile. "I've heard a lot about you." He racked his brain to remember all the things Dixie had told him about Vera on their way to the pancake house.

"Me too!" Her eyes were curious but friendly. "I was out shopping and thought I'd drop by with those shoes I told you about." She handed Dixie a bag, saying to Morgan, "They don't fit right. I've been meaning to let Dixie try them. She's about the right size."

Morgan glanced down at Vera's feet. They were quite a bit bigger than Dixie's.

Vera saw him looking and said, "They're my daughter's." She smiled. "Sorry to barge in. I didn't know you were busy." She threw another pointed look up the stairs. "I'll be on my way."

"I was just giving Morgan the grand tour," Dixie said. Overly effusive, Morgan thought. "Come in and sit down."

Morgan returned to the barrel chair, Dixie and Vera sat on the couch. He felt Vera scrutinizing him. "Beautiful day out there," he said lamely.

"Ice cream, anyone?" Dixie sprang up nervously.

"I'll take a little," Vera answered quickly.

"Me too," Morgan said.

"Dixie tells me you're from Chicago," Vera said after Dixie left for the kitchen.

He nodded warily. Why had he ever opened his big mouth about Chicago? "I consider myself a Buckeye."

"How long have you lived in Ohio?"

"Long enough to feel at home."

"Dixie tells me you were an officer at the bank."

"Yes."

"What do officers do exactly?"

"It depends. I did loans mostly."

"When did you retire?" she asked.

This was getting to be a cross-examination. He smiled kindly but firmly to let her know it wasn't any of her damn business!

"Dixie and I have been friends for years. We're in bridge club together. We tell each other everything and look out for each other too." Vera wore a pleasant look, but her eyes were serious.

Sounds like a warning, Morgan thought.

"Need some help out there?" Vera went into the kitchen. Morgan heard her say, "He's cute but nearly mute." Then their voices dropped.

He strained to hear what they were saying. Dishes clattered. Their murmurs were broken by fits of giggles. He was getting annoyed. He stood up, about to barge into the kitchen, interrupt their tête-à-tête.

Just then Dixie bubbled into the living room, followed by her tall friend. "Sorry we took so long," Dixie trilled, handing him his dish. Vera flashed him an innocent smile before she sank down on the couch and dug into her ice cream.

Morgan ate in silence, then waited, grimly polite, for Vera to leave so he and Dixie could take up where they left off. Vera remained glued in place, chatting with Dixie about people and places he didn't know. "It's late. I'll be getting home," he said after half an hour. He'd come over expecting to be the center of attention. Now the friend with the stringy hair was monopolizing Dixie.

Dixie jumped up. "I'll take you."

"Don't bother," he said brusquely. "I'll call a cab. Where's the phone?"

"You'll do no such thing. I'll be right back," she said to Vera.

He knew the two were going to talk about him. Their hilarity in the kitchen was just the prelude.

When he got in the car, he felt something behind him, jabbing him in the back. He pulled it out and held it up. The maple syrup. "Look what we forgot."

"I'll think of you every time I use it," Dixie said.

"Well, I'll have to keep you supplied!" He tried to make his voice jovial but he was tired. It had been a big day, with more talk than he was used to. "Thanks," he said as he left the car, "for a nice time." Marred only by the entrance of Vera. "You have a beautiful home."

He let himself into his apartment, curious about Dixie working two jobs. From the looks of her home, one would think she was well off. And what was the real story about that husband of hers? More in the next installment, he decided.

It came to him then. He'd been set up. It all made sense—Vera's phone call to Dixie while they were on their way to the pancake house, her nervousness as she jabbered on and on about her friend. The delivery of the shoes. He wondered if Vera even had a daughter.

Dixie had invited him to her home not because she had the hots for him, but so Vera could stop by and check him out. He felt tricked.

❧

Dixie carried in the jug of maple syrup. "His first gift," she said proudly to Vera, holding it in the air.

"Sweet," Vera said.

Dixie made popcorn in the microwave. "Let's get comfortable." She took off her suit jacket and her wig. The two slipped out of their shoes and settled on the couch, each with a bowl of popcorn. Jiggs, on the floor between them, hungrily eyed the path of the popcorn from hand to mouth. "Well, what do you think?" Dixie asked, reaching down to let the little dog nibble a few kernels from her hand.

"I think I arrived here just in time," Vera chortled. "You said two-thirty. I was late. You two were standing by the stairs. Did I interrupt something? He looked daggers at me."

"He'd all but asked to see the bedrooms." He'd also been about to kiss her, she was sure, but she wouldn't spoil it by telling Vera.

"Oh, God, they're all alike." Vera laughed raucously and went into a fit of coughing.

"Better cut down on those cigarettes."

"I only had one while you were gone," Vera said, adding hastily, "I smoked it outside." She stuffed a handful of popcorn into her mouth and chewed thoughtfully. "What else do I think? He's sharp. I think he guessed I was lying about the shoes!" She hooted with laughter again.

Dixie giggled. "I noticed you invented a daughter you don't have."

"He's personable. Nice looking. Well groomed."

"His apartment was a pigsty." Dixie grinned. "I deliberately made up an excuse to get inside."

"Red flag," Vera said. "You're a stickler for cleanliness and order."

"I can train him."

"Famous last words. How old is he?" Vera asked.

"What do you think?"

"Older than you."

"He's cagey about telling me."

"A sure sign he's a lot older than you are. Any ailments?"

"He hasn't said."

"You don't want to get stuck playing nursemaid. You don't need that after what you've been through."

Vera was right. Still, you had to follow your instincts, take a chance. "I like his sense of humor," Dixie said.

"Well, I certainly didn't see much evidence of it."

"He's shy. He just met you. And I heard you from the kitchen giving him the third degree."

"He's very good at keeping secrets." Vera grinned. "I have better luck with my husband."

"We've had some real conversations. He listens." Argues too. He liked to have the last word.

"So what's next?" Vera asked.

"I'll wait a few days. If he doesn't call me, I'll invite him over for a meal. From the look of his wastebaskets, he lives on TV dinners when he isn't eating out."

Vera chuckled. "The best way to a man's heart . . ." She became serious. "I'll be interested in what Barry finds out. Under no circumstances, do not, I repeat, do not continue on to Step Three of that plan of yours until you do more digging."

"I won't," Dixie promised.

As she lay in bed that night, Dixie whispered, "Please, God, let this work out," exactly what she'd wished for in the restaurant when her little finger was entwined with Morgan's.

4

Royal Flush

"Hello," Morgan said. When he heard Nate's voice at the other end of the phone, he had to admit he was disappointed it wasn't Dixie. He'd been putting off calling her since the visit to her home and the ambush by her friend Vera. Vera with the stringy hair. He'd been the goods; Vera, the appointed inspector.

"How'd you like to see us perform Saturday afternoon?" Nate rumbled in his mellifluous baritone. "Open rehearsal for the Swinging Seniors District Barbershop Championship."

"I don't have wheels."

"I'll pick you up. Have to be there an hour early to warm up. Your car still in the shop, huh?"

"They can't find the part."

"If you don't want to go early, ask Dixie to bring you."

Morgan grunted.

"I'd like to meet her."

"I'll think about it." To tell the truth, he wasn't sure he needed the excitement and the uncertainty of Dixie at this stage of his life.

"Are you still sulking about that trick she pulled?"

"No, it's just that—okay, I admit I didn't like being examined by her friend. Like some sort of prize hog!"

"Better lay off those desserts, or you could take home the blue ribbon."

Morgan laughed.

"Think of it this way. Dixie can now be examined by me."

He'd like to get Nate's opinion. Not that he'd ever followed his advice. Nate had met most of his girlfriends and hadn't thought a one of them measured up, except—what was her name? Lucy? Lucy the Listless.

"Anyway, buddy," Nate continued, "you should feel honored that she wanted her best friend to meet you."

Well, that was another way to look at it. "I'll let you know."

After he hung up, Morgan found Dixie's number in the phone book and dialed it.

She answered right away. "I was just about to call you. It must be ESP."

"If you were about to call, I guess that means I passed inspection," he chuckled.

"Vera says you're a doll."

Vera's opinion shouldn't matter, but it did. "She's a doll too." He felt expansive. "And she has good taste in men!"

⊙⊹⊙

Dixie was acutely conscious of Morgan's hand on her arm, guiding her through the crowd. She hoped she hadn't overdressed. Morgan wore a sport coat. Others were dressed casually, in slacks or jeans.

"How do you like my outfit?" Dixie asked. "You haven't said." It had been a favorite when she worked at the ad agency years ago, dark brown, trimmed in fake leopard skin at the wrists and collar. When she'd unearthed the matching leopard-print scarf, it seemed to be an omen.

"Don't worry. You look fine," Morgan said.

Only fine? And what did he mean, don't worry? Barry, her former boss, had called this combination dramatic and eye-catching.

"You have a new hairpiece," Morgan said.

Spoken doubtfully. "Not a hairpiece. It's a wig." Oh, God, she should have asked Vera to give her the once-over before she decided on this getup.

Morgan added, "You really have a thing for wigs."

"What does that mean?" Now she felt like sinking into the floor. *Get a grip, Dixie.*

"It means you like wigs, that's all!" He smoothed back his hair and grinned. "I just get fed up with all the emphasis on youth. No gray allowed. It puts pressure on me."

"You'd look great with a spiky cut, dyed blond," she laughed.

"There's Nate." Morgan stopped at the poster outside the auditorium. The headline was THE ROYAL FLUSH—ENJOY THEIR FULL, RIPE SOUND. Underneath it: THRILL TO THEIR FOUR-PART CLOSE HARMONY A CAPELLA STYLE. Morgan pointed to the photo in the center. "He's the one with the mustache."

"They all have mustaches," said Dixie.

"He's the tall one," Morgan said.

Nate's hair was dark, Dixie noticed, with only a bit of gray on his sideburns. His mustache had no gray. Maybe he touched it up.

They squeezed past the others in the row and sat. Dixie felt her skirt hike up. She tugged at it, trying to cover her thighs. She hadn't worn this dress in years. It was tight across the seat. "How'd you meet Nate?" she asked.

"The bank."

"Oh, so you worked together here, in Columbus?" Dixie thumbed through the program.

"Yeah," Morgan answered. "He's good. Sings baritone. His group's won some prizes."

She read the brief bios. A sentence caught her eye. Together, the members of The Royal Flush have a combination of 162 years of experience. Divide that by four, she thought, and you get an average of over forty years' experience for each. That, plus the photo out front, made her curious. "How old is Nate?"

"He's twenty years younger than I am," Morgan mused, "so that would make him . . . 69." His head suddenly swiveled her way, his mouth agape.

Dixie was ecstatic! She knew she'd get it out of him one way or another. So Morgan was 89. He was glaring now at the back of the woman's head in front of him. Dixie didn't want him to brood throughout the concert. She nudged him and winked. "I have a thing for older men."

He flushed and cracked a weak smile. "I may be older but I refuse to grow up."

She laughed. "Vera thought you were in your seventies." It was a little lie but it produced a big grin.

The house lights dimmed and the stage lights came up. The Royal Flush marched out, each dressed in a black shirt with a white collar, white suspenders, and a white and gray tie. They tore enthusiastically into their first song, "When My Sugar Walks Down the Street."

Dixie forgot about her tight dress. She swayed to their ringing tones as they sang everything from gospel to Broadway show tunes to blues, swing, and country songs. The ballad, "Tie Me To Your Apron Strings Again," was a showstopper, the last chord floating cleanly and gently to the ceiling. "They're wonderful," she whispered to Morgan. The first set ended with "Inka Dinka Doo." The applause was loud and long.

At the intermission, Dixie turned to Morgan, "Did you notice? Nate's right shoulder lifts and lowers each time the pitch changes."

Morgan nodded. "He gets a lot of kidding about it." He turned to her and smiled. "He's looking forward to meeting you."

"Me too." Now she felt jumpy again. She wanted to go home and change before she met Nate. "Excuse me, I have to go to the little girls' room," Dixie said. She gave herself a quick once-over in the bathroom mirror. Maybe her outfit was too dramatic for an afternoon program in a high school auditorium. She tried taking off the leopard printed scarf. Worse. It left her too nude at the neck. She put the scarf back on again.

She went inside the stall, removed her blonde wig, and put it in her purse. Back at the mirror, she brushed her hair and fluffed it out, then blotted off some extra lipstick.

When she sat down again beside Morgan, he noticed. "What happened to your wig?"

"I thought you didn't like it."

"You don't need it. Your own hair is," he searched for a word, "beautiful." He blushed.

"I think it makes me look mousy."

"You're a standout in this room."

She glowed, and the glow stayed with her through the next half of the show. The Royal Flush opened with "Red Roses for a Blue Lady," followed by "Forgive Me." Dixie melted and felt goose bumps on her arms. But soon she was bouncing again to "Jeepers Creepers." When the group launched into "I Wish I Had My Old Gal Back Again," Dixie was right there with them, trembling, dizzy with feeling. "Nate's crying," she whispered to Morgan. She was crying too.

"His wife. He misses her," Morgan whispered back. "She's only been gone six months." He took out his handkerchief and blew his nose.

The song ended. Over the din of the applause, Dixie heard the tenor gasp, "Oh, man," and the bass's ecstatic, "Awesome." They knew and the audience knew that something special had just happened. The Royal Flush received a standing ovation.

During their encore, "Heart and Soul," Dixie was transported. She stole a look at Morgan. He had a soft smile on his face. His eyes were closed.

Dixie was silent, Morgan too, after the program ended. Dixie finally sighed, "I'm sorry it's over." The Royal Flush exited the stage into the auditorium. Flashbulbs popped and family and friends swirled around them, offering congratulations. Morgan stood and waved, and soon Nate loped their way, pausing now and then to murmur thanks or shake a proffered hand.

"Terrific," Morgan said, clapping him on the back. "Fantastic," Dixie added.

Nate, who towered above Dixie, did a half bow. "So this is Dixie."

"Hello, Nate," she said. "You had me crying, laughing, practically dancing in my seat." She felt Nate giving her the once-over. She was sure by the look on his face that she'd dressed all wrong.

Nate introduced them to the other members of his group, bass, tenor and lead. "I love the way your mustaches wobble when you sing," Dixie told them cheerily, determined not to feel self-conscious about her dress. She'd bluff it through.

"Want to join us for a brew?" Nate turned to Dixie.

"What do you think?" Morgan asked.

"Why not?" Dixie flung her scarf back over her shoulder—with flair, she hoped.

At the Knotty Pine, Morgan, Dixie, and Nate sat at one end of the long table, Nate's buddies, their wives, and friends at the other. A few regulars watched television from the bar. Otherwise, the place was theirs this late afternoon.

"Just half a glass for me," Dixie said as Nate poured beer from the pitcher. "I'm driving." A beer would ease the butterflies, but she'd have to be careful. She had a low tolerance for alcohol. It made her talkative, then sleepy.

"Here's to you." Morgan lifted his glass to Nate. "And winning the district gold medal."

Nate nodded, his eyes excited. "We'll be heading for Cinci tomorrow, and if we're lucky, on to Indianapolis for the international competition."

"Do you travel a lot?" Dixie asked.

"Four to five times a year. We do concerts as well as competitions. That plus rehearsals and my consulting at the bank keep me busy. Just the way I want to be."

"Morgan told me. I'm sorry about your wife."

He looked away and seemed almost angry that she'd mentioned it. She could have kicked herself.

Morgan said hurriedly, "Tell Dixie what you do to get ready for a contest."

Nate smoothed down his mustache and cleared his throat. "You have to train like an athlete. I don't mean just practicing the songs." As Nate talked on about the rigors of his training—what he could eat and drink—Dixie relaxed. Thank God for the beer. She took a big swallow. "It must be worth it, the thrill of a good performance after all the discipline leading up to it."

Morgan chimed in, "He also has to remember to have his outfit cleaned, and have the right colored socks on. A tall order for our absent-minded friend here."

Nate's eyes sparkled. "Morgan's heard it all many times."

Morgan was grinning from ear to ear. His face was flushed and a lock of his hair drooped over one eye. He looked almost as young as Nate. "Morgan said you've won quite a few gold medals."

Nate nodded enthusiastically. "The adrenaline flows. Each time we do a contest, each of us worries, Did I keep us from winning?"

Morgan topped off Dixie's beer, poured more into Nate's glass and his and signaled for another pitcher.

She was about to protest, but what the heck, she was eating peanuts. Still, she found herself talking too much, rambling on about the songs sung that afternoon, and the memories they brought back. She clinked her glass against Morgan's and Nate's. "Here's to the good ol' songs of the good old days!"

Nate smiled. "I think of Momma's peanut butter cookies when we sing 'Tie Me to Your Apron Strings Again.'"

"I could taste those cookies." Dixie felt a definite buzz.

"I always loved my mom's sugar cookies," Morgan sighed. "I could eat a half a dozen at a sitting."

"I liked to dunk my mother's oatmeal cookies in milk," Dixie said, "straight from the cow." She sipped her beer. Her glass seemed to be full again. How did that happen? "Don't you wish sometimes, with all our progress, we could just slip back in time and enjoy the slower pace?" Then she was off on a jag of reminiscence, talking about sitting on the porch at the farm, playing the old games, hide-and-go-seek, Simon says.

"That was when you got your windshield cleaned, oil checked, and gas pumped, without asking, all for free," Morgan said.

"And you didn't pay for air and you got trading stamps to boot," Nate added.

"Speaking of gas stations—" Morgan excused himself to go to the bathroom.

They'd polished off two pitchers of beer, a bowl of pretzels, and a bowl of peanuts. "When did everyone leave?" Dixie asked Nate. The rest of The Royal Flush and friends had disappeared. "It's been such fun."

Nate nodded, smiling broadly.

"Morgan said you worked together at the bank."

"Yeah. We've been good buddies for almost forty years."

He must have known Morgan's wife. She wondered what she'd been like. Why they'd parted ways. Nate was smiling so pleasantly, she decided to ask. "What was his ex-wife like?" Despite the wary look in his eyes, she forged ahead. "I just wondered if she was anything like me." Nate frowned. He probably thought she was taking a lot for granted.

"Never met her." His smile was apologetic.

That was a shock. "Never?"

He shook his head. "Morgan was divorced before he transferred here from Chicago."

So his divorce had been decades ago. "But he told me," she blurted out, "he'd lived alone for just eight years."

Nate looked mystified, then said, "Oh! That was—" He clammed up then, rubbed his face, and scratched his head.

The beer made her reckless. "Tell me about her."

"Better ask Morgan."

"I heard my name," Morgan said, sitting down. "Better ask Morgan what?"

"If he wants coffee!" Dixie proclaimed. She put on her brightest smile. "I need coffee before I drive us anywhere." Morgan's eyes darted from her to his friend. He didn't look pleased.

Nate stood. "I have to leave you two now. Very early day tomorrow. Dixie, it was a great pleasure." He thrust a ten-dollar bill in Morgan's direction. "My share."

Morgan waved it away. "It's on me."

"Treat her right, pal. You hear?" Nate turned to Dixie, raising his eyebrows and nodding, as if to say, *ask him*. Then he made his way toward the exit.

"How about something to go with that coffee?" Morgan asked.

Dixie nodded.

Morgan ordered a hamburger. Dixie asked for a chef salad.

"So you and Nate were talking about me while I was in the john?"

"Were your ears burning?" she asked with a laugh.

"What do you want to know?"

Well, that was easy. She didn't have the courage to say, "Everything, about your wife, your girlfriend, your mysterious Chicago past." So she asked, "You and your ex, how did you meet?"

"College sweethearts."

He was silent for so long she thought that was all he was going to say on the subject.

"We didn't get married right away." He laughed mirthlessly. "I had the bad luck to graduate college in 1933."

"The start of the Great Depression," Dixie said.

"Banks were failing all over. I couldn't get a job in my field, accounting, so I joined the Civilian Conservation Corps. Luckily, I could swing an axe and wield a spade."

"Brawn as well as brains!" She smiled. "What did you do in the CCC?"

"Helped with forestry and drainage projects around the country."

"So you lived out of a suitcase?"

He nodded. "For almost a year. Then I landed the job here in Columbus at the bank. As a teller."

"Lucky break."

"Yeah, it was. We were married then. We were both 24. My wife didn't like living here; she called it a cow town. She left me. I should have said to hell with her. But I wanted her back. I was ambitious. She was beautiful, vivacious, a blonde with a terrific figure. Pretty foxy ornament to have hanging from your arm."

Even in my prime, Dixie thought, I've never been considered a foxy ornament. "Did she make a lot of noise?"

"What?"

"The ornament. Did she jangle?"

He laughed. "Just my nerves. Anyway, to please her, I started looking for another job. When I became an accountant with a bank in Chicago, she moved there with me." He gave Dixie a wry grin. "She liked Chicago. The raise in pay and prestige helped too."

"So life was good for awhile?"

"We stuck it out for twenty-three years." He shrugged. "That's about it."

That wasn't nearly it, but she knew by the look on his face that's all she was going to get today. "Then you came back to Columbus?"

He nodded grimly.

Should she broach the subject of the live-in girlfriend? "Never wanted to remarry?"

"Not on your life!"

"Any children?"

"Three, a boy and two girls."

"You have pictures?"

He shook his head.

"The kids, they're all still in Chicago?" she asked.

"As far as I know." He gave her a fake grin. His eyes were sad.

"You don't keep in touch?"

He shook his head. "I put them all through college. After that—" He threw up his hands.

"What a waste!" she blurted out. "You don't know how lucky you were. I would have given anything—"

He looked sheepish.

"You could be surrounded now. By your children, your grandchildren, your great-grandchildren!" Her eyes filled with tears. "You really blew it!"

"How do you know? You weren't there," he snapped, suddenly angry. "Anyway, it's none of your damn business!"

"You're right. It's none of my business. Nothing is my damn business as far as you're concerned." She pushed away her half-eaten salad and stood. "If you're ready, I'll drop you off at your place," she said icily.

"I'm still eating," he said, taking a bite of his hamburger. "I'll call a cab."

"Fine." She gathered up her purse, flung her leopard-print scarf over her shoulder, and flounced out the front door of the Knotty Pine.

⚭

Morgan put down his sandwich. He'd barely touched it. He signaled the waitress over and paid the check. Ouch! It left him just a dollar. Damn! He should have taken that ten-spot Nate had offered toward the bill. How was he going to pay for a cab?

His chest felt tight. He drew his inhaler out of his jacket pocket and puffed at his Albuterol. He closed his eyes, concentrating on his breathing. In and out. In and out. Better. He took a second puff, then a third.

The ragweed season this year was hell on his asthma. So was this dame Dixie, rummaging around in his past, stirring up all those best-forgotten memories.

She was like a camel. Once she got her nose in the tent, you couldn't get her out.

Now, how to get home? He could call Nate and ask him to pick him up. And lose face. He could ask the cab to take him home and wait while he ran in to get the fare. Come to think of it, he had no cash at home. He'd carried it all with him today. Well, he could walk the mile or so to his apartment. He'd walk. It would do him good.

Outside, he took long strides, breathing the cool night air deep into his lungs. By the time he arrived home he'd worked up a light sweat. His head was clear. He felt in control.

⚭

Self-centered, selfish bastard. Dixie undressed, throwing her clothes on a chair in her bedroom. Cold-hearted, egotistical boob, not giving a damn about his kids! Who knows how many girlfriends he'd had after his divorce? She didn't need a report about him from Barry. Or Nate! She had a report, all right. The way he'd yelled at her with no regard for her feelings.

She put on her nightgown, her eyes straying to the photo of the little boy on her nightstand. He'd been such a great kid, bright and sensitive. The best thing that had ever happened to her. If he'd lived, he'd be 48 now. He'd have children. She'd be a grandmother, a great-grandmother.

Her life would be rich and satisfying, filled up with family. No need for her to go out and find someone at this stage of her life.

She climbed into bed, picked up the book on the nightstand, and tried to read. None of it was sinking in. She snapped off the light. Selfish jackass! No wonder his wife had divorced him. He couldn't keep a wife, couldn't keep a girlfriend. Good riddance!

At two AM she was still awake, fretting and fuming. She went downstairs and made herself a cup of warm milk.

◦╬◦

Morgan woke up in a panic. He couldn't catch his breath. He took three puffs from his inhaler, waited, then took three puffs of his Azmacort. He lay back down. Not much better. Shakily, he walked to the closet and took two pillows off the shelf. By the time he'd stacked them on his bed, he was gasping for breath. Calm down, he told himself. You're making it worse. He lay back on the pillows, breathing through his mouth. Yeah, it was better with his head raised like this. He was able to relax. He drifted off, then jerked awake, sweating, from a nightmare. Someone was trying to smother him.

He took another puff from his inhalers, dozed, and woke up again. The night dragged on. The more puffs he took, the worse his breathing grew, it seemed. Imagination, he told himself. Things always seemed out of proportion at four o'clock in the morning.

By dawn, he was afraid to lie down, afraid he'd go to sleep and be asphyxiated. He sat on the edge of his bed, taking rapid, shallow breaths, not thinking very clearly, willing the medications to kick in and allow him a few good breaths of air. He was starving for air. It was five AM. Too early to call anyone. He took more medicine. At six-thirty, he tried Nate. No answer. Then he remembered Nate was leaving early for Cincinnati.

He felt light-headed. He couldn't let himself pass out. He picked up the phone, wondering if he was dying.

◦╬◦

When the phone rang, it seemed to Dixie she'd just closed her eyes. "Hello."

The voice at the other end was thick, unrecognizable. She couldn't understand the words. "Who's this?" She looked at the clock. Seven in the morning!

"Morgan." His voice cracked.

"My God! What's the matter?"

"Having . . . trouble . . . breathing."

"Did you call emergency?"

"I'll be OK." She heard his breaths, quick and shallow. "Soon as the medicine—"

"I'm getting help." She hung up the phone and dialed 911.

She threw on her clothes and arrived at Morgan's just as the emergency squad was pulling up.

"I'm the one who phoned." She ran alongside the two young men as they hurried up the walkway. They tried the door. Locked. They pounded. No answer. Just as they were about to break the door down, Morgan pulled it open. He was in his skivvies and an undershirt. His eyes were glassy. "Sorry," he apologized to Dixie. "I tried Nate first."

One of the men grabbed his arm to steady him as they pushed into the apartment. He gently sat Morgan in a chair, hooked him up to an IV and oxygen. "What medications are you on?"

"Asthma," Morgan gasped, pointing to the table beside his bed.

Dixie heard one of the men mumble to the other, "Or congestive heart failure. No heart meds?" he asked Morgan.

Morgan shook his head.

The two attendants put Morgan on the gurney, covered him up, and rolled him out the door. His eyes were closed. His chest rose and fell rapidly as he sucked at the oxygen.

Dixie found his keys and locked his apartment. She followed the screaming ambulance to the hospital, whispering over and over, "Please don't let him die."

5

Breathless

The waiting room of the emergency room was jammed this early Sunday morning. Some people dozed, sprawling over the hard chairs. Others, with dull eyes, stared at nothing.

Each time the doors flew open, Dixie, half-sick with hope and dread, expected news about Morgan. But each time the attendant veered toward someone else, ushering him or her through the double doors.

Morgan had looked so awful, his face haggard, his lips blue. Was he alive or dead?

She had a headache. She found a vending machine and bought herself a cup of foul-tasting liquid that billed itself as coffee. Scalding hot, it burned her tongue and tasted like cardboard. She took it back to the waiting room and drank it.

She'd known Morgan almost three weeks, but she'd never once seen him take anything for asthma. Didn't asthmatics use a spray? What else was wrong with him? His heart? Was he diabetic? Well, she had her secrets too. Don't get too emotionally involved, she told herself.

Maybe he'd gone into cardiac arrest. What if they were zapping his heart right now? She could stand it no longer. She stood up abruptly and as she did, a few people jerked awake, looking as if they feared she was crazy.

She pushed through the swinging doors. Hallways and cubicles were filled with narrow cots occupied by people, fat and thin, silent or moaning or grunting in pain. Where was Morgan?

A harried-looking woman in green scrubs blocked her way. "May I help you?"

"I'm looking for Morgan. Bryce Morgan. I've been waiting a long time." Her heart was thudding. "How is he?"

The woman frowned at her clipboard, looked up, and sighed. "Over there." She pointed to her right.

Dixie found him in the last partition, sitting on the edge of the bed in his undershirt, a light blanket over his lap. A plastic mask covered his nose and mouth. Clouds of white vapor spilled out around the edges, billowing up around his head. The mask had a small hose attached to a nearby nebulizer. Morgan sucked in the vapor and breathed it out. After a few puffs, he started to cough, and as the cough built to a paroxysm, his face grew red and his eyes watered. He pulled off his mask, coughing so hard she was afraid he was going to have a stroke or heart attack.

Gurgling and hacking, huffing and puffing, he spit out brownish hunks into a bowl that rested beside him.

Dixie was horrified. "He's spitting out his lungs," she said to the young man in a white coat who stood near Morgan. Surely he wasn't the doctor. He looked so young, his face pink and cherubic. But he wore a stethoscope around his neck.

"Mucous plugs," the young man said.

When the coughing subsided, Morgan put the mask back on and sucked in the vapor. The cycle of coughing and spitting repeated.

"He needs to get the plugs out so he can breathe," the young man said. "I'm Dr. McBride." He offered Dixie his hand.

"Pleased to meet you." She hoped he knew what he was doing.

After the breathing treatment was over, Morgan hawked and spit for several more minutes, trembling violently.

"Why is he shaking so hard?" Dixie asked.

"The medications," the doctor replied. "He's had to have high doses to make the treatment work."

"That awful coughing must be hard on his heart."

"That's why he shouldn't wait until he's in this shape to get help. Luckily, his heart's strong. He's in good condition for—what is he? 75?"

From the corner of her eye, Dixie could see Morgan perk up considerably. She almost smiled.

"Actually," Morgan replied breathlessly, with a weak grin, "I'm 89."

"89? You're kidding!" the doctor said. "Good genes."

"This is the first time," Morgan's voice was ragged, "my meds didn't work." He cleared his throat over and over.

"It's a worse than usual allergy season this summer—grass, mold spores, ragweed," the doctor said.

"I guess I got the asthma going when I walked home from the Knotty Pine," Morgan murmured, almost to himself.

"What?" Dixie cried. "You walked all that way?" Unbelievable. "Stubborn mule."

The doctor glanced at Dixie quizzically, then asked Morgan, "How much water do you drink a day?"

"I'm not much of a water drinker."

"Make a conscious effort to drink six to eight glasses a day. It will help thin your mucous. Do you take antihistamines for allergies?"

"Sometimes," Morgan said.

"They dry you out. If you have a tendency to form plugs, which you do, they make it worse." He added sternly, "Next time, don't wait this long. That's how people die. Thousands die unnecessarily every year."

"And you could have been one of them," Dixie said tartly.

"There won't be any next time," Morgan said, hollow-eyed, with an attempt at bravado.

"Also—" the doctor hesitated. "Anxiety and nervous stress can increase asthma symptoms and aggravate an attack."

"I'm retired," Morgan said. "No stress in my life."

"Right!" Dixie muttered. After the doctor left the cubicle, she hissed, "I can't believe you walked all that way."

"I wanted to blow off steam," he said sheepishly.

Dixie, muttering to herself, went off in search of Dr. McBride. "That's all that's wrong with him, just the asthma?"

"Are you his wife?"

"A friend."

"You mustn't think of it as 'just the asthma.' Asthma is dangerous, tricky. He has to learn to treat it with respect."

Dixie nodded slowly. "I'll make sure he does." Morgan's heart was strong; his only malady, besides pigheadedness, was the asthma. He seemed fourteen years younger to the doctor than he was. He had fourteen more years in him, at least.

The young doctor smiled down at her. "He's very lucky to have a friend like you. You got him here just in time."

In fourteen years, she would be 93. Well, she knew for certain she wouldn't last that long. Morgan would have to go on without her. Slow down, Dixie, she told herself. Remember, you don't know everything about this man.

When Morgan was released, Dr. McBride handed him a prescription. "Prednisone. Take as directed. It will help your lungs return to normal." He added, "Use your inhalers. See your own doctor in a week."

Dixie drove Morgan home, swinging by the drugstore to pick up his prescription. She pulled up to his apartment a little after noontime, just as his neighbors were flocking from church or going out to Sunday dinner. Morgan emerged from Dixie's car, wearing only the white blanket furnished by emergency, his underwear, and socks.

Dixie hesitated, but wrapped her arm around his waist to steady him, expecting him to push her away or to say something grumpy at the very least. But he was docile. Together they wobbled up the walkway to his apartment, meeting a young man and woman on their way out. Morgan gave them an embarrassed wave.

Dixie couldn't resist. "The strip poker game got out of hand."

The couple smiled uncertainly.

"Now why did you say that?" Morgan demanded, when the two were out of earshot. "They're new here. What will they think?"

"They'll think I'm a good poker player."

He gave a chuckle. "You're unbelievable." At his front door, he patted his underwear. "Oh, God, where are my keys?"

"Right here." With a flourish, Dixie extracted them from her purse.

He gave her a long look. His eyes were red-rimmed, his chin dotted with salt and pepper stubble. "Thank you, Miss Dixie," he said gently. "I think you saved my life."

She was so surprised she could think of no reply. Her eyes filled with tears. She ducked her head quickly and unlocked his door.

"I'm going to fix lunch for you," she announced when they were inside.

He sat in a chair, the white blanket draped over his shoulders, looking like a once-powerful chieftain who'd lost an important battle. "I'm not hungry. Think I'll hit the sack. I didn't sleep much last night."

She was pleasantly surprised to see the refrigerator held a carton of milk, still fresh enough to use, orange juice, and bread. Corn flakes, bananas, and a couple of apples sat on the counter.

She fixed cereal and poured out a glass of orange juice. "Eat, so you can take your medicine." As he ate, the blanket slid from his shoulders. She noticed the muscle definition in his bare arms. Morgan indeed was in good shape.

"Let me help you to bed," she said when he finished.

"I'm not an invalid," he protested, pulling the blanket once more around his shoulders. But he let her walk him into the bedroom.

When he was settled in bed, he reached for her hand and held it to his lips. "You're an angel." He closed his eyes.

Confused, shivery, she slipped her hand from his. She softly closed his bedroom door.

She cleared the dishes off the table and washed them, along with the stack of dirty dishes in the sink. She couldn't find a dishtowel so she dried everything with paper towels. As she thought over how she'd responded in this crisis, in this matter of life and death, she felt flushed, almost radiant. Like an angel. That's what he'd called her. An angel.

She emptied the wastebaskets, picked the newspapers up from the floor, and stacked them on an empty tray table. She scrubbed his bathroom sink, toilet, and tub, and put out a fresh towel and washcloth.

She glanced in the bathroom mirror. What a mess you are, Dixie. She'd dashed from her house without makeup, her hair in a frizz. Her jeans were old and paint-spattered, her blouse faded. Maybe, she decided, this episode, terrifying as it was, might have a benefit, fast-forwarding their relationship to another level. She'd seen him in his underwear, scared and sweet; he'd seen her looking as if she'd just climbed out of bed. They could cut the cat-and-mouse games and get down to serious business. When he was well, she'd invite him to her house for dinner and lay her cards on the table. But first, she'd take Vera's advice. Call Barry and prod him to dig a little harder.

She cracked Morgan's bedroom door and peeked in. He was asleep, snoring softly.

❦

Morgan woke with a start. It was dark outside. The clock on his nightstand showed it was almost midnight. He'd slept over ten hours. He had a headache. He felt nervous, hyper. *Don't start thinking. Go back to sleep.*

No dice. He got up, found a note from Dixie on the kitchen table,

"Call me when you read this." He didn't think she'd appreciate a call this late. He was hungry. He put in a TV dinner. He'd read while it cooked. Wait a minute! The apartment looked strange. What the hell! She'd cleaned the place up. It looked damn good.

He'd gotten careless in the last few years without a woman around, someone to invite over, to impress. Someone to clean up after him. If he didn't watch it, he could turn into one of those people who smelled bad and talked to himself.

He'd never had an attack like this. He'd think of it as a reminder for him not to get too full of himself, believing he was immortal. He had to admit, he'd never been so scared in his life.

Where would he have been without Dixie? He'd been too addled or stubborn to call 911 himself.

On the other hand, if he were living at Whispering Pines, he'd just have to signal for a nurse. That was their job. He wouldn't have had to impose on a friend. An acquaintance, really.

His brain was churning. His apartment lease was about to run out. Should he renew? His car was falling apart. Should he buy another, maybe a used one? This relationship with Dixie. It was unsettling. Now he felt grateful to her. And obligated.

If he'd died, it would have been simpler. All his decisions would be made in one fell swoop. He had to grin. His sense of humor was getting warped.

What if Dixie hadn't answered when he called her? She could have been in the shower and not heard the phone. He was right back to Whispering Pines and the security it offered.

He dug through a stack of papers, found the retirement center's packet of materials, and looked up their charges for a one-bedroom apartment in independent living, plus meals. God, it would kill him to pay good money for those meals! But they'd be a notch above his TV dinners, he supposed. He added up the figures—his pension, Social Security, interest on his CD. He could just squeak by with something left over for incidentals. If he had any unusual dental or medical problems, forget it. He'd have to break into the principal of his CD. The longer he lived the chances of his going into assisted living increased. He looked up those rates. Whew! Quite a jump in the monthly nut. Inflation had to be factored in. Would his small savings see him through? He could cut expenses by getting rid of his car. How much longer would he be able to drive anyway? He felt the walls of the prison spring up around him.

Why had he been such a jerk when he was younger? The grasshopper who partied while the hard-working ant worked and saved. Or was it vice versa? He ate his TV dinner, then tried to sleep, but his life—all the terrible, gut-wrenching, catastrophic mistakes he'd made—played over and over in his brain.

6

The Proposition

Dixie scurried around the house, cleaning cloths in hand, zapping newly settled dust particles and smudges on windows and mirrors. In the dining room she paused. The table looked beautiful. The cloth napkins matched the tablecloth. Her best china and crystal glasses gleamed. The good silverware glittered. New candles stood tall and white in ornate antique candlesticks. Music played softly in the background.

She knew in her heart today was the day. All seemed auspicious. Barry had found out zilch, except that Morgan had started at the Ohio Bank forty years ago. That sounded right. Nate and Morgan had been friends for almost forty years.

His ex-wife, superficial bimbo that she was, must have turned the children against him and he'd pulled up stakes as soon as he could after the divorce. That's why he didn't want to talk about Chicago. Too many bitter memories. No wonder he'd blown up when she accused him of not caring about his children.

Vera, of course, had been riveted, rendered speechless (momentarily) by Dixie's breathless account of the part she'd played in Morgan's life-and-death struggle. When Vera finally spoke, she said, "89 and asthmatic, huh?"

"But the doctor thought he was 75."

Vera laughed her gravelly laugh. "Estranged from his kids? If his kids don't like him, doesn't that tell you something?"

"His ex-wife was a bitch. She poisoned their minds."

"What about his finances? You've struggled long and hard to get out of the mess your husband left. You don't need someone who can't keep up his end."

"There comes a time in your life when you have to reach for the brass ring, or just give up! I feel close to him. I know underneath his I-don't-give-a-damn exterior beats a kind, gentle, lonely heart."

"That doesn't pay the bills. What did Barry find out?"

"Nothing at all!"

Vera finally sighed. "I guess you believe in that old adage—when you save a person's life, you're responsible for him for the rest of his life."

A daunting thought, but if she could mold him to her habits, it could be beneficial for them both.

Lastly, to be absolutely certain she was up for this, she'd made a special appointment with her doctor, who'd told her, "Go for it!"

And that's what she'd do. She applied mascara and eye shadow and dabbed on perfume. She changed from her housecoat into her robin's-egg-blue dress with the bolero jacket.

⚛

Morgan rang Dixie's bell. He felt listless, almost blue. He'd nearly canceled. They'd been on the phone with each other all week. What else did they have to talk about? And whew, she was a big phone person! Still, she made him smile and his spirits were high for a long time after she'd hung up.

When Dixie opened the door, he put on a big grin as he handed her a bouquet of flowers and a bottle of cabernet.

"How thoughtful!" she said.

He stepped inside. "Smells wonderful."

"Pot roast. My mother's recipe."

The tiny dog danced around him, its shaggy reddish-blonde fur brushing over the floor and its toenails clicking. "Hi, Jiggs." He bent to pat him. Damn, the little thing licked his face, almost caught him full on the lips. He was quick for an old dog.

"He absolutely adores you," Dixie said.

With a rueful smile, Morgan dried off his face with his handkerchief.

"You're looking good," she told him.

She was looking pretty nifty herself. The blue dress set off her eyes. "You're just saying that because the last time you saw me I was in my underwear, spitting up my lungs." Now he was glad he'd come. Actually, he'd been on top of the world until yesterday, when out of nowhere he felt as if the stuffing had been knocked out of him. It must be that new medicine they gave him.

He had a lot to be thankful for. He was alive. His car was back in operation. They'd found the part. It cost much less than a new transmission. Things were back to where they were a month ago, except for the entrance of Dixie into his life. "Nate said you were a heroine. You made a good impression there." He followed her into the kitchen.

"So he's back from Cinci. Did they win the gold?"

"Second place."

"Oh, no. Poor Nate! How's he taking it?"

Morgan felt jealous. "What's all this about Nate?"

"He's a fine man. Quality!"

Morgan guessed his bad temper made her think less of him. That, and knowing his age too, and that he had a chronic illness. Nate had raved on and on about Dixie. If Morgan wasn't careful, he'd lose out. He didn't want to spoil this, like he'd spoiled almost every other relationship in his life.

"What does that make me?" he asked with what he hoped was a teasing smile.

"*Superior* quality."

"Sounds good." The little dog was jumping up on him, wagging his tail. Morgan bent down, patting his bushy head. "Hey, Jiggsy, you sure know how to make a fellow feel important."

"I hope you won't be allergic to him."

Morgan waved his inhaler in front of her. "Just in case."

"Dinner will be ready soon." She tied an apron around her waist. "Keep me company while I finish up. Some wine before dinner?"

"Good idea. Let me." He took the corkscrew from her, his fingers brushing her hand. "Umm," he said, leaning her way, "you smell almost as good as the roast."

While he opened the wine, she arranged his flowers in a vase. "They're gorgeous."

He beamed. The flowers and the wine had set him back over twenty dollars. Well worth it!

"The wine glasses are on the dining room table," she said. "Here, take the flowers in."

He placed the flowers in the center of the massive table, admiring the elegance with which it was set, the beautiful plates, the gleaming silver, and spotless goblets. Even cloth napkins with napkin rings. And candles. He felt honored. "Dixie, the hostess with the mostest," he said as he carried the wineglasses into the kitchen.

"I remember! Pearl Mesta, the biggest party-giver in Washington! She was the hostess with the mostest!" Dixie cried. "What was it she said? 'Any dame with a nice dress and a million dollars can be a great hostess in Washington'?"

"Well, you have the nice dress," Morgan offered.

"But not the million dollars," Dixie said.

He poured the wine. They clinked their glasses together. "Long life," he said.

She said, "Here's to us, because we're beautiful."

"Damn right!" He'd heard that toast before. He sat at the kitchen counter. What was the rest of it? *We're beautiful*—no, *you're beautiful because you're good, You're good because God made you, I wish to God I could*. He gave her a startled look. Did she know that toast? He watched her face, serious, intent, as she donned oven gloves and lifted the roast out of the oven. She sure had a gift for the unexpected. Disconcerting but highly attractive.

Jiggs was growing more and more excited, running from her to him.

She put the roast on a platter and made gravy. "Let me fix a dish for Jiggs." As he scampered around her legs, Dixie put dry dog food in his bowl, covered it with gravy, and added tiny bits of the roast. "That's my good little boy!" she crooned, rubbing his neck and head as he attacked the food.

"Pampered dog," Morgan observed.

She dished out the carrots, potatoes, and gravy. He helped her carry the food into the dining room. "Sit here." She handed him a large knife and fork. "You can carve."

He sat at the head of the table and pierced the meat. The juices ran. He sliced off thin slabs of roast beef. God, this felt good! Master of his domain. He surveyed the long length of the table. It could seat ten more guests easily. If she were agreeable, he could have his poker gang over for a big spread.

She lit the candles, then closed the drapes to keep out the late afternoon sun.

He eyed his full plate. He was starving. He could cut the meat with a fork. It melted in his mouth. Everything was delicious, well-seasoned, and flavorful. "Fantastic," he sighed. "It's good, what there is of it." He grinned. "Er, I mean—there's plenty such as it is."

She seemed taken aback.

He chuckled. "Dad used to say that every Sunday dinner. Mom always laughed. It was his way of complimenting her."

"Hmm," Dixie said. "I'd rather have real compliments."

"*You're* fantastic!" he burst out, then amended with, "a fantastic cook." The dishes of food, Dixie's face, all had soft edges. He hadn't had a candlelight dinner for years, not since he'd been with Miranda. He noticed for the first time the music coming from the living room. She must have a radio in there. He felt as if he were in a movie. It all seemed too good to be true.

He ate two helpings of everything, then dug into his apple pie with ice cream. "As good as my mom's," he proclaimed when he finished.

"I made the pie dough from scratch," Dixie said.

"Hey, you're gonna spoil me if you're not careful."

She stood and began to gather up the dirty dishes. "I'll just stack them in the sink and wash them later," she said. "Two's a crowd in my kitchen. Go in the family room, watch TV."

Hey, this was great, being waited on. He stretched out in the stuffed chair and loosened his belt buckle. He could hear rumblings from the laundry room off to the side. Why not keep his apartment for another year and see what happened? He could come over here for meals, maybe even bring his dirty clothes over. She could wash them and he wouldn't have to send them out. He clicked on the TV. The specter of Whispering Pines receded.

⚭

Dixie rinsed the dishes. She wasn't setting a good precedent, not letting him help. Well, he'd catch on. She needed time to get her thoughts together. She would be unemotional and businesslike.

After the dishes were rinsed and stacked, she marched into the family room, determined to speak her piece. Instead she asked, "Did you see Regis yesterday?"

"What?" He turned down the volume on the TV set.

"Regis! Remember, I told you to be sure to watch."

"I forgot," he said apologetically. "I'm not much for talk shows."

She told him all about it anyway, a blow-by-blow—who the guests were, what they said. "I loved the show," she sighed, "when Kathie Lee was on. She's been through so much." Here was her chance to add, *Just like me,* and move on into her agenda. No, that approach was too self-pitying.

He yawned widely.

She could tell he was getting bored but she kept blabbing, skipping on to the *Antiques Road Show*.

"I'm not a big TV fan. The news. *Sixty Minutes*, baseball games. That's about it."

She felt her palms sweating, her heart going a mile a minute. Just as she was ready to get to the nitty gritty, he said, "Last time you gave me the tour, but I never saw the upstairs. Vera interrupted." His eyes twinkled.

Okay, they'd finish the tour. Give him a peek at the whole package.

As they climbed the stairs, she chattered on about other favorite TV programs. At the upstairs landing, she announced, "Three bedrooms, each with ample closet space," flinging out her arm with a flourish, as if she were a real estate agent. "Two bathrooms, one with a whirlpool tub." He seemed properly impressed. "These two smaller bedrooms are fully furnished but haven't been used for some time."

He dutifully peered into the smaller bedrooms, mumbling, "Very nice," then added, "Don't you get afraid, or lonely, rattling around in this big place?"

She did get lonely and frightened. Every night she prayed for strength. "My memories keep me company," she said brightly.

"Good memories, I hope."

She sighed. "Both kinds. My bedroom," she said of the larger one, "that I share with Jiggs. It has its own bathroom."

Hearing his name, Jiggs dashed into the room, scrambling up on the bed, where he surveyed the two of them magisterially.

"I see who's in charge." Morgan walked over to the window. "Your backyard's like a park with all the flowers and shrubs. Must be a devil to mow."

"I have a power lawn mower," she said.

"Your repertoire of disguises?" He smiled, indicating a variety of wigs, each on its stand, lining her dresser.

Dixie wrinkled her nose. "I'm not what I seem."

"I like it natural." He touched her hair.

She stepped aside nervously. "I have a proposition."

His eyes lit up.

She had to get them out of the bedroom. "Let's talk about it downstairs."

"Who's this?" He stopped at her nightstand, picking up the photo.

"My son."

He looked mystified. "You said you didn't have any kids."

"He died when he was seven." She didn't want to take this tangent, but she heard herself say in a tiny voice, "He went to the hospital for a minor operation. You see his ears? They're large and protruding. The kids teased him about looking like Dumbo. The doctor was going to fix his ears. Minor surgery, they said." Her voice broke. "He died on the operating table, from the anesthesia. The anesthesiologist made a mistake." She sank onto the bed, her fists over her eyes, sobbing. Jiggs, startled, stood up behind her, then pushed his head into her lap.

"I'm sorry." Morgan gently nudged his handkerchief into her hand.

She blew her nose. "I think about him every day. Imagine what he'd be like now as a grown man of 48. What his children would be like. My grandchildren." She broke down again. "My husband and I wanted more children, but they never came. I was 39 when my son Ronnie died."

He sat beside her and awkwardly patted her shoulder.

"I've ruined your handkerchief." She shrugged off his hand and stood. "I'll wash it and give it back." She walked unsteadily into the adjoining bathroom, Jiggs at her heels. She splashed her face with cold water. Her eyes were swollen, red. She held a cold cloth against them. When she came out, Morgan was waiting uncomfortably by the bedroom door. Jiggs, who'd followed her out of the bathroom, looked up at her with sad eyes.

She felt ready to cry again. "Want some tea?" she asked.

"Sure." Morgan followed her back downstairs. Jiggs trekked along behind. "Did you sue the hospital?"

She shook her head.

"Why not?"

"That just wasn't done then. Well, what do you think?" she asked, when they were back in the kitchen. "Now that you've had the full tour?"

"It's beautiful, a showplace."

"Nice part, it's all mine. Except for the last few mortgage payments." She filled the teakettle and put it on the burner. They sat at the counter waiting for the water to boil. "This house and upkeep on it, it's getting to be too much for me. Even though I work, every year it gets harder to make ends meet. I've even thought at times of taking someone in. A paying guest." She gave him a pointed look. "But it would have to be someone who'd help me with chores and the yard."

His eyes widened. He looked shocked. Then he said, "Well, you'd have to screen them pretty thoroughly. You wouldn't want just anyone living with you."

He didn't get it. Or if he did he was pretending not to. She felt humiliated, but she decided to go for broke. "Think about it. Moving in here. As an alternative to Whispering Pines."

The teakettle shrieked. Dixie made the tea. The two drank silently, immersed in their thoughts.

"I will," he said slowly. "I'll think about it."

7

Indecision

Morgan drove home from Dixie's in a daze. Her home was beautiful, an attractive place in which to spend the next few years.

Slow down now, he mumbled to himself. Don't be a sap. Think it through carefully.

She wanted help with the lawn, the chores.

Her yard was huge. Even with a power mower, it would be hard work to keep it looking good. There'd be the shrubs to trim and all those flowers to plant and prune. What other jobs did she have in mind?

Her mortgage was *almost* paid off, she said. What did that mean? Then there'd be taxes, insurance, and upkeep to factor in. Maybe he'd end up paying more at Dixie's than at Whispering Pines.

As soon as he returned to his apartment, he called her. The line was busy.

He sank down in his easy chair and tried to read the paper. If she wanted a gardener, why didn't she look for a younger man to move in and do the work?

She'd asked him. Morgan! She must really like him!

Or maybe she thought he was rich. Like Miranda, who'd dropped him like a hot potato when she found out he wasn't.

๑๖๑

"He said he'd think about moving in," Dixie exclaimed to Vera over the phone. "I skipped church and worked all morning fixing that meal. I waited on him hand and foot. He left without a thank you."

"No manners. A bad sign."

"I was going to send some of the roast home with him, for sandwiches." Dixie sat and kicked off her shoes. She was dead tired. "He was out the door before I could mention it."

"I keep telling you, find out more about this guy."

Maybe she scared him off, crying the way she did about Ronnie. Well, if Morgan was frightened by a little honest emotion, best to know now rather than later. "I won't be hearing from him again," Dixie sighed. Nothing ever turned out right. "Let's change the subject. What did you and Paul do today?"

⊕⊕

Morgan stood by his phone. He'd try calling her again. Dixie was good-looking. She was a terrific cook. She had a sense of humor and a good head on her shoulders. Look how quickly she'd gotten help for him when he was having trouble breathing.

Or was it all part of her larger plan? Charm and manipulate?

God, he was a mess, see-sawing back and forth as if he were a teenager. It had to be those damn pills. He picked up the information sheet that came with them and read: *Prednisone is a corticosteroid.* He scanned down the page. *Side-effects: May cause hirsutism (excessive growth of body hair), weight gain, high blood sugar, hypertension, bone thinning . . .* He laughed. The cure was as bad as the disease. He read on, *irritability, mood swings, an excited or nervous feeling.* There it was in black-and-white. Mood swings. He wasn't going nuts.

Only one pill more left, and he'd be back in control.

He dialed Dixie's number. Still busy. He called every five minutes for the next half hour, growing more and more impatient as he continued to get a busy signal. What could she possibly have to say that would take so long?

Maybe she'd taken her phone off the hook.

One thing for sure, if he decided to move in, he'd get his own phone line.

⊕⊕

"The sweethearts' dinner dance at the Elks!" Vera exclaimed as Dixie was about to hang up. "Bring Morgan. You can double date with Paul and me."

"Only if he calls me first. I'm not calling him!" After Dixie said good-bye to Vera, she asked Jiggs, perched in her lap, "Is he worth the trouble?" Jiggs licked her hand. Dixie sighed. She found the little dog's leash and fastened it on. "Let's go for a walk!"

⟨⟩

Morgan fumed. Her line had been busy for over an hour, and now she wasn't picking up. He hung up when her machine came on. She was obviously avoiding him. PO'd because he'd rushed out of her house like a scared rabbit!

He chuckled at the image, then picked up the newspaper. He read for awhile and went to bed.

⟨⟩

The next morning he got through to Dixie. "Are you mad at me?"

"Why do you ask?"

"Last night I tried to reach you," he said. "The line was busy for almost an hour. Then no answer."

"I was on the phone," she said sweetly, "but not for an hour."

It had been an hour. But he wouldn't argue. "Talking with Vera?"

She made a noncommittal sound. "Then I was out walking Jiggs. Are you sure you called? There wasn't a message on the machine."

He cleared his throat. "I wanted to apologize. I left without thanking you for one of the best meals I've had in years."

"It was nothing." Silence.

"Sorry I had to rush off." He rummaged for an excuse. "I'd just got my car back from the repair. I didn't want to get caught driving after dark, in case the transmission gave out on me again."

"I understand," she said quietly.

"I've been doing some thinking." He cleared his throat again. "About your son. Terrible accident."

"I didn't mean to get so upset."

She sounded choked up, ready to cry again. "Look, how would you like to go for a movie tomorrow night. Dinner first? We can continue our talk from where we left off." He waited for her reply with bated breath. If she asked, "Where did we leave off?" he would have to say, "Where you asked me to move in." And she might answer, "Where did you get that idea?" And he would have to think he'd dreamed it.

"I've been wanting to see that new Julia Roberts picture, *Runaway Bride*," Dixie said. "And you're right, we have a lot of talking to do."

Runaway Bride? Morgan swallowed hard. What was he getting into?

8

Running the Gauntlet

The next night, during the movie, Morgan stole sideways glances at Dixie. She was enraptured. He thought the film was pretty light-weight, a woman's film. But Dixie's laughter was infectious, and about halfway through he found himself joining in.

"I loved it that Julia Roberts was a kickboxer," Dixie said, with a Cheshire-cat-like smile, as the two of them sat in the ice-cream shop after the movie.

Morgan squirmed. "That kinda turned me off."

"I'm not surprised," she said lightly.

"Now what does that mean?" he tried to grin, but he was feeling im-patient. We have a lot of talking to do, she'd said. They'd done a lot of talking this evening but not about his moving in and what might be ex-pected of him.

She finished her strawberry ice-cream soda, then licked her spoon dreamily. "Anyway, they overcame their differences and were married."

"Unrealistic," he pronounced through a mouthful of his double chocolate brownie slathered in chocolate ice cream. "She'd already been married four times."

"You didn't like it!"

Maybe Dixie had changed her mind. Should he bring it up? The evening was almost over. "I did. I did. Life should be more like a movie. That's all."

"Well, we're here for a purpose," she said briskly. "To discuss your moving in."

"As a paying guest," he said.

She hemmed and hawed, and finally ventured, "You can be stubborn."

"I'm not alone there," he laughed, trying to sound casual.

"Compromise is important," Dixie offered.

He agreed. He thought hard. "And then there are personality quirks."

She nodded. "Some little foible could drive one or the other of us crazy."

"And don't forget the moral issue," Morgan laughed. "Some of your friends may accuse you of living in sin."

"My friends will be informed you're renting a room," she replied stiffly.

Morgan hesitated. "The big question is . . . Can we stand each other on a daily basis?"

And so they roughed out a plan, at the end of which a decision would be made. With no hard feelings, they both decided.

⚭

For the next few weeks Morgan and Dixie met almost daily. They ate breakfasts together at the pancake house, or late lunches or dinners at Morgan's favorite restaurant. They always went dutch.

They became an item throughout the area, a "star" couple greeted with interest and anticipation, for Dixie usually had a funny or dramatic story to impart. She told anyone who cared to listen how she and Morgan met so violently at the front door of Whispering Pines. That it was a relationship ordained from the beginning.

One day she said proudly to a new waitress at the pancake house, "Meet my friend. He's 89."

"He doesn't look that old," the woman murmured.

"And he still has all his teeth." Dixie nudged Morgan. "Open your mouth and show her."

She'd surprised him again. He grinned, showing his teeth. "I feel like a horse!" he joked.

The waitress smiled, properly impressed.

Sometimes they had dinners at Dixie's home. Dixie cooked while he relaxed in an easy chair. Jiggs treated him like a member of the family, jumping up in his lap, expecting to be petted and scratched, getting in a quick lick of his face. Morgan vowed he'd train him not to do that when—if—he moved in.

Neighbors of Dixie rang the bell and traipsed in to look him over. Then the postman dropped by, and the woman who delivered her newspaper, followed by the man who cleaned the swimming pool down the block and the boy who mowed the lawn next door. Dixie told them all about their dramatic meeting, how old Morgan was, and asked him to show his teeth.

To some she confided that she'd saved his life. That embarrassed him. It was true, he supposed, but as the days went on the incident seemed less dramatic. He wanted to forget it.

Finally, after a neighbor left, he said to Dixie, "Please stop saying you saved my life. We've heard it enough." He didn't mind showing his teeth. He was proud of them.

"But I did. And you called me an angel."

"I'd have called 911. Or gotten better. The medicine would finally have kicked in," he growled. "Probably!"

"Probably, schmobably," she replied, rolling her eyes.

He met her bridge club (Vera was a member) and played a few hands, badly. Again, he showed his teeth without demur. Dixie honored his request not to mention in front of him that she'd saved his life. But a few of the women came up to him privately, praising Dixie as a heroine. He, of course, agreed. What else could he do?

Even though he was an agnostic, Morgan went to church with Dixie three Sundays in a row. He usually fell asleep during the sermon, which seemed to drone on and on. Each Sunday, Reverend Carmichael shook his hand effusively and said, "Morgan, it's great to have you worship with us!" Each Sunday, Morgan was introduced to every member of the congregation Dixie could accost. It made him feel like a celebrity. Too bad he couldn't get with the whole religion thing. He'd save that discussion for later.

Of course, before every outing, they debated about whose car to use. Dixie didn't trust his car to get them there. Morgan thought her car was too cramped. Besides, he wanted to drive. She drove if they took her car.

"Don't be so cheap," she said. "Buy a new one."

"They're a little pricey," he said pointedly, hoping she'd understand the delicate state of his finances without his spelling it out. Besides, he knew if his car expired for good, he could use hers, if he moved in. A cramped foreign car was better than no wheels at all.

Dixie met his poker club, of which Nate was a member, when she invited them over for a potluck. They played several games around her long and elegant dining room table, staying until eleven PM, leaving behind a stack of dirty dishes and several empty beer bottles.

Morgan left when they did, Dixie insisting Nate take him home since Morgan's car was back in the shop. But it left the mess for her to clean up. She complained about it the next day. But she'd been the one to insist he leave, he grumbled to himself. He'd been geared up to stay overnight with her.

The pace was fun but exhausting. He'd have preferred a slower approach. But the renewal on his apartment lease was looming. Whispering Pines was beckoning. And Dixie seemed determined to move things along in double time.

The Elks dinner dance climaxed this giddy period of their lives.

❧

Morgan, in his rented black tux with tails, caught a glimpse of himself reflected in the florist's window. Not bad looking, for an old man. He threw his shoulders back and sauntered into the shop. The female clerk smiled.

"May I help you?" she asked, almost flirtatiously, he thought.

"I need some advice." He leaned in confidentially, elbows on the counter. "On a corsage for my date. I'm on my way to collect her. Big dance tonight."

The young woman beamed. "What will she be wearing?"

He didn't know.

"Her favorite color?"

"Her eyes are blue, very striking."

"Ah," she said.

He wanted to buy the perfect corsage, one that expressed her uniqueness. "And she has a dramatic flair, an unusual way of seeing things. Everybody likes her . . ." He stopped, surprised at himself for going on this way.

"Black Magic," she said.

"Yes," he answered, chuckling. "You might say that."

She showed him. "Black Magic roses." They were a deep, velvety red. "Flown in from Central America."

"Very nice."

Then the young woman appeared with more flowers. "Stephanotis, also known as the Madagascar jasmine. Smell."

Their fragrance was subtle, tantalizing. "Perfect."

She deftly intertwined the red roses with the white jasmine, adding some greenery and a sheer white ribbon.

Morgan felt almost dizzy, wondering what the evening would bring. Tonight was, in effect, the conclusion of the compatibility experiment between Dixie and him. Soon a decision would be made about the future, his and Dixie's. He swallowed hard.

෨෨

"Who's the elegant stranger?" Dixie asked as she opened her front door. Morgan did look distinguished, like someone from a movie set, with the black tux and tails, and the red carnation in his buttonhole.

Grinning, he looked her up and down and whistled appreciatively.

She slowly pivoted, lifting her arms so the long, wide sleeves of her black sequined jacket floated behind them. The black, she knew, set off dramatically her floor-length blue gown with the silver sheen. She'd paid top price for the ensemble but it was worth it, judging by the look on Morgan's face. She saw him glancing at her blonde wig. She knew he didn't like her to wear it, but she wasn't going to be seen in this outfit with her own mousy gray hair.

Morgan handed her a small white box.

She lifted the lid and parted the tissue paper. "Red roses," she sighed. "My favorite. What are the white flowers?"

He said proudly, "Jasmine, all the way from Madagascar."

"Madagascar! They must have cost a fortune!"

He stood close, his fingers fumbling, as he pinned on the corsage. She breathed in the spicy scent of the roses and jasmine, mingled with his musky aftershave and her new perfume. Intoxicating.

He sneezed.

Oh, dear, she hoped he wasn't allergic. "God bless!"

He took his inhaler from his jacket pocket and sucked at it twice. "People used to think a sneeze was the body's way of expelling a little evil spirit," Dixie pronounced. "*God bless* is a small prayer for divine help."

"Your request for divine help must have been ignored," he grinned roguishly, trying to look down her dress front. "My thoughts now are just as ornery as before I sneezed."

❦

At six o'clock a horn tooted. "Paul and Vera!" Dixie said to Morgan. The two hurried out to the car and scrambled into the back seat, Morgan making sure the tails of his dinner jacket were tucked safely under him before he slammed the door.

"We're late. It's my fault," Vera chortled as Paul backed the car out of Dixie's drive. "Morgan, my hubby, Paul," Vera said. "Nice to meet you," each said to the other.

Paul drove like a madman, mumbling under his breath, his bald head twisting and turning from side to side. His scalp was so smooth that Morgan wondered if he shaved it.

Dixie and Vera chattered excitedly about their gowns, expectations about the evening, the food, the orchestra. Morgan watched and listened, dazzled by their energy.

Vera's long hair, not stringy now, was piled up on her head very becomingly, and she wasn't wearing her glasses. She was better looking than Morgan remembered.

"I'm quitting smoking," Vera announced.

"Good for you," Dixie squealed.

Amazingly, Paul found a parking spot in the front row of the lot. The two couples spilled out of the car and soon were trotting up the front steps of the Elks.

Vera was almost as tall as her husband, Morgan noticed.

Paul gave Vera a boyish smile and grabbed her hand. Morgan wondered if he should take Dixie's hand, but she beat him to it, linking her arm in his. He glanced up at the red-lettered sign draped across the entrance of the massive yellowish stone building. The banner read, SWEETHEARTS' DINNER DANCE. Morgan reached for his handkerchief and wiped the perspiration off his forehead.

❦

"May I have this dance?" Morgan asked, his lips close to Dixie's ear.

His breath tickled. She felt a thrill run from her ear down her neck. She stood up to the strains of "Some Enchanted Evening," enveloped by the music. The band had a big, lush sound, too loud for much conversation, which was fine with her. She loved to dance.

Morgan led her to the dance floor. Overhead, multicolored ribbons of crepe paper looped sinuously, balloons swayed and bobbled. We make a nice fit, she thought as he put his arm around her and pulled her toward him. "Not too close." She indicated her corsage.

With a regretful grin, he allowed more space between them. "I only know the two-step."

"Me too," she said.

He apologized the first time he stepped on her foot. "I haven't danced for some time."

After a series of missteps, Dixie feared her stockings would be shredded and her feet black and blue. She took over the lead during the next dance, but he wrested back control and marched her around the floor, their arms sawing up and down. She worked to keep her feet out of harm's way. I'll be a wreck, she decided, if this keeps up all night.

Finally, to her relief, he stopped trying so hard, relaxed into the rhythm, and guided her around more gently and intuitively. She went with the flow. As the evening progressed, he was grinning and she was grinning. They were having fun!

During "Haunted Heart," he started sneezing. "The battle between good and evil in my sinuses seems to be continuing!" he said in her ear.

She removed her corsage and took it back to their table. He had a long puff of his inhaler and waited on the dance floor.

She glided back into his arms, putting her head on his shoulder. They danced the next dance. And the next and the next.

The band hit favorites from every decade, the twenties through the seventies. A kaleidoscope of memories and feelings enveloped Dixie. Morgan seemed wistful too. "A penny for your thoughts," she said, as the band finished "It Was a Very Good Year."

"Too many pennies for you to carry," he sighed.

They sat out the jitterbug and swing from the forties and the rock and roll from the fifties. Morgan bought another round of drinks for everyone. He and Dixie watched Vera and Paul do a pretty mean

Charleston. They came back to the table, huffing and puffing, and the band took a break.

Morgan couldn't resist a story. "I remember when the Charleston became the rage back in the twenties," he said, "I begged my older cousin Rachel to take me as her dancing partner. 'No way,' she told me. 'You have two left feet!'" Morgan threw a rueful look at Dixie.

"Not true," Dixie smiled.

"Rachel and her partner Ted," Morgan continued, "had already won three contests. I remember standing on the sidelines—I was about ten at the time—while contestants leaped and whirled in a mad frenzy. One couple created quite a stir. The girl did a back flip that brought down the house." He grinned. "To get the attention of the judges, she'd worn no panties."

Dixie glanced worriedly at Vera, who wore a polite smile. Vera disliked off-color stories told in mixed company.

"Ah, those feminine wiles," Paul said to Morgan conspiratorially.

"Her gamble paid off and she took home the evening's grand prize," Morgan laughed. "Rachel and Ted had to be content with honorable mention."

"I was only a year old in 1920," Dixie said. "But I'm a flapper deep in my heart."

Vera was nervously tapping the side of her soda glass with her nail. She looked bored, Dixie thought, but maybe she was just hankering for a cigarette.

"The crazy things people did," Morgan mused, "all in the name of fun. Flagpole sittings. Dance marathons."

"Speaking of dance marathons . . ." Dixie took off a shoe and rubbed her foot.

Vera sighed. She drummed her fingers. She couldn't seem to relax. Finally, she drew a pack of cigarettes from her purse. Paul patted her hand.

She rolled her eyes apologetically. "I'm dying for a cigarette."

"The twenties were a period of great prosperity," Morgan went on. "My dad was a janitor. His wages rose, his work hours were cut back . . ."

Dixie gave Morgan's leg a nudge under the table. Vera's eyes were glazing over.

Morgan ignored her. The drinks seemed to be making him reckless. "Arguments developed over the ethics of contraception, get-rich schemes and women smoking. My grandmother smoked a corncob pipe. She had to hide in the bathroom to do it. Now women smoke walking down the street, just like the men."

Vera sat up, suddenly alert. "You think we should still be hiding in the bathroom?"

"Of course not," Dixie said quickly.

"I just meant . . ." Morgan sputtered.

Paul cut him off, smiling. "I was born at the end of the twenties. In 1929. Vera too." He finished his martini with a quick gulp.

Good, Dixie thought. We're on smoother waters.

"Ah, October 1929," Morgan said half-heartedly. "The stock-market crash."

"And Roosevelt's New Deal," Paul added.

"Let's don't get started on the thirties now," Dixie said nervously.

"Please, no," Vera groaned. "My nicotine-deprived mind can only hold one thought—when is the next hit coming?"

That cleared the air. Everyone laughed.

The band filed back in and launched into a fast number. Vera stood. "Gotta keep movin'," she said to Paul. The two hightailed it to the dance floor.

"I think I monopolized the conversation," Morgan said to Dixie with a grimace. "I also think I put my foot in my mouth."

"Both feet." Dixie was sure she'd hear from Vera about it later. "That's the most I've ever heard you talk."

⚬❧⚬

What stamina, Morgan thought, as he pulled Dixie against him and performed a whirl and dip. It was nearly eleven and they'd danced almost every dance. His gimpy leg, with whatever was going on in the hip joint, didn't even hurt. He was patting himself on the back when he caught a glimpse of a familiar figure. Could it be? Yes, it was. She was plumper, but still Miranda. She wore a flashy, expensive-looking necklace. Her hair, blacker than he remembered it, was swept up and held in place by a large, jeweled comb. She wore bright blue eye shadow and her cheeks were heavily rouged.

She was dancing with a fat dark-haired man, his face coarse and jowly. Was that the guy she'd left him for eight years ago? Her rich guy? Or had she moved on from that rich guy to another?

Morgan spun Dixie the other way, and they finished their dance.

As he and Dixie made their way back to their table, he was face-to-face with Miranda. She stared at him coolly, gave Dixie an appraising glance. He froze. If Miranda said hello, he'd have to introduce her. She evidently didn't want to chat any more than he did. She turned the other way, hooking her arm in the arm of the fat man. They headed toward the bar.

Morgan was glad Dixie was dressed so splendidly tonight, in her blue dress, black sequined jacket, and yes, even the blonde wig. She looked younger and classier than Miranda, who, with her extra weight and too much makeup, made him think of an aging tart.

"I think that woman knows you," Dixie said as they approached their table. "She's been staring at you all evening."

"Because I'm so handsome," Morgan replied as he sat down. Oops, mistake. He should have said, *What woman? I didn't see any woman staring.*

"What's because you're so handsome?" Vera asked with a bright smile.

Morgan grinned. It looked as if Vera was back on his side.

"His effect on women," Dixie said thoughtfully. She whispered something in Vera's ear.

"No secrets now, gals," Morgan said with what he hoped was joviality.

☙❧

"Did she tell you about her husband?" Vera asked Morgan while Dixie was dancing with Paul.

"Not much," Morgan said.

"He was a womanizer. Selfish. He brought her to the brink of financial ruin. She was too good for him. She's waited all her life for someone. She deserves the best. Someone who's loyal and . . . solvent." Her eyes widened as if she expected him to reply.

Did she think he was a freeloader? He'd bought two rounds of drinks during the evening. Didn't she know he was going to be a paying guest and not a husband? That is, if he moved in.

Vera was saying something else. She was hard to hear over the music. "Well, you know her worth," Vera went on. "She saved your life."

"I'm grateful," Morgan said. The music swelled. "But I'm tired of being reminded daily of her good deed."

"What?" Vera asked.

"I said I'm tired of being told over and over that she saved my life." His voice was louder than he had intended. "The repetition is getting annoying!"

She stood up and stared at him, looking frayed around the edges. "It's been ninety minutes since I've had a smoke. But who's counting?" she asked with a raspy laugh. She grabbed her purse and pushed through the milling crowd to the front door.

"Where's Vera?" Dixie asked when she and Paul returned to the table.

"Out having a cigarette," Morgan said glumly. "I think."

"But it's not time," Paul wailed. "She's not due for another thirty minutes."

Morgan lifted his hands. Paul left to find Vera.

Dixie threw Morgan a questioning look, which he ignored. What the hell. He wasn't going to live with Vera. When Vera visited Dixie, it didn't mean he had to be there too.

9

The Kiss

Morgan and Dixie waved. Vera fluttered her fingers. Paul tooted his horn twice and backed his car slowly down Dixie's driveway. The car lurched into the street and headed right.

"Beautiful night," Dixie said.

"Yeah." The sky was clear. Thousands of stars twinkled.

She suddenly laughed.

"What?"

She pointed. Paul's car was stopped at the stop sign under the streetlamp. "Vera will be twisted around in the front seat, trying to get a look. To see if you get in your car. Or come inside."

"Let's give them a show." Morgan moved toward her, grinning, arms outstretched.

Dixie turned away and walked up on the front porch. Morgan followed. He'd better let her set the tone.

Her dress rustled as she lowered herself on the porch swing. "Let's sit out here." She patted the seat.

He sat, draping his arm casually around her shoulders.

The sequins bordering her sleeve seemed to glitter and glow. She ran a finger over them. "Stardust," she said.

"Or maybe light reflected from the street lamp?" He noticed Paul's and Vera's car had moved on.

"You're such a realist," she said with a sigh. "I had a wonderful time."

"So did I," he answered.

"I hope Vera didn't spoil the dance for you. She was pretty jumpy."

"Like a fart in a skillet."

"I'm relieved she's quitting smoking. It's about time."

"Yeah." He didn't want to talk about Vera.

"You and she were deep in conversation while Paul and I were dancing."

Should he tell Dixie he'd yelled at Vera? That was why she'd left the table in a huff to grab an extra smoke, and why she was so quiet in the car just now on the way to Dixie's.

"I was happy to see you two chatting. I want you to get along."

No, he'd let Vera do the carping and then he'd defend himself to Dixie. "She was telling me your late husband was a skunk."

"That he was."

The porch swing squeaked as the two swayed gently to and fro. The crickets chirped, almost like a serenade. Morgan was very conscious of her thigh touching his and the warmth of her back and shoulder where his arm rested.

Finally, Dixie spoke. "Alfred left me with this beautiful house, huge mortgage payments, and almost $98,000 in debt, including $4,500 for a ring he'd just bought for his sweetie."

Morgan withdrew his arm quickly. "$98,000?"

"That was twenty-seven years ago. I've pinched every penny since then, most of the time working two jobs." She faced him with a smile. "I even worked cleaning houses."

"Sounds rough." She'd told him her mortgage would be paid off in two years. She hadn't mentioned any debt. "$98,000 was real money then."

"I've paid off every cent and managed to keep up my mortgage payments too."

"That takes gumption," he said.

"It's one thing I have plenty of."

Jiggs yelped from behind the door. "He's afraid he's missing something." Morgan faked a laugh. That was a bombshell—the $98,000 she'd owed—and paid back, she said. He wondered if he was getting the whole story there. Or maybe something else needed attending to, like a new furnace? Now that he thought about it, Vera had strongly hinted that Dixie needed financial shoring up.

"My late husband loved to gamble. He was also a philanderer. He died in the arms of his mistress." She fixed a suspicious eye on Morgan. "That striking woman who kept looking at you at the dance. Who was she?"

The crickets sounded very loud. "I wouldn't call her striking," he blustered.

"I would!"

He'd better come clean. Well, not entirely. He didn't think she would appreciate his checkered past one bit, not after having Alfred for a husband. "Someone I used to date, eight years ago. Her name's Miranda."

"She looked like she was still attracted."

Hmm. Interesting. He thought she'd eyed him very coldly. "I doubt it. As far as I know, she's married to that ugly, fat guy she was with."

"He wasn't fat. He was buffed. And he was ugly in a handsome way," she said briskly.

He could tell she was in a mood to be contrary.

"Why did you break off?"

Okay, he'd tell her. "She thought I was rich because I was a banker. When she found out I wasn't, she went looking elsewhere."

"Aren't all bankers rich?" Dixie asked lightly.

"Not if they were taken to the cleaners after a divorce. Not if they had to pay child support and use up their savings to put three kids through college. Not if they changed jobs at age 49, losing out in seniority and pension." He felt breathless after that mouthful. He took a hit of his asthma medication.

"You didn't transfer from the bank in Chicago to one of their branches here?"

"I took a job with another bank. I started over."

"That was . . . brave," she said.

"Foolhardy. Now you know it all, including her name."

"Her first name."

"That's all I know. I'm sure she's married."

"She looked pretty restless to me."

"That's Miranda for you."

Jiggs was scratching at the door. The crickets sang, the swing creaked. He checked his watch. "Almost midnight." He stood. "It's been fun!"

He leaned over, kissed her lightly on the mouth, afraid he'd blown it by telling her too much. She rose up from the swing, surprising him, kissing him back. They swayed, arms around each other. The kiss continued.

He'd have liked to stay the night, he said later. She said that she would have liked it too.

❦

Vera called Dixie first thing Sunday morning and apologized for being such a grump at the dance, adding ruefully, "I'm dropping down to three cigarettes today. It's like losing a best friend, but I'm determined to keep smiling." She also felt obliged to mention Morgan's rudeness when Dixie was dancing with Paul and his disrespect for the fact that Dixie had saved his life.

"It makes him feel too vulnerable." Dixie sloughed it off.

"He *is* vulnerable," Vera shrieked. "He's almost 90."

"Oh, Vera, you know as well as I do age is only a number. And don't blame him for blowing off steam at you. Blame my big mouth for making such a big deal out of calling an ambulance. That's all I did."

Vera sighed. "Yeah, I blew off steam at him too. After you pointed out that woman who seemed to know him—which he denied—I worried you were getting yourself another loser like Alfred. Womanizer, spendthrift and all."

"I know." Dixie was touched by Vera's concern. "We had a talk last night. He told me about her. Miranda. They used to be an item eight years ago."

"Ahh. She's history."

Dixie hoped so. She wondered if there were any embers left.

"Did you tell him about Alfred?"

"Oh, yes. $98,000 debt and all. That woke him up." She giggled. "He settled down when I said I'd paid it off." She hadn't told Morgan about her credit cards, four of them, still charged to the max. Even Vera didn't know about that. "I want you two to like each other."

"He can be charming," Vera admitted. "Paul likes him." But she gleefully pounced when Dixie let it slip that he'd started all over again at age 49, when he left Chicago. "I wonder if he was fired," Vera mused. "Caught skimming?"

"They would have checked before they hired him here. Banks, of all places, are meticulous."

"Maybe you should get a private eye . . ."

"Vera! Don't be so cynical! I thought you wanted this for me."

"Just don't let him take out life insurance on you." Her gravelly laugh was cut short by a fit of coughing.

After Vera caught her breath, Dixie said impatiently, "You read too many mysteries."

"Just kidding. I feel protective, babe. You seem to have an affinity for playboys. First Alfred, then that dork in the neighborhood—what was his name? Frank? The one who almost moved in with you. You were pretty high on him at first too."

She didn't like to be reminded. Frank had been married and divorced three times. He'd no thought of being a companion. He wanted a housekeeper, a concubine, and a place to stay, with the freedom to come and go as he pleased.

"If Morgan decides to move in, you better draw up a formal agreement," Vera advised. "Start tough! You can loosen the reins later, once he knows the drill."

෴

That night Dixie confided to Morgan, "When you kissed me, I felt like a woman for the first time in years."

He took a deep breath. She was sweeping him off his feet. He hoped he could measure up.

"It felt so right. I knew you were the answer to my prayers." She said she hoped theirs would be a commitment for the rest of their lives. Maybe even marriage eventually.

"There are tax advantages to staying single," he replied slowly. He wondered if he might not be better off at Whispering Pines.

"I have no family," she said. "Your family might like it better if there are no marriage vows, if our estates are kept separate."

What estate? He had no estate to speak of. If she thought he had money, he'd have to set her straight. Of course, she was probably thinking of her magnificent home, what it would bring on the market.

His kids wouldn't give a damn. They didn't know a thing about his life. He hadn't been in touch since he'd put them through college. Still, the family could be contentious just for the hell of it. Like his ex-wife was. "Why not do what the dropouts of the 1960s did?" he suggested. "Move in together. Share expenses. See what happens."

"It will be like starting over," Dixie smiled. "Life could be exciting again. Just sharing meals will be fun."

Morgan vacillated.

"I like your looks and your sense of humor," she murmured. She continued briskly, "And your tolerance of my shortcomings—if there are any!"

Whoa! He hoped she was joking. He was in big trouble if she thought she was perfect. "There are still many practical questions to be answered," he hedged. Could he adjust to the change and excitement? Would he live long enough to adjust? He didn't want to dwell on that one. It made him short of breath.

"I've decided! You're the one," she gushed. "I can't let you go."

Surprised by her fervor, he heard himself stammer, "Your home is lovely. It's a very agreeable neighborhood. I'll feel like I'm being entertained by a princess."

"You will be," she said, "if you agree to my terms." She smiled wickedly.

The look in her eye sent his heart racing. "What terms are those?" he asked slyly.

She raised her eyebrows. "You'll find out!"

Hell, he wasn't dead yet, not by a long shot. He'd take a chance.

He gave notice on his apartment the very next day, a week and two days before his lease came up for renewal.

⚬⚬

Tony scoped out the territory. It looked like the surface of Mars—rocks, spindly trees, and bushes. Sweat was pouring into his eyes. His feet were sore and swollen. He took a gulp of water. He wanted more, but forced himself to screw the cap back on.

He felt a surge of anger. How could they do this to him?

A guy, his face dirt-caked, was suddenly beside him. "I'm out of water. You got some? My toes are cramping up."

Tony hesitated, then offered his canteen. The guy took a long pull. "Hey!" Tony grabbed his arm. "We got another two miles, anyway."

The guy handed back the water jug. "Thanks." He wiped his mouth on the back of his hand. "You're new."

Tony shrugged. "I've been in orientation."

"What are you here for?"

"Cars," Tony said."I like to drive."

"Me, too." He grinned. "I'm Eddie."

"I'm Tony." He grinned back. "The food sucks. Rice, oats, trail mix. I feel like a horse."

"Wait till Sunday dinner. You'll get your own brick of cheese. It's weird. I never thought cheese would be that good."

Brown hills in the distance shimmered in the heat. "Any way out of here?" Tony asked in a low voice.

"Not easy," Eddie answered. "I heard three guys did it last year. It's about a hundred-mile trek to the nearest piece of pavement."

Tony was tired. Dead tired. He'd think about it later.

"I've been here four weeks," Eddie whispered. "I got some advice. Tell them what they want to hear. You'll get out sooner."

10

This Will Never Work

Friends said they were opposites in every way. They had different backgrounds, different tastes. He had a temper and was alternately passionate and moody. She was vivacious and garrulous. It was one thing to date, another to live together. Especially since they'd known each other for only two months and one week.

Vera said that her friend's wrinkles were from smiles and her pleasant manner masked a fierce desire to have things her own way.

Nate said that Morgan was the sort of man who demanded to be in charge. He was methodical and didn't like surprises. He'd never cooperate with a woman like Dixie, who had a strong mind and will.

Morgan's poker club was offering ten-to-one odds against the success of the partnership.

So their friends clucked and shook their heads when Bryce Morgan and Dixie Valentine met to place their stamp of approval on a just-completed agreement, one that Dixie, with all good intentions, had created that very morning after talking with Morgan (and then Vera) on the phone.

Dixie thought they'd live together without benefit of marriage, go places together, share the expenses and the duties. Morgan had been hesitant about some of the details and let Dixie know he had an aversion to dusting, cleaning, and cooking.

✧

At three o'clock on an October afternoon, the first rifts rent their revolutionary relationship. To celebrate the three-month anniversary of their meeting, the two walked into the Sugar Bowl Tea Shoppe, sat down across the table from each other, and ordered lemon-spice tea and rolls.

After finishing their snack, she smiled and handed him a piece of paper and a pen. He scanned the paper and shook his head. She said something. He shook his head again. Nearby diners sensed a quiet argument was under way between the slender gray-haired woman and the man with the ruddy face.

The elderly couple, who seemed to onlookers to be in their early seventies, had intended to celebrate while deciding more concretely how they could live together in harmony. How would they share expenses? She owned the house but had to meet mortgage payments, insurance, and taxes. Then there were the urgent matters of housework, cooking, laundry, and upkeep. Such problems could not be ignored. No wonder he frowned; he sensed he was about to become a housewife.

Morgan, very much the macho man, had always been pampered. "I never did housework and I am not about to start," he declared.

She smiled, but was unconvinced. "This is a fifty-fifty proposition," Dixie explained. "Each of us has to do a fair share of the work and pay half of the expenses or the deal is off."

He hesitated. The deck was stacked in her favor. She had the house, the bedrooms, all the facilities. He'd thought this woman would make concessions just to have him around, to have someone to talk with, someone to escort her to restaurants and movies. Stubbornly, he shook his head. If she wouldn't relent, he'd find another angel to help finance his remaining years. He folded up the contract she'd presented for his signature and shoved it in his pocket.

Diners had been watching surreptitiously as the tableau unfolded and were surprised by its sudden ending. Dixie, who in her youth undoubtedly had been a golden-haired beauty, quietly arose, walked around the table, and smilingly led her companion away.

I've got her on the ropes, Morgan exulted to himself. *She's still smiling.* He paid the cashier for their rolls and tea. *I'm about to move into a new home with board, room, and services provided.* He swaggered down the street with the suddenly more desirable damsel at his side. *If it works out, I might even insist we get married. This looks like too good a thing to pass up.*

He almost placed his arm around Dixie's waist as he strutted along. He grinned at an approaching shopper and gallantly doffed his hat. Boy, did he feel happy and at peace with the world. He wished he could make a permanent record of this moment so he could relive it from time to time.

The way to Dixie's home was short. He hardly noticed the blister that had formed on his heel. However, he was beginning to feel a little tired, a feeling that was becoming more frequent since he'd passed his eighty-ninth birthday. He began to think of the easy chair and the air-conditioned comfort that awaited him.

Inside Dixie's house, he sat down with a sigh. *I'll put my feet up and ask Dixie to bring me some lemonade. Some ham and cheese on rye would be nice too.* His reverie was shattered by Dixie's voice. "Morgan," she said, "I realize how much you dislike doing any sort of housework so I'm letting you off the hook. You go your way," she continued, her chin jutting out, "and I'll go mine. I'll start looking for another companion, someone who'll be more sharing. You can get yourself a patsy who'll let you sit around on your duff while she works herself to death trying to please you. I'll be interested to know how you make out."

Momentarily speechless, he rose from his chair and blindly stumbled out the front door. He climbed into his car and slammed the door, expecting at any moment to see her imploring him from her doorway. When she didn't appear, he yelled a few choice words through his open window, gunned the motor, and sped away. The trip back to his dreary one-bedroom apartment seemed long. The blister on his heel had broken and was hurting like the devil. He unlocked his front door, limped into his living room, and stared miserably at the boxes stacked there. He had to move out in two weeks. He'd soon be homeless.

☙❧

Nate listened to his friend's criticism of the woman who'd bitterly disappointed him. "I never thought this relationship would fly. I've thought this since the day you two met."

Morgan laughed gloomily. "You seemed to enjoy her company when we had beer at the Knotty Pine."

"I found her attractive and fun, but . . . ."

"But what?" Morgan flared.

Nate shrugged.

"She talks too much. She can be nosy," Morgan admitted. "But who's perfect?"

Nate nodded slowly.

"You think she's too dramatic? She overdresses?"

Nate raised his brows and threw up his hands.

Morgan found himself getting irritated by Nate's criticisms but tried to hold his tongue. "She's generous to a fault," Morgan finally exploded. "She invited the whole gang of us to her place to play poker."

"Yes," Nate said.

"She may have made the guys edgy. As soon as we set a dish down, she grabbed it away and washed it. She was nervous, trying to impress everyone." He threw Nate a questioning look. "But I think they all had a good time."

Nate scratched his head.

"Didn't they?"

"A couple of the guys . . ."

"Who?" Morgan demanded.

Nate waved his hand. "Forget it."

Morgan said stiffly, "She fed us, fixed that big dish of potato salad, baked beans, and hot dogs. Made room in her refrigerator for the beer. Cleaned up the mess we left. She really put herself out." Okay, Morgan said silently, so the next day she complained to him about the rings on her table from beer bottles and the dishes used as ashtrays when she'd specifically asked smokers to go outside. One of the guys had even smoked a cigar. Who could blame her for being annoyed?

"Okay, she's a saint," Nate laughed, then clapped him on the shoulder. "But *you're* not!"

"Oh, I'll be glad to do more than my share in financing the deal, helping with the mortgage payments, the insurance, the operation of the automobiles, but . . ." He spluttered, "Dusting? Washing the kitchen floor? Doing the laundry? Defrosting the refrigerator? These are things she should do."

"You wash and clean now, don't you?" Nate asked drily, with a quirk of his eyebrow.

"As little as possible. Besides, as you know, Dixie's standards are much higher than mine."

◦❧◦

Morgan felt abandoned. What was wrong with a woman who'd choose loneliness rather than see to his simple wants? "I should ride past her house and toss ripe tomatoes on the porch, or write her a nasty letter," he said under his breath. "I should never have given her the time of day."

He turned on his TV, surfing channels, hoping to find a baseball game. He thought she'd appreciate his help with expenses, the comfort he could give her during the long winter evenings. Instead, she wanted him to perform menial chores only a woman should do.

He clicked off the TV in disgust. "Unreasonable shrew!" he burst out. "I'll never live with her even if she begs me to return on my own terms."

He should have listened to friends who warned him about false expectations.

As for Dixie, whenever she felt herself relenting toward Morgan, she fanned the flames of her indignation. Vera was right. *Hold the reins tight. You can loosen them later.* If she'd done that with Alfred, he wouldn't have treated her like a doormat. She'd hold out for what she wanted. Morgan had better shape up, or—well, she'd just look for someone else. And keep looking until when? When would she throw in the towel and admit no one was out there for her at this time of her life?

❧

Like two ships—with their lookouts asleep—that pass in the night, Dixie and Morgan went their separate ways. Both were relieved. She told her bridge club friends she'd prayed for help in finding a companion but "if this man was the answer, the Lord must have been listening on his cell phone."

Her friends insisted, "He'd have been too demanding and too inclined to put everything off on you. He'd blame you for anything that went wrong."

His poker friends agreed to a man: "She was too bossy, too particular about her house. No reason for Morgan to change his ways."

❧

Three days later, Morgan strode into the lobby of the Whispering Pines Retirement Center and Nursing Home. If he bumped into Dixie, so be it. He'd be cordial, as if nothing had happened. They'd both agreed, no hard feelings if the Compatibility Experiment turned out to be a bust.

The square, cheerful face of Mrs. Fontana beamed at him from behind the reception desk.

He pushed his dry lips into a smile. "I'm seriously considering your offer of a one-bedroom apartment in independent living." Okay, so he'd keep running into Dixie there. So what! He could take it if she could. It was the most reasonable and nicest place in the area. He could park his car in the lot, using it until it gave out. Then he would simply rely on cabs and Nate to get him where he needed to be.

He handed Mrs. Fontana his admission papers and added, with a wry grin, "In case I can't find a substitute housekeeper, cook, and caregiver for my remaining years."

She gave him an indulgent smile, waved him back into her office. She examined his documents, saying most likely there'd be an opening in a couple of weeks when the snowbirds left for Florida. "Furnished or unfurnished?" she asked.

"I have furniture," he said.

"We'll need a thousand dollar deposit."

He wrote out the check, signed it with a flourish, and handed it over.

He left her office and stopped dead in his tracks, mesmerized by the parade of pale figures shuffling slowly from the dining room. He broke out in a sweat and told himself he'd get used to it. He'd soon be one of the gang.

Oh, oh, there was Dixie, the last person he wanted to see, pushing a frail little lady in a wheelchair. He ducked back into Mrs. Fontana's office. Her dark brows lifted in surprise. "I guess," he said, stammering, searching for an excuse for returning, "I . . . uh . . . better leave you my phone number."

She blinked. "It's on your admission papers."

He tapped his forehead, chuckling inanely.

He left her office on heightened alert, racking his brain for something breezy to say if Dixie nailed him. But she and the wheelchair-bound lady had disappeared.

He crossed over to the other building and scurried up the back stairs to visit Stan, a member of his poker club who was recovering from a hip replacement. Morgan was saddened by the resigned way Stan accepted the rules that dictated when he would rise, eat his meals, entertain guests, and even go to the toilet. Morgan feared that would be him too soon.

He listened to Stan's complaints that this place wasn't like home, that the help had no sympathy for a sick man, that he couldn't do what he wanted, that he had to conform to their hours, and he, if had his druthers, would rather have a nice woman stay with him and cook for him in his own home.

"That sounds ideal," Morgan said.

Cautiously, he left Stan's room, on the lookout for Dixie. All clear. He hurried down the hall, turned a corner and almost ran into her.

Her eyes widened. She was about to speak.

"Excuse me, ma'am," he mumbled, ducked his head, and kept on moving. He felt her staring daggers at his back. "Imbecile," he heard her mutter.

"Harpy," he muttered back. She brought out the worst in him.

Maybe it would be a relief to live in this beautiful place, he thought momentarily. Hallways and rooms had color-coordinated wallpaper and carpets. Scenic paintings hung from every wall. Eye-catching light fixtures adorned every public place. The wide windows opened on a panorama of pine trees that gave the institution its name.

Residents lived in a carefree setting, with every need provided for. Better than doing half the work at Dixie's, with her barking out orders and cracking the whip.

Dixie watched Morgan's retreating back and saw her future receding too. She didn't want to live in a place like this in her later years. She loved to help the residents and many had become her friends, but she didn't like the occasional sickroom smell and the pervading odor of bodily functions.

I have a lot of living to do before I'll be ready to give up my home and my independence, she told herself. I just need to find someone to share expenses.

Morgan was having similar qualms. His economic outlook was truly bleak. If he moved in here, he'd soon be dipping into his CD, and when that was gone he'd have no cushion. If he didn't move in, he'd have to find another apartment. Quickly. Or a room—that would be cheaper still. He felt a wave of self-pity, and saw himself staring at lonely walls, opening a tin of cat food for lunch, and taking his asthma medications every other day to save money.

He was starting to regret his cavalier rejection of Dixie Valentine's offer of companionship.

After all, she was attractive. She had a beautiful head of hair—when she didn't wear those darn wigs—and wonderful blue eyes. She was small and fit nicely in his arms. She was a good cook. She was, he had to admit, fun to be with, never boring! If only he could prevail on her to curb her sharp tongue.

The more he thought of his plight, the better Dixie Valentine looked, and the more desirable became her plan of sharing duties, expenses, and companionship over the remaining years.

Could he make amends for his earlier mistake? He must, or he would die trying!

ふ

Morgan practiced his apology in his apartment in front of the bathroom mirror. He knew it would take more than a simple "I'm sorry." He'd been too abrasive in rejecting the original deal. He vaguely recalled calling her a *hoyden* or some other unkind word as he sped out of her driveway that day she'd turned him down. He couldn't remember the details.

Dixie was partially to blame. But he should not think that, or mention it. He squinted at his image, then added artificial tears to his eyes, turned the corners of his mouth down, and broke out laughing. His act was going to need more practice.

At last he was ready. He waylaid her at Whispering Pines, in the hallway by the pool table. She jumped and stifled a scream. He could see she didn't want a scene and so allowed him to escort her to a quiet corner. There, behind the elevators, his eyes bright and the corners of his mouth turned down, he blurted: "Dixie, I'm sorry. I'll fulfill every part of the agreement. I'll do my share of the work. Pay half of all living costs including the mortgage, insurance, and operation of the car. Please give me another chance."

She studied him briefly. "I haven't arranged for another companion yet," she said, "but I'm not sure I want to gamble on fickle you."

Now was his chance. He dropped to his knees, hoping it would bring a smile to her face. "I'll do my work cheerfully. I'll shave and shower every morning before breakfast. I'll even dress for dinner each night and take you out 'on the town' every week."

Dixie replied coolly, but he thought he saw a twinkle in her eye. "That sounds too good to be true. But a two-week trial can be arranged. We'll start it the day you bring me the signed and notarized contract."

Morgan's jaw dropped. Notarized? Wasn't his signature enough? Now Morgan was truly sad. He'd committed himself, expecting Dixie to excuse him from some of the shared duties. She was taking advantage of him.

I should walk away, he thought as he struggled to his feet. Patience, he reminded himself. I can work on rule changes after I'm firmly established. Morgan managed a weak smile. "Agreed," he said and stuck out his hand. Dixie ignored it and offered her cheek for a dutiful peck.

As he turned away, he waved his hand in what he hoped was an airy salute. "Here's to a long and happy relationship."

"I hope so," she replied with little enthusiasm.

11

Boot Camp

After checking her watch countless times, Dixie heard a car door slam. She rushed to the window, peeking out from behind her living room drapes. Morgan, a dazed look on his face, emerged from his disreputable-looking four-door sedan. A checked cap perched roguishly on his head. She wanted to run out, throw her arms around him, and lead him into his new home. *Keep your head, Dixie.* She continued to watch as he opened the back door of his car and pulled out two suitcases. *Be all business until you know what's what. No more losers!*

He rang the bell. She slowly counted to ten before she opened the front door.

He handed her his signed and notarized agreement, plus a check, then asked to be shown to his room.

Dixie smiled briefly. "You'll have the guest room up the stairway and down the hall to the right."

"I thought I'd be sleeping in the master bedroom," he teased.

"That's off limits." She took one of his suitcases, leading the way upstairs. "For now," she added softly. *Now how did that pop out?*

"Say what?" he asked, alert.

Stay strong, Dixie. She pictured Vera's face in her mind and ignored his question.

Jiggs followed them up the stairs.

"And there's *your* bathroom," she said, gesturing towards the open door at the end of the hall.

"His and hers bathrooms?" he asked, grinning and puffing slightly from the trek up the stairs.

She nodded. When they got to know each other better, maybe she'd invite him to use her whirlpool tub, big enough for two.

"Here we are," she said proudly. She'd worked hard on his room, cleaning it the day before. She'd also added a bright blue-and-white-checked bedspread with ruffles, matching curtains, and two blue and gold throw rugs.

He entered the bedroom without comment. She winced but held her tongue as he lifted a dirty-looking suitcase onto the pristine spread. He unpacked his shirts and she helped him hang them in the closet. As he put away his underwear in the chest of drawers, she noted his undershirts and skivvies were frayed and dingy-looking. She'd have to give him some instruction about using bleach.

They made two more trips to the car, lugging a small trunk, two suits and four pairs of shoes up to his room. Jiggs happily scampered behind them each time.

His car certainly was an eyesore, Dixie thought. She didn't want it sitting in her drive day after day, to be seen by nosy neighbors who might be offended by an arrangement such as theirs. She'd give him the other side of the garage after it was cleaned out. Good idea, she'd add that to the list of chores he could do while she was at work tomorrow: Clean out garage and drive your car inside.

"Iced tea?" Dixie asked as he continued to unpack.

"Sounds great."

While the kettle boiled, Dixie made a quick call to Vera. "He's unpacking now," she whispered excitedly. "I'm sticking to your advice to hold the reins tight."

"Heigh ho, Dixie!" Vera rasped. "Call me if you weaken. I'll talk you through it."

ॐ

That night, Dixie woke up and slipped across the hall to look in Morgan's room, just to be sure he was really there.

That same night, Morgan, on his way back from the bathroom, stopped at Dixie's door, pushed it open, and peeked in. Jiggs hopped off the bed. Morgan eyed him stonily. Jiggs growled and gave a yip. Morgan slunk back to his bed.

It had come to this. He was a rival with a dog. Morgan lay awake for several minutes, brooding. She'd said the master bedroom was off-limits, but he was sure she'd murmured something that sounded like, *For now*. That half-heard promise tantalized and guided him for the next several weeks.

⁊⁊

They were like a newly married couple. That first week, Morgan forgot he was supposed to do the laundry on Monday, while Dixie was at work. He had to be reminded when it was his turn to empty the trash or mop the kitchen floor. Dixie excused him from cleaning the bathrooms because he objected so much. He did run the sweeper but did no dusting. He was willing to mow the lawn but it was late in the season and the grass refused to grow.

The second week, Dixie followed through on a tip she'd picked up from one of the women's magazines. Before she left for work, she filled a wide-mouthed mason jar with slips of paper assigning his jobs for the day. "Close your eyes and draw out a slip." Her blue eyes were merry. "It will add a touch of mystery and fun."

On a par with a root canal or an IRS audit, Morgan thought, bristling. He put off doing his assigned tasks as long as he could, Jiggs eyeing him solemnly as he dallied over the morning paper and watched TV. "What are you contributing to this household?" Morgan railed at him more than once. "I want you to know I'm looking for a good taxidermist!"

Morgan preferred the weekend or late afternoon each day, when Dixie was home. He wandered around the house, asking her what he should do next. The two often bumped into each other as they went about their housework. "Fancy meeting you here," Morgan quipped one day as they tried to pass in a doorway, and he stumbled against her, hoping she'd fall into his arms.

Dixie stepped out of his reach with the grace of a dancer. "We wouldn't meet so often if you knew what you were doing."

Dixie had made a copy of his notarized agreement. It was displayed on the wall next to the job jar where it reminded Morgan that he'd better toe the line during this trial period or he'd never make it into the Master Bedroom.

So far there'd been no arguments, thanks to Morgan's careful self-control, although he let her know with loud, drawn-out sighs and sad looks that he felt put-upon, since he had no voice in what was going on. It was a mistress/servant setup. He'd envisioned a friendlier environment, with Dixie seeking his advice and affection.

Toward the middle of the second week, he decided to change tactics. He knew it tickled her to get his goat. Well, he'd show her she wasn't fazing him

So when he forgot to transfer the washed clothes to the dryer and she found them the next morning smelling of mildew, he ignored her upraised eyebrow and cheerily offered to rewash the clothes. "I always sent my laundry out to be done," he apologized, asking her to write down all the steps he should follow, how to sort the clothes, when to put in bleach and softener and how much to use, proper time and temperature settings for the washer and the dryer. "You're a gifted teacher," he said finally, kissing her hand. She seemed somewhat disconcerted when she left for work that morning, he was pleased to note.

He was starting to feel at home.

When he didn't remember to take the roast out of the freezer and thaw it for their evening dinner, he ordered Chinese food, which was delivered minutes before she arrived. "I thought we needed a change," he proclaimed with a half-bow as she walked in the door. The food was arranged on the dining room table, in Dixie's best dishes, piping hot. Sweet-and-sour soup, crispy shrimp with walnuts, and lemon chicken.

As for Dixie, she was touched. He'd remembered her favorites. The food smelled delicious and he looked so appealing, it took all her self-control not to hug him. But that might lead to other things she wasn't ready for. And, she sternly reminded herself, it was a two-week trial period and two weeks it would be.

After three days of finding dirty dishes in the sink, Dixie exclaimed half-jokingly, "Morgan, I'm beginning to wonder if your forgetfulness is intentional. I may have to haul you into court to compel fulfillment of the agreement."

"Do that," he quipped back, "and I may be forced to buy you an automatic dishwasher!"

What? That tightwad would never part with his cash for a dishwasher! Would he? She was stunned into silence.

Dixie grew upset with friends who continued to insist that she and

Morgan were much too different to exist in harmony. She'd do her best to preserve the relationship. After all, she'd gone to the Supreme Being to ask for help in finding a companion. She refused to believe that both He and she could be wrong.

☙❧

"They'll never make it," Nate said to himself as he watched Morgan escort Dixie from the restaurant where the three had just dined. "It's definitely not a union made in heaven."

In another part of town, Vera told Paul, "If it succeeds, it will be because both stubbornly refuse to give up or they become experts at compromise."

☙❧

I've been using the stick. Now I'll offer the poor, confused man a carrot, Dixie decided early one evening. She was finding his earnestness and awkwardness increasingly appealing as he went about his loathsome household tasks. She thought about fixing a romantic candlelight dinner, maybe with champagne, but quickly discarded the idea. Such an approach too soon might undo all the progress she'd made in his education as a housewife.

He has a certain charm and carries his age well. I'm almost 80 and not getting any younger, went Dixie's train of thought. While she was hesitating, Morgan sensed an opening and took it.

"Get your jacket. I'm buying dinner tonight at the Red Lobster. We need a break in the prison routine. Besides, there's a domestic problem we should discuss in a neutral setting." Morgan marched off to get her car, which he now was driving as if it was his own.

They were no sooner seated in a secluded corner of the restaurant than he launched his assault. "The pet industry is a multi-billion-dollar annual business," he ranted. "Records show that an owner pays an average $979 a year just for veterinary bills and medications. We can't afford it."

"What is eating you?" the astonished Dixie demanded.

Morgan was almost as astounded by his outburst as she. He'd meant to calmly discuss with her that she sometimes gave Jiggs more consideration than she gave to him.

"Are you starting a campaign against all pets and the animal-rights people?" she asked. "Or do you just have a burr under your saddle?"

"Last night when I went to the bathroom," he blustered, "I was confronted by that furry animal who presumes to be an accredited member of your household."

Dixie smiled to herself. She knew why Morgan had been accosted. He'd lingered outside her bedroom again in the middle of the night. Jiggs was being protective.

"I'd not been told that part of my financial aid would be going to support anyone or anything except you and me. I consider this a reason to renegotiate our agreement."

Dixie stared at Morgan. "I'd begun to doubt my early opinion of you," she said icily. "But now I'm convinced that not only will you do anything to get out of housework—"

"Do I complain?" he exploded. "Never! I do more than my share of the housework, while Jiggs looks on, pampered as a prince." Other patrons in the restaurant were looking their way. He lowered his voice to a hoarse whisper. "Why is it that I get the worst jobs from the job jar?" he asked with a savage grin. "The whole thing's fixed."

She was speechless for a brief moment. Then she rallied, carefully biting off each word. "I can't believe it. You're jealous of Jiggs. You're jealous of a dog! I'm sorry, Morgan, but Jiggs is not negotiable." She threw down her menu. "I hate to think we have an unbreakable contract to live together for the rest of our lives. I'm no longer hungry." She stalked out.

"Who said it was unbreakable and for the rest of our lives?" he yelled, hurrying after her, oblivious to the stares and murmurs of onlookers.

She waited while he unlocked the car. They drove home in silence.

He found her minutes later furiously scrubbing the toilet in the downstairs bathroom.

He went up to his room early and heard dishes clanking angrily below. He guessed she was fixing leftovers. His stomach growled. He waited for her to invite him to join her, but she didn't. Damned if he'd go downstairs and share the table with her. His mouth watered for that lobster dinner he'd missed out on. All because of her. He got mad all over again.

The next morning, Dixie was still cool. That night, Morgan apologized reluctantly. "I want you to know that I love dogs. I'm sorry I complained about having to share the expenses for Jiggs. He's been a little standoffish since I moved in but we became better acquainted last night. When he growled, I offered him a piece of cheese I'd taken from the refrigerator for a midnight snack."

"A bribe, is that it?"

"For what?" he asked innocently. Had she seen him lurking by her bedroom door? "He sat up and begged for more. He can be a cute little cuss." Morgan realized he almost believed what he was saying.

Jiggs was truly a beautiful animal, if dogs can be beautiful. He was 13 years old, no longer young, but was still slim, graceful, and playful. He weighed eleven pounds. His reddish-blonde coat was glossy. If only, Morgan said silently, we weren't rivals.

"He's the only male to sleep with me since my husband died." Dixie explained that Jiggs always snuggled close to her back on cold nights or warm, occupying his own little blanket.

Morgan searched for something flippant to say. Instead, he burst out, "Jiggs has no chores, contributes nothing to the household kitty. He's allowed to share your bed. He gets better treatment than I do." Morgan wanted to add, "We should send him to a kennel so you and I can get better acquainted," but a glance at her solemn features shut him up.

"Vera brought Jiggs to me the day after I retired from the PR agency. At the time, I was lost and lonely, searching for other jobs to continue paying off my debts. This little doggie," she scooped Jiggs up and fondled him in her arms, "has been my closest friend and confidante ever since."

She went upstairs into her bedroom leaving Morgan uncertain as to whether he'd been forgiven. *I may not get another chance if I leave now!* Morgan retreated to his own room, dusted the furniture, ran the sweeper, and hoped the tempest was over.

Her bedroom door remained closed. *Perhaps she's still angry.* He went into the laundry and did the week's washing.

⚅

For the next few days, they did their respective chores, nodding curtly when they met face to face.

"This is childish," Dixie muttered to herself. But she wouldn't be the first to give in. Give an inch now, it would be a mile later.

"This is stupid. All because of the dog!" Morgan thought. But Jiggs was the tip of the iceberg.

Jiggs sensed the tension, growling at Morgan without provocation. Morgan was angry with himself for having brought about the cooling of relations and the possibility that he might have to move out. "I'll go visit Nate for a couple of weeks," he told Dixie after cornering her on the stairway. "That will give us time to reach a decision about the terms of our relationship. Will we continue, or call it quits?"

He smiled to hide the ache in his gut, then made a hasty exit to his room as Jiggs sniffed his trousers and raised a leg. Dixie might have smiled at Jiggs' farewell gesture but she was in the bedroom wiping a tear from her eye.

Morgan left in his car a short time later with a heavy heart and a change of underwear.

Terms of the partnership, which Dixie said was made in heaven and which Morgan blasted as a conspiracy to place him in petticoats, brought sleepless nights to both. Would Dixie liberalize her housekeeping rules? Would Morgan more willingly don an apron? Or would they agree the relationship was so volatile they should go their separate ways?

ᑌᕮᑌ

"She owns the house," Nate said, handing Morgan a cup of hot chocolate. "She's used to being boss of her life. You've been alone for the last forty years and are set in your ways. You'll never take orders or even treat this relationship as a joint venture. Give up the idea of staying together."

The poker club met that night and raised the odds of a successful relationship to fifteen-to-one.

ᑌᕮᑌ

Dixie told Vera she could put up with him if he'd just change his ways a little, tone down his temper, and not be so contrary.

Vera and the rest of the bridge club met the next Saturday at Dixie's to lend her emotional support. For two hours the women deliberated. "Live it up," was Ruthie's conclusion. "Try to reason with the man," advised Joanne. "If he doesn't like Jiggs, it doesn't look good," retorted Karen. "I give it about a fifty percent chance of succeeding," Hilda intoned somberly.

Vera was more optimistic when she talked with Paul about it. "She's grown to like Morgan very much," she told him, "and will go to any length to keep him under her thumb. I predict she'll do all the housework if necessary. She'll agree to let him have two nights a week with the boys. And she'll welcome him into her bedroom where he'll share the bed with her and Jiggs."

"That's just speculation," Paul replied drily. "If I know Dixie, she'll continue to study the challenge."

෧෨

Morgan was in a quandary. Thank God he'd hedged his bets and put his furniture in storage. Should he look for another apartment? Or bite the bullet and check into Whispering Pines?

The days slipped by. Each did a lot of thinking about the future and the past. Each steadfastly refused to call the other.

When the letter arrived with the Chicago postmark, Morgan almost tossed it. He kept it for two days before he finally tore it open. Inside were a handwritten note and a clipping, brittle and yellow with age. He read them both, his chest tight, his stomach churning. He walked around for days weighted down with the past he'd tried to forget.

Morgan later admitted to Dixie that the separation period was the longest two weeks of his life. Nate was on tour most of one week. Morgan hated looking at the walls of his lonely bedroom. He dreaded the arrival of each morning and the thought of eating three meals by himself or across the table from Nate, if he was there. He and Nate weren't meant to live together.

Morgan discovered he missed Dixie's voice, her bossy ways, and that little smile that crossed her face when he pleased her.

He found she'd become so important that he was willing to abide by her rules, do the most depressing household chores, and even walk Jiggs each morning if it would make her happy.

Morgan telephoned early on the fifteenth day to warn her he was on his way. "Have my room ready and prepare to put up with me for the rest of my life," he told her. "I'm going to hold you to the terms of our agreement." But he didn't tell her that he loved her. She (and he) would find that out later.

Dixie had missed him, it was true. But she'd kept herself busy working overtime at Whispering Pines and doing the chores around the house that both should have been doing. She tried not to think about that often grumpy man who'd agreed to share her home, her life, and her expenses.

"I guess he's come to his senses," she told Vera. "He says he's ready to try again." She admitted to Vera what Vera had suspected all along, that she was willing to relent a little on the contract she'd made him sign. In fact, Dixie sometimes fantasized about sleeping with him. Would she have the courage? Only if the lights were out, she decided.

Dixie viewed Morgan's return as a victory and as another of their anniversaries. She recorded the date, November thirteenth, ten days before her eightieth birthday.

BOOK II

STAYING TOGETHER

12

What Could They Have Been Thinking?

Morgan felt a warm, wet kiss in his ear. "Ummm," he sighed, smiling. He stirred in the narrow bed. Where was he? In Heaven, being greeted by an angel?

An even wetter kiss was planted on his cheek. It was coming back now. He was at Dixie's. What a welcome!

Then she was nuzzling his throat, her hair tickling his chest. "You vixen," he murmured. His power over women hadn't failed him.

Wait a minute! Too much! His eyes snapped open.

He sat up with a jerk, arms flailing. Jiggs yelped and bounded off the bed onto the floor.

What was going on? It was the crack of dawn.

"Time to get up," Dixie trilled from outside his bedroom, "if we're going to catch the early service."

"Early service?" he croaked. He rubbed the sleep out of his eyes. Her small figure, dressed in a long white robe, materialized at his door. She carried something in her hands.

"Church, silly," she said. "It starts at nine AM."

Did paying boarders have to join their landladies for church? Church was ungodly at any hour. But nine AM was satanic. "That's not in my contract," he growled, sinking back into the bed.

"You haven't been to church for weeks. They've been asking about you."

This was no time to start a fight about it. Today was his first *real* day back. You couldn't count yesterday when, after his arrival, they'd both behaved like polite strangers, Jiggs eyeing them warily, waiting for the next explosion, tantrum, or ice storm. "What's wrong with the eleven o'clock service?" Morgan asked. He felt tired. The on-again off-again shenanigans of the last few weeks had taken their toll.

"Well, since we're up . . ."

How could she be so perky? "Yeah, since we're up . . ." He glared at Jiggs, who stood by his mistress in the doorway, his beady eyes darting back and forth between the two, his little tongue hanging out. It almost looked as if he were laughing.

He shouldn't be so hard on Jiggs. Dixie most likely had put him up to barging into the room.

"I already had coffee," she said, entering his bedroom. "I've brought you some." She lifted a mug of steaming coffee and a glass of juice from the small tray she carried and put them on the nightstand.

"Well," he said, surprised and touched. He took her hand. "You look like an angel in that outfit."

"It's just an old robe." She smiled, slipping her hand out of his. "I thought we might have brunch at the pancake house after church."

Church it would be. "Sounds good." He'd straighten out the church issue with her at a later date. He threw back the covers and realized he was in his underwear. So what? He sat up on the edge of the bed to drink his coffee.

"Put on something. It's chilly," Dixie called, as she scurried out of his room and into hers. He heard her door close.

The coffee helped. He felt more awake. A hot shower took the kinks out. He shaved, humming tunelessly, thinking it would be like old times—when they were dating—to go to the pancake house. They hadn't been there since August, when they were conducting their Compatibility Experiment. What a relief to be normal, after the weeks of seesawing emotions!

Morgan put on a slightly wrinkled but still serviceable white shirt, and chose his gray suit over the navy blue. He pulled on his trousers, stuffed his shirt in his pants, and buckled the belt. Hmmm, a little tight. He sucked in his stomach. After he was dressed he started downstairs, remembered the coffee cup and glass on the nightstand, and went back for them.

As he walked into the kitchen carrying the dirty dishes, she said, "Well," placing her hand on her chest in mock astonishment. "Just leave them in the sink."

He could see he'd made some points. "You mean I don't have to wash and dry them immediately?" She was wearing that damnable blonde wig. *Keep quiet, Morgan.* "Nice dress. Very cheery."

"We have OSU colors! My scarlet dress and your gray suit!" She eyed him speculatively. "You need a handkerchief for that pocket." She ran upstairs and brought down a square of reddish-pink material that matched her dress. "It picks up the color in your tie," she said, folding the cloth carefully before she tucked it in his jacket pocket.

He smelled her perfume, wanted to wrap his arms around her waist. "The scarlet lady," he murmured, leaning in. "And blonde to boot! What will the congregation think?"

"Who cares?" she answered lightly, dancing away, busying herself filling Jiggs' dish with food, petting and crooning over him while Morgan watched enviously.

They donned their winter coats and hats and walked through the door into the garage. He pushed the button on the wall. The door lifted, groaning.

The brisk November day was overcast. The trees were skeletal, the lawn covered with dead leaves. Raking leaves would be one chore that would get him out of the kitchen, if it didn't stir up his asthma. "Your car or mine?" he asked.

"Don't even ask! Yours is too unpredictable!" she exclaimed.

"Just have to know how to handle it. Like a woman," he grinned, hoping to get a rise out of her.

She looked away. "Expensive, keeping two cars."

"For sure." He should get organized. Scrap that junk heap. Bring over his favorite chair. Get rid of his furniture still in storage. Storage costs weren't cheap. Oh, yeah, and pick up his deposit from Whispering Pines. Well, he'd wait. Until when? Until he was sure? This was it. Wasn't it?

"Why don't you drive?" she smiled, handing him her keys.

"My pleasure," he said.

He backed the car out of the garage.

"Wait a minute! There's Pauline," Dixie said. "Wave."

"Who's she?" Morgan stopped the car and put it in park. Where was she?

"Up there," Dixie said. "In the bedroom window."

He looked up to see a smiling face with curious eyes in the upstairs window of the neighboring house.

Dixie flung her arms back and forth wildly. "She can't see me in here. Wave."

Pauline must really be a good friend, Morgan thought. He rolled down the car window and waved.

"You remember Pauline?" Dixie asked.

"Dimly." She'd been one of the stream of people who'd trickled in and out of Dixie's during their experimental period.

"Well, you made a big impression on her."

"Now what does that mean?" Morgan asked.

Dixie grinned. "She keeps an eye on things in the neighborhood."

He groaned. He hoped Pauline hadn't been watching from the window the day he shouted at Dixie and, gunning his car motor, screeched out of the driveway. Or the day he'd slunk away to Nate's, with only a few toiletries and a change of underwear.

Pauline flung open her front door and called out, "How was Chicago? Any snow up there?"

Morgan threw a quizzical look at Dixie, who seemed embarrassed.

Dixie leaned across him, yelling toward the open car window. "He said no snow. Just a cold wind off the lake. We're off to church. Come over later, why don't you?"

"Chicago?" Morgan asked Dixie, as he rolled up the window.

"When the neighbors wondered where you were, I told them you were called up there, to visit family."

His chest felt tight. He took out his inhaler.

She shrugged. "When I think of you, I think of Chicago."

She knew there was more to that story than met the eye. He sucked in two puffs of Albuterol. Eventually, he'd have to tell her. He could start off the conversation by showing her the clipping. But she might believe it. Best leave that alone.

"Are you okay?" she asked.

"Yeah." He backed the car down the driveway. "It's the dead leaves."

⚘

As the two walked into church, Dixie saw heads turn in their direction. "You see, he's back," she wanted to crow. There were a few here, she wouldn't mention any names, who'd asked about Morgan when he didn't come to church with her anymore and who'd eyed her skeptically when she'd answered, "He's away. Family crisis." They'd never expected to see him with her again. Well, she hadn't been so sure herself. That's why she'd said crisis, to leave her an out.

They slid into the pew. Dixie removed her scarf and shrugged off her coat. When she and Morgan stood to sing the opening hymn, she felt several pairs of eyes drilling into them. She'd chosen her scarlet dress, the matching swatch of scarlet for Morgan's pocket, and her blonde wig carefully. She wanted to be extremely noticeable.

As the two filed by Reverend Carmichael at the exit, he gave them each an effusive smile. "Welcome back," he said to Morgan, pumping his hand. "Hope Chicago was not too taxing."

"No," sighed Morgan.

"There's Betty and Jack," Dixie announced quickly and, waving, skittered over to the couple. She herded them toward Morgan, thinking how smart he looked today in his black topcoat and hat.

Betty beamed at Morgan. "I hope things are okay in . . ."

"I love your scarf!" Dixie quickly said. Why on earth did everyone remember where she said he'd been? And why did they have to parrot it back?

But all in all, church had been a triumph. Dixie grabbed Morgan's arm and the two of them paraded toward Dixie's car. People nodded and smiled. A few looked envious, she was pleased to note, then chided herself for her uncharitable thoughts on church property.

At the pancake house, their favorite waitress greeted them. "Flash me a smile," she said to Morgan.

He did.

"Yep, you still got them," she said, referring to his teeth. "How was the Windy City?"

"*Very* windy," Morgan said with a short laugh. After the waitress left to fetch their water with the slice of lemon, he stared at Dixie thoughtfully.

"Well, now you know. You were asked about while you were gone," she said pertly.

"And talked about, profusely."

She felt her face grow red. She didn't want him thinking she didn't have anything else to do but chitchat about him, as if she'd missed him.

Just then the waitress delivered their water. "Those sports drinks," Dixie, flustered, said to Morgan, as she squeezed lemon juice into her glass, "do you know why they taste like sweat?"

"OK, why do they taste like sweat?" he grinned.

She was glad to see the shadow leave his face. "They analyzed the sweat of football players, created a liquid with a similar composition, and added lime or lemon flavoring."

"No kidding?"

She nodded.

"You got a lot of important information under that blonde wig of yours."

"Trivia, that's my strong suit. No digs about the wig, now. We're in the non-arguing section of the restaurant."

He lifted his glass of water in a toast.

⟊

While Morgan stood in line to pay the check, Dixie waited off to the side, relieved he'd accepted her share of the money for brunch. She didn't want him paying for extras and expecting extras in return. Money had a way of ruining things between people. Slow and easy was the way to go.

Was that—yes, it was—Barry, sitting in the waiting area over by the window. He didn't look much older than when she'd worked for him at the agency, heavier maybe, a sprinkling of gray in his hair. She turned away. She didn't want to run into Barry, not with Morgan in tow.

Too late. "Dixie!" Barry's tall, slightly stooped figure towered over her. His wife, still seated by the window, smiled and waved. "You look stunning," Barry said, taking her hand, giving her a peck on her cheek.

"Just my church duds," Dixie said deprecatingly.

"Say, I was about to call you. I'm going up to Chicago on business in a week or so. I'll do a little more pointed sniffing around about Mr. Morgan. If," he grinned broadly, "the situation still warrants looking into."

She shook her head, starting to tell him to forget it, but was interrupted by Morgan, who suddenly arrived at her side.

"What's going on?" Morgan shoved his billfold in his pocket.

Dixie smiled guiltily. "Morgan, look who's here! You know Barry!"

"Well, my God," Barry stopped in mid-grin. "Bryce Morgan!" He looked from Morgan to Dixie and back, nodding, sucking in his lower lip.

"Barry, yeah." Morgan smiled.

Dixie could see Morgan's antennae were up. She was on pins and needles. If Morgan ever suspected she'd asked Barry to check up on him—

"You still with Kiwanis?" Morgan asked.

Barry nodded. "Lookin' good, buddy!" He grabbed Morgan's hand and shook it. "What's new?"

"What's new?" Morgan's eyes glinted. "I got a new landlady." He grinned toward Dixie. "Moved in yesterday."

Now why did he have to blab that? What would Barry think? All of a sudden, the guy she'd been suspicious enough of to ask Barry to check up on had moved in with her.

"Yesterday! Okay!" Barry slapped him on the back.

Dixie's face felt hot. That was a congratulatory slap as if Morgan had scored. "I've been looking for a *roomer*"—she emphasized *roomer*—"for quite some time," she said, trying not to show her irritation with both of them. Boy Talk. They only thought of one thing.

Morgan winked at Barry. Dixie felt like throttling him.

"By the way," Barry said to Dixie, looking serious. "We finally discussed your project."

She had to think a moment. "Oh," she blurted out, "the project!" It had been an afterthought, the fake reason for her first call to Barry.

He turned to Morgan. "Dixie and I talked—" Barry paused "—when was it?"

"July? August?" She held her breath, praying Barry wouldn't let something slip.

"That long ago? Well, we'll be voting on it next month."

"Project?" Morgan asked.

Barry smiled quickly. "About Kiwanis establishing a fund for Whispering Pines to hire people to read to the sight-impaired residents." He winked at Dixie. "Very positive vibes during the discussion."

"Well," Dixie said, taken aback. "That's great!"

Barry's feet seemed glued to the floor. He looked ready to talk until his table was called. The more he talked the looser his tongue might get. She looked at her watch and then at Morgan. "We're going to be late!"

She patted Barry's arm. "Thanks for your support." She led the way to the exit, Morgan following. She turned to wave at Barry, who was watching with a bemused smile. "I'll phone when I know more," he called. More about the fund? Or more about Morgan? Oh, God, what if he found out something fishy? He wouldn't, she was sure. Morgan had left Chicago so long ago.

"Why did you hurry us out of there?" Morgan grunted as they walked to the car.

"You men. You could talk standing up all afternoon. I've got to get out of these heels. My feet are killing me."

With guilty, sideways glances at Morgan, Dixie talked feverishly about the project as Morgan drove, naming all the residents at the center who were blind or nearly blind. "Some have no visitors, no one to read the paper to them," she said with a sigh. "That must be the worst thing about growing old, losing your sight after being used to it all your life."

"I've heard it's even more isolating to be deaf," he answered.

"We're lucky," she said.

"So far," he murmured.

They were silent for the rest of the ride home, wondering what tricks old age would have in store for them.

After Morgan drove into the garage, he shut off the engine and took Dixie's hand. "That was terrific, what you did."

"What do you mean?"

"Talking to Barry. Getting Kiwanis to fund readers for the blind residents."

"It's not started yet," Dixie said uncomfortably. Morgan seemed impressed by her altruism, but she'd been more interested in herself than in the well-being of the blind at Whispering Pines. Not that she didn't care about the blind.

But wasn't that the way life was? The things you didn't care about that much seemed to happen. The things you cared about too much—well, that was another story.

"I bet you get your funding," Morgan said

His face was inching toward hers. He was going to kiss her. "Better get in the house," she said with laugh. "Jiggs will be wondering where we are." She opened the car door.

"I'm sure he will," Morgan murmured.

"Want some of the paper?" Dixie asked from the couch.

"Sports section," Morgan said, heaving himself up from his chair.

Dixie shuffled through the thick Sunday newspaper, spreading it beside her, fishing out the pages.

He took them from her, their fingers grazing, setting off an electric spark. Both jumped. She laughed nervously. "The news today must be shocking," he said, sitting again in his chair. She'd changed from her church clothes into slacks and a blouse, a deep blue blouse that made her eyes bluer. Her blonde wig was now resting on its stand upstairs, leaving her hair in its natural state. It curled softly around her face. He wanted to touch it.

As they read, Jiggs dozed in the middle of the family room floor.

Dixie seemed embarrassed when she made the first overture. "While we're dawdling, life is passing us by," she declared. "We've set aside our differences. Let's spend part of every day from now on doing the things we want to do."

Morgan perked up. Did that mean he didn't have to defrost the refrigerator after he finished the paper, as indicated on the slip he'd plucked from the job jar? Maybe she was easing the rules. Maybe a little romance might find its way into their lives. He remembered the passion of her kiss that night after the dance, the stars glittering above them. And hadn't she said that he made her feel like a woman again for the first time in years? He came over to the couch, ostensibly to pick up another section of the paper, and sat down beside her. He gave her a melting smile. Feeling like a teenager on a first date, he slid his arm awkwardly around her shoulder. Who knew what might happen on this lazy Sunday afternoon?

He felt her relax against him. He pressed her closer, ready to nibble at her ear. Abruptly, she stood and walked away. "I have an idea. Instead of reading the paper, let's play a game—remembering the things that charmed or shocked us during the twentieth century." Smiling brightly, she perched on the chair he'd just vacated. "They say this sort of exercise prevents Alzheimer's."

Prevents me kissing you, you mean. "What is this? Musical chairs?"

"Clark Gable," Dixie exclaimed. "Do you remember? He created such a furor when he slapped his leading lady that he became an overnight star." She stood again and disappeared into the kitchen, calling to him, "While you help me make soup for dinner, we can reminisce. Let's start with the thirties." She added, "You pretty well covered the twenties at the dinner dance."

He reluctantly made his way to the kitchen. The sweethearts' dinner dance. He'd been a half-hearted sweetheart then. Now it seemed he'd skipped the sweetheart period altogether and was being thoroughly and numbingly domesticated.

She lifted a beef roast out of the refrigerator. "I remember my father called a family conference when he lost his job at the metal stamping factory. It was 1933. I was 14, had started wearing lipstick, and was an ardent admirer of—guess who? Clark Gable."

Morgan sat down at the kitchen table. Okay, he'd be a sport and play the game. "I thought your dad was a farmer."

"We lived on the farm for ten years and loved it. Then we moved to the big city of Columbus for more opportunities." She wrinkled her nose, then ducked her head, cutting the meat into cubes, as she described the impact of the depression on her family.

Morgan listened. He enjoyed watching her. Her movements were deft, almost graceful. "I like your blouse." Shiny, like silk, it fit her snugly, outlining her breasts.

"This old thing! It's too small." She wiped her hands on a towel, flung open the refrigerator door as if she were angry. Had he stared too obviously at her chest? She pulled out bags of raw vegetables and lined them up on the counter top. "You do the carrots." She thrust a primitive-looking gadget his way.

So much for just sitting idly by, while she talked and he listened. He stood beside her at the sink, smiling to himself. The poker club gang would never believe this—he was actually learning to peel a carrot. "How do you work this thing?"

"Don't gouge, just skim over the surface." She took hold of his hand and guided it. "Long, light motions, like this."

He got into the rhythm. Hey, this was fun.

"Let's keep it businesslike," she said with a teasing smile, removing her hand. "Your turn."

He was getting mixed signals. "My turn to what?" he asked with a rakish lift of his eyebrow.

"To talk!" She hacked off the end of an onion.

As they made the soup, they ploughed up their memories of the thirties—the Ohio River flood, the Easter Sunday fire at the Ohio Penitentiary, Hitler's invasion of Poland, the prelude to World War II—each trying to top the other.

Finally, Dixie held up a triumphant fist. "And the thirties ended, with Clark Gable and Vivian Leigh getting starring roles in *Gone With the Wind*." She opened the freezer and pulled out packages of frozen vegetables. "It won sixteen Academy Awards, did you know that?"

"Frankly, my dear," Morgan grumbled, "I don't give a damn." She giggled. Maybe she wanted him to sweep her off her feet and carry her upstairs to the bedroom, 'a la Clark Gable. He had to chuckle. He could imagine the emergency squad asking, "And how did this happen, that you both sustained multiple fractures simultaneously?"

"People lined up around the block to see *Gone with the Wind*." She opened the packs of vegetables and dumped them in the simmering soup.

"We stood in line too," he said. 1939. Barbara had joined him in Chicago. She was pregnant with Clay, their first child, their only son. Morgan had hoped it was a great new beginning for the two of them.

Now with Dixie he felt the same. The testing period was almost over, he felt it in his gut. They were moving toward commitment and intimacy. He hoped he wasn't mistaken, as he'd been with his wife.

The phone rang. It was Vera. Why did she have to ruin the afternoon by calling?

As Dixie talked with her, Morgan stirred the soup and learned to boil a cabbage. When the call went on for an hour, he decided he'd definitely have to put in a separate phone line for himself. "I mean," he faked a grin after she'd hung up, "if it's okay with my landlady."

"Of course," she answered breezily. "Have your own line. Conduct your secret life."

"You make me sound like the CIA." He gave a short laugh. So did she.

After dinner, from separate chairs, they watched *Sixty Minutes* and then a show about angels, one of Dixie's favorites.

When they parted for the night, he patted her on the shoulder, watching as she disappeared into the master bedroom. She reopened the door, called to Jiggs. The door closed firmly.

No kiss goodnight, not even a hug. He lay awake, brooding. If

Dixie's agenda was, as she said, to discuss the highlights of the past, decade by decade, he might as well be at Whispering Pines, looking at life through the dining room window. This was the moment to plunge forward, not stand still. How much time was left?

On the other hand, what if she took him up on his hints and winks? It might just be embarrassing. He hadn't been with anyone since Miranda, eight years ago.

He took a puff of his Albuterol. Empty. He turned on the light and got up. As he pawed through his underwear drawer, looking for another inhaler, he unearthed the Chicago letter.

He swallowed hard. He'd have to make a decision soon. If he went, he'd have to tell Dixie why.

Meanwhile, in her room, Dixie said her prayers, kissed the photo of her son, and lay awake. It had been a good day. She felt closer to Morgan, but she'd have to feel much more secure to let him into her bedroom. She'd have to be surer of his feelings for her.

Now he wanted his own phone line.

She lay tensely on the bed, her brain racing. The real truth of the matter, she finally admitted to herself, did not lie with him. But with her. She was afraid her body would turn him off.

She climbed out of bed, snapped on the light, and stood in front of her mirror. She unbuttoned the top of her nightgown and slid it off her shoulders, forcing herself to take a good, long look. Hideous! What could she have been thinking? He'd give her a disgusted glance, turn on his heels, and leave forever.

13

Strange Doings

Someone had him by the shoulder, shaking him. Tony jerked away and buried his face in the pillow.

"You got hair dye all over the bathroom." Eddie was standing over him. "She's hoppin' mad," he hissed. "She's giving me a hard time. You better leave."

Tony stumbled out of bed, breathing hard. He struggled into his clothes, making sure his billfold was in his pants. "I dreamed I was back at the camp."

Eddie was looking apologetic. "Give me a call. Later. After she goes to work."

"Yeah." Tony shrugged on his jacket and hurried down the stairs and out the front door. He didn't want to run into HER. He stopped for breakfast at a fast food place a block away. The redhead at the counter gave him a big smile. He smiled back.

He dawdled over his egg sandwich and coffee. He remembered there was a library in the neighborhood. But where? He asked the redhead. "Turn left at the corner," she said, looking him up and down. He knew it was because of his new look, the blonde tips in his hair, the mustache, the tiny earring in his right ear. "Later, babe," he said as he turned away.

He found the library and hurried in, glad to get out of the cold. He searched through the stacks, pulled a murder mystery from the shelf, and sat down, trying to read. He had the jitters. He waited an hour, then found the pay phone and called his friend.

"She definitely wants you out," Eddie said. "Sorry, pal."

Stay cool. Keep your head. You're not going back home, that's for sure. "My clothes are still over at your place."

"Where are you?"

"The library."

"Hey, I got an idea. Let's have some fun. I know where her keys are. I'll pick you up in the car."

Tony laughed. "You got some balls."

"She won't be home 'til six. I'll bring your clothes."

Tony hung up the phone. How much dough did he have? He counted. It would last for a week, maybe two if he was careful.

Suddenly, the thought just rolled into his brain. Out of the blue, like it was hiding there all along in some dark corner.

He flipped through the ragged phonebook by the pay phone and found what he was looking for.

Why not? Yeah. Why not?

He walked over to the woman at the reference desk and asked to borrow her pen and a piece of paper. He jotted down the information from the phone book. Then he waited just inside the door, watching for his friend.

"You know where this is?" he asked, as he got into the car. He handed Eddie the slip of paper.

"We can ask," Eddie said. "But first I need something to eat. How much money you got?"

⟡

Dixie clicked on the TV, surfing the channels. She heard Morgan clattering around in the kitchen. "You up?" she called out.

"Just barely." He peeked around the corner and waved.

She twisted around in her chair. "You gotta see this! Regis has a woman wrestler on. She's six foot tall. Weighs two hundred pounds."

"I never watch the morning talk shows," Morgan said. "Too much fluff!"

"Fluff? This woman is a pioneer. One of the few females in wrestling."

"I do like her outfit, the studs on her bra!" Morgan disappeared back into the kitchen.

She heard the toast pop up, the refrigerator door open and close. Finally, he made his way into the family room, a glass of tomato juice in one hand, his toast resting on a napkin in the other. He sat on the sofa and placed his breakfast on a nearby TV tray.

"I almost forgot," Dixie said, during the commercial. That was a lie. How could she forget? She turned the volume down. "Tonight I'll be late getting home."

"Oh?"

"Staff meeting." She had a doctor's appointment after work, her usual checkup, with all the usual tests. She felt fluttery thinking about it. But then she always did.

"You always dress up like that for a staff meeting?"

"Umm hmm." She wore something special for these visits. It gave her a morale boost in advance, in case there was bad news. "Why don't you use a plate?" she grinned. "Afraid you'll have to wash it?" He was dressed in baggy gray pants and a green plaid shirt. His hair was rumpled, as if he hadn't combed it yet this morning. But he'd shaved. She could smell the aftershave. He looked vulnerable and cute. She almost could have kissed him. "Look at Regis!" she cried out. "Look! He's showing off his muscles." Dixie turned the volume up. This was a show that really cheered her up, even when she was way, way down.

From the corner of her eye, Dixie could see Morgan feeding Jiggs pieces of buttered toast. She tried to ignore it. "If he gets sick—" she finally burst out.

"He won't."

"—you're going to clean it up."

"You treat this dog like a prima donna," he said airily.

"He's an old dog. Fat does not agree with him." The show was drifting into a cooking segment. She looked at her watch. "Nine-thirty. Better put on my face. That was fun." She handed the remote to Morgan.

"Yeah." Morgan clicked off the TV. "Pretty sexy, that female wrestler rolling around on the floor with Regis."

"Is that all you think about?" She padded upstairs in her stocking feet, brushed her teeth, and put on green eye shadow and lipstick. Today she'd wear the auburn wig! It made her feel like Shirley MacLaine.

❦

Morgan dropped another piece of bread in the toaster. He always made sure he was up to see Dixie off in the mornings. And he tried to watch the shows she liked. The days she worked were pretty much the same routine. Now he knew how housewives felt and no, contrary to what Dixie said she believed, being surprised by what the job jar held for him on those little slips of paper did not make the day more exciting. The work was boring, tiring. Besides, after he'd cleaned everything up, the place just got dirty again. Talk about Sisyphus!

The toast popped up. He buttered it and spread it thickly with jam. Jiggs was underfoot. "You like this, do you?" he broke off a hunk and fed it to him. When he and Dixie were better established, maybe she'd quit that job. They could sleep in, indulge in some hanky panky in the mornings. That was a better time for him than late at night. He had more energy. He knew she was attracted to him, he could feel it in her glances. But she was still treating him like a paying guest.

He chuckled to himself. Next Tuesday was her eightieth birthday and he had a plan that might change things for the better around here.

Jiggs made a choking sound and threw up on the kitchen floor. Morgan grabbed some paper towels and, almost losing his cookies himself, wiped it up.

Yikes. It still smelled. Morgan searched the cupboard, found some lemon-scented cleaner and squirted it on the floor. He threw down another paper towel and wiped it around with his foot. Then he squirted the lemon scent into the trash can. Better.

"Mama's boy," he said to Jiggs.

Jiggs hung his head.

"Just kidding, pal." Morgan scratched his silky ears. Jiggs licked his hand, his little tail wagging furiously.

❦

Dixie swept downstairs, green and blue scarves flying, just in time to see Jiggs lick Morgan's hand. Her heart soared. Morgan and Jiggs were bonding. She had to be careful to give them equal attention. One always jealously watched the other. She sniffed the air. "What's that smell?"

"What smell?"

"I don't know," she frowned. "Something lemony?" She sniffed again. Underneath the lemon, something sharp and sour. Morgan looked guilty.

"I thought I'd do the kitchen floor maybe," he said quickly, holding up the bottle of lemon cleanser.

Dixie knew Jiggs had gotten sick, but she held her tongue. Jiggs looked none the worse for it. She laughed. "It's not for linoleum." She studied a moment. "But good idea. You could do some dusting with it." She took her coat out of the front closet. "Maybe after you defrost the refrigerator. You know, we never did get around to that."

"No, *we* never did!" he said, helping her on with her coat.

ҩ

He waved as she opened the door to the garage. Jiggs yelped good-bye. The two then segued to the front door, as they always did. Jiggs stood up, his shaggy paws on the glass sidelite, his nose pressed against it. Morgan opened the front door and waved again.

Usually, the days seemed long without her. But today Morgan was excited.

How to begin? He'd never shopped for clothes for a woman before. His secretary had always done it. He went upstairs and into Dixie's bedroom, looking through her closet. Dresses, blouses, and skirts were bunched so tightly together it was hard to jam his hand in and get a look at sizes. Frustrated, he rummaged through her dresser drawers. He'd better take something with him. Okay, this would do, for the first part of the expedition anyway. Feeling a little like a pervert, he pulled out a pair of Dixie's underpants and stuffed them in his pocket.

He backed out of the garage and down the drive, his ramshackle car smoking and grunting. It was a beautiful autumn day and he was going shopping.

ҩ

Morgan wandered around in circles, past the perfumes, purses, blouses, dresses, and pants suits. After hitting one dead end after another, he finally ended up in brassieres, hundreds of them hanging from hooks or stuffed in boxes stacked on tables. His head was whirling. No one was around to ask. He trudged on, getting more tired and impatient by the minute. At last, miracle of miracles, he stumbled into underpants, a maze of all sizes, shapes, and colors, hanging from little white hangers.

He felt as if he were in a jungle surrounded by exotic blooms. He fingered a pair of black lacy things. Let's see. What about size? He took Dixie's underpants out of his pocket and dangled them next to the black ones. He needed something a little larger.

"May I help you, sir?" a voice behind him asked politely.

He jumped and turned around to see a buxom middle-aged lady. She wore no coat. Must be the sales clerk. Had she been following him? "I need something in black, about this size." Embarrassed, he held up Dixie's underpants.

The sales clerk stared, her eyes magnified behind her glasses.

"These are mine. Not mine," he stammered. "They're hers. My friend's. Not the store's."

The clerk inspected them. "Size six." Her hand darted from one rack to another, sorting through the collection. "Do you want a brief? Bikini? Hi-cut? Thong? Freeform? Cotton, nylon? Chiffon? Microfiber?"

"Uhhh." His head was swimming. He didn't know he'd have to make so many decisions. "Definitely no thongs. Can I see everything else in black, size six?"

She sighed. "They're grouped by brand, all over the department." She made a sweeping gesture with her arm.

"Well." He pointed to the black lace panties on the rack. "Do you have these in size six?"

She rummaged again through the racks and handed him an identical pair, showing him the label.

He held the two garments together. "Just right."

"Just one pair, sir?" she asked.

"For now." He cleared his throat. "I'm also looking for, uh—sleepwear."

"For yourself?" She managed a smile. "Your friend?"

Oh, ho, what was over there? Some very shapely mannequins draped in a variety of nightgowns or negligees or whatever they were called. He quickly walked over to the display. She followed.

He eyed a stunning, floor-length maroon number, low cut, with a lace bodice, and see-through jacket. "What do you think?"

"The peignoir?" The woman's eyes twinkled. "She'll love it!"

❧

Elated, Morgan returned home from the department store. He hid the gift-wrapped packages in the closet in his room. For lunch, he ate a bowl of soup. He and Dixie had been eating it since they made it Sunday, but he was too lazy to fix himself something else.

He felt wonderful, light as air, as he ignored the slip of paper that instructed him to wash the kitchen floor and run the sweeper. Ignored the can of lemon cleaner that Dixie wanted him to use while dusting. And, no, thank you very much, he wasn't going to defrost the refrigerator as Dixie had cheerily suggested.

He donned his coat and cap, looped a scarf around his neck, and opened the door from the family room to the garage, punching the button that lifted the garage doors. He called to Jiggs, "Freedom, boy, how does that sound?" Jiggs hesitated, then scampered after him. Dixie never let Jiggs play in the front without a leash. He was allowed only in the fenced-in backyard.

Morgan lifted the rake off the wall hook. Jiggs nipped at its quivering prongs. The two marched into the front yard.

Morgan took a deep breath. The sky was clouding up. It seemed snappier than earlier. He attacked the leaves with gusto as Jiggs danced beside him, growling at the rake, his silky coat dotted with twigs and dried leaves.

Morgan was feeling pretty frisky, working up a good sweat. Then he noticed his breathing was ragged. Better slow down. He did, but he was still huffing and puffing. Finally, he sank down onto the front stoop, breathing hard. *Asthma attack, you numbskull!* He took three hits of his inhaler and sat, conscious of his every breath, until the medicine kicked in. He glanced over at the house next door and thought he saw the upstairs curtain flutter. Had what's-her-name, the neighborhood gadfly, been watching? Jiggs darted over and licked his face. Morgan laughed. He'd caught him by surprise again.

Jiggs was getting friendlier. Morgan would get his leash out and take him for a long walk.

But first he was determined to finish the leaves. Morgan pushed himself up off the concrete porch. He felt a little wobbly. He stood still for a few seconds. Okay, all systems go. He wrapped his scarf around his nose and mouth to filter out the dust. He raked the leaves into several piles. Each time, Jiggs leaped in the middle and rolled around. He'd never seen Jiggs so frisky! Laughing, Morgan distracted him by throwing his glove for him to fetch. Only then could Morgan bag the leaves.

He was feeling damned good. "We'll do the backyard, Jiggsy. But first we need some sustenance." He dragged the bulky, leaf-filled bags over to the curb for the trash collector. Then he went into the house, Jiggs trotting alongside. He filled Jiggs' water bowl and fixed himself a cup of hot tea. As he drank it, he savored his surprises for Dixie. He couldn't wait to see her face when she opened the gifts. It would be hard to wait until her birthday.

๑๑

Dixie tiptoed over to the bed. The sleeping figure was almost swallowed up by the bedclothes. Her little face peeped out, scrubbed, with sunken cheeks. She looked like a shiny-faced little gnome.

Effie's eyes fluttered open. "Who's there?" she croaked.

"Me, Dixie. It's Dixie," she repeated more loudly, seeing the confusion on Effie's face. "I just wanted to say we're glad you're out of the hospital and back here at the convalescent center."

"Me too." Effie took several shallow breaths. "The doctor had trouble finding the right antibiotic," she said hoarsely.

Pneumonia. The old people's friend. It takes them quickly. Well, it hadn't taken Effie. She couldn't walk, was almost blind, couldn't hear very well, but even so she was alive, thanks to modern medicine. "We miss you at bingo."

Effie smiled.

"I won't stay. Go back to sleep now." She placed the tangerine she'd brought for Effie on the bedside table.

"I have to get out of this bed . . ." Effie's trembling fingers found the button on the bed rail and pressed it. ". . . if I'm gonna make it to 101." The mechanism squeaked and rumbled, lifting her head and upper body into a sitting position.

"You gotta show that new great-granddaughter the ropes!"

Effie gave a dry chuckle.

"I brought you something from the dining room." Dixie held out the tangerine.

Effie's eyes lit up.

Dixie peeled the piece of fruit. Soon the room lost its stuffy sickroom odor and was filled with the clean, fresh smell of tangerine.

"I don't know what they did with my teeth," Effie fretted.

"Suck out the juice." Dixie gave her a slice.

"Just what the doctor ordered," Effie said after four tangerine slices. Her little eyes, deep-set in her bony face, sparkled. "How's that friend of yours?"

"Morgan?" Dixie had told Effie a little bit about their ups and downs. "He moved back in last Saturday. You were still in the hospital."

"What's that?"

"He moved back in," Dixie repeated with more volume. Her words reverberated, swirling around her, like one of those spooky voice-overs in a forties movie. Like *Rebecca*.

"I'm glad," Effie said.

"Why are you glad?" Maybe Effie had some special second sight.

"You seemed so sad the last time I saw you."

Dixie sat in the chair next to the bed and leaned towards Effie's ear. "This is hard, at my age, living with someone again."

"It takes courage," Effie said.

"Maybe more than I have. Every time he's moody, I wonder what it is I've done." Dixie found herself blabbering and she couldn't seem to stop. "And he wants more than I can give. Right now." Dixie felt her eyes fill up with tears. Her face was burning. "I'm on pins and needles," she stammered, "afraid he'll leave." She felt Effie's hand, soft and dry, on hers.

"He's on pins and needles too, I bet."

Was he? He seemed so sure of himself.

"You trust him?" Effie asked.

"I do," she said more forcefully than she felt. She laughed nervously.

"I caught a glimpse of him outside the room at my hundredth birthday party. Nice looking man. Lots of character. You can see it in his face."

"He does have a nice face." You can't tell a book by its cover, her mother always said. "And he's opinionated. And stubborn. And secretive."

Effie leaned forward, her eyes burning. "There's no better time than right now to be happy." She squeezed her hand, hard.

Dixie was silent.

Effie looked embarrassed. "I just wish I'd had your gumption when my husband died. I've been alone almost thirty years. My kids are there for me, but that's not the same."

"No, not the same," Dixie murmured. She didn't have a kid. But she had Jiggs.

"I'd like to meet your friend. Tell him not to take you for granted."

"I'll bring him by." Dixie bent and kissed her forehead. "I came here today to make you feel better. You turned the tables on me!"

Dixie drove on to her doctor's appointment. What a grande dame Effie was! Dixie hoped she'd have half her spunk when she got to be 100!

⚬⚬

Tony rubbed his hands together and blew on them. He was freezing. He needed gloves. He could smell his sweat through his jacket. The cold wind slapped his face, making his eyes tear. Don't start feeling sorry for yourself, man.

He blinked at the square of paper he held in his hand. This was the address, according to the woman at the first place he'd tried.

Expensive-looking house. Big too. Looked like he was rich, as they'd been claiming all these years. A rich, fat banker.

He walked up the drive and onto the porch.

A dog barked inside. Two magazines were rolled up in the holder below the mailbox. He bent down and read the address label on the bottom one. Dixie Valentine. Maybe he was at the wrong place.

Inside it was another, thinner magazine. He peered in through the glass sidelite. No one in the hall. He furtively adjusted the thinner magazine so he could see the label. Aubrey Bryce Morgan. This was the place all right. And he was living here with some woman.

There was the bell. All he had to do was ring it.

His mouth was dry. What if he answered the bell? What would he say? You owe me? I need you to help me?

Well, I'll just ask, Are you the rich slob who ruined our lives? Or will I be too mad to speak?

His heart was pounding loud. He felt dizzy.

⚬⚬

Dixie left the doctor's office, high heels clicking. Everything looked good, he'd said. The gloom that had shrouded her all day lifted. Still, it was hard to relax. She'd been so tense. And she still had to wait for results from the usual tests. On a whim she stopped by the supermarket and picked up two filet mignons and some red wine. By the time she made it through the checkout it was late, later than she thought she'd be. Would Morgan be worried? Well, if he was, he could always call her on the cell phone. He'd be pleased when she showed him her surprises.

As she drew closer to the house, she saw a figure hurry down their drive, then cross the street. As she passed him, she strained to see a face, but his hood obscured much of it. Still, she saw a dark mustache, a pinched white face. Someone selling something? But he carried nothing in his hands. No need to get worked up. A new neighbor perhaps, stopping by to introduce himself. In her rearview mirror, she saw him running as he turned the corner.

She wondered if he'd been up to some mischief. This neighborhood had always been safe. She was just edgy. She shouldn't have had that coffee at two this afternoon. But it had geared her up for the doctor. In fact, maybe she'd been a little too hyper, cracking jokes to hide her nervousness.

She came into the house from the garage. "I'm here!" she called. Where was he? His car was in the garage when she'd driven in. "Morgan?" She hurried upstairs to his room to see if he was lying down. No sign of him. She came back downstairs, still wearing her coat, her sack of groceries in her hand. Where was he? And where was Jiggs? "Jiggs," she called. "Jiggs!" She was feeling panicky.

She heard a muffled bark. Was he outside?

She rushed over, looked through the sliding-glass door into the back yard.

Morgan, his back to her, his long, black raincoat flapping about his legs, was filling a plastic bag with leaves. Jiggs romped beside him. Relief swept over her. She slid open the door. "Hi, I'm home! Were you worried? I'm very late."

He turned around, his nose and mouth covered by a cream-colored scarf.

"You look like a bandit!" Dixie said.

He ripped the scarf away. Grinning, he sidled up to the door. "I've been working incognito," he said in a fake whisper, "to confuse your nosy neighbor. What's in the sack?"

She felt deflated. He wasn't worried about her at all. But she'd been worried sick about him. Men!

⚜

"He's living with some broad," Tony said after he climbed into the car.

"No kidding? So, what did he have to say?" Eddie asked.

"I'm still casing the joint. I looked at the mail. That's how I know."

"Next time I'll come with you." Eddie pulled away from the curb. "How about a beer?"

"I gotta find a place to crash first." What was he letting himself in for? He should go back to Chicago.

⊙⊷

"Be careful!" Dixie exclaimed as Morgan started through the sliding door.

He froze mid-motion.

"Don't track leaves in on the rug!"

"Yes, ma'am."

"Please," she added.

Sighing, Morgan lowered himself onto the back stoop, took off his shoes, and slapped each one vigorously against the edge of the step.

Jiggs jumped over his arm, through the open door, and ran to Dixie, his tail wagging. "Oh, Jiggs," she moaned. "You're a mess." She plucked off the dead leaves and twigs tangled in his shaggy coat. "I'll have to take you in for a trim! And look at the rug!"

Shoes in hand, Morgan stepped into the family room in his stocking feet and slid the door closed.

"Should you be raking leaves? What about your asthma?" *Shut up, Dixie.* She wished she could stuff the words all back in. Nothing out of her mouth but criticisms. Why couldn't she seize the moment, as Effie had advised?

He waved his scarf at her. "Perfect filter. Don't try to baby me like you do Jiggs." He gave her a close look. "I'd hoped for a friendlier greeting." He slid out of his coat.

"The yard does look better," Dixie admitted. "But you don't want to get another attack. Like before."

"And you'll have to save my life, like before!" he replied, a little tartly, she thought, but with a smile.

"Don't joke about it." She walked into the kitchen. "There's plenty for you to do inside." She set the grocery sack on the kitchen table, opened the refrigerator, and put away the package of steaks. "For instance," she made her voice casual, "I see you didn't—uh—get a chance to defrost the refrigerator."

She heard an expulsion of breath from the family room, then mumbling.

"What?" she asked, peering into the room.

"I was talking to Jiggs," he grunted, sitting in the chair, putting on his shoes.

What did it matter about the refrigerator? She had the filets and wine. They were going to have a good meal. It was Friday. She'd let herself relax, let him relax.

She hung up her coat in the front hall and brought in the mail. Nothing but bills and a few ads. She left it on the hall table. She went upstairs. She slipped out of her high heels and into slippers, took off her wig and put it on its stand beside the others. She rubbed the base of her neck. She was looking forward to unwinding with a glass of wine and talking to Morgan about her day. What a gift it was to have someone here at night to talk to! Why couldn't she leave her other habits behind and let herself realize her good fortune? But before she did anything, she'd sweep up the mess Jiggs had made, get that off her mind.

⚘

She was tired, Morgan realized. But he was put out that she hadn't been more effusive about his work on the yard. He took the sweeper from the utility cupboard and ran it over the carpet where Jiggs had tracked in the leaves. He knew if he didn't, Dixie would. He cut off the sweeper and realized she was standing in the kitchen watching him. "Well, well," she said, rather smugly, he thought, as if she had him in her pocket.

"What do you want to do for dinner?" he asked, then decided it was time to assert himself. He was being namby-pamby. No wonder she was still ordering him around, treating him like Jiggs.

"There's the soup . . ." she said, with smile.

He cut her off. "I had soup for lunch. And soup every other day this week." Where were those delectable meals that had been implied, the tantalizing roasts and home-made pies? "Let's talk," he demanded. He sat down at the table. Eyes wide, she sat opposite him.

"You've been setting the rules," he said. "Now I have some rules that would improve our relationship. For one, let's get rid of that job jar. I had a damn good time out there today, playing in the leaves. And so did Jiggs! And the yard looks a damn sight better!"

She opened her mouth to speak.

He held up his hand. "Two, no more soup. Put on your best bib and tucker, I'll take you out for supper at the Downtown Inn." *And perhaps*, he continued to himself, *I'll kiss you goodnight!*

Her lower lip quivered. He thought she was going to cry. She reached over and squeezed his hand. "I picked up a surprise for dinner. When I got home I was so flustered that I forgot to mention it." She opened the refrigerator and held up the package of filet mignons.

"Why were you flustered?"

She shook her head, mute, then burst out, "Effie. She's had pneumonia, did I tell you?"

He shook his head.

"So frail. I think we're going to lose her soon. Then the doc—the staff meeting went into overtime. I was running late and stopped by the supermarket for steaks and wine to celebrate." She pulled a bottle of wine from the sack on the table.

He took it from her and went over to the sink, scrabbling through the drawer for the corkscrew.

"And I don't know why—it gave me a chill. I saw a someone in a dark hooded jacket walking down the drive here at the house, then he started to run. I had a terrible feeling . . . I rushed in to see if you were all right. I couldn't find you. Did someone ring the bell just before I came home?"

He shrugged. "I was in the backyard. Someone in a black jacket and hood, you say?"

"You know him?"

"Did he carry a scythe?" Morgan asked with a twinkle in his eye. He handed her a glass of wine.

"That's not funny."

He clinked his glass to hers. "What are we celebrating?" he asked.

Dixie's face was blank for a moment, then she laughed. "Well, it's the weekend. TGIF."

☙

As Dixie turned to face him at the sink, Morgan said, "Delicious meal," and quickly kissed her on her lips before she had a chance to dodge away. He threw a grin at Jiggs. *See pal, I'm learning your tricks.* But Jiggs was too busy gobbling down his steak dinner to notice.

Dixie looked Morgan in the eyes and took a deep breath. "We have a lot to talk about before I jump into bed with you."

"A hug or a kiss is not the same as jumping into bed," he protested.

The dishes clattered loudly as she rinsed them. "One thing leads to another," she murmured.

"By talking, you mean we have to go through the highlights of all the decades before I get a hug?" They'd gone through the forties on Thursday. Five more to go.

"By talking, I mean there are things I don't know about you," Dixie said. "And things you don't know about me." She turned off the faucet and dried her hands. "Let's go into the family room."

This must be serious, Morgan thought. She'd left the dishes soaking in the sink. He grabbed their glasses and the remaining wine and followed her into the family room.

Each took a chair. Morgan plunked the wine bottle and glasses on a tray table between them. Silence was thick.

She seemed to want him to say something first. He squirmed. "I'm a Republican," he finally said.

"And I'm Democrat!" she replied.

"I voted for Dewey instead of Truman. I believe that Nixon was railroaded out of office, and I campaigned for George Bush," he said in a rush.

"You voted for Tricky Dick!" she shrieked.

"No editorializing."

She blinked. "I chose Roosevelt—"

"And Eleanor and their little dog Fala," Morgan interrupted. "I remember well those fireside chats when the country—"

She interrupted briskly "—and I voted for Kennedy and for Clinton. Now there was a man who led the nation through crisis after crisis."

"Despite his apparent inability to keep his trousers zipped," quipped Morgan.

Dixie raised her eyebrow. "You've set the rules. No editorializing!"

He waved his hand for her to continue.

She thought for a moment, opened her mouth, and closed it again.

What could she have to say that was so important? Maybe she'd changed her mind about the two of them.

"I believe in labor unions for the working man," she finally said.

Relieved, he countered, "I believe that businessmen should set the wage scale and workers should work at that rate or go elsewhere."

"Looks like we disagree on just about everything."

More silence. He poured them more wine. "Maybe we don't disagree on the important things," he said slowly.

Dixie took several sips. "Like?"

He'd start with generalities. "I grew up in a home full of love, hard work, and high expectations."

"You sound like a politician." She gave him a steady look. "We're almost strangers. I still don't know much about you or your past life."

He shrugged. "Dad was a janitor at Macy's. Mom altered clothing for customers at a dress shop near home. They saved every penny they could. I helped too, from the time I was 14. They paid my entry fees to Columbia, bought me a new suit of clothes, then told me the future was my responsibility."

"So you weren't a spoiled rich kid who had everything handed to him?"

He shook his head. That all came later, when he was old enough to know better.

She waited.

"You know about the rocky start to my career—"

She nodded. "But thanks to President Roosevelt, whom you refused to vote for," she intoned with mock seriousness, "you got a job when most of the country was out of work."

"Digging ditches!" He smiled ruefully, then frowned. "My marriage. Also a rocky start, but my wife came back to me after I took the job at the Illinois Banking and Trust."

Her eyes lit up. "That's what I want to know! What your life was like in Chicago. What was her name, your beautiful, sexy wife? Your ornament."

"Barbara."

"What about your children?" she asked softly.

"My son Clay was born nine months after Barbara and I got back together." The names felt clumsy on his lips. "Two years later Evelyn was born. Sara came along in 1943."

"Clay, Evelyn, and Sara," she said slowly. "You were a very lucky man."

"I took it all for granted." He fingered the stem of his wineglass. "I was an executive. My wife enjoyed the prestige, being in the right social circles. I became," he hesitated, "a playboy."

"A playboy." She nodded thoughtfully.

The doorbell rang. Jiggs, who was now dozing in the center of the family room, looked up, then drowsily dropped his head again.

"Who could it be?" Dixie glanced at her watch. "Almost eight-thirty."

"Vera?" Morgan asked.

"She wouldn't come this late without calling," Dixie said.

"I'll see who it is." Morgan jumped up, relieved to be off the hot seat. If it were Vera, for once he'd be glad to see her. He flicked on the porch light, then peered through the sidelite. Not Vera. It was someone he didn't know, holding a package.

14

The Playboy of the Midwest

Morgan opened the front door.

"Who is it?" Dixie called.

He was still trying to figure that out when the woman, wearing a blue and yellow stocking cap and a bright red coat, stepped into the hallway, cradling something wrapped in a paper sack. "Hi, I'm Pauline," she said, with a cheery smile. "Your next-door neighbor."

"Pauline." He was used to seeing just a corner of her face peering out from her upstairs window. She was short and round, with bright gray eyes.

"I met you here at Dixie's a couple months ago. Before you moved in." She pulled off her stocking cap. Her grayish-black hair stood up in electrified tufts. She smoothed it down, beaming at him.

"Yes, yes," he said. "Didn't recognize you with the cap."

"I hope I'm not interrupting anything." She thrust the package toward him.

"It's your neighbor," Morgan called out to Dixie, as he took the parcel. It was warm. "She's brought us something."

"It's lasagna, Dixie," Pauline suddenly yelped. "I made too much."

Morgan sniffed the top of the package. "Smells wonderful."

"Come on in," Dixie called from the other room. "I don't want to get up. What a day it's been!"

"I hope I'm not imposing," Pauline said as she stepped into the family room.

"We always welcome donations of food!" Morgan said heartily. He saw her eyes take in the wine bottle and the two partially filled glasses on the tray table. "Would you like—" he was about to say *some wine* but he could see Dixie frowning and shaking her head over Pauline's shoulder. "—to sit down?" He indicated the chair he'd been sitting in.

"I can't stay." Pauline unbuttoned her coat.

"She's a wonderful cook!" Dixie said.

"Well, let's take a look!" He set the package on the tray table and, as he fumbled to open the sack, knocked over a glass of wine.

"Oh," Dixie cried, springing up.

The red liquid was spreading quickly across the table. It shouldn't—it couldn't—reach Dixie's rug. Morgan groped in his pants pocket for his handkerchief. Ah, there it was. He pulled it out and began blotting at the wine. Wait a minute! He didn't own a peach handkerchief! With lace trim! And holes for legs! Holy Toledo! He was using Dixie's underpants. He'd forgotten to take them out of his pocket after his morning shopping expedition.

Had Pauline seen the underpants? Her lower lip was caught between her teeth. Was she trying not to smile? Thank God Dixie hadn't seen them. She was already heading toward the cleaning supplies in the kitchen.

Pauline's eyes, thoughtful, followed Dixie. Morgan stifled a laugh. She was probably thinking of Dixie minus her undies, and that she'd interrupted an amorous encounter. Fat chance!

Now what to do with the underpants, soaked with wine?

Dixie was back with some kind of spray and a cloth.

"I caught it before it hit the rug," he said, not daring to look at Pauline, "with my handkerchief." He grabbed the dish of lasagna and danced out to the kitchen, underpants wadded up in his hand. "I better put the food away." He slid it into the refrigerator. "Thanks, Pauline." He dropped the sodden underpants into the trash, washed his hands, then tied up the sack and carried it to the can in the garage while Dixie and Pauline talked.

When he returned to the family room, Dixie had finished her final wipe-up of the tray table. "Morgan, Pauline saw—"

Morgan twitched guiltily.

"—the fellow I told you about. In the hooded jacket."

"Oh," Morgan laughed, "him. He probably was selling something. Or asking for a handout."

"Well, yours was the only house on the block he went to," Pauline said. "He got out of a car . . ."

"A car? I didn't see a car," Dixie said.

Pauline nodded ominously. "The car turned the corner after it let him out."

"Hmmm," Dixie mused.

"Then he made a beeline for your porch."

"If he rang the bell I didn't hear it," Morgan said. "I was out back." He frowned. "What did he look like?"

"Blondish hair, dark underneath. Dyed, maybe."

"I didn't see his hair. He had his hood up when I saw him!" Dixie exclaimed.

"Something sparkled in one ear. Maybe an earring!" Pauline glanced from one to the other, pleased to be the center of attention.

"He had a mustache," Dixie said. "That I saw. Before he ran around the corner."

"Where the car was waiting," Pauline said, her round eyes rounder. "Did he put something in your mailbox?"

"I brought in the mail. Nothing unusual," Dixie said.

"You gals are making a mountain out of a molehill," Morgan said. "He rang the bell. No answer. He'll be back if he wants something."

"Well, I'll let you get on with—" Pauline threw a cheerful look at Morgan—"whatever you were doing before I barged in." She headed for the front door, Dixie and Morgan following.

"By the way," Pauline turned to Morgan, "I was worried about you this morning."

"Oh?"

"When you were raking leaves out front and collapsed."

"Collapsed?" Dixie exclaimed.

"I didn't collapse. I sat down on the front stoop to rest." He felt Dixie's eyes boring into him.

"I thought you might be having a heart attack. I was ready to call emergency."

"Just a touch of asthma," he said. "But I appreciate your concern." He wished Pauline would shut up.

"We'll return the dish when we're finished, Pauline," Dixie smiled, edging her toward the door. "Thanks again."

After their neighbor left, Dixie said, "You didn't have the sense to stop raking?"

"She's a drama queen," Morgan replied gruffly. "Collapsed, my foot. You saw me. I had my scarf over my nose and mouth. Once I did that, I was fine."

Dixie sighed.

"She knows how to push your buttons," Morgan grumbled as they returned to the family room. "She probably cooked the lasagna as a pretext so she could come over here and scare the wits out of you." Morgan poured the remaining wine into their glasses. "Might as well finish off the dregs." He yawned. "It's getting late." His muscles were starting to stiffen up. Maybe he'd overdone it today.

"Do you want me to try to get that wine out of your handkerchief?" Dixie asked.

"Handkerchief? Oh, that! It was," he stammered, "old. I threw it away."

Dixie sat, curling her legs up in the chair. "Where were we? Oh, yes, you said you became a playboy."

"By that I meant," he cleared his throat, "I was careless." How was he going to get out of this? "Spent more than I earned." He lowered himself into the chair and took a mouthful of wine. "I bought a yacht. I took clients and friends out. I learned to navigate the unpredictable waters of Lake Michigan." He put his hand to his chest and grinned. "Commander Morgan emerged."

"Commander Morgan," Dixie mused. "The Playboy."

Get her off the playboy tack. He babbled on. "I never liked my sissy name—Aubrey Bryce Morgan. I finally shortened it to Morgan. Barbara said it was an affectation; she persisted in calling me Bryce right up to the divorce. She knew it got my goat."

Dixie's eyes were wide. "I thought only princes and tycoons had yachts!"

"Well, who do you think you're looking at?" he teased. "As yachts go, it was small. A forty-five-footer. Called *The Merry Maid*. A motor yacht, with two staterooms, each with head and shower. It had a galley and a small dining salon. Quite a nifty little vessel!"

"Forty-five feet. That's almost twice the size of this room. You operated it yourself?"

"Mostly. For parties, I hired someone to cook and serve drinks." A heady time! He thought it would last forever. What a jerk he'd been, arrogant, self-indulgent!

"What was your job when you bought this yacht?"

"Well," he admitted, "I had to take a loan to buy her. I'd just been promoted to First Vice President. I saw it as a job investment. My wife didn't argue at first. Later she called it 'Bryce's Boo-Boo.'"

"To get your goat!"

He nodded, grimacing. "With the wining and dining of clients, the job at the bank became round-the-clock. I became estranged from my wife. I never took the time to get acquainted with my son and two daughters. I tried the father-son thing with Clay when he was seven. I let him row me out to a favorite fishing spot and told him interesting stories. I threaded worms on his hook. He complained the entire time, wondered what his friends were doing, and splashed the water to scare my fish away. We both were disgusted and never tried it again."

Dixie clucked her tongue. "Poor husband, worse father."

"Barbara filed for divorce. We'd been married twenty-three years."

"What reason did she give?"

"Don't remember." Like hell he didn't. "Mental cruelty or something. She was granted the house, funds for herself, and money to put the three children through college. That was 1959."

"The year my son Ronnie died," she murmured. "A bad patch for both of us." She rubbed her eyes with the heel of her hand.

She'd lost her son. He'd left his kids without a backward glance. "If I'd been here, I'd have"—he searched for an appropriate revenge—"had those fool doctors fired, sued the hospital! Broadcast their incompetence to all the newspapers!"

"We were more polite in those days." She gave him a fragile smile. "What happened to *The Merry Maid*?"

"I had to sell her for a fraction of what she was worth. I needed cash. Fast. Commander Morgan, reduced to cabin boy." She still looked ready to cry. He rose from his chair and kneeled in front of her. "Now I come to you on bended knee with a new perspective." He'd meant to be facetious, but found himself oddly stirred, almost believing what he said. "I thank you, Dixie, for the chance to work, and live with you. It's your turn to bare your soul." He had a little trouble getting to his feet again but, with her help and the arm of the chair, he managed. By then, she was laughing.

⚛

Okay, Dixie thought, she now knew what bank he'd worked at in Chicago. She knew he was a self-admitted playboy, though he'd tried to slough it off. She still didn't know why he'd left his high-paying job in Chicago to start over in Columbus. Something to do with his divorce, she suspected. It happened so long ago. Was it even pertinent now? "My life was drab compared to yours!" She grinned. "At the time I graduated from Central High School, women were considered second class. College was not an option for me. You with your fancy degree from Columbia!" she snorted. "But I got two years of secretarial school."

"How fast could you type?"

"Eighty-five words a minute and darn proud of it!"

He whistled.

"I met Alfred Valentine my last year there. Al was tall, dark, and handsome, fun to be with. We were married. They didn't draft him for World War II. Heart murmur. He started with the gas company and worked his way up to supervisor of warehouses. I took a job too, as a secretary in an insurance firm. During the war, thanks to Rosie the Riveter, it became okay for women to work."

"You loved each other?"

"Yeah." She laughed softly. "We loved to dance. Before we were married, we could dance all night. Then we got too busy. We wanted a house, kids. We'd all but given up hope when we had Ronnie. We were thrilled. I quit my job. I was a housewife and mother. For seven years." She felt her mouth quiver.

Morgan leaned over and squeezed her hand.

"I blame myself. I never should have let Ronnie have that surgery." Her voice broke. "*Minor* surgery, the doctor said!" Tears were rolling down her cheeks. "It will make such a difference in his quality of life!"

"Hey, hey," he said gently. He patted her hand, then abruptly stood up and disappeared.

Had she scared him off? She struggled to control herself. She heard him in the bathroom. Suddenly he was thrusting a wad of tissues in her hands. "Thanks," she squeaked. She blotted her face. "When they finished with him, he didn't have to worry about quality of life. He had no life." She sniffled. "Big ears—they wouldn't matter when he grew up."

"Not a bit." He thumped her awkwardly on her shoulder.

It required all her self-control not to fall into his arms blubbering. She took several deep breaths. "After I got myself together—it took almost a year—I landed a job in Barry's PR agency. Executive secretary. Lots of glitz and glamour. I heard inside dope about his clients, most of them big shots in town, that would make your hair curl."

"That must have saved you some trips to the beauty parlor," he said deadpan.

She gave a watery giggle. She blew her nose and sighed. "Al and I grew apart. When you lose a child, it's a big strain on a marriage. We tried to have another. By then, I was over 40. We gave up." *Al, with all his faults, had loved Ronnie, had spent some time with him. Pitch and catch. A fishing trip.* "You ever hear from your kids?" she asked Morgan.

"I received invitations to their weddings. Sent them each a hundred dollars, which I couldn't afford. Didn't get a thank you, except from my youngest, Sara."

He couldn't afford a hundred dollars each? Quite a comedown from his yacht days. Where did his money go? Dixie wondered. Surely not all of it to his wife and kids. "How can you stand it, not knowing how they turned out?"

"I know only," Morgan said abruptly, "that Sara married a successful accountant; Evelyn, a Chicago politician; and my son Clay married a social butterfly whose father set him up in the retail clothing business." He pressed his lips together, shrugging his shoulders.

She could see he wasn't going to talk anymore about his past.

"Somehow we're back to me, but it's still your turn," he added lightly.

"You know the rest, pretty much. Al died of a heart attack in the bed of another woman. I almost had a heart attack myself when I found out how much debt he left me in."

"$98,000," Morgan said. "Plus mortgage payments on the house."

"You remembered!"

He smiled. "I'm a banker."

"I thought nothing more could go wrong." She paused.

"What else went wrong?"

Ten years ago I got bad news from my doctor. She couldn't do it.

She couldn't tell him. Anyway, it was too late to get into that chapter tonight. "Only that I get tired and discouraged sometimes. I've worked hard since Al died, trying to pay off everything. Each year it gets harder to break even on Social Security and the money I earn at Whispering Pines and the church."

He waved a hand. "By the way, you're entitled to know about my finances. I pay no alimony or child support. That stopped when my last child graduated college in 1965. I own no real estate. I have $1,343 in a checking account at the Ohio National. A $50,000 CD. My bank pension and Social Security payments total over $3,000 a month. I have no outstanding debts."

She looked at him in disbelief. "You're rich, compared to me. You should be helping me with mortgage payments, insurance on the house and car, and all the utilities."

Morgan grinned sheepishly. "I planned to offer a little more aid after we got established. You seem to be a better manager. Just make a list of monthly food and utility expenses, add the pro rata cost of insurance and home maintenance, and for good measure include the real-estate tax. I'll pay my full share. Perhaps we can have a little surplus for an occasional night out." He added expansively, "And maybe you can quit your job."

"We'll see." She couldn't—wouldn't—quit her job until she trusted him, until she had bared herself totally. Until he had filled in some gaps. For instance, why would he have jeopardized his career and financial future just because of the divorce?

He stood and held out his hand.

Maybe if he contributed more per month, she could get that mortgage paid off faster and start whittling down her credit-card debt. Maybe even get those new windows for the house she'd been wanting for the last ten years.

She jumped up and impulsively gave him a hug. "Now we can get better acquainted."

Morgan put his arms around her.

"We won't rush things," Dixie warned, sliding out of his embrace. "Before we wind up in bed, we have lots more to talk about. I don't even know your favorite movies, your hobbies. Do you enjoy art? What's the best book you've ever read? What about the upheaval in the Middle East? Do you think our weather patterns are changing?"

Morgan toppled back into his chair in a daze. "Well, right this minute, the only observation I can make with conviction is about the weather. Like the weatherman, I figure it will be partly sunny with possible rain."

"And we still have the rest of the decades," she added weakly, "to thrash out."

"It will be three years before I can steal a hug, give you a tender kiss on the cheek or an affectionate pat on the butt. At my age, you can be sure of one thing—in three years I'll be dead or will have lost all interest in sex."

"Now who's the drama queen?" Dixie asked edgily. "A conversation about world problems could be vastly more enlightening than a tumble in bed." She stood and stretched. "Come on, Jiggs. It's past our bedtime." She picked the little dog up in her arms, and traipsed out of the family room and up the stairs.

⊙❦⊙

Morgan stayed behind. Why had he told her to quit her job? It was the wine talking. Now we can get better acquainted, she'd said, *after* he'd told her about his finances.

Maybe she was just a tease. Maybe it was money and companionship she wanted from him, nothing else. In that case, could he stay?

If he helped pay off her mortgage, he was purchasing part of her home. After an investment like that, could he leave?

He'd ply her with champagne on her birthday, then give her the see-through nightgown. She loved to dance. Maybe they could take dancing lessons.

He'd been hearing a lot about Viagra. He should check with his doctor. It wouldn't hurt to be prepared.

15

Secrets, Lies, and Tears

Dixie carefully ironed out the tiny wrinkles on the collar of her favorite blouse. The staff at Whispering Pines just might throw a little party for her today. The big 8-0. Could it be? She felt, maybe not 39 anymore, but not more than 60.

Suddenly, the cord spat sparks and the air was filled with an acrid odor. "Darn." She pulled out the plug.

"What happened?" Morgan grunted from the kitchen.

She licked her finger and touched the iron. Cooling rapidly. "The iron gave up the ghost." Oh, well, her blouse looked fine. She threw it over her arm, gathered up the folded clothes stacked on the dryer, Morgan's underthings among them. She chuckled softly. He hated to wash clothes as much as he hated to wash dishes. Maybe, just maybe, she'd give in and be the washer lady for the household.

She rushed upstairs, stuffing her underclothes into the drawer of her dresser. Hmm. She seemed to be missing a favorite pair of panties, peach with lace filigree around the waist. She'd look for them later.

She hurriedly dressed and dabbed cologne on her ears. She put on her blonde wig, fluffing out the bangs with her fingers. She didn't look a day over 70.

Funny, Morgan hadn't said a thing about her birthday, or even left a card for her on the kitchen table.

She heard the shower in Morgan's bathroom. The door to his room was open. She stepped inside, his clean underwear in hand.

What a mess! Two pairs of pants and a shirt were piled on a chair. Socks littered the floor. The bed was unmade. The top of his dresser was covered with wadded handkerchiefs, loose change, more socks, inhalers, and sprays. Not wanting to add to the clutter, she opened the drawer and slid his clothes in, neatly folded.

What was that? An envelope half buried under some socks. A Chicago return address. She pulled it out of the drawer. Handwritten to Morgan, sent to his old address, but forwarded to him at a PO box.

What's he doing with a PO box? He lives here. She felt scared.

The shower was still running. Should she? Did she want to know? Her heart was thudding. She slid out the letter and read.

I don't expect anything from you and never have since the day you left (42 years ago). But I'm writing to tell you that Mom is dying. She's had some strokes and memory problems the last several months. Her second husband, our stepfather, died three years ago. He was steady, a good provider, but now all she talks about is you, the yacht, and the good times you had together hobnobbing with Chicago's rich and famous.

Good times? Were there good times? Not according to Morgan. Dixie's cheeks felt hot.

Mom forgets the times when you were running around on her, making a mess of all our lives.

I looked you up in the phone book in the library so I guess you're still alive and still in Columbus. If you get this, I hope you'll have the decency to see Mom before she dies.

Your daughter, Sara

P.S. I came across this clipping (enclosed) when I was helping Mom clean out her things. She'd kept it all these years. We both started crying.

Dixie checked inside the envelope. No clipping. She quickly searched to the bottom of his pile of socks. Nothing. He would be out of the shower soon. She'd look for the clipping later. She examined the postmark, squinting. The tenth, two weeks ago. She didn't want to get messed up in his family problems and absolutely didn't want Morgan fretting about them again either.

The water had stopped running in Morgan's bathroom. She quickly stuffed the letter back into the envelope and jammed it between his socks where she'd found it.

The clipping his daughter said she'd enclosed—that Morgan's ex-wife had kept all these years—what was it about? Their wedding announcement, maybe? Dixie felt a twinge of jealousy.

In slow motion, she descended the stairs. The post-office box did not bode well. Was that her hand, taking her coat from the closet? She heard Morgan call, "Dixie! Are you here?" She didn't want to talk to him. She needed to think this over. She opened the door and stepped into the garage.

◦⁊◦

Dixie leaned into the mirror of the staff bathroom. In one more hour, her work day would be over, thank the Lord. She applied fresh lipstick. Her makeup had caked, leaving deep creases around her mouth. All that forced smiling she'd done over lunch at the surprise birthday party the girls had arranged. Now that same lunch threatened to make a reappearance.

One sentence from his daughter's letter had stuck in her brain, repeating itself throughout the day: *Mom forgets the times when you were running around on her, making a mess of all our lives.* Dixie hoped it wasn't a prediction for their relationship, hers and Morgan's. Morgan the playboy. The philanderer. A man planning to stay doesn't keep a post-office box.

She heard herself being paged. She blotted her lips. She pushed open the restroom door. Before she reached the front desk, she heard "Dixie!" Barry, leaning against the pillar by the dining room, waved and started towards her. "You got the money! We voted yesterday—to hire readers for the sight-impaired residents. I wanted to come by and tell you myself." He smiled broadly. "We'd like to call it the Dixie Valentine Fund."

"Oh, Barry," she wailed and started bawling.

"You don't want it?"

"It's my birthday. It's the best thing that's happened to me all day!"

"Don't worry, folks," he said to a couple of ladies who hovered with worried looks. "It's good news." He gave Dixie his handkerchief and patted her on the shoulder. "Your enthusiasm about the people you work with was just contagious. We voted on a pretty-good-sized check."

"I don't know what to say." She felt breathless. What a roller coaster of a day!

"We'd like a report on its use and a financial report."

"Barry, thanks. We better talk to the business manager."

"First, can we find someplace private to talk?" His voice was grave. "I hope you won't think I'm nosing in where I shouldn't."

Her heart full of dread, she found an empty recreation room on the second floor.

Barry was silent, with a scowl on his face, when he blurted out, "I don't want you to get hurt. I found someone who knew your friend way back when in Chicago."

"Morgan," she mumbled numbly.

"I was at a party for one of our Chicago clients. Someone was there from the Illinois Banking and Trust. Bigwig at the Trust now. He'd just started working there before your friend was . . . let go."

"Let go?"

"Resigned, actually. Under pressure. All kept very hush-hush. Rumors of embezzlement." Barry's face was red. He hated giving bad news. "I wouldn't be telling you, except that any possibility of shady dealings, no matter how long ago, I thought you should know."

Her head was swimming. "He's told me," she lied.

"Even about the suspicious death?" he blurted out.

"Suspicious death?"

"The husband of his, uh, office manager." Barry's face grew redder still. "The paramour," he mumbled.

By sheer force of will, she made her face blank. "Yes. He told me that too." She felt physically sick. "All of it, a terrible mistake. But thanks for your concern."

Somehow she took Barry to the business manager, stayed to chitchat, a smile frozen on her face, and stumbled through the rest of the day. Embezzlement. A suspicious death. Had he been in jail?

She'd gotten herself another lemon. Perhaps the worst lemon of her life! That banker's pro rata double talk he'd given her about helping her with home maintenance, insurance, and real estate taxes! *I'd planned to offer a little more aid after we got established.* She might have to work forever, supporting herself and another loser, who might just flit off and find another woman with more money. Not *might*, planned to. Don't forget that post-office box, Dixie. He probably thought she was rich when he glommed on to her, the house and all. Well, she'd done the improvements on her home with the help of many credit cards, which she now was having a hard time paying off. She patted the tears away with her handkerchief. No, it was Barry's. She'd forgotten to return it. She'd wash and iron it, mail it to him.

At three o'clock, quitting time, she went into the Whispering Pines dining room and drew herself a cup of coffee, black and bitter. She drank it all. When did he plan to leave? she wondered. A terrible thought hit her. Maybe he was going back to Miranda. An image of Miranda, as she'd looked at the Elks dinner dance, floated into her brain, glamorous, voluptuous, her black hair held in place with an elegant jeweled comb, her dark eyes lingering seductively on Morgan. They'd been an item for eight years, Morgan had admitted after Dixie pressured him, but Miranda broke it off when she found out he wasn't rich. That's what he'd said.

⊛

Morgan chuckled to himself as he slid a bottle of champagne from the refrigerator and set it in the silver bucket filled with ice. Was Dixie going to be surprised or what? In the center of the dining room table, set with her best dishes, was a vase of large yellow and white chrysanthemums. Alongside it rested the birthday cake decorated with yellow and blue roses and eight yellow candles. Greeting cards he'd been intercepting from well-wishers fanned out over the table. A fire crackled in the fireplace. Music played in the background. He did a two-step over to the refrigerator, drew out a lemon, and began to slice it.

The garage door creaked open. Her car drove in. He wiped his hands on his apron and stood at attention, a grin spreading across his face.

"What smells?" she asked when she stepped from the garage into the family room. Her face was grim, like stone.

Bad day at work, he thought. "Just a little dinner I threw together, with help from the gourmet shop at the supermarket. May I?" He helped her off with her coat, Jiggs bouncing between the two of them.

"How about a pick-me-up?" he asked heartily, lifting the bottle of champagne from the ice bucket. As he tore off the foil, he noticed she was giving the flowers and the cake the once-over. Still, she didn't say a word. She made no comment about the chef's white apron he wore, or the red plaid suspenders. He'd been sure his get-up would get a laugh. In fact, every time she glanced his way she seemed to look right through him, as if she was in a daze.

The champagne cork popped. He poured the bubbly into two fluted glasses. "Sit down. Kick off your shoes." He pulled out a chair. She sat stiffly, a bewildered look on her face. He felt a twinge of uneasiness, then decided that he must have really pulled it off! She was speechless with surprise.

"Before we have the shrimp cocktail," he said, emphasizing shrimp cocktail, one of her favorites, "would you like to open your birthday gifts?"

She nodded slowly.

He handed her a paper bag. "I didn't have time to wrap it."

She pulled the box out of the sack, looked briefly at the picture of the iron on the box, and put the package on the table. "Thank you."

"Essential to the running of a proper household," he said jovially, expecting some kind of crack about his needing to learn to use it, or surprise that he'd remembered her iron had burnt out that morning.

Her face was frozen. She must be disappointed that his gift was so practical. "How about something a little more frivolous?" He handed her the large parcel wrapped so elegantly by the department store. With a dry mouth, he watched as she fumbled with the ribbon and mechanically tore off the paper. She opened the box, lifted the see-through maroon and black negligee out of the tissue paper, and burst into tears. She went upstairs without a word.

"Dixie?" he called from the bottom of the stairs.

"I'm going to take a bath," she answered in a muffled voice.

Nonplussed, Morgan walked back to the dining room. Of all the scenarios he'd imagined when Dixie opened his gift, bursting into tears was not one of them. She was unpredictable, that was for sure. She must have come home tired, too tired to respond. He'd rushed her, as usual.

The package lay on the floor, the black and maroon gown spilling out of it. She must have hated it. He sat down, leaning over to stuff the negligee back into its wrappings. He didn't want to look at it. He closed the lid. He'd return the damn thing tomorrow.

Morgan felt Jiggs nuzzling his hand with his wet nose. He patted his lap. Jiggs scrambled up and licked Morgan's face. Morgan gave him a squeeze. Okay, so she didn't like the negligee. What about the champagne, the decorated cake, the flowers? He'd spent the better part of two days planning this birthday surprise. What did he have to do to please her? He stood, sliding Jiggs off his lap.

Morgan snapped off the oven and took out the beef stroganoff and the potatoes au gratin. He was about to dump them in the wastebasket, but his thriftiness got the better of him and he slid the casseroles into the refrigerator. He eyed the two untouched glasses of champagne. Shame to let them go to waste. He slugged one glass down as if it was water. Whew! He felt better already. He poured the other glass back into the bottle, stuffed a paper towel in the opening, and put the bottle in the fridge. He ripped off his apron and flung it over a kitchen chair. He marched into the family room, plunked himself down in a chair in front of the fireplace, and tried to read the paper.

ᏬᎨᏬ

Upstairs, Dixie dried her eyes as the hot water filled her tub. Why would a man keeping a secret post-office box go to all this trouble for her birthday? Was it his way of apologizing for getting her hopes up and dashing them? I'm sorry but I'm not the man of your dreams. I'm a womanizer, a man accused of embezzlement, implicated in a suspicious death.

Dixie turned on the wall timer, stepped into the whirlpool tub and sank into the hot water. She pushed the button. Water pulsed from the jets. She closed her eyes. She was growing quite used to him. He was learning the ropes, doing the household chores. She didn't want to have to search for someone else and train him. Frankly, she needed the money he provided.

And, she had to admit, he made life fun. She started to cry. She wondered what her horoscope had to say about this awful day. She soaked a washcloth in cold water and covered her eyes.

If he were going to leave, why did he give her a negligee? Sheer, at that. Wham, bam, thank you, ma'am?

Did he think she was easy? Desperate was more like it. She knew she'd disappointed him often. The tears flowed again.

The whirlpool wasn't helping. She felt as tense as when she started. She pushed the button on the tub, turning off the throbbing jets of water. She soaked another ten minutes, then made herself get out. She wanted to crawl into bed, but this had to be settled tonight.

In her robe, she walked over to Morgan's room. She wanted to find the clipping his daughter had enclosed in her letter. She didn't think it would be a wedding announcement. She looked in his underwear drawer. She rifled through all his dresser drawers. No letter from Sara even. He'd gotten rid of the evidence.

She applied extra make-up to her red and swollen eyes. She shoe-horned herself into a tight-fitting sweater and slacks and sprayed on perfume. Morgan's sordid past astonished her, yes. Vera had told her she should hire a private eye to check up on him. She shuddered, remembering Vera's warning, meant to be a joke: Don't let him take out life insurance on you.

She'd let him talk, hear his side of it. Because people change. He was almost 90. He'd had forty years to mature.

Fifteen minutes later, Dixie came downstairs. He was reading the newspaper calmly as if nothing had happened. Her brain was teeming, boiling over with anger, hurt, frustration. Why hadn't he told her everything? Why had she had to hear it from Barry? Why did she have to stoop to snooping?

Morgan turned to look at her. "Are you going somewhere?"

"To my birthday party," she said with a brittle laugh. She put on her brightest smile and ducked back into the kitchen, grabbing some peanuts out of a jar on the kitchen shelf.

"If you're hungry," he said gruffly, "we could eat some of that dinner I picked up. Cost me an arm and a leg."

He looked so stern. She prepared herself for his announcement that he was going to leave. She said, chewing on some nuts, "Did you know that peanuts are one of the ingredients of dynamite?" hoping to break the ice. Why did she always babble when she was nervous?

"Not surprised. They give me terrible gas," he mumbled, without interest. He went back to reading the paper.

"Morgan, look at me."

He did.

She had no idea what she was going to say. "Why, why," she wailed, "do you have a post-office box?"

His jaw dropped. He flushed. "Well," he said, not meeting her eyes, "I wasn't sure, with all our ups and downs, where I'd end up."

"Maybe at Miranda's?" Her throat felt tight.

"Are you out of your mind?" he exploded. "What's she got to do with it?"

"I thought maybe you were up to your usual philandering tricks."

"I haven't gotten around yet to closing the post-office box. Is that a criminal offense?" he blustered.

"You're the expert on criminal offenses. You tell me."

"What do you mean?" He narrowed his eyes.

He didn't know that she knew, thanks to Barry, about the rumors of embezzlement and the suspicious death. She shrugged. Let Morgan tell her. She prayed he would.

"I do know," he said slowly, folding his newspaper, "that reading someone else's mail is a federal offense."

She felt her face grow red. "When I put your clean clothes away this morning, I saw the letter, from Chicago, forwarded to you *at a post-office box*. Why wouldn't I be curious?"

He nodded, his jaw clenched. "You may remember, I gave notice at my old place prematurely." He looked at her steadily. "I was to move in here, then I wasn't."

"Because you were too darn hardheaded to sign the contract."

He gave her a twisted grin. "When I did move in, I was out again in two weeks, staying with Nate, wondering where I'd end up—at Whispering Pines or another apartment. I didn't want my mail forwarded here if I wasn't going to be here."

She nodded slowly, digesting his explanation. "I'll go along with that."

"Anything else?"

"Yes, as a matter of fact." She took a deep breath. "Your daughter mentioned a clipping." A clipping that she said made her cry. "It wasn't in the envelope."

He closed his eyes.

"Is it something I should know about?"

He slid his billfold from his pocket, cracked it open, and fished out a folded paper. "A lot of lies were printed about me at the time." He handed it to her, his face grim.

Perching on the edge of the chair opposite him, she opened it carefully so the brittle newsprint wouldn't crumble. She felt herself taking rapid, shallow breaths. She swallowed, then read aloud, voice hoarse, the headlines: "BANK OFFICER AND MAN ABOUT TOWN AUBREY BRYCE MORGAN CAUGHT RED-HANDED IN OFFICE MANAGER'S DRAWERS. WAS HIS OTHER HAND IN THE TILL? AUDIT PROMISED. SWEETIE'S HUSBAND

THREATENS TO BREAK MORGAN'S KNEECAPS." She looked at Morgan. "He said that?"

He nodded uncomfortably.

Under the headlines were photos. She held the clipping under the lamp to see more clearly what Morgan looked like forty years ago, and she was curious about his sweetie. Morgan's hair was dark and thick, flecked with gray. He wore glasses and a no-nonsense expression. He was in a suit and tie. His face was fuller.

The woman had blonde hair, soft and wavy, almost to her shoulders, with long, fluffy bangs. Her lips were full, her eyes sulky.

"It was true I was having an affair," he said slowly. "My wife and I had stopped sleeping together. I'd had some flings, nothing to amount to much. Then we got a new office manager." He barked out a derisive laugh. "Just my type, blonde and dumb, great figure, not much upstairs."

"I hope your taste has improved," she said tartly.

He winced. "We were flagrant. Long weekends on *The Merry Maid*, just the two of us. We cruised the nightclubs. At first, the gossip columnists were discreet. 'What important figure in banking circles has been seen club-hopping with his office manager?'" He spoke from the corner of his mouth, the words staccato.

Just like Walter Winchell, Dixie thought.

Morgan pushed out a laugh. "When they got around to naming names, it embarrassed my wife because of the social circles she traveled in. It was the fifties. Affairs were supposed to be hush-hush. Barbara didn't give a hoot what I did as long as it was kept quiet. As long as I continued to keep her in the style she was accustomed to."

His eyes were full of pain. She almost told him to stop.

He put his head in his hands and groaned, "I didn't think she'd do it. File for divorce. But she did. The whole sordid story hit the papers as we fought over who'd get what."

"That's why you left Chicago? Because of the divorce?" she asked softly. She hoped he'd tell her everything that Barry had told her and more—the results of the audit, how and why the man who'd threatened to break his kneecaps died. She was afraid to hear it but she had to, in order to trust him.

He shook his head. "It wasn't just the divorce. I'd made a lot of enemies. I was an arrogant SOB. Some people at the bank were jealous of my extravagant lifestyle, wondering how I'd been able to afford the yacht," he said bitterly.

"How *did* you afford it?" she asked.

"I took out loans. I was deep in debt when I got socked with the divorce papers."

She knew how it felt to be deep in debt. "They went after you, the people you worked with?"

He nodded. "I was a first vice president. I came into work early, I worked late—often alone. Opportunity for embezzlement, they said. They wanted to get rid of me because of the scandal, not because there was a cash shortage. One of the men especially had it in for me. I'd been promoted before he was."

"People can be rotten," she said.

"They thought I had it coming. Maybe I did." He fumbled in his pocket, brought out his inhaler, took two deep puffs, his hand shaking slightly.

She wanted to believe him. She didn't want him to have an asthma attack. "Let's drop it. I get the picture."

He shook his head, his face a mask. "First, they did an internal audit. Nothing amiss. But the auditor was a good friend of mine. So they did an external audit. Again, no money missing, but word of the audits got around. You read the clipping from the tabloid. 'Was his other hand in the till?' Some people," his brows rose, "including friends and family, believed I embezzled money from the trust company and got away with it, hid it in a Swiss account."

"What a nightmare." One thing she knew for sure. If he had money in a Swiss account, he wouldn't be living with her.

"I was asked to resign. If I did, they'd give me a decent letter of recommendation. Otherwise they'd fire me with no recommendation. One thing in their favor, they gave me a financial settlement, which immediately went to alimony, child support, and college tuition for my first child, Clay." He dug his knuckle into the corner of his eye. "I'd been at the place for twenty years."

"So you came to Columbus."

"Back to where I'd started." He sighed heavily. "I was relieved to put some distance between me and my 'loving' family, and the former mistress whose husband was threatening to break my kneecaps."

"Was he," she hesitated, "involved with organized crime?" If so,

Morgan's blonde girlfriend would have been mixed up in it. Morgan too?

"Who knows? He died suspiciously. This was after I left town. But I heard my name was brought up in connection with it," he said with a wry smile. "The authorities finally ruled it was a suicide."

"Maybe he was upset his wife was running around on him?"

"Maybe."

"Or maybe she killed him and made it look like a suicide."

"Could be."

"You were lucky you weren't the one killed."

"Leave it to you to find a grain of luck in the whole mess."

"So many lives ruined." She wouldn't tell him that Barry had come to her with information. It would make him feel worse, knowing that the sleazy story was still remembered in Chicago banking circles after forty years.

"I'd left Chicago as a first vice president. I started over in Columbus at age 50 as a loan officer." He gave a sour laugh.

"Didn't they ask questions at the bank here?"

"The guys in Chicago were so glad to get rid of me they covered for me. The guys at the bank here believed me when I said that I left because of the unpleasantness of the divorce. I implied I received a terrific severance package. I said I loved Columbus and had always wanted to return. Nate's the only one I ever told—one night when we got drunk together." His face was pale, his eyes watery and red-rimmed. "Do you want me to leave?"

"Are you crazy?" she asked. "Just when things are getting interesting?"

He laughed raggedly. "Better than TV."

"I thought I saw some champagne around here," she said, getting up. He followed her to the kitchen. She opened the refrigerator and pulled out the bottle. She poured champagne into the two fluted glasses sitting on the kitchen counter.

He clinked his to hers. "Happy birthday."

"I have one last question," she said.

"Fire away."

"When you came back here, you were—fifty?"

He nodded.

"Didn't you think about remarrying?"

"Never." He shuddered. "There were other women, of course. But as far as getting married again, I was gun-shy."

"How many women?" She was jealous. Yes. Of his other life, of the women, the string of indiscretions before, during, and after Barbara, including the office manager, and especially including Miranda.

"I don't remember. I don't even remember their names, except for Miranda." He took a sip of champagne. "How about I turn on the oven and warm up that dinner? Are you hungry?"

"Starving." She looked at the table. "It's all so beautiful. The cake, the flowers. Those cards—are they all for me? I wondered why none came in the mail." She leaned over and kissed him on the cheek, leaving the bright red imprint of her lips. "I've branded you," she laughed, rubbing the lipstick off with her fingers. To cover her confusion, she reached for the iron. "You remembered that it burned out."

"Your training paid off," Morgan said with a dry smile. His eyes dropped to the package on the floor. "I can see the iron is the biggest hit of your birthday."

She hesitated, bent down, and lifted the lid of the rectangular box. She shook out the peignoir and held it against her, running her hand over it. "It's lovely." Soft and filmy. *I'll never measure up. He's seen and had them all.* "Really gorgeous."

"You like it?" Morgan asked, his face lighting up. "Try it on."

"I will," she said, surprising herself. "When the right time comes."

"When's that?"

Why, oh, why had she said that? Now she'd set herself a time limit. No, she decided, *the right time* was friendly but vague enough not to put undue pressure on her. "You'll know," she said firmly, carefully folding the gown and placing it back in its box.

He cocked his head at her. "So now I'm a mind reader." He poured them each more champagne. He handed her his final gift, his eyes teasing.

"There's more?" As she opened it, she oohed and aahed, "So beautiful! The wrapping paper, the ribbon!" Suddenly silent, she held up the black lace panties. "Well, aren't these"—she searched for the right word—"fancy?"

"I think you like the wrapping better than the gift."

She peered at the waistband. "Just the right size. How on earth did you manage that?" She'd never owned black underwear. She'd always felt it was somewhat scandalous. "Now I have a replacement for the pair I lost."

"Lost?" He shook his head slowly. "I borrowed them," he confessed with a sheepish smile.

"Why on earth did you borrow them?" What else was he holding back?

He laughed as if he'd read her mind. "To show the saleslady, to help me choose the right size." He took a gulp of champagne, his face reddening. "Then I forgot I still had them in my pants pocket that night Pauline came by. When the wine spilled, I jerked them out, thinking they were my handkerchief, and wiped up the mess. Pauline saw."

"She saw my peach underpants with the filigree come out of your pants pocket?" Dixie asked, eyes wide.

"She kept apologizing, hoping she wasn't interrupting anything," he reminded her pointedly.

"Oh, nooo," Dixie squealed. "You mean . . . ?" she pointed to Morgan and back to herself.

He nodded.

Her face felt hot. Her lips trembled. She dissolved into laughter.

Morgan joined her. "You should have seen her expression," he grunted out between guffaws. Soon they were laughing so hard the tears were running down their cheeks.

"What happened to my underpants?" Dixie spluttered.

"I had to throw them away." Morgan wiped his eyes. "You insisted you wanted to wash out my 'handkerchief' for me. I was afraid I might have to retrieve them from the trash barrel in the garage and tell you everything then and there."

"Pauline, dear Pauline." Dixie giggled, then said in a hushed voice, "She's probably spreading the word all over the neighborhood. You're not a roomer, after all. We're living in sin."

"Better she thinks we're living in sin than I'm living in your underpants," Morgan said merrily, pouring them each another glass of champagne.

They exploded into another fit of laughter. Dixie got the hiccups. "I'll have to hold my arms above my head and pant like a dog," she said, and that's what she did.

Jiggs, curious, ambled into the kitchen, gave them each a disgusted look, and disappeared. Their laughter bubbled up again. Dixie's hiccups continued.

"Close your eyes, hold your breath, and think of ten bald men," Morgan advised.

Dixie closed her eyes. For some reason, she saw Morgan's face instead of ten bald men. The hiccups stopped.

"We better simmer down and get some food in our stomachs." Morgan put on his chef's apron and served the shrimp cocktail. Dixie breathed, "My favorite," and both fell silent as they ate.

"I think," Dixie said, pushing back from the table after the beef stroganoff, potatoes au gratin, cake, and ice cream, "it's the very best birthday I ever had."

Morgan beamed.

She hated to destroy the mood, but she needed to ask. "What did you do with Sara's letter?"

"It's in my billfold." He gave her a rueful grin. "I was going to show it to you. Once I decided what to do." He stacked his dishes as he sat, chewing on his lower lip. "Of all my kids, I felt closest to Sara. I remember," he murmured sadly, "her screaming at me when I moved out. She was 14. Skinny kid with straight black hair. She'd always been the quiet one."

"Will you write to her?" *He'll want to see her again. Erase that memory from his mind.*

"What do I say? They all hate me."

"Are you going back?" She felt a little flutter in her chest.

"I'd be walking into a battle zone. Let Barbara—and everyone—remember things as they want to. I can't go back into it again. I'm too old."

That surprised her. He never talked about his age. He never seemed almost 90. But tonight he looked weary with the weight of it—the pain and sadness, the wasted years.

"On the other hand," he raised his brows, "it seems a crime not to honor a dying woman's request."

"You'd be like a lamb going to the slaughter," Dixie replied. It made her half sick to think of him going back. She didn't want to lose him to Chicago.

16

Battle of Wills

"We've loafed long enough," Dixie announced as she and Morgan finished breakfast on a gray Saturday in December. "You wash the windows on the inside," she said briskly. "I'll wax the kitchen floor. After lunch, if there's time, you can sweep the leaves off the sidewalk while I bake us a cherry pie."

Morgan gulped the last of his coffee. It was almost three weeks after Dixie's birthday celebration, a landmark occasion, when he'd sensed a change, a welcome to a friendlier environment. But she was still bossing him around as if he were the hired hand.

She stood, stacking their dishes on the kitchen table. "Oh, yes, and Vera's coming by this afternoon for coffee and dessert."

So that was the reason for the cherry pie. "Like clockwork. Vera on Saturdays, and church on Sundays. We're getting in a rut," he growled. He knew Dixie wouldn't like it if Nate barged in here every week. And Dixie's bridge club was coming next month, but she kept putting him off when he said he'd like to have another poker night here, even though he'd promised her there'd be no smoking inside the house. He was contributing more cash than ever to the household. He hoped he wasn't putting money on a dead horse.

"I'm not about to cut Vera out of my life," Dixie said firmly. "She's fun, she's upbeat. I wouldn't have survived without her support all these years."

"I'm not asking you to cut Vera out of your life." Dixie was exaggerating, a typical female ploy. "But does she have to be here every week?" Whenever Vera visited, the two conferred often, it seemed, whispering in another room. He felt left out. If he tried to talk to Dixie about it, it started a fight. Or she changed the subject.

"I want you to get to know her. I want you two to like each other," Dixie repeated for the umpteenth time as she carted dishes over to the sink. "Do you want to argue politics with me while we do the dishes?"

"That's what confuses me about you." He'd almost said *annoys me* but thought better of it. "You tell me what we'll do without consulting me. I don't want to discuss what's wrong with the country, how Social Security should be changed," he muttered, "or if America should bail out every country in the world from their own mistakes." *I don't want Vera coming by as if she owns the place*, he added silently. He went over and stood beside her as she filled the sink with sudsy water. "What I'd like to do is sit down in front of the fireplace with you, listen to the music of Guy Lombardo or Lawrence Welk, and munch on popcorn. If you let me hold your hand, I'll whisper sweet nothings in your ear."

She smiled. "That would only lead to further overtures and you would suggest that we adjourn to my bedroom to ruminate about the starving people in Ethiopia and the hole in the ozone layer, through which our existing weather is escaping."

She looked him in the eye. "However, the AIDS epidemic is an issue we definitely should be discussing. I want you to know that I won't go to bed with you until you've been tested for AIDS and other social diseases. Frankly, your playboy years worry me."

He was speechless. While he'd waited in vain since he'd given her the negligee, waited for the "sign" from her that she said he'd know when he saw it, she'd been cooking up another delaying tactic.

"You don't know about me either," she added sweetly, handing him a dish towel, "so when you get ready, I'll go with you to the doctor and have similar testing."

She must be bluffing. Morgan was sure she'd never slept with anyone other than her own husband. "I've never had a social disease," he said huffily. "Your demand for testing is an insult to me and the women I've known. Hell will freeze over before I come to you with a doctor's statement attesting to my purity."

"Very well," Dixie replied. "It's no big deal. We're getting along nicely under the present arrangement." He thought he detected more than a little relief as she delivered this latest edict.

⚬⚬

Morgan dumped the dirty water from his window-washing efforts into the sink in the laundry room and hung up the wet rags to dry. He stopped in the kitchen to watch Dixie pummel a ball of dough, roll it out flat, and place it in a pie plate. She poured in the cherry filling. "Smells delicious," he said, tempted to scoop up a finger full. She quickly rolled out another crust, laid it over the cherries, sliced off the excess, and crimped the edges, fingers flying. He was mesmerized. He was also hungry. The doorbell rang.

"Can you get it while I put the pie in the oven?" Dixie asked.

He opened the front door. Before he could say *hi*, Vera called to Dixie over Morgan's shoulder, "I want you to know I'm still nicotine-free. I have more energy than I've had in years."

Morgan blanched. She was unbearably cheery. He thought of buying her a pack of cigarettes.

"I'm so proud of you!" Dixie squealed, slamming the oven door shut. She hurried into the hall and kissed her friend on the cheek. Then she stepped back, giving Vera the once-over. "You look great. Your face has filled out. You have some color in your cheeks."

"I've gained ten pounds," Vera moaned.

"I agree, you look great," Morgan chimed in with phony heartiness, feeling left out already.

Vera preened and did a little shimmy. "And how are you two getting along?" she cooed, slipping out of her coat and hanging it in the hall closet.

Every week Vera asked the same question. She thought he was too old for Dixie, he knew. Too poor. A risk for flight. "If you really want to know . . ." he said, feeling out of sorts from the mindless exertion of washing all the windows. He was still irritable about Dixie's demands for an HIV test, and he still didn't know whether to visit his dying ex-wife's bedside.

Vera smiled and nodded. "I really want to know."

"During the week since you last were here," he reported with fake cheer, "we've taught each other always to place the toilet seat down, cap the tooth paste, hang up our clothes as we remove them, and wash out the bathtub after each use. We've also learned," he continued, pleased with his snappy presentation, "that there can be no argument if one keeps quiet when the other becomes angry." He chuckled to himself. He was getting Vera's goat. Dixie didn't look too happy either. "We already enjoy the same kind of music," he added glibly, hand over his heart, "are committed to discussing rather than fault-finding, and have agreed to settle each day's disputes before retiring for the night."

Dixie blinked. Vera had her arms crossed.

"Each morning," he quipped, "we join in a brief ceremony welcoming the new day. We slide in our dentures and hearing aids, put on our glasses, our wigs, and other falsies." He finished with a flourish. "It's great just to be able to stand in a vertical position."

Vera looked at Dixie, who shrugged. "He thinks he's a comedian," Dixie said. "Come on upstairs. I want to show you my new bedspread." Vera followed Dixie up the stairs. "What did . . ." Vera's voice dropped to a whisper.

Morgan lingered at the bottom of the steps, straining to hear. Vera was asking something about the doctor and tests. He felt a rush of anger. Had Dixie told Vera about his checkered past? Maybe her demand that he get an HIV test was really Vera's advice. If so, it would be too big a betrayal to ignore. He heard Dixie say, "Shh. Later." Their voices became even more muffled. He supposed the two were in Dixie's bedroom by now. He crept halfway up the stairs. His confession had been meant for Dixie's ears only. Vera already doubted him. If she knew about the supposed embezzlement, the suspicious death, and his womanizing, she'd be more than willing to fan the flames and maybe even insist that Dixie kick him out.

"The spread is beautiful," Vera cried. "How much?"

"I bought it on sale. A present to myself."

"So—everything OK?" Vera asked in a low voice. More murmuring.

Morgan quietly climbed to the top of the stairs. The door to her bedroom was cracked, not closed.

"Got the results of the tests last week," he heard Dixie say. "Still holding my own."

What did that mean? He tiptoed down the hall, past the master bath, to the edge of Dixie's bedroom.

"That's great, kiddo. You see, things are on the upswing."

He smiled. Good. Their voices were as clear as if he were with them in the room.

"I keep pinching myself."

"You'll tell Morgan?" Vera asked.

Dixie laughed huskily. "I'll have to." He heard papers rustling. Dixie murmured, "Morgan . . . for my birthday."

"Oh," Vera sighed. "Sexy. Try it on."

He heard swishing and more rustling. "Here, let me help," Vera offered. More murmurs and mumbling. "You look gorgeous. I love it. It's perfect," Vera exclaimed.

Morgan felt his mood lighten. He sidled closer, hugging the wall, eager to catch a glimpse of Dixie in the negligee.

"I take it he hasn't seen you in it?" he heard Vera ask.

"Not yet."

"Go for it, girl! You only live once!"

Maybe Vera was in his corner after all. Maybe Dixie had kept his confidences. He shouldn't be so suspicious. Ah, here he was at the bedroom door, invitingly ajar. He peeked through the crack, catching a glimpse of swirling maroon chiffon.

What was that noise behind him? He turned to see Jiggs, who'd evidently been dozing in the spare bedroom, galloping toward him, tail wagging.

"What's that?" Dixie asked. The bedroom door started to open.

Morgan scuttled down the hall, Jiggs at his heels. He ducked onto the stairs just as Vera exclaimed, "It's only Jiggs."

"Morgan?" Dixie called.

She was in the hall now, Morgan thought as he hurried down the steps. When he reached the kitchen, he faked a coughing fit. "Dixie, did you want me?" he yelled, out of breath.

Dixie called from the top of the stairs, "How's the pie doing?"

"I was in the family room," he puffed guiltily.

"I said, how's the pie doing? Has the timer gone off?"

"Fifteen more minutes." He sank down at the kitchen table, breathing hard. Seemed Dixie still had her secrets. Test results? Whatever they were for, Vera obviously was in on it. He felt a pang of jealousy. Still, Dixie had told Vera she'd tell him.

The cherry pie and ice cream were delicious. Morgan, happy that

Vera approved the negligee he'd given to Dixie, was the life of the party. Vera laughed at his jokes. She ate two pieces of pie. And she didn't cough once.

"Why, Bryce Morgan," Dixie said after Vera left. "I could just kiss you for being so nice to Vera." And she gave him a big smooch on the forehead, sending a hot flush to his face.

"Don't restrain yourself," he said, grinning. "Feel free."

"Don't push it," she replied, grinning back.

That evening, while Dixie was feeding Jiggs, Morgan sneaked upstairs and into Dixie's bathroom. He opened her medicine cabinet. Was she a diabetic? Heart problems? He found a couple of prescription bottles, labeled with unpronounceable names, but none of them said what ailment the pills were for.

ollo

"Did I hear Vera say something about a doctor's visit you had?" Morgan asked the next day as they were getting ready for church.

"I don't think so," Dixie said, surprised. She distinctly remembered she and Vera had talked about it in her bedroom, with the door closed.

"When you two were on the way upstairs to look at the new spread."

"Oh, that? Just a routine checkup. I like to get one every year. And so should you." She was glad to see the worry on his face. Maybe she should tell him the truth now. It might keep him from going to Chicago, if he thought he was leaving her, poor, sick Dixie, behind. But, no, she'd bide her time. She'd convinced him to wait until after the Christmas holidays to go to his ex-wife's bedside—if he really was determined to go. Anything might happen by then.

ollo

One night followed another as Morgan waited in vain for Dixie to suddenly appear in the maroon and black negligee, crooking her finger at him like the goddess Circe, inviting him into her bedroom.

Instead, the two exhausted topic after topic. They discussed endlessly the attitude of young people in today's society. Was Dr. Benjamin Spock to blame for the permissiveness? Kids today seemed to think that hard work was for squares, that things that had taken their parents a lifetime to acquire—the car, the house, the credit, and the prestige—should be theirs immediately.

Should children be seen and not heard, as our grandparents thought? Or should children be treated as young adults, allowed to make decisions they're unqualified to make?

Dixie spoke with sympathy of the choices made by the flower children of the 1960s. "They were so idealistic. *'Make love, not war.'* Poor things. They left secure homes to live on the street and ended up sick, poor, or addicted to drugs."

"Well, I don't feel sorry for them," Morgan snorted. "They were spoiled brats who had no clue about the sacrifices their parents made to give them an easier life."

These friendly debates, which went no place and brought about little agreement, were a needless waste of time and effort, Morgan thought, when more romantic possibilities existed. He was beginning to reconsider HIV testing.

They discussed religion, Dixie maintaining, "The Bible says if you want to enter the Kingdom of Heaven you must believe that Jesus is the son of God."

"If I don't believe that, you mean I'll burn in hell?" He was in the mood that night for a good argument. "I have my own beliefs, based on the Ten Commandments," he said, sounding somewhat sanctimonious to himself. "I don't cheat. I treat everyone like I would want to be treated. I try to be kind and considerate—"

"You have to do better than that," Dixie interrupted. She was staring at him as if he were a heathen.

"The example I set must have some influence with God," he burst out. *If there is one*, he added silently.

"Your good works come from God working through you," she explained.

"Okay, I can accept that interpretation. But you're saying I have to believe in Jesus to qualify for everlasting life? What about the Jews, Muslims, Hindus, and Buddhists? Are they as doomed as I am?" Surely she'd see the logic of that.

She veered, avoiding logic. "I'd really like it if you'd go to church with me without complaining. And quit frowning. It won't hurt you."

Morgan tried to look contrite.

Her face was flushed. "I know you don't understand my faith and you think I'm asking for too much in my prayers, but miracles do happen through prayer."

Illogical or not, her position was heartfelt. It was part of her. He must accept it along with the rest, he decided.

Each evening, darkness trapped Morgan and Dixie before the fireplace. They played cards or Scrabble, munched on apples and popcorn, watched the news on television, telephoned friends, and waited for the clock to chime the "good night" hour, sending them to their separate beds.

"You know, members of my family were real characters," Dixie confided one night. She then proceeded to confound him with breezy anecdotes about people he'd never met. Her Uncle Floyd who had a romantic streak and bicycled fifty-three miles every weekend to court her aunt Lizzie; her cousin, a judge, who embezzled money from a client, and then paid it back; her four-foot, eleven-inch Grandma Ruby who spouted aphorism after aphorism: Waste not, want not. If wishes were horses, beggars would ride. A stitch in time . . .

Just as Morgan was feeling almost comatose, Dixie slid Jiggs, who was in a similar state, off her lap. She stood and stretched.

Morgan widened his eyes, gave his head a quick shake to jumpstart his brain. He watched expectantly as she held her hands toward the dying flames in the fireplace, awaiting the invitation that never came.

"Bedtime, Jiggsy. Come on, sweetie." She picked up the little dog and, crooning sweet nothings in his ear, carried him out of the room and up the stairs.

Morgan put his head in his hands, groaning and laughing. She'd broken him in less than two weeks of endless evenings of boring games, idle chatter, and friendly debates about the world's rights and wrongs.

It was three days before Christmas, time for hell to freeze over. He'd call his doctor tomorrow and get his HIV test. He'd probably be the first 89-year-old in history to get one. Perhaps he and Dixie could then find something romantic to do.

Or would she come up with another hurdle? Talk about the Seven Labors of Hercules.

BOOK III

THE INTRUDER

17

What a Mess

*T*ony huddled against the building, warming his hands under his armpits. Not many people out tonight. Saving themselves for tomorrow, he guessed, New Year's Eve. The slush in the gutters was freezing. Patches of icy snow glittered under the streetlights.

His stomach knotted. Would Eddie even show? He'd give him ten more minutes.

"About time," he muttered when the white car pulled up. He opened the door and slid inside. "Hey, man, it's cold."

"Had to wait till she went out." Eddie grinned and held up a small wad of bills. "Look what I found."

"She's gonna bust your chops," Tony said.

"She won't remember how much she had. What you wanna do?"

"I'm hungry, man. Let's get a burger."

"I just ate."

"They kept me late at work. I stood out here in the cold for a half hour waiting for you. I could have eaten."

"Quit bitchin'," Eddie said.

"You'd bitch too if you lived in a dingy room, if you worked a stinkin' job."

"It's not my fault, birdbrain. I told you not to dye your hair in the bathroom. You made a mess. She didn't like it."

"Yeah, blame it all on me. I thought you were gonna get a job."

"I'm looking, man."

As long as Eddie had three squares a day, a comfortable bed, and no hassles, he didn't give a damn about finding a job. And if he didn't have a job, he couldn't afford an apartment with Tony. And Tony couldn't afford one alone. "Let's go to the Blue Moon, over near the campus. They have draft beer for a buck. And food."

"Maybe we can find some college girls," Eddie grinned.

The Blue Moon was empty except for a couple of serious drinkers. "No college girls," Tony muttered to Eddie. "It's the holidays." They sat at the bar. At the end of it, not far from Tony, a man nodded into his drink. Tony ordered a cheeseburger and fries, along with a beer. He could smell his hands as he ate. He smelled like the greasy, mildewed rag he cleaned the tables with at work. "I stink, man. The job stinks. This town stinks. I wouldn't be here if it wasn't for you."

"What about that rich guy who owes you?"

"Yeah?"

"Ask him to pay up."

"I'm planning to," Tony said through a mouthful of food.

"Stop whining then."

"So where're you looking? Job-wise?" Tony asked when he was on his second beer and Eddie was on his third.

"I got two interviews lined up next week." He smiled mysteriously.

Eddie always had big plans, but as Tony was learning, they never quite panned out.

On the good side, Eddie had showed him the ropes at the camp. They'd made it through the program together, tough as it was. There was a bond there.

Tony finished his beer. He looked at the empty face of the drunk at the end of the bar. That could be him ten years from now. "Let's get out of here," he said to Eddie.

They headed downtown and drove around, half-heartedly looking for girls. The streets were deserted except for a few guys in thick coats, shoulders hunched, leaning into the wind. "I'm still thirsty," Eddie said. He pulled into a carryout lot, left the motor running, and went inside the store.

Tony felt woozy, half sick. He rubbed his forehead. He hated them for making him live like this—working as a busboy at a two-bit greasy spoon, going back at night to a one-room hole-in-the-wall, sharing a *bathroom with some geeks. It was as bad as Wilderness Valley. His eyes smarted. Hang tough, man, he told himself.*

Eddie flung open the car door.

Tony took the beer that Eddie offered and chugged half of it down in one gulp. They both finished their beer as they sat in the carryout lot.

"What do you wanna do?"

"How long you got the car for?"

"She gets off work at midnight. But she always goes out after."

"Let me drive," Tony said.

"You're drunk." Eddie's blonde hair, limp and damp, clung to his forehead. "She'd tear me apart if the car got smashed."

"You're drunker than me."

Eddie revved the car and they left the lot.

"Where you going?" Tony asked as Eddie returned to the freeway. "I don't want to go back to the room." Depressing, antiseptic, institutional green, YMCA room. At least he wasn't scared there, like he'd been at the homeless shelter. Eddie had promised him a place to stay. That's the only reason he came to Columbus. Now he was stuck.

"I got an idea," Eddie said.

Tony opened another beer.

"Crack me one, too," Eddie said. "We're going visiting."

Twenty minutes later they were driving slowly down a neighborhood street, past homes with Christmas decorations. One had a reindeer in the front yard, another a plastic Santa Claus on the roof. Tony felt homesick, until he remembered what waited for him at home. In the next block, he mumbled, "There's the playground. We're almost there."

The house was dark, except for a dim light coming through the sidelite of the front door. Eddie stopped the car at the curb, engine idling. "They must be away," Tony said, relieved.

"Or in the back watching TV." Eddie turned onto a side street and parked the car. He switched off the motor and slid out. He waited a few moments and then opened Tony's door. "What's the matter? You scared or something? You been burning my ears off about this guy and what he owes you."

"Sit on it." Tony climbed out of the car, swaggered across the street, up the driveway, and onto the porch. The cold air cleared his head. He

felt buoyed up. He'd confront him, make him sweat. He rang the bell. No answer. He rang it again.

Eddie, beside him, put his forehead against the window panel, peering inside. "No one. Let's go around to the back. Scope it out."

Tony followed Eddie around the right side of the house. The house next door was dark. He looked behind him. Across the street, the houses were black and still, except for an electric candle in one window. Further down the block, Christmas lights outlined a door. Through the window, he could see a TV screen flickering in the front room. Someone was home there. "Too dark to see anything back here," he hissed at Eddie.

Eddie took a small penlight out of his pocket and directed the beam on the crusted snow. The only sound was the crunching of their feet as they made their way to the back.

"Big place," Eddie said.

The house was a shadowy hulk. No one was watching TV. "Let's get out of here," Tony whispered.

Eddie unlatched the gate in the fence. Tony followed him through the snow to the back door. Eddie shined the penlight through the glass.

"We're trespassing," Tony said, glancing nervously at the dark house on the far side. He thought he detected a crack of light at the back second floor window. He took Eddie by the arm. "Let's go."

Eddie shook him off. "You keep telling me he owes you big-time." He took something out of his pocket and fiddled with the sliding-glass door.

"What are you doing?"

Laughing softly, Eddie shined the penlight on his credit card as he slipped it into the crack between the door and doorjamb, jiggled it, and tried the door.

"Are you nuts?" Tony hissed.

"Open up, you turkey." He kept working at it until the door slid open. He chortled, "Just like butter on toast," and entered the house.

"C'mon," he whispered. "You said you wanted to see how he lived with his secret bank accounts, all that money he stole. Here's your chance."

Tony stepped inside. He felt scared, but it was thrilling. And he was very curious.

Eddie flashed the penlight around the room. "Fireplace, TV set," he murmured.

"Hey, man, they'll see us. We better close the curtains." Tony pulled the heavy drapes over the sliding-glass door.

Eddie's beam caught a small Christmas tree. "No gifts under the tree. Mr. Morgan and his girlfriend must be away for the holidays. On their yacht in the South Seas." Eddie snickered.

"What if they're upstairs asleep?"

"No one's asleep this early." Eddie handed him the penlight. "Here, go up and check."

Tony caught a glimpse of Eddie's face in the dim light, his blue eyes cool and measuring, daring him to do it. "Don't be a wuss."

Tony made his way into the kitchen, Eddie following. Tony found the staircase at the end of the hall and tiptoed up the stairs, every nerve in his body tingling. Halfway up, he heard a sound behind him. He whirled, pointing the light down the steps. No one. His imagination was working overtime. Where was Eddie? He must have stayed downstairs. He almost laughed aloud. How could Eddie call him a wuss, now that he, Tony, was the one up here? Well, Eddie had gotten sloppy since they left the camp. Too much beer.

He stopped at the landing, listening. Not a sound. No heavy breathing or snoring. His heart rat-a-tat-tatting, he shined the light on the floor of the room to his right and slowly raised the beam. The bed was empty. Wait! What was standing at the foot of it? He licked his dry lips.

Only a bicycle. Must be some kids around. What was he getting himself into?

To his left, a door was open. He thrust his light in. Bathroom with a big, circular tub. Very FANCY. Next room on his right. Another empty bed. A chest, the top of it cluttered with handkerchiefs and socks. He took a deep breath and let it out. Two rooms remaining. At the end of the hall, another bathroom. Empty.

Sweat was pouring down his face. The door on the left was partially open. He gave it a push, shining the thin beam on the floor. Bedroom, larger than the other two. He heard a noise. Someone was in bed. With his heart in his throat, he switched off the penlight and jumped back. A thud. Bare feet touching the floor. Someone was moving toward him. Something was brushing along the floor. A nightgown? Pajamas? Tiny clicking noises.

"Don't shoot. I'm sorry," he whispered, flicking on the penlight to show his face.

A *small bushy dog, his face half covered by fur, was padding toward him, his toenails clicking over the floor. What a weird-looking animal. He looked like a mop, except for his beady eyes. Tony flashed the light around the room. Empty. The dog was at his feet. Would he bark? Would he bite?* "Nice boy, nice boy," *Tony murmured. Slowly, he reached down and patted his head, then scratched his ears. The little dog licked his hand, then shuffled back into the room.*

When Tony came downstairs, he found Eddie at the refrigerator, its door open, the light casting a ghostly glow on Eddie's face. "All clear?" *he asked.*

"Except for a vicious watchdog. I fought him off." *Tony snickered to himself.*

Eddie took a step toward the hall. "What's that noise?"

Tony aimed the light into the hall. The dog had followed him downstairs.

Eddie laughed. "Vicious watchdog, my ass." *He opened a package that was in the refrigerator and threw a slab of something at the dog, who jumped back.*

"What's that?" *Tony asked.*

"Cold cuts."

The dog went over to the meat, sniffed, and began to chew noisily.

"That ought to keep him busy." *Eddie unscrewed the top of a liquor bottle and took a long drink. He handed it to Tony.* "Good scotch."

Tony took a slug. It burned his throat. His eyes watered. He turned away so Eddie wouldn't see. "Yeah."

Eddie opened the freezer door, rummaging around inside. "Give me some more light." *As Tony focused the light on Eddie, he saw that drawers near the sink had been pulled out, their contents emptied on the floor.* "I thought we were just going to have a look around."

"Have another drink."

Tony took a gulp of scotch. It went down easier than the first one. He kept the light on Eddie as he shoveled items from the freezer into a black plastic leaf bag. "What do you want with all that food?"

Eddie laughed. "Peace offering."

"Hurry it up."

"What's the rush? They're away."

"What if they come back tonight?" *Tony took one more drink from the bottle.* "We don't want to get caught."

"*Anything interesting upstairs?*" Eddie asked.

"*A bike. Looked new.*"

"*Let's get it.*"

"*Sure. We're gonna carry it out to the car, right under the street-light.*"

"*I'll drive the car around to the playground. There's a parking lot in back. We'll take the stuff through the backyard of the folks next door and through the playground. Hey, don't be stingy with that scotch.*"

Tony handed him the bottle.

"*Find any money?*" Eddie asked.

"*No.*"

"*You checked the drawers?*"

"*Yeah,*" Tony lied.

"*Maybe Mister Big Shot has a safe.*"

"*I didn't see one.*"

Swigging from the bottle, Eddie walked into the dining room, shining his thin beam over the walls.

"*Hey, man, they're gonna see us.*" Tony jerked at the drapery cord in the back window. The drapes didn't budge. Impatiently, he jerked again. And again. The cord broke.

"*Uh-oh,*" Eddie said mockingly. "*Now look what you've done.*"

"*Someone's gonna see us, moron, the way you're flicking that light around.*" Tony tried forcing the drapes shut with his hands. There was a loud rip.

"*Born to raise hell.*" Eddie laughed. "*What's in here?*" He opened the corner cupboard, fingering a shelf of books. He pulled one out and examined it. "*An old Bible,*" he said contemptuously, letting it fall to the floor. "*Look at all these pigs. I've never seen so many.*" He pawed through the collection of porcelain and metal figurines. Chuckling, he held one up. "*Here's one with wings. An angel pig.*" He hesitated, then put it in his pocket.

"*Why do you want that?*" Tony asked.

"*Souvenir. Maybe it's worth something. Get one for yourself. Here's one taking a bath, something you ought to do once in a while.*" Eddie thrust the small figure in Tony's face. "*Oink, oink.*"

"*Cut it out.*" Tony slapped his hand away, sending the pig and the half-empty scotch bottle tumbling to the floor.

"*Asshole!*" Eddie yelled.

Tony darted into the living room. Eddie tackled him, knocking over a lamp, shattering the glass. As they wrestled over the floor, they toppled a chair, breaking a vase on a table beside it. Tony felt a murderous rage, took a good punch at Eddie's face. "Fuckin' asshole!" Eddie cried. "My nose. It's bleeding."

Tony wanted to pummel him more, but forced himself to break away. The two lay on the floor, breathing hard.

"What's the matter with you?" Eddie asked, wiping his nose with the back of his hand.

"You started it." Tony got up. "This place smells like a brewery." He found the penlight. "Where's that pig? That old pig of mine," he sang. He found the pig taking a bath unbroken on the floor, beside the scotch bottle. He put it in his pocket. He picked up the bottle and jiggled it. "What do you know? There's a little left." He gulped it down.

Eddie grabbed it from him and tipped his head back, sucking at the bottle. "Jerk, you didn't save me any!" He threw it at Tony, who ducked. It smashed against the wall.

∽✦∾

Dixie brushed tears from her eyes as the closing credits rolled. Her son Ronnie would have been just like the young hero, charming and loving as he struggled to find himself and make a life. The lights came up. She took her hankie from her purse and blew her nose.

Morgan gave her a questioning look.

"I thought about Ronnie."

He nodded gravely.

She wondered if the movie reminded Morgan of his children. They were lost to him, but not the way her son was lost to her. Morgan could make a quick journey and find them again, along with his dying ex-wife. And open a trunk full of bitterness and half-forgotten memories. She turned to ask him what he'd decided. "Good film," she said instead, losing her nerve.

He nodded. "Glad you saw that review."

"Want to take a ride?" Morgan asked when they reached the car. He turned the key in the ignition. "See how the rich folk decorate for Christmas?"

"Why not? I have tomorrow off," Dixie answered. "Then let's stop by The Creamery and pick up a quart of ice cream."

"Make a night of it." Morgan drove onto the freeway. The lights of downtown Columbus twinkled off to the side.

"You're awfully quiet," Dixie said.

"Mmm hmmm."

"What are you thinking?"

"It's a surprise."

He'd already bought a new dishwasher and had it installed two days before Christmas while she was at work. You could have knocked her over with a feather. She never thought he'd part with that much money for a household item. On the other hand, she knew how he hated to do the dishes. "Another surprise?" She glanced his way. His eyes, lit from the dashboard, were hollow, his lips a straight line. She was certain. He'd decided to go up to Chicago. "Good surprise or bad?"

"There are only good surprises," he said. "Otherwise, it's a shock. Or an outrage."

They left the freeway. Morgan zigzagged through the streets, chasing the glitzy decorations. They oohed and aahed, entertained by the ingenuity of some. They reached a strip of homes ablaze with too many lights, front lawns packed with angels and creche scenes, and Santas and elves. "Little competition going on here," Morgan chuckled.

"What a waste, when people are homeless and starving," Dixie murmured.

"Well, people amortize the cost over several years," Morgan explained.

"I'm ready for that ice cream. How about you?" Maybe over ice cream he'd tell her his surprise. Dixie half dreaded it. Why? He'd told her there were only good surprises.

⟡

"Let's get out of here." Tony felt edgy.

"Get that bike. I'll take care of the TV," Eddie said.

Tony went upstairs. "Hey," he called down to Eddie. "It's only an exercise bike."

"She'll like that. She's always trying to lose weight," Eddie answered.

Tony reluctantly carted the bike down the stairs and into the family room. Taking a couple of pigs was one thing; stealing a bike and a TV was another. Besides, he didn't want to lug the stuff through the back-yard of the people next door. What if they woke up? What if a security guard patrolled the school playground? "We get the cops on our tail, we're done for."

Eddie unplugged the TV, hefted it up, and carried it over in front of the sliding-glass door. Puffing, he set it down. "Weighs a ton."

"It's old," Tony said. "Leave it."

"It'll be OK for my bedroom," Eddie replied. "I thought you said this guy was rich."

"It's too heavy. It'll take both of us to carry it," Tony said.

"I got an idea." Eddie opened the door to the garage. He was back in a few moments with a wheelbarrow. "We'll put the stuff in here."

Tony heard a yip. Eddie quickly flashed the light around the family room and into the kitchen.

"It's the dog, man," Tony said.

Eddie's beam caught the shaggy little animal, who growled, then hiccoughed.

"He's puking up those cold cuts." Tony's stomach lurched. He held his breath.

"Ughh. Get him out of here."

Breathing through his mouth, Tony reached for the dog, digging his fingers through the fur, and found his collar. "C'mon, boy, let's go back up to bed." He pulled him toward the stairs. He hoped to God the dog was finished being sick. Near the front door the little creature rolled over on his back. Tony laughed. "Feeling better?" He rubbed the dog's stom-ach.

Eddie was rummaging through the debris he'd dumped from the kitchen drawers.

"What are you looking for?" Tony asked.

"We ought to leave a note. What are you doing?"

"He wants to play."

"Aw, leave him." Eddie returned to the family room and climbed up on the couch. "Come here." He handed Tony the penlight. "Give me some light." Tony aimed the penlight at Eddie, as Eddie wrote across the wall in large red letters.

∞

"Our neighborhood looks pretty shabby by comparison," Morgan laughed as he turned the corner onto their street. "A dented Santa Claus and some ratty-looking reindeer." He was bursting to tell Dixie his surprise. Scared too, he had to admit.

He took a deep breath. He'd picked up his test results from the doctor today. He had the proof Dixie wanted, that he was HIV-free and free of everything else—but lust. He fingered the bottle of Viagra in his pants pocket. He wouldn't need to tell her about the Viagra. Let her think what she would. He drove past the playground. Almost home.

"What are you grinning about?" Dixie asked.

"Just thinking of that ice cream," Morgan said.

☜☞

"Shit! They're back!" Tony screamed from the hall. He dashed into the family room.

"Get my sack of stuff," Eddie yelled. "From the kitchen."

Tony grabbed the bag of food Eddie had collected from the refrigerator. He was shaking so badly his kneecaps were jumping. The stuff weighed a ton. What did he have in there? He half-carried, half-dragged it into the family room. "C'mon, man! They're in the drive!"

Eddie hefted the TV up into the wheelbarrow. He lifted the handles and tried to force the wheelbarrow through the drapes covering the sliding-glass door.

"What do we do with this?" Tony pointed at the bag of food. He felt as if his head was going to fly off his body.

"Hold the curtains back, man," Eddie grunted. A ball of fur appeared from nowhere and, with a growl, jumped at his legs. "Get away, mutt." Eddie kicked at him and, as he did, he tipped the wheelbarrow. The TV fell with a crash onto the metal track of the sliding door. The little dog yelped. Tony jumped away to miss the splintering glass. Eddie flailed backwards, grabbing at the drapes and the plant stand, bringing both down as he thudded to the floor.

"Shit! We're cooked!" Tony felt like he was going to throw up. Where was the little dog? Under the TV? Mangled by the plant stand? Why had he let Eddie get him into this?

☜☞

"Oops," Morgan said, "forgot the ice cream." He doubled back to the car and plucked the sack out of the backseat while Dixie opened the door of the family room.

He heard her shriek, "Oh, my God! Morgan!"

"Dixie? What's wrong?" Silence. Had she fallen? "Dixie?" He quickly entered the house. The sight that met him stopped him in his tracks. The plant stand was overturned. Clumps of dirt, green leaves, and flowers were scattered over the rug. The sliding-glass door stood open. Cold air blew in through the flapping drapes, or what remained of them. One panel was partly torn off the track and hung there twisted around the front wheel of the wheelbarrow. The television set was on its back, its screen broken, surrounded by shards of glass. "Dixie?" he called, his voice cracking. The kitchen lights were on. Why didn't she answer? Had someone been waiting inside for them to return? Had Dixie been attacked? Knocked out? He hurried back out to the garage and snatched the first thing he saw, the hedge shears hanging on the wall.

He heard his heart beating a mile a minute. He hoped he was up to this. Gripping the handles of the metal shears, he edged into the kitchen, ready to lunge. Dixie stood in the middle of the floor, tears rolling down her cheeks. Silverware, utensils, tools, dishcloths, cookbooks, nails and screws, glue and string, nutcrackers, plastic bags, pens and pencils, thumbtacks, buttons, phonebooks, old lotto tickets, and miscellaneous bric-a-brac littered the floor. Every drawer in the kitchen had been pulled out, its contents dumped. Morgan reached for the phone and dialed 911. "We've had a break-in," he reported in an unsteady voice. Was the culprit still in the house? He picked up the shears again, grasping them in one hand, as he gave the dispatcher their address.

"Jiggs! Where's Jiggs?" Dixie cried. "Jiggs, here, boy!"

"Stay calm," the dispatcher told Morgan. "Leave everything untouched. An officer is on the way."

"The police are on the way," Morgan yelled at the top of his lungs in case anyone still lurked. "What did you say?" he asked the dispatcher. "No, no injuries. We were out at a movie. The place is a wreck."

"You'd better leave the house," the dispatcher said.

"Jiggs, where are you?" Dixie wailed and started toward the hallway that led to the stairs. "What have they done to Jiggs?"

"Dixie, stay with me," Morgan ordered. "Jiggs, our dog, may be missing," he said into the phone. He let go of the hedge shears to fumble for his inhaler and took two quick puffs. "It smells." He sniffed the air. "Like vomit." He saw a mess on the floor at the door between the kitchen and the hall. "And alcohol." The cupboard was open where he kept his scotch whiskey, the bottle missing. "He drank my twelve-year-old scotch and got sick all over the floor. Dixie, where are you? What did you say?" he asked the woman at the other end of the line.

"Leave the house," she urged, "until help arrives."

Dixie, who had drifted from the kitchen into the family room, cried, "Morgan, look at this!"

"We're on our way out." He hung up the phone. In the family room, he found Dixie pointing to the wall that abutted the garage. They'd both missed seeing it on their way into the house. Above the couch HAPPY NEW YEAR, YOU PIG had been scrawled in red paint.

"What does it mean?" Dixie whispered.

"It means we're leaving until the police arrive," Morgan said, hustling Dixie into the garage. He opened the garage door. The two, still bundled in their coats, Morgan clutching the hedge shears, stepped out onto the driveway. Dixie cried on his shoulder as he hugged her—oh, so tenderly. "Who would do this to us?" she sobbed.

"We'll find out," he said grimly. "Lucky we weren't here."

"Do you think they hurt Jiggs?" She broke down again. "Or killed him?"

He hugged her tighter, fervently hoping nothing had happened to Jiggs. Dixie would never be the same.

18

The Police

Dixie clung to Morgan, afraid she'd collapse if she let go. "You're shaking," he said, drawing her closer. "I thought it was you," Dixie answered through chattering teeth. They followed the two police officers through the garage, squeezing between their cars, their coats wiping dust from doors and fenders.

The officers halted outside the door to the family room. Dixie held her breath. "Stay here," the older officer hissed. *What did he say his name was?* Dixie searched her rattled brain. *Barzini, that was it.*

Both officers drew their guns, just like on TV. Barzini slowly opened the door and sprang inside, grasping his weapon with both hands. The female, Officer McGinty, followed. "Police! We're coming in!" Barzini boomed. Then all was eerily silent. The door gaped open. Dixie, frozen, felt Morgan propel her over to the far corner of the garage where they crouched, half hidden behind Morgan's car.

Dixie prepared herself for a shootout, or a crazed vandal fleeing past them. She could bear it, whatever happened, if only Jiggs were found unhurt. She imagined Jiggs maimed, hiding under her bed. Jiggs killed, his broken body found in the house. Jiggs kidnapped, carted away to an abusive family. Jiggs, in terror, running through the open back door, wandering the neighborhood in a daze, hit by a car blocks away. She might never see him again, might never know what happened. She brushed tears away with the heel of her hand.

Morgan squeezed her arm.

She jumped when Officer McGinty, framed in the doorway, beckoned them inside. "All clear. We've checked upstairs and down."

Dixie took a step and stumbled. Morgan grabbed her, gently pushing her in front of him. He took her elbows, nudging her up the step into the family room, into the chaos and destruction.

It took her breath away—her beautiful, expensive drapes, only three years old, dangling like filthy rags, tangled in the wheelbarrow, which lay on its side like an obscene beast, its underbelly mudencrusted. Chunks of glass gleamed among the clods of dirt. Green and purple remains of plants were scattered over the carpet. The rug would have to be professionally cleaned. Her African violets would never survive this outrage. Would soap and water wipe off the frightening message on the wall?

"We've been seeing a lot of this lately," Officer Barzini said grimly.

So much glass, surely not all from the crushed TV. Or from the broken pottery that once held her plants. The sliding-glass door to the patio. Was it shattered too? She stepped over a clay dove planter, broken in two, the spider plant uprooted, and made her way around the overturned plant stand. The patio door was open. She reached out to make sure the glass was intact.

"Please, ma'am, don't touch anything." McGinty pushed strands of blonde hair back under her cap.

"He most likely left by the back door when you two walked in," Barzini offered.

Dixie scanned the back yard for signs of movement. "Jiggs," she called hoarsely. She felt Morgan behind her, his hands on her shoulders. She prayed she'd see a reddish-blonde streak against the white snow, bounding toward her. "Jiggs. Don't be scared." She heard a noise behind her, a little yip. She whirled around and there was Jiggs. Dixie almost fainted. He jumped up against her, then leaped back to Morgan, flinging himself between them like a ping pong ball.

McGinty smiled. "We found him upstairs on the bed. Asleep."

"Asleep? Through all this?" Morgan gave a shaky laugh, scratching Jiggs' ears. "So much for our watchdog."

A dazed Dixie scooped up the little dog. Her precious boy. She buried her face in his fur. "I thought I'd lost you."

Barzini cleared his throat. "We'd like you, when you're ready, to go through the house with us and check if anything's stolen."

She didn't want to see the rest of the house. She wanted to wake up from this nightmare.

Morgan touched her arm. "Ready, Dixie?"

She held Jiggs closer, told herself it didn't matter what was missing, torn, or broken. She had Jiggs. She looked around the family room. "Not much here worth stealing. Except the TV. But it's—it was pretty old."

"Did you have any gifts under the Christmas tree?" Barzini nudged.

Dixie shook her head.

"Well, let's check out the kitchen," he said, leading the way.

Dixie stepped into the kitchen and gently lowered Jiggs beside his bowl of water. She didn't want him stepping on the broken glass in the family room. She offered him a dog treat from the box in the cupboard. He turned away disdainfully. She'd never known Jiggs to refuse a treat.

"Did you keep any money or valuables here?" McGinty asked, her gray eyes taking in the empty drawers, their contents spilled out over the kitchen floor.

Dixie shook her head. "Kitchen stuff. Odds and ends. Junk, most of it." Had the intruder been looking for something? Or was it just malicious mischief? She had a sudden, terrible thought. Her new dishwasher. She opened it with trembling hands. Pulled out the racks, top and bottom, filled with dirty dishes. "It's new," she explained to Officer McGinty. "I hope he didn't break it." Dixie knew she'd made a bargain with the Lord, not to care about anything as long as Jiggs was safe. But she'd never had a dishwasher. And it was a gift from Morgan. Unexpected. Special.

"Try it," Officer McGinty suggested. Dixie shut the door and pushed the buttons. The dishwasher whirred to life, sounding as smooth and efficient as ever. McGinty nodded. Dixie sighed with relief, catching Morgan's eye. He gave her the thumbs-up.

Dear Morgan. He's being such a soldier through all this. She smiled brightly.

"Let's move on," Barzini suggested, making a face as he stepped into the hallway over the vomit on the kitchen floor. Dixie gagged at the smell, but pressed forward to the entrance of the living room. She steeled herself, turned on a lamp, and peered inside. Not so bad at first glance. An overturned chair, a broken lamp. The strong smell of alcohol overpowered the stink of vomit.

Dixie moaned, pointing. The ivory paint on the far wall was chipped and spattered with light brown stains. "I think he broke the scotch bottle against the wall." Chunks of dark glass lay on the table under the ruined wall. A vase was shattered too. "I hope I can get the smell out," Dixie worried. The table would have to be revarnished, the wall painted. How much would it cost to put everything to rights? How much would the insurance pay?

"The holidays bring out a lot of meanness." The creases around Barzini's mouth deepened.

"Why tear up the place?" Dixie burst out angrily. "Why not just steal?"

He shrugged.

"Any rebellious teenagers in the family? Family members who carry a grudge?" asked McGinty.

"I have no family alive," Dixie said. She turned to look at Morgan.

"And you, sir?" Barzini prodded.

"My family are as good as dead," Morgan murmured, frowning, staring into space.

The quartet moved on to the dining room. Those drapes too had been ripped, Dixie noted sadly, but they were old. The carpet here reeked even more strongly of alcohol. The paned-glass doors of her corner cupboard, formerly Grandma Ruby's, stood open. But on inspection, she found no broken glass. A Bible from her collection lay on the floor. She snatched it up and flipped through the pages, relieved to find it was undamaged, as were the three remaining Bibles on the cupboard shelf.

"Anything missing?" Officer McGinty asked.

Dixie scanned her collection of dolls and pincushions. They seemed to be as tightly jammed as ever on the shelves.

"Take your time," McGinty said gravely.

Dixie counted her dolls. All twelve were there, Miss January through Miss December, as were her pincushions—the Victorian heart, the turn-of-the-century pewter pincushions, lion, camel, dragon, and owl.

"May I use your phone, ma'am?" Barzini asked.

"Help yourself. In the kitchen." The shelf containing her collectible pigs seemed to be in disorder. One by one, Dixie lifted them out of the cupboard and lined them up on the dining room table—the patchwork pig bank, the pig toothbrush holder, pigs in a carriage, salt-and-pepper-shaker pigs, two pigs dining, her windup dancing pig, the three little pigs, Piglet.

Oh, no. She clapped her hand to her face. "Grandma Ruby's pig taking a bath is gone! And my angel pig." Favorites. Her eyes stung. She squeezed them shut, brushing away the tears. So she lost two pigs. She had Jiggs. She had Morgan, friend and comforter.

"Pig taking a bath and an angel pig," McGinty murmured, writing in her notebook. "What are they worth?"

"Not over a hundred dollars, probably. But priceless to me." The angel pig had been good luck for almost ten years. Vera had given it to her when she was in the hospital.

Dixie had another awful thought. She hurried over to the china cabinet, threw open the doors, and lifted out the chest that held Grandma Ruby's silver. She counted out the pieces. "It's all here," she said, astounded. Why would he leave the silver and steal the pigs?

Barzini stepped back into the dining room.

"Some collectibles are missing," McGinty told him.

Barzini nodded grimly. "Detective Bernson will be here soon. Shall we take a look upstairs?"

The officers led the way. Dixie trailed behind Morgan, preparing herself for the worst. Amazingly, the rooms upstairs appeared to be untouched—until they entered Dixie's bedroom.

"He's been looking through my things!" she cried out. Clothes from her closet—skirts, blouses, dresses, still on their hangers—were piled in a tangled heap on her bed.

"Sorry, ma'am," McGinty apologized, "it was me. Your closet was pretty jam-packed. He could have been hiding behind your clothes."

Hiding until the police left, standing over her as she slept. Dixie felt weak in the knees.

"Nothing missing from the upstairs then?" McGinty asked.

Dixie shook her head uncertainly. No costume jewelry stolen from her room. No checks or money taken from Morgan's dresser.

"Wait a minute," Morgan exclaimed, "I may have overlooked something." He ducked into the spare room and out again. "My exercise bike. It's new. So it didn't register at first. It's gone."

Dixie groaned. She'd used her charge card, dangerously overloaded, to buy it for Morgan for Christmas. "He stole an exercise bike," Dixie murmured, "but left Morgan's cash untouched."

Morgan speculated, "The vandal saw our headlights through the window or," he gave a hollow laugh, "our ferocious watchdog frightened him away before he finished ransacking the whole house."

"I notice you two have different last names," Barzini said. "Are you related?"

"He's a roomer," Dixie answered hastily.

Morgan raised his brows, then nodded. "A paying guest."

"You both were out tonight? Separately?" McGinty asked.

"We saw a movie together," Dixie admitted. Her face grew hot and even hotter when she saw Morgan wink at Barzini. Flustered, she turned away and started toward the stairs. "I think we're finished here." She wanted to sit down. She had the beginning of a headache. She heard them behind her on the stairs. Her stomach was upset. Smelling the vomit didn't help. "Can I clean up—where he got sick?" Dixie asked when the four of them reached the downstairs hall.

Barzini nodded. "I'd be much obliged."

First she'd take an aspirin with juice. She opened the refrigerator. It was bare. "The orange juice is missing," she said incredulously. "And a dozen eggs, one pound of bacon, a package of cold cuts, and a gallon of milk."

She checked the freezer. "The porterhouse steaks we bought for New Year's Eve have been stolen." Officer McGinty wrote in her notebook. "Also packages of pork chops, sausages, wieners. And a bowl of homemade chili."

The bread was not in its container, nor anywhere else—until Morgan found it floating in the downstairs toilet.

◦✧◦

Detective Bernson, the crime scene investigator, found no broken windows. Entry had been made through the sliding-glass door into the family room. The tracks in the snow showed that two individuals were involved, and both wore athletic shoes. "You ought to keep a wooden rod in the track of this sliding door so it can't be pushed open," he advised Morgan. He found the exercise bike in the backyard, near the gate in the fence. "Is that where you usually exercise?" he'd asked with a glint in his eye, beckoning Morgan to the door.

When Bernson discovered what looked like drops of blood on the living room rug, Dixie whispered, "You don't suppose they wrote the message on the wall in blood?" Morgan, white-faced, blinked. She brooded about it until the detective found a red felt pen near the couch and bagged it as evidence. HAPPY NEW YEAR, YOU PIG. Better to be written in ink than in blood.

"We'll run the prints through the database," Bernson said as he was leaving. "And I'll be back tomorrow to ask the neighbors if they saw anything suspicious."

"Be sure to ask Pauline, next door." Dixie pointed to her right. "She knows everything that goes on in the neighborhood."

"In fact," Morgan added, with a short laugh, "I'm surprised she isn't over here now, offering us a casserole of macaroni and cheese."

After the police were gone, Dixie, with Morgan's help, blotted the excess scotch from the carpet. As he dumped the sodden paper towels into the wastebasket, Morgan quipped half-heartedly, "I'm almost tempted to wring these out over a glass."

She mustered a smile.

It was nearly midnight when the two trudged upstairs to bed.

⚜

Morgan, in his pajamas, came out of his bathroom. He met Dixie in her nightgown and robe.

"I'm almost afraid to sleep alone," she said.

He stepped toward her. He thought she was going to invite him into her room.

She waved her hand apologetically. "I have a splitting headache."

"See you in the morning." Disappointed, Morgan left. He was bone tired. But they could have lain side by side, worried together, talked as the feeling stirred them. He might have told her about his doctor's visit today, that he was HIV-free. Something for her to think about, so she'd be ready when their lives got back to normal. "Better leave your door open. Call me if you want me." He lingered in the hall, hopeful she might change her mind. Finally, he went downstairs and checked the outside doors. He turned on the kitchen light. He'd leave it burning the rest of the night.

⚜

Dixie lay in bed with Jiggs snuggled beside her. She was as wide awake as if she'd had three cups of coffee. Why had they trashed *her* place?

Singled *her* out? "Oh, Jiggs, if only you could talk." She stroked his silky fur.

What would she have done without Morgan? He'd taken command with the power of what? An executive. She knew one thing—she'd be in a hotel right now if he wasn't here.

What if she and Morgan had been at home tonight when the thugs arrived, bent on destruction? She hated to think what might have happened. She pulled Jiggs closer.

HAPPY NEW YEAR, YOU PIG. It was nasty. A threat even. Would they be back? She broke out in a clammy sweat.

ଙ୍କ

Morgan tossed and turned. He thought he heard Dixie calling, "Help me, Morgan." He leaped from the bed and cracked his knee against the nightstand. The quiet was broken by his moan of pain.

He hurried down the hall, listened outside her door, heard nothing, and went back to bed. He was suddenly aware of the drip, drip, drip of water. Who forgot to turn off the faucets? The vandals? The police? He checked bathtubs and lavatories, the sinks and laundry equipment. Mystified at finding no leaks, he opened the sliding-glass door in the family room. A warm front had moved in. Melted icycles and snow dripped from roof and eaves. Bare ground showed in places where an endless sheet of white had covered it earlier.

He shut the door and locked it. He went into the garage, found a broom, measured it, sawed it off, and placed the wooden rod in the track of the sliding-glass door.

When he turned around, HAPPY NEW YEAR, YOU PIG greeted him from the opposite wall. Well, he didn't want to look at that day after day until they were able to paint. He pulled out one end of the couch, his slippered feet crunching on bits of dirt and glass. He brought a ladder in from the garage. With a rag and soapy water, he tried to scrub away the message. It blurred into a pale red smear. The wall looked worse than ever. But at least the hateful message was now illegible.

He put away the ladder. *They stole two pigs and wrote* you pig *on the wall. Pigs seemed to mean something to them.*

He poured himself a glass of milk and sat at the kitchen table, sipping slowly. *Pig meaning greed, meaning dirt.* Had the message on the wall been directed at him? Not as he was now. But as he used to be?

❧

Dixie willed herself to relax. She had to get some sleep. Her frazzled brain whirred on. The sinister man in the hood, with the mustache, whom Pauline had seen on their porch. Had he been scoping the place out? Looking for something? Or someone? That someone being Morgan?

She was being silly, stupid. It was a—what time was it?—a four-o'clock-in-the-morning thought. The thought stuck in her mind like a fly to flypaper. It was followed by another. The husband in Chicago who'd wanted to break Morgan's kneecaps, his suspicious death. The newspaper clipping from the scandal sheet. *Was his other hand in the till?*

Lies, unfounded rumors, Morgan said. Barry had heard differently. Was she living with a criminal? A man wanted by someone, if not the police? A man who'd brought the mess of his life into hers?

She'd make herself a cup of hot milk. She needed to settle down, try to think this through.

The kitchen light was on. Morgan sat at the table, both hands wrapped around an empty glass, staring into space. "I couldn't sleep," he said.

How could he sit there in the middle of the piles of stuff that had been dumped all over the floor? She swept past him and began to toss the silverware back into an empty drawer.

"What the hell—shouldn't we wash that first in the dishwasher?"

"Here," she said, scooping up a batch of spoons and forks and handing them to him, "you do it."

He awkwardly took them and laid them on the table. "I'm sorry."

"What about?" she asked, staring him down. Was he going to tell her, yes, I brought this on us?

He threw up his hands. "This—mess." His eyes had dark shadows under them.

"Nothing like this ever happened to me before you moved in."

"You're blaming me?" he spluttered.

"Why would strangers break into my place, write *you pig* on the wall? Out of the blue? Rifle through the drawers?" Flushing angrily, she picked up an eggbeater, held it above a drawer that still lay on the floor, and let it fall. The scissors followed, then a sieve. The clatter was music to her ears. "Are they looking for something you have?"

"What would that be?"

"Hidden bank accounts?"

He tried to laugh. "Not you too."

"Or are they paying you back?"

"For what?"

"For what you did in Chicago—wrecking a family, two families if you count your own. That man, your girlfriend's husband, died because of you."

"He committed suicide."

"You said it was a suspicious death."

"The police ruled it a suicide." He glowered.

"Didn't he threaten to break your kneecaps? Didn't he have ties to organized crime?"

"Why are we rehashing all this crap? What's wrong with you?"

"Did you know the rumors are still flying all over the place up there in Chicago?" she blurted out.

"Flying all over the place?" He looked confused.

"Well," she turned away uncomfortably, "some people still talk about it. Besides your former family."

He rubbed his forehead. "How would you know?"

"Barry told me."

"Barry? Your ex-boss?"

She nodded.

He looked as if she'd slugged him.

"He was at a party for a Chicago client. Someone was there from the Illinois Banking and Trust."

"Who?" he demanded.

"Someone who'd just started work at the bank when the investigation and the rumors started."

"So you asked Barry to check up on me?" Morgan rose from the table. "Did he tell you anything new?"

She hesitated, shook her head. "Only that the rumors are still—active."

"I think you've been watching too many cop shows. It's been forty years, for God's sake. Who would still be after me after forty years?"

She had to admit it was a logical question. If they'd been after him (whoever *they* were), surely they'd have found him long ago. "I'm worried, with all that's happened," she swept her arm around the kitchen, "that you haven't told me everything."

"I have," he said savagely. "I told you too much. If I'd kept quiet, you wouldn't be giving me the third degree. I'm going to bed." He left the kitchen.

 infinity

He heard her slamming things into the kitchen drawers as he climbed the stairs to his room. His bed was hard and unrelenting. So she'd asked Barry, her former boss, his former colleague in Kiwanis, to check up on him. He felt sick, hollow inside. Had Barry stirred up stuff?

Was that why he'd heard from his daughter, Sara? After almost forty years of silence?

He took two puffs from his inhaler. Sara's letter, then this break-in. Coincidence? Or were the two related? Preposterous! The past was finished.

What's the matter, Morgan? Guilty conscience? Because you haven't answered Sara's letter, saying yes, you'll honor your ex-wife's dying wish and visit her? A wave of sadness overwhelmed him. His wife had been so beautiful. Those first years were good years.

infinity

He felt groggy, his eyes full of grit. He looked at the clock. Almost noon. He stood up on rubbery legs and peered across the hall. Dixie's bedroom door was closed. He hurriedly dressed, splashed water on his face, and tiptoed down the stairs.

In the kitchen, the floor was clean and the mess from the emptied drawers cleared away. So Dixie finished the job before she went to bed. He made some strong hot coffee and gulped it down. He should start the cleanup of the rest of the house.

He felt hemmed in. Every room downstairs was a disaster, except the kitchen. Jiggs softly padded in. Surely that meant Dixie was awake. He didn't want to see her. He had to get out of the house. He quickly fed Jiggs. He put on his coat, climbed in his car, and drove away.

Two hours later, when he returned, he found Dixie in the dining room. She was in her robe, staring at the table, which was still covered with her platoon of pigs. "Oh," she said, "you scared me." She combed her hair with her fingers. Carefully, she placed the pigs back on the cupboard shelf, then slowly closed the paned-glass door. Her back was to him. Her shoulders began to shake. He put his arms around her. "Look," he said, trying to keep his voice even, "we're both off kilter. Let's not jump to conclusions."

"I thought you'd left me," she cried.

"No, no. I just had to go out for something."

"Mail from your post-office box?"

He laughed. He threw his arms around her. "Oh, Dixie, I gave that up weeks ago. Right after you found Sara's letter and we talked." He couldn't keep it to himself any longer. "I went out and bought a new TV! A twenty-seven-incher! To be delivered next week." He thought she'd be ecstatic. She was always complaining about how dim the picture was on the old TV. She looked glummer than ever. "Aren't you happy?"

She forced a smile.

"That old junker we had. We needed a new one anyway."

"Yes. Good thing they trashed it. Expensive?" she asked pointedly.

"A bargain. After-Christmas sales." He felt deflated by her lack of enthusiasm.

Later, at the kitchen table, as he poured her a cup of coffee, he insisted, "Look, it's random. A random crime."

She nodded uncertainly.

"Officer Barzini said they'd been seeing a lot of this. It's a typical holiday crime. Thieves after expensive Christmas gifts. When they don't find them, they tear up the place."

꧁꧂

When the doorbell rang, Morgan sprang up from the kitchen table. He opened the front door, with Dixie at his elbow.

Detective Bernson nodded hello. "I just wanted to bring you up to date. We visited every household within two blocks," he reported. "We found three people who saw two young men cruising the streets last night in a white car, possibly of Japanese make."

"Young men, you say? What did they look like?" Dixie asked.

Bernson smiled broadly. "We have a good description, ma'am. We also have a partial license tag number and possible leads from the fingerprints. If one or the other has been in trouble with the law, we'll have them."

He'd sidestepped Dixie's question, Morgan thought irritably. "What did they look like?" he repeated. "Short? Tall? White? Black?"

Bernson gave Morgan a thoughtful look. "Just wanted you to know, ma'am, the inquiry is far from over."

What did that look mean, Morgan wondered as the detective turned and walked away.

Shape up, he told himself. He was imagining looks and moods that weren't there.

"Well, Bernson didn't say much," Morgan fretted after the detective left. "'If their fingerprints are in the database, we'll have them.' You'd think a neighbor would have seen something more conclusive than a white car cruising the neighborhood. The guys in the white car were probably out gawking at Christmas lights."

"You'd think someone, especially Pauline, would have seen them going in our back door," Dixie mused. "Or spotted lights inside the house, or seen them running down the street."

Morgan frowned. "The police have murders and drug busts and armed robberies to investigate. They won't spend much time on our case, you can be sure." He didn't want theirs to be an unsolved crime, with Dixie and him fearing the vandalism was just the beginning. What was wrong with him? He took a deep breath. This wasn't going to be a repeat of Chicago with one disaster leading to another. "More coffee? Hot chocolate?" He went into the kitchen and put some water on to boil.

"I'll have tea." Dixie picked up the phone and dialed. "Let's see what Pauline knows." She drummed her fingers on the table. "Pauline, you sound awful." Dixie was silent, nodding, making sympathetic noises. She covered the mouthpiece. "She has a terrible cold." Morgan waited impatiently as Dixie described the break-in to Pauline. "Well, that's a first!" Dixie exclaimed, hanging up the phone. "She slept through the whole thing. She'd taken cold medicine to unstuff her nose."

"Who can we count on if not Jiggs or Pauline?" Morgan asked, trying to make a joke. He put a teabag in Dixie's cup and spooned hot chocolate into his. The kettle shrilled.

"She said she'll bring over a dish of spaghetti and meatballs after she's well."

"We could use it now," Morgan said. "There's no food in the house."

"You should have picked up something when you went out earlier." She fixed him with a reproachful look.

So much for the new TV. He poured water into the cups. They drank in silence. He hoped they'd get concrete answers from the police soon. Maybe Dixie's mood would improve. "Want some soup?" He rummaged in the bottom cupboard, found a can of chicken noodle, and held it up.

"Fine," she said, sitting there like a lump.

He heated the soup, determined not to let her goad him into another fight.

After the soup, it was nearly three. He felt rocky from so little sleep. But Dixie mulishly headed to the family room, insisting on starting the cleanup.

"First," Morgan said, working hard not to show his irritation, "we have to take photos for insurance."

By the time they finished the photos, it was five. Dixie was back in the family room, repotting her plants. What else could he do? Morgan untangled the drape twisted around the wheel of the wheelbarrow, flipped it upright, and hauled it around the room, dropping into it chunks of glass from the TV, assorted broken pottery, and clods of dirt.

Dixie ran the sweeper furiously, the roar of the motor matching her frown. With a sudden yank, she tore down a panel of the mutilated drapes. "These drapes were just a few years old," she burst out.

The next thing he knew, she was in the dining room on her hands and knees, rubbing at the carpet with cloth and spot cleaner. "My bridge club is due here next month. The house will smell like a bar."

She was like a whirling dervish, Morgan thought glumly. "We can burn incense," he suggested.

"Incense reminds me of funerals." She stood up, hair in disarray, shoulders slumped. "We'll have to have the carpet steam cleaned. What if they have to tear it out and patch it?" she wailed.

"The insurance will pay," Morgan grunted.

"Not the cost to replace."

"I'll take care of it," he said, managing a smile.

She gave him a steady look and nodded. As if it was the least he could do.

How much would it be? He'd already plunked down over $500 for a new TV.

He was beginning to feel grumpy. It was hard work keeping cheerful, like stirring a vat of molasses. She hadn't even noticed he'd put the broom handle in the track of the sliding-glass door. Or that he'd worked on cleaning off the wall.

He went out to get them Chinese food for dinner. When he searched through his coat pocket for his gloves, he found the Viagra. It seemed like a century ago, another life. One filled with hopes and dreams. He almost threw it away.

At nine o'clock, stumbling with fatigue, he went to bed. Dixie stayed downstairs listening to the radio, her eyes fluttering sleepily. She wanted to stay up to celebrate the New Year. So she'd said.

He wondered if she was concocting ways to get rid of him.

◑◐

The next morning she brought him coffee in bed, along with the newspaper. Jiggs danced alongside her.

"What's all this?" he asked, surprised.

"Happy New Year!" Dixie was grinning from ear to ear.

Jiggs jumped up on his bed. "You're both frisky this morning." Morgan patted the little dog on the head.

"Listen to this." Dixie read from the paper. "The police are investigating a dozen new burglaries. They think two youth gangs may be involved."

Morgan took the paper from her and read. Youth gangs. A dozen new burglaries. Not some dark plot against them. Not his ugly past erupting.

She smiled. "We were chosen at random!"

"I told you," he beamed. "A random hit. Well, nothing is really random," he pontificated, feeling expansive. "We were sitting ducks. They could get in easily through the sliding-glass door. Not any more. I put a rod in the track. And first thing when I get dressed," he said with a raised eyebrow at Jiggs, "I'm going to post BEWARE OF DOG signs in the front and back windows."

19

The Contract

On Monday, the phone rang just as Dixie was about to leave for work. When she picked up, a voice growled, "Sergeant Kelly. We've found your men. We need you to come down and file charges."

"Morgan," she shrieked, elated. "They've found them."

"What?" he yelled down from upstairs. The whine of the exercise bike stopped. She heard his footsteps from the spare bedroom to the landing. "Dixie?" he shouted "Did you want me?"

"They've caught them. The criminals!" She asked the sergeant, "Did they belong to a youth gang?"

"No," he said slowly. "One is from Chicago and has had some run-ins with police up there."

"Chicago?" She stammered, "My friend who lives—rents—here is from Chicago."

"We have reason to believe he'll be able to provide us with more details," the policeman said briskly.

Morgan, in his sweatsuit, stood beside her, panting slightly and frowning. "What's that about Chicago?"

"We'll be right down," Dixie said slowly. She hung up the phone. "One of the thieves—he's from Chicago."

Morgan looked stunned.

"Someone who's had run-ins with the police up there." She locked her eyes into his. "Sergeant Kelly said he hoped you'd be able to provide him with more details."

"I have no idea what he's talking about." Morgan walked away, blotting his face with his handkerchief. He turned back to Dixie. "Look, I'll take care of this. You go on into work."

"Are you crazy? I'm coming with you." Her chin jutted out. Did he have more dirty linen to hide? No matter. She'd stand by him. Wouldn't she? She called Whispering Pines to tell them she'd be late.

⚭

Morgan started the car. The motor squealed, then stopped. He tried again. It whined.

"Flooded," Dixie said.

He waited, shoulders slumped. What was all this about? Some kind of conspiracy? He pumped the gas pedal and turned the key. A groan. "We better take my car," he muttered.

"Give it a few minutes," Dixie said.

He looked at Dixie from the corner of his eye. She was sitting upright, tight and still as if she'd been made of metal. "You shouldn't have asked Barry to check up on me," he said.

She sighed, covering her eyes with her hand. "Barry was afraid I'd get hurt." She shifted in her seat. They were face-to-face. "I informed him you'd told me all about the Chicago mess, that none of it was true."

"Thank you," he mumbled.

The silence was thick. She asked softly, "Why did the sergeant say he has reason to believe you'll be able to give them more details?"

"I wish I knew," he grunted. He turned the key in the ignition. The motor fired. He sat there, gunning it.

⚭

Dixie clutched the dashboard as the car bounced into the street. Its undercarriage scraped the pavement. "Careful," she squealed, "there's a car parked right behind you."

"I see it," Morgan said, narrowly missing the fender.

Dixie fumbled with her seat belt.

His lower lip sticking out, Morgan jerked to a stop at the stop sign.

Dixie closed her eyes. She hoped they'd arrive in one piece. Who would they be up against? These days anyone could hire someone to kill or maim for a few hundred dollars. By the grace of God she and Morgan had been out of the house when they came. It was a miracle Jiggs was still alive. Her head throbbed, her stomach ached. Were the two thugs backed by a gang of racketeers intent on finding the money Morgan supposedly did or did not run away with? "Slow down. There it is. On the left."

⦿⦿

Dixie held onto Morgan's arm as the two walked into the station. The pudgy, balding policeman at the front desk eyed them sternly. She almost felt like a criminal herself. She glanced around furtively. The place definitely needed some sprucing up. The walls were drab and stained. The desk was dilapidated, its paint scarred. Morgan stepped forward and gave his name. The policeman escorted them upstairs to a dingy room that smelt of stale cigarette smoke.

"I'm Jim Pfeiffer," said the earnest-looking, dark-haired man behind one of two battered desks. The other desk was empty. Pfeiffer shook hands with them and closed the door, motioning for them to sit on the metal chairs. With an odd smile on his face, he asked, "Does the name Anthony Morgan mean anything to you?"

"Why, that's the same last name as my friend here," Dixie burst out.

The officer clamped his arms over his chest, waiting.

Morgan blinked, as if he'd just awakened. "You say he has a Chicago address?" he asked. "Morgan's a common name. But he could be a relative, I suppose." In response to the policeman's questioning look, Morgan explained that his divorced wife and their children had gone their separate ways with little communication for almost forty years. "I could have a dozen grandchildren and great-grandchildren and not know it," he said, trying to be offhand.

Pfeiffer nodded, his eyes cool. "Tony's been complaining about a rich relative, a once-prominent banker who abandoned his wife and small children, leaving them in dire circumstances." The officer paused, then continued, "The vandalism of your home may have been an act of retaliation."

Morgan glared. "Your Tony, if he's talking about me, is mixed up on the facts. My divorce was a friendly one."

Oh, yes, Dixie thought, so friendly they hadn't spoken with one another for years.

"I made generous support payments until every child became 21 years old," Morgan fumed. "I was never rich. And now I'm living on a fixed income from pension and Social Security."

The policeman didn't seem interested in his financial report. "He's in another room. Why don't we mosey over there and discuss what he plans to do with his life?"

"What about discussing how he plans to make good on all the damage?" Morgan sputtered, his face red.

Dixie put a calming hand on his arm.

"Am I the criminal or is he?" he asked her.

"What about this man's accomplice?" Dixie asked. "I thought two were involved."

"Eddie Navotka. His mother claimed him earlier. They were using her car."

"His mother?" Dixie exclaimed.

"He's a juvenile," the officer said. "Won't be 18 until next month." He handed Morgan his card.

"Jim Pfeiffer, Juvenile Bureau, Alternative Services Program," Morgan murmured to Dixie as they followed the officer down the hall into another room.

Why, he's just a boy, Dixie thought when she saw the figure slouched in the metal chair. His long legs, encased in ragged jeans, were sprawled in front of him. A black sweater with raveled cuffs, buttons missing, gaped open to reveal a dingy shirt, once white. He had a ragged mustache and stubble on his face. He looked to be about 15. She'd been picturing a tough-looking hooligan.

He eyed Morgan sullenly. His shoulder-length hair was dark brown, tipped with blonde. Bleached. What kids did these days to make a statement. An earring glinted in his right ear. "He's the person Pauline saw on our porch last month," Dixie exclaimed. "I saw him too. But his hood was up. He must have come by to case our house before he broke in." She looked into the boy's dark eyes for corroboration. He looked away.

Pfeiffer rolled over two rickety wooden chairs that rested near the far wall and placed them opposite Tony. "Please." He indicated for Morgan and Dixie to sit.

Looking stricken, Morgan lowered himself into the chair. Dixie sat too, after brushing off the seat. She slipped off her coat.

"So you're Anthony Morgan," Morgan mused. "Who do you belong to? Who sent you?"

"My name is Tony," the boy said softly, staring at the floor. "No one sent me."

Morgan cleared his throat. "Who's your dad?"

"Clay."

Morgan gave a short laugh. "Figures."

Tony smiled with bravado. "My dad looks like you. And I'm supposed to look like my dad."

So Tony was Morgan's grandson. She would have guessed great-grandson. He looked so young. Clay must have been pretty well up in years when Tony came along. Dixie studied the boy's face, the full lips and heavy-lidded eyes. He did resemble Morgan, except Tony's skin was darker.

"How did you find me, Tony?"

"I looked you up in the phone book." The boy's lips moved as if his jaw was wired.

"My current address is not in the phone book."

"I got it from a woman where you used to live."

"You went to a lot of work to track me down."

"I needed a decent job," he mumbled.

"Do you have any idea what you've put us through?" Dixie exploded. "We've been nervous wrecks, wondering who was out to get us."

Tony sighed and slumped further down in the chair.

"Funny way to ask for help finding a job," Morgan said gruffly. "You break our TV, write threats on our walls, ruin our rugs, and . . ." He flailed his arms, searching.

"Stole from my collection of pigs. And food from our refrigerator too," Dixie jumped in.

That last item seemed to boggle Morgan's mind more than the other crimes. His voice rose. "What's the matter, are you starving?"

Tony's eyes flashed, then he looked away.

Officer Pfeifer said, "They'd been drinking, Eddie and him."

"My twelve-year-old scotch."

"And a few beers before that." Pfeiffer fixed the boy in an unblinking gaze.

"Then you got sick all over the floor," Morgan said, disgustedly.

Ease up a little, Dixie almost said.

"It was the little dog that got sick," Tony said softly.

"Jiggs?" Dixie cried. "What did you do to Jiggs?"

"We fed him some cold cuts." Tony's eyes were apologetic.

"Cold cuts?" Dixie moaned.

"Then he disappeared." Tony ducked his head, glanced up at her. "Is he—okay?"

So Jiggs had been downstairs, romping with the two boys as they wrecked the house. And she'd been so worried that they'd killed him. He ate food she never allowed him to have, got sick, and went up to bed while the rampage continued. Jiggs had just been one of the boys. "He's fine," she sniffed.

Tony looked relieved.

"Where do you live?" Morgan asked.

"The Y." The boy examined his hands.

Officer Pfeiffer walked over to a desk jammed up against the wall and opened a drawer. He held up a figurine.

"It's Grandma Ruby's pig in the bathtub," Dixie said in hushed tones. She took it from him, grateful and amazed.

"Good condition?" asked the officer.

She examined it, then nodded. "No nicks or missing pieces."

The officer threw a hard look at Tony, who muttered, "I'm sorry I took it."

Pfeiffer then handed the angel pig to Dixie. "From Eddie, with his apologies."

It too was unbroken. "Thank you." Dixie smiled at Tony. "These are precious to me, for sentimental reasons."

He blushed.

Officer Pfeiffer said, with a twinkle in his eye, "My wife collects too. Hummels."

Dixie carefully wrapped the two figurines in her scarf and put them in her purse.

"You have a job now?" Morgan asked.

The boy made a face.

"He works as a busboy," said Officer Pfeiffer.

Morgan shucked off his coat. He wiped his face with his handkerchief. "For the record," he asked with a half smile, "where's that food you took?"

"It was found in the trunk of the car," Pfeiffer said. "You wouldn't want it back, believe me."

"What a waste," Dixie murmured.

"You get your meals where you work?" Morgan asked.

The boy nodded.

"Why steal our food?"

Tony twisted in his chair.

Morgan closed his eyes and sighed. He turned to the officer. "Has Clay been notified?"

"I don't want him involved," Tony said sharply. He suddenly unwound from the chair and stood. He was tall and slim, verging on thinness. "He wouldn't care anyway. I don't want Fulkerson—" he spat the name out—"messing around either."

"Who's Fulkerson?" Morgan asked.

Tony sat down again, fists clenched, a ferocious scowl on his face. Dixie realized he was trying not to cry.

"His stepdad," Officer Pfeiffer said. "This young man," he told Morgan and Dixie, "just turned 18 in November, the same month he was released from a wilderness camp in Utah."

"Wilderness camp?" Dixie asked.

"Juvenile boot camp. He came to Columbus with his pal Eddie, whom he'd met at the camp, instead of returning to his folks in Chicago."

"They don't want me."

"There he was going to have to work to pay off repairs on his mother's car," Officer Pfeiffer said drily, "which he'd taken for a joyride and nearly totaled. That's why he was in the boot camp."

"Mom didn't care if I used her car," the boy said angrily.

"She certainly cared that her car was nearly totaled," the officer replied.

"That was Fulkerson's fault. He called the cops on me. I was just trying to get away," Tony finished lamely.

Officer Pfeiffer looked almost fatherly as he told Dixie and Morgan, "The only other crime on Tony's record was that he stole a tape recorder when he was 14. He was placed on temporary probation then. He dropped out of high school his senior year. After he wrecked his mom's car, his stepdad thought boot camp would straighten him out." He made a sour face, then signaled Dixie and Morgan out of the room into the hall. "Want to file charges?" the officer asked softly. "The kid could be tried as an adult."

"I ought to—to scare him," Morgan said. "Him and that other hoodlum—what's his name? Eddie?"

"I told Eddie and his mom I'd be in touch once you decided what to do."

"Eddie's a juvenile," Dixie burst out. "How can his mother let him run wild, using her car at all hours of the night? If he were mine—"

"He didn't ask, he just took. She's a single mom; she works as a waitress." Officer Pfeiffer glanced down at the floor and back at them, squaring his shoulders. "It's my experience that teenage boys are looking for a new identity as they grow up. They're moving away from their family. So you move away and you do a lot of things that are experimental," he explained, rocking back and forth, his hands clasped behind him, "and often those things, including the testing of law and order, just frighten the hell out of society."

"They sure scared the bejesus out of us, wrecking the place, leaving threatening messages around. What do you think of a boy who writes *you pig* on the wall?"

"Someone who needs some family guidance," the officer said, his eyes drilling into Morgan. "Most juveniles who commit crimes come from a dysfunctional family."

Dixie looked at Morgan, who glanced away.

Pfeiffer stroked his chin, then revealed, "Actually, his friend Navotka confessed he wrote that message on your wall. He also said Tony wanted to leave the premises when no one answered the bell. Navotka did the actual break-in."

"Well, Tony didn't stop him," Morgan said. "What about our broken TV?"

"Navotka said he dropped it accidentally—"

"When he was trying to get it out the back door," Morgan said with a cynical smile.

"They were pretty soused."

"But to deliberately vandalize, destroy property," Dixie said. "Was it done to get even with Morgan? The boy had never met him."

"They claimed it was accidental. They got into a fistfight. I think that caused a good bit of the damage," Officer Pfeiffer offered, shrugging and holding out his hands.

"Whose side are you on?" Morgan raised his brows.

Pfeiffer massaged his forehead. "Everywhere a boy turns—the movies, TV, advertising, computer games—he's force-fed speed, violence, sexuality, and alcohol. No wonder he often follows through." His eyes were gloomy.

He looked as if he'd seen it all and cared about each boy he met. "It's true," she said softly, turning to Morgan.

"Families are key. Good family relationships." Pfeiffer frowned. "Your Tony told me he doesn't want to go home to his stepdad. And his real dad Clay, your son," Pfeiffer gave Morgan a meaningful look, "doesn't involve himself much in the boy's life. His sisters are grown up and married." He eyed the two of them evenly. "We look for alternatives to locking up young offenders."

"What about paying us for the damage and loss?" Dixie asked.

"Restitution is part of our diversion program," Pfeiffer said.

"On a busboy's salary?" Morgan sighed. "The TV was pretty old, anyway." He rubbed his chin. "Well, at least he—they—can help us clean up the mess."

Pfeiffer smiled. "Eddie and Tony seem to be a volatile combination. We're warning them to avoid contact with each other." He shook hands with Morgan and then with Dixie. "Tony has a lot of anger," he added. "He needs to learn to channel it." The three filed back into the room where Tony was waiting to hear his fate.

"I won't press charges if you cooperate," Morgan said grimly. "Clean up your act. Your friend Eddie—well, Officer Pfeiffer and his mom can deal with him. From what I've heard, you two better stay apart." He added, "I'd like to start by asking you to help us paint the walls and clean up the place."

Tony mumbled something that sounded like, "Okay."

"That will be your sixteen hours of community service," Pfeiffer told him, suddenly brisk and businesslike.

"Sixteen hours?" Tony groused.

"It will take longer than sixteen hours, young man, to get my walls painted, the rugs cleaned, the table refinished—" Dixie said sharply. Tony's eyes were wide. He seemed surprised by her outburst. "And my African violets, my pride and joy—well, there's nothing to do except buy new plants and invest months in nurturing them." He looked almost bored. Didn't he understand? "It'll take time to fix what you've broken. You young people think you have all the time in the world. Well, we don't!" At last, the boy had the sense to look ashamed.

"Sounds like you're getting off easy, Tony, with sixteen hours," Pfeiffer said drily. He removed some papers from the desk drawer. "In these nonviolent cases," Pfeiffer looked at Morgan and Dixie, "we require a contract, signed by the diversion officer and the offender so he'll know exactly what's expected. He'll come in for counseling. You two will be his community site supervisors, the site being your home. He'll also be required to attend an educational program. The contract"—he handed it to Tony, holding him in his gaze—"also stipulates that if you don't complete the program, you'll be facing criminal charges."

Tony glanced down at the paper, rattling it in his hands. He saw Dixie looking at him, stood, and swaggered to the other side of the room. He turned away, pushing a hand through his hair, while he read.

He looked so lonely, Dixie thought, wearing indifference like a badly fitting coat.

"Come by next Saturday at one, Anthony," Morgan said. "You know how to find us. We'll be ready to paint by then."

Pfeiffer gave Morgan a sheet of paper. "Keep track of the dates and times he works, sign it, and return it to me after he completes his service. Now," he said to Tony, "you and I will hash out the other contract details."

Morgan and Dixie were silent on the way to the car. Dixie's brain was spinning. If Tony were her grandkid, she'd have been sobbing, thinking of the meeting today as a real reunion, a chance to get close. She might even have invited Tony to dinner, a social visit, before his official visit on Saturday, so he'd *want* to help them. So he'd feel Morgan was real, and not a cardboard cutout manufactured by bitter relatives.

On the other hand, Tony had broken into her home, destroying belongings she'd scrimped and saved for over several years. Even if it was Eddie's idea, as Pfeiffer maintained, Tony should have shown some backbone. She and Morgan had been put through the wringer, practically in fear for their lives. And the boy had the nerve to be offended at the prospect of spending a measly sixteen hours to right his wrongs. Well, his upbringing was at fault. Parents like his shouldn't be allowed the privilege of raising kids.

"He dropped out of high school. He'll never be able to get a decent job," Dixie ventured when they were in the car.

"He has a lot of anger. You heard what Pfeiffer said," Morgan grunted irritably, as if he'd detected a tinge of sympathy in her voice. He turned the key in the ignition.

"I heard," Dixie sighed. Tony was an unknown. His judgment was immature. He could turn out to be a bigger handful than either of them wanted at their age. She remembered with a chill that one of the Columbine boys had a history with the police long before the massacre. Best keep things businesslike, with Pfeiffer as the buffer.

"So Tony belongs to Clay." Morgan started the car. "Well," he said grudgingly, "I'm willing to look at the vandalism with a tolerant eye if Tony will be a little more forgiving of the dumb decisions I made all those years ago."

Dixie gave Morgan the thumbs-up sign. She prayed that Tony had sense enough to complete the program to everyone's satisfaction.

20

The Cleanup

M organ stepped inside the front door, knocking snow from his boots onto the mat. "I've cleared off the driveway," he announced, pleased to see Dixie coming down the hall to greet him.

"Officer Pfeiffer just called," she said worriedly. "He wants you at the station. Grandson Tony was picked up again last night."

"What? I don't believe it!" He looked at his watch. "He's scheduled to be here in exactly three hours, to help us with the cleanup." Morgan gave a short laugh. "Guess this is his way of getting out of work." Just like Clay, hard-nosed and irresponsible.

"I hope you're not too disappointed."

"Why would I be disappointed?" he snapped. "I'm a realist. I expect the worst of people."

What kind of trouble had the darn fool gotten into now? Morgan fretted as he drove the few miles to the station. It had only been five days since the kid's last run-in with the law. Didn't Tony realize he was flirting with a term behind bars? Had he misjudged the boy's intelligence?

Coddling Tony was turning into a full-time job. Ready to wash his hands of responsibility for Tony's future, Morgan burst into Jim Pfeiffer's office. "He must think the world owes him a living," Morgan fumed, "that the laws don't apply to him. Does he even know what it means to work hard, to accept responsibility? His trouble is he wants to start at the top; he thinks he knows more than the qualified operators of business, law and order—"

"Calm down," Pfeiffer ordered. "He was only disturbing the peace. He and Eddie got into a brawl at their favorite pub, The Blue Moon."

Morgan sputtered, "He's not supposed to be with Eddie. In addition, he was supposed to come by at one today to help paint the walls. I suppose that's out of the question now. Has he kept any part of his contract with you?"

"He has," Pfeiffer said smoothly. "He's been in for counseling. And he's enrolled in an adult education class to study for his GED."

"Well," Morgan muttered, "something positive."

"Look," Pfeiffer said earnestly, his forehead creasing, "the first month or two after they get home from boot camp, most grads do well. Then they start to have problems for a few weeks. Then they get better. They need support from parents or," he gestured toward Morgan, "their substitute."

"So now I'm a substitute parent?" He threw up his hands. "You know how old I am? Almost 90. I don't need this stress."

"90? I'd never guess." Pfeiffer's eyes crinkled. With an arm over Morgan's shoulders, he led him out of his office and down the hall. "He looks a little raunchy. He's been in the holding cell since he was picked up at midnight. With your help, we'll keep a potential lawbreaker off our lists and add in his place an industrious, law-abiding citizen. Now let's go in and scare the crap out of him." Just outside the door, he whispered to Morgan, "We need to hold out hope that there's something better for him in the future."

Tony started guiltily when Morgan stepped inside the room.

Pfeiffer closed the door and stood with his arms crossed over his chest.

Morgan felt a twinge of sympathy. Tony's eyes were puffy. Dried blood caked his nostrils. Blood smeared one cheek. His lower lip was split, his shirt torn and filthy. His hair hung in greasy clumps. He needed a shave.

"Tony," Pfeiffer began grimly, "you've violated two terms of your agreement, to stay away from Eddie and to abstain from the use of alcohol."

"The guys in the bar started the fight." Tony's face flushed. "Eddie and I hadn't even finished our beer."

"You shouldn't have been in the bar in the first place," Pfeiffer said.

"I only had a beer and a half," Tony protested.

"Do you know what the penalty is for underage drinking?" Pfeiffer continued. "Five hundred dollars and sixty days in jail. You could be incarcerated with hardened criminals. The camp you were sent to would seem like a vacation in comparison," he said sternly. "You hear me?"

Tony gave an almost imperceptible nod.

"Your grandpa here has gone out of his way to give you a second chance. He's disappointed, he's disgusted . . ." Pfeiffer looked at Morgan, eyebrows raised.

"Even though you're my grandson, I'm ready to call it quits." Morgan continued severely, "If you persist in this behavior, I'll have no choice but—"

"I'm sorry," Tony shouted, clenching his fists. He exhaled loudly, then swallowed, his Adam's apple bobbing. "I'm sorry," he repeated in a whisper, adding something that sounded like *Grandpa*.

"In your favor, Tony," Pfeiffer said, swaying from side to side, "you've attended one counseling session and have enrolled in night school." Pfeiffer paused, nudging Morgan with his eyes.

"You have to make up your mind, young man," Morgan said. "Get your act one hundred percent together or face criminal charges as an adult."

Pfeiffer said matter-of-factly, "You just got a taste of what it's like behind bars."

Tony looked down, then raised his head, licking his hurt lip. "I know I messed up. I know I can do it." His eyes seemed to plead for a second chance.

"Do what?" Pfeiffer demanded.

"Get my act together."

"Okay." Pfeiffer rubbed his hands together. "Tell us your plans for this next week."

"Look for a better job. Then I can pay you something toward the damages," he said to Morgan solemnly.

Pfeiffer nodded.

"I'll come to counseling. Go to my class at night school."

"Good," Morgan said.

"And maybe," Tony said, looking hopeful, "after I get my high-school diploma, I'll take some college courses."

Morgan felt optimistic. "It would increase your job options." The kid must have some smarts. Clay did, but never had the discipline to keep his grades up.

"And no hanging out with Eddie," Pfeiffer admonished. "He's been warned, twice now, as well."

"It would help if you found some new friends in night school," Morgan suggested.

Tony nodded.

"Now about your community service," Peiffer said, glancing at his watch. "It's to start in two hours."

The boy was bushed. "Look," Morgan said, "go"—he started to say, *home*—"back to your room at the Y. Wash your face. Get some sleep. Normally, I'd ask you to come over at eight AM tomorrow. But I don't want you scaring Dixie with that face. If it's okay with you," he turned to Pfeiffer, "he can start next week. There's plenty to do." If Tony came while Dixie was at work, he and his grandson might have a chance to get to know each other. He thought aloud, "We need the painting done, but it's much more important for you to get yourself fixed up and look for a job, Anthony, something more satisfying than your current one as a busboy. Come by, let's say, next Friday, one o'clock." If all went smoothly, maybe he'd ask Tony to have dinner with them.

Pfeiffer pushed out his lips, thinking. "Okay," he finally said. "Friday at one."

"In the meantime," Morgan said, slapping Tony on the shoulder, "promise me you'll be out looking for a job." He handed Tony three twenty-dollar bills. "Get your hair back to its normal color, get it cut, get rid of that earring, and buy yourself a new shirt! I want to be proud of my newfound grandson."

"Thanks, Grandpa." Tony smiled, wincing through his split lip, and stuffed the bills in his pocket.

His car skidded twice on the icy streets as Grandpa Morgan joyfully made his way home. "Today I helped a young man turn his life around," he announced to Dixie as he bounded into the house. Morgan shed his overcoat. "I think Grandson Tony has seen the light. He's continuing his education and looking for a new job and new friends. If he messes up, he goes to jail. If he follows through, I'll pat him on the back and give him new challenges. I may even pay his fees for more schooling." He nodded to himself, pleased that the problem seemed to be resolving itself so quickly.

"Well," Dixie replied dubiously, "that was easy."

"I gave him some money," Morgan admitted, "so he could get a haircut and some new clothes. He needs to look presentable if he's going to get a better job."

"So he's coming at one to help with the painting?"

"Well," Morgan stammered, "he looked terrible. They kept him all night in the holding cell. He'd been in a fight at the bar. His nose was bloodied."

Dixie nodded solemnly.

"I told him to go home and get some sleep. He's coming by next Friday." He grinned. "I thought that way he and I could get acquainted while you're at work."

"Sounds good."

"Pfeiffer's making him toe the line. Tony's already been to counseling, and he's enrolled in night school."

"All's well that ends well." Dixie nodded briskly. "We'd better get to work cleaning up the place—without Tony. My bridge club and your poker club will be here in a few weeks."

"Did you say my poker club?"

"But they have to do their smoking outside." She smiled.

He opened his arms wide, marched over to her, and gave her a bear hug. Humming a little tune, he waltzed her around the kitchen.

She pulled away, laughing. "Down to business, pal. We've got painting to do."

"Don't we want to leave it for him to do on Friday?"

"Well, we'll save the living room for Tony. We can get started on the family room today."

He saw the urgency in Dixie's eyes. The mess made her nervous. She wanted it cleaned up as quickly as possible. "What do you mean, *we*? It's my responsibility. He's my grandson."

"We'll each do thirty minutes. I don't want you keeling over on me."

⁂

Morgan had no clue, Dixie thought, as she changed into her painting clothes. He was too hard on Tony one minute, too lenient the next. She wasn't sure he should have given Tony that money. And it would have been good discipline for Tony to work today, as scheduled, tired as he was. They could have let him go early. Well, Morgan hadn't done too well with his kids. She felt a pang of guilt at her disloyalty. She was beginning to feel like a ping-pong ball, being batted back and forth between the two.

Why do I even care about this kid? she wondered. She was just setting herself up to be let down.

She went downstairs into the family room. "Open the door. You need ventilation," she called to Morgan after he disappeared into the garage to mix the paint. Several minutes later, he returned carrying a paint bucket. "Where's your mask?" she asked, cracking the sliding-glass door for ventilation. "I don't want you breathing those fumes."

Sheepishly, he took it out of his pocket, fastened it over his nose and mouth, climbed the ladder, and began to paint.

He's quite nimble, she thought, and he makes every movement count. He stretched to reach a distant smudge and his jeans tightened across his buttocks. "You know," she told him confidentially, "you have nice buns." She felt her face flush. She walked into the kitchen and pretended to work, banging around a few pans.

"You're really throwing yourself into cleaning up the kitchen," Morgan called cheerfully.

❧

As Morgan worked, he whistled tunelessly. She'd said he had nice buns. She'd been responsive when they danced around the kitchen, almost melting in his arms. Now, man. Do it. Tell her. He should ease into it, so he wouldn't startle her. *You asked me to get tested and I did. But that night our home was trashed and*—Should he be more direct? *The doctor said my tests were okay. It's time for you to get into that sexy negligee.* He studied all the angles. Before he knew it, they'd both done their thirty minutes and the first coat of paint had been applied to the damaged wall.

After Dixie climbed down from the ladder, Morgan took a deep breath and jumped in with both feet. "Honey," he said, deciding on the subtle approach, "I'm tired. Let's relax. Let's lie down together for awhile."

She laughed. "You never give up, do you? Why can't we just go to the kitchen, sit across the table from each other, and drink a cup of hot chocolate?"

"You're the one," he said, trying to be light, "always thinking someone is about to trick you into doing something you don't want to do." He blurted out, "I received the all-clear from the doctor. I'm HIV-free." Seeing her look of dismay, he added quickly, "But I'll have the patience to wait until you're ready to welcome me with open arms."

Dixie took his hand. "Come and relax with me in front of the microwave oven. We'll drink a glass of sherry. I'll hold your hand to keep you from making any forward passes." She poured them each a glass of sherry, took his hand, and continued shyly, "Just to set the record straight, I visited my doctor too. I don't have the HIV virus or any other social disease."

Morgan couldn't stop grinning. "Let's go out to dinner tonight and celebrate the start of a whole new relationship."

"Hold on," she said, looking as if she were about to say something serious. She seemed to change her mind, stood, and said chirpily. "Why not? At least we can forget the mess we're leaving for a few hours."

꙳

Morgan stepped out of the shower and admired his sleek torso in the mirror. The exercise bike was starting to produce results. *Nice buns.* He chuckled.

He wore his best suit. Dixie, perfumed and bewigged, appeared in a stunning outfit Morgan had never seen before. "How about prime rib?" Dixie asked.

After they were seated at the steak house, Morgan, almost tongue-tied, gazed at Dixie. In her electric blue dress, she seemed to charge the atmosphere. "They were surprised," he said, after rummaging through his mind for the perfect opening, "when I came in to take the test for HIV."

Dixie pressed her lips together and shifted in her chair.

The waiter brought the bread and wine.

Morgan cleared his throat. "The nurse told me that ten percent of new AIDS cases occur in people over 50. So we old folks are obviously," he heard himself chuckle inanely, "not over the hill." He took a gulp of his wine. "She thought I was in my seventies. When I told her my age, you should have seen her face."

Dixie gave him a piercing look, her eyes like sapphires. "The nurse told me anyone who had any," she paused delicately, "careless behavior since the mid-1970s could be at risk."

"What does that mean, careless behavior?" he asked with a sly smile, trying to make her blush.

She did. "Well, sharing needles for one."

He leaned forward. "I didn't share any needles. Did you?"

"No, but you had Miranda and plenty of others to be careless with during those twenty-five years," she shot back.

"So you're still worried about Miranda? She doesn't hold a candle to you." He chewed on his lower lip. "What about you during that time?"

She gave him a mocking smile. "I don't kiss and tell."

Aha, just what he thought. She hadn't been with anyone other than her meandering hubby. "I told the nurse I was in a new and serious relationship. And it was only fair to my significant other that I get tested." He clinked his glass against hers. He hoped he got it right. "I told her I'd never be content with a woman who wasn't beautiful, talented, who didn't have a sense of humor, and who wasn't wanted by another man." He winked. "I told her that was you, to a T."

She laughed. "Uncle Floyd's blarney to a T. I'm surprised you remembered."

He chuckled, pleased with himself. It was the one thing he'd heard that evening when she was going on and on about her relatives until he was nearly comatose. "Well, the guy was impressive, pedaling fifty-three miles on his bike to court his girl."

When the food arrived—prime rib, baked potato, and salad—the two dug into it with gusto.

Over cheesecake and decaf, Dixie chattered on about the new millennium and their broken vow to finish rehashing highlights of the decades by then.

"Well," Morgan argued, "2000 isn't really the New Millennium. 2001 would be. So," he countered, smiling hugely, "we have twelve months to finish that project. Plenty of time for frivolous pursuits as well as intellectual."

By the time they arrived home, Morgan was having trouble keeping his eyes open.

Dixie yawned. "There's still a lot to do around here."

"Maybe we should get a good night's rest and be fresh to tackle this mess again tomorrow. A belated happy new year," he said, drawing her into his arms and kissing her on the lips, their first real kiss since that night long ago on the front porch after the Elks dinner dance. He felt her hug him back. He buried his face in the hollow of her neck.

"Happy new year," she whispered. "We have a lot to talk about when things calm down." She gently slid out of his arms.

Her response to his kiss boded well, Morgan thought happily, as he undressed for bed. He'd better get in shape for the BIG MOMENT. He'd make it a daily habit, using that exercise bike. His head barely touched the pillow before he fell into a sound sleep.

21

The Blow-Up

Dixie opened the front door. "Why, hello, Anthony," she said, surprised. "We expected you yesterday." Morgan had waited for him for hours. She'd left work early to pop over to the house to check on things. She'd had a panic attack about leaving Morgan alone with Tony.

"Hello, Mrs.—" Tony held himself stiffly, his shoulders hunched. His dark eyes bored into her.

She felt uneasy. Was he angry that Morgan reported his absence yesterday to Pfeiffer? "Valentine," she said, "Dixie Valentine." His shirttail hung below his hooded jacket by several inches. His baggy jeans bunched on top of filthy-looking sneakers.

"Something came up yesterday." He looked down. "A job interview." He pushed off his hood. His gold earring peeked between two matted clumps of hair. "I came by to apologize."

"You should have called us."

"I forgot your last name, ma'am, to look up your number in the phone book."

"You could have rescheduled with Officer Pfeiffer."

"I tried to. I had to leave a message."

Surely, Morgan would have told her if Pfeiffer had passed along Tony's message.

The boy shifted from one foot to the other.

She should ask him to leave and come back later, when Morgan would be home.

Just then Jiggs appeared, wagging his tail and sniffing at Tony's leg. Tony's face lit up. He squatted down to scratch the little dog's ears. "Hi, Jiggs!" Jiggs exuberantly licked his hand.

The boy was shivering. That jacket was too thin for a day like today. She made up her mind. She hoped she wouldn't be sorry. "Come inside. Let me close the door."

He stepped in, towering over her. His hands were red and raw from the cold. He had no gloves.

"Uh," Tony hesitated. "Is Grandpa here?"

"He's at the paint store, buying more supplies." *Mistake, Dixie. You shouldn't have told him you're alone.*

He smiled ruefully. "I was in the neighborhood. Over at the mall. Maybe I should come back." He turned as if to leave.

Trust the boy, Dixie. He needs trust. "Would you like some hot chocolate?"

"Yeah," he said, his face brightening.

She led him through the hall to the kitchen. When she turned around, she saw him gawking at the chaos in the living room, where furniture, draped in paint cloths, was pushed away from the wall. Paint cans and a stepladder waited in the middle of the tarpaulin-covered carpet. "We've done the family room. It took two coats of paint to completely hide the red felt pen," she said pointedly. "And the rug still stinks of scotch. We'll have to get a professional cleaner in."

"I'm sorry," he mumbled, looking shamefaced, "about the damage."

"Sit down at the table." She smiled. "Take off your jacket." She lifted the milk out of the refrigerator and measured out two cups into a saucepan. "Your grandpa should be back soon." She turned on the burner, stirring the cold milk slowly.

"What kind of dog is Jiggs?" he asked, throwing his jacket over the back of his chair.

His shirt, a faded blue, was wrinkled, with grease stains down the front and sweat stains under the arms. He'd said he came by to apologize. Maybe he came to ask for money. Or maybe he'd stay and help them after Morgan returned. "A Lhasa apso."

"I had a dog."

"In Chicago?"

"Yeah. His name was Barney. He was a collie. He died."

"You get so attached. I don't know what I'd do if I lost Jiggs."

He nodded, his eyes sad.

The boy seemed so forlorn. She wanted to put her arms around him. Instead, she spooned the chocolate into two cups, and when the milk was heated, poured it in and stirred. She dropped two marshmallows into the cups. As she set his cup in front of him, she caught a whiff of mildew.

"Thanks."

"Have you ever thought about going back to Chicago?" she asked gently. She supposed Pfeiffer could call a juvenile officer in Chicago and he could fulfill his contract there.

Tony put his elbow on the table and rested his chin in his hand, staring at the tablecloth.

She sat down across from him. "I'll bet your mom is worried to death. Have you called her?"

"*He* always answers." Tony spooned out a marshmallow and ate it.

"Your stepdad? What's his name? Fulkerson?"

"Yeah."

"I bet you could find a time when your mom was alone. Why don't you like him?" She hoped his stepdad wasn't physically abusive.

He blew on his hot chocolate and took a sip. "He orders me around, yells at me, treats me"—he swallowed hard—"like they did at the camp. He's an ex-Marine." He glared into space.

"How long were you at the camp?" she asked. She'd heard terrible stories about those boot camps.

"Three months."

She nodded sympathetically. "What about your real dad Clay? You get along with him?"

"He's too busy chasing after every skirt he can get his hands on," he burst out. His face reddened. "Sorry, ma'am."

"What's he do for a living?"

"A big-shot executive for a department-store chain." He looked away. "They got divorced when I was 14."

A bad time for a kid to go through divorce. But any time was a bad time. No wonder he stole that tape recorder at age 14.

"I don't see him much." Tony drained his cup.

"How about your sisters? Are you close?"

"One's 27, the other 31. They have their own families." He shrugged.

He was a forgotten child. A mistake, most likely. "Would you like a sandwich? Grilled cheese?"

"Sounds great!" He watched her slice the cheese. "We ate a lot of cheese at the camp. I like it."

She sliced it thick. "What else did you eat?"

"Peanut butter, rice, beans, trail mix. We had to ask for more fruit."

Dixie made a sandwich, buttered both sides of the bread, and put it in the toaster oven.

"What was it like at the camp?" she asked him after he'd wolfed down half the sandwich and she was making him another.

He was silent. She could see in his eyes he was deciding how much to tell her. "The first two weeks were tough," he finally said. "I hated every minute."

"What made it so tough?" she asked, trying to sound casual. She hoped she could keep him talking about his real feelings.

"Couldn't even take a piss without someone telling you when." He gave her a sheepish smile and mumbled, "Sorry." He continued indignantly, "At six o'clock every morning, the counselor called, 'Five Minutes!' In five minutes, my clothes had to be on and all my gear had to be 'plumb and square.'"

"You were able to get your gear plumb and square, just like that?" She snapped her fingers.

"Yep," he said proudly.

"That's great."

"We chopped and sawed wood." He paused. "We marched from camp to camp. Every day, rain or shine. With heavy backpacks. Forty-five pounds."

A growing boy, she thought indignantly. A wonder it didn't hurt his back permanently. The grilled cheese was done. She opened the toaster oven.

"We slept in shelters made out of tarps." He smiled mirthlessly. "We learned survival skills. How to start a fire without a match."

She took his plate and put his sandwich on it.

"Thanks." He took a big bite. After he swallowed, he said, "At night we had classes. I was so tired from marching I looked forward to the classes."

She smiled in commiseration. "Good—that you had classes."

"We got high-school credit." He grinned. "I was the third highest in the math test and literature."

So he was a decent student. He must have dropped out of high school as an act of defiance against his stepdad. "I hope," she said tentatively, "you'll have the fortitude to get your high-school diploma."

"Yeah," he said. "I'm taking night school now to get it."

Dixie nodded, smiling. "Tell me more about the camp."

"We had counseling." His lips twisted. "Changing your coping strategies," he mimicked. "Rites of passage. All you needed to do was tell them what they wanted to hear." He gave her a cynical look, as if he dared her to speak her mind.

"You don't learn to change by holding yourself above it all, figuring out how to beat the system," she said steadily. "That's a loser's game." Was he telling Pfeiffer, telling them all, only what they wanted to hear?

He looked away and concentrated on eating his sandwich.

She reached across the table and before she knew it, she'd grabbed his wrist. "I hope you're not telling Morgan what you think he wants to hear. It would kill him." His startled eyes met hers. "Your grandpa believes in you. He told me. He was terribly hurt when you didn't show up yesterday."

He was silent, digesting what she'd said. He finally nodded.

She took her hand away. She searched for neutral ground. "Tell me about Eddie. How did you hook up with him?"

"We were on a hike. Eight miles through the desert. He ran out of water. I gave him some of mine. Then we all ran out. We had two miles to go. It was almost a hundred degrees. We got cramps in our toes."

He could have died.

"It was the worst day in the program." He took a bite of his sandwich, chewed, and swallowed. "The first week we hiked two miles a day. We worked up to fifteen miles a day. With water breaks only at intervals." He grinned proudly. "When I graduated, I was in better shape than I ever was in my life. My body never felt like that. I could run three miles without feeling it."

"Good for you."

He finished the sandwich and brushed his lips with the napkin.

"You and Eddie had a lot in common?" Dixie asked.

Tony shrugged. "Eddie was there from Youth Corrections. The program accepted kids from the courts for free. If he didn't make it through, he'd have to spend time in juvey hall. If he finished, the felony would be taken off his record. There were some tough kids. Some fights." He tapped his chest. "Then there were kids like me, sent by parents. Well, it cost." He smiled crookedly, then spoke contemptuously in a rush. "Clay paid $40,000 for me to be there."

She bit her lip to keep from exploding. He'd ignored Tony all his life, and then spent the price of a luxury car to send him away for ninety days.

"Eddie had been at the camp longer than me. He kinda showed me the ropes. At graduation—there was a ceremony when you finished. Parents were supposed to come. Clay was too busy. Mom planned to come, but she couldn't get away at the last minute." A muscle twitched in his jaw. "They sent me money to fly back to Chicago. I took the bus to Columbus with Eddie and his mom."

"Eddie's mom came to graduation?"

He nodded.

Eddie's mom just went up a notch in Dixie's book.

"I stayed with Eddie and her." He sighed. "Until she kicked me out."

"You two must have been a handful."

He shrugged, giving her a sheepish grin.

"So you moved into the Y?"

"A homeless shelter, until I got a job."

"Homeless shelter? How awful."

"I got three meals a day. And they helped me find a job. Busboy." He grimaced.

He was bright enough. He could get a better job. "How about an ice-cream sundae?" she asked.

⚬❦⚬

"There was a huge line," Morgan grumbled as he burst into the family room from the garage. "The clerk was new and didn't know what she was doing!"

"Tony's here," Dixie called from the kitchen. "We've been talking."

What the hell? "You were supposed to be here yesterday! What happened?" Morgan carried his shopping bag full of painting supplies into the kitchen, expecting to see the new person Tony promised him he would become. He looked as seedy as ever.

"Want a grilled cheese?" Dixie asked Morgan. "Some hot chocolate?"

Tony stood up, swallowing his last bit of ice cream. "Hi, Grandpa."

"Hello, Anthony. What happened yesterday?"

"A job interview came up. You told me to start looking for a job."

His clothes looked as if he'd worn them to bed last night, or maybe for the last week or two. "I hope you told Pfeiffer you broke your appointment with us."

"Pfeiffer wasn't in. I left a message."

"I left a message with him too," Morgan said emphatically.

"I was in the neighborhood today, so I stopped by." Tony spoke in a rush. "I applied for a job in a shoe store at the shopping mall up the street. The man told me he didn't have anything. He took my name but that was all—"

"I don't wonder that he turned you down." Morgan cut him off, his voice ragged. "You look like a bum. I gave you money a week ago to get yourself fixed up. What did you do with it?" Was the boy here for another handout?

"Morgan," Dixie interrupted. "Tony was telling me—"

Tony's face turned dark but he continued evenly, "I thought maybe you might give me a recommendation. Help me find something. I'll take any kind of a job. Except busboy."

"Get your hair cut. Wear some decent clothes. Get that earring out of your ear. You look like a girl. Make an effort to show the prospective employer that you understand how to take care of yourself."

"I knew I shouldn't come here," Tony glowered. "You said you'd help me out but I can see you don't believe in giving kids a break."

"I don't have anything against kids," Morgan said. "It's just that I'm fed up with you fellas who think you have the world at your fingertips without even trying to meet an employer's expectations. You think you should start at the top. I started at the bottom and worked hard for what I got."

Tony sneered. "And ran around with all the women and got written up by the gossip columns."

"Why don't you go on home, get spruced up, go out and get a job, and then come back and talk to me? I'd like to hear about your plans for the future but right now I can see you don't have any."

"You said you'd help me!" His voice was accusing. "You're rich. You have connections."

"Who said I was rich?"

Tony simmered for a few seconds, then blurted out, "My dad, Clay. He told me how you stole from the bank and hid the money in secret accounts so you wouldn't have to give it to the family."

"Horse manure!" Morgan spat. That damn family of his! "Furthermore, when you go out to meet someone, look him in the eye. Don't keep looking down. It gives the impression that what you're saying is a lie. Practice before a mirror. Look at yourself." He marched over to the boy, his face close to Tony's, biting off the words. "Stare right in your eye in the mirror and explain what you're trying to do, how you're going to go about it, and when you've mastered that and you got yourself a job, I'll go all-out for you." Morgan felt lightheaded. He forced himself to breathe in deeply, breathe out.

Tony looked him in the eye to glare at him. "You're as bad as Fulkerson!" He grabbed his jacket and stomped out of the kitchen.

"Go back to Chicago. Ask Clay for help!" Morgan sat down heavily in the chair Tony had vacated, taking a puff from his inhaler.

"They're right—everything they've said about you!" Tony yelled before he slammed the front door shut.

Dixie was staring at Morgan.

"What's the matter?" he asked truculently.

"He and I were having a wonderful talk before you barged in."

"He didn't come here to help. He wanted to get a job recommendation out of me."

"You tore into him before he had a chance to say much of anything!"

"Anyone who looks like he does," Morgan spluttered, "well, I'd hate to have him around for the neighbors to see." He paused, drumming his fingers on the table. "The subject is finished! There's nothing to do until Tony returns looking like a normal human being. If he ever does."

Dixie looked at him askance.

"He's 18, old enough to cut it. If not, he can go back home."

"To his wonderful, concerned family," she said drily. "Did you know—"

Morgan broke in on her. "In the meantime, we'll go along as if he'd never shown up." He rose from the table.

"Your grandson has a contract with Officer Pfeiffer. We agreed to be part of it."

"I'll call Pfeiffer tomorrow and tell him Tony has to look for another community site to sponsor him." He walked down the hall to the stairs.

"At least I'm not pressing charges, even though he didn't keep his part of the bargain. I'm going to change my clothes and get to work."

❦

"Why don't we wait to paint?" Dixie asked when Morgan appeared in the kitchen wearing an old shirt and slacks. His face was pasty, with dark smudges under his eyes. Tony had worn them both down. "We can do it tomorrow."

"And miss church?" he smiled wanly.

"I made you lunch."

"I'm not hungry."

She marched him over to the table and sat him down. "I want you to eat before you start." She lifted a grilled cheese out of the toaster oven onto a plate and set it before him. She plunked a mug of hot chocolate beside the sandwich.

He ate lunch silently, but afterward, Dixie was pleased to see some color in his face. "Let your food digest. I'll paint first."

He ignored her, bringing the can of paint into the living room from the garage.

So damn stubborn. She raised a front window and propped it open with the stick she kept in the windowsill.

"Let me help," she said, as he slowly climbed the ladder, lifting the paint can each step of the way. He seemed shaky. "Let's leave it for today," she begged. "I'm fine," he snapped. She hovered as he began to paint. "Are you watching to see I do it to suit you?" he asked.

He was as grumpy as a bear with a sore behind. He was feeling guilty about the way he'd treated Tony, most likely. She left for the kitchen and waited, on edge, until twenty-five minutes were up. She couldn't stand it any longer. She burst into the living room. He was standing near the top rung of the ladder, not moving, a dazed look on his face. "I think the fumes are getting to you." No answer. "Morgan, it's time for you stop." She thought he'd give her a hard time about quitting, but he meekly descended the ladder. She stood behind him, to steady him if needed. Once he reached the floor, he tore off his paint mask, breathing hard. "Can't tell if that damn thing helps or hurts," he puffed.

"Let me wipe the paint off." She dipped the rag in turpentine and rubbed the smudges off his forehead and his cheek. "Go get cleaned up," she told him, patting him on the face. "Lie down. It's been a long, hard day."

⁕

After Morgan took a shower, he lay on his bed. He felt leaden, his arms and legs so heavy. He felt slightly nauseated too. He wondered if he was coming down with the flu. Naw, he'd just pushed himself too hard. He had to remember that Dixie, after all, was ten years younger. He didn't need to keep trying to keep up. Why had he let his temper get the better of him with Tony? Just like he'd done with Clay when he was growing up. He rolled over on his stomach, pushing his face into the pillow.

The next thing he knew Dixie was in his room, standing over him in her robe, whispering, "Will you want some dinner?"

He turned and sat up quickly. Too quickly. The room spun.

"Are you okay?" she asked.

"Just waiting for you, my dear." He reached for her and pulled her down on the bed beside him.

"Vera called while you were asleep. I was painting. I couldn't talk," Dixie pleaded, getting up. "I told her I'd call her back."

"Oh, yes, Vera," he sighed, as Dixie left his room.

Morgan lay in bed, listening to the white noise of her voice, rising and falling, on the downstairs phone. Dixie was undoubtedly filling Vera in about the latest troubles with Tony. The call should take just about an hour. He was surprised when after forty minutes Dixie hung up. He heard the TV click on. He roused himself and went downstairs.

"I finished the wall," she said.

"You didn't wait for me." He joined her in front of the television set.

"We'll have to paint the rest of the room, to make it match." Dixie smiled. "I can't get over this new TV. The picture is so much bigger and brighter."

"I'm glad you like it," he said, glowing.

She pressed the mute button. "Nice nap?"

"I was mostly lying there, thinking," he said gravely. "I've decided I'm not going to Chicago." His ex-wife would have to die without him. "I've had enough of family. I'll write Sara tomorrow."

⁕

Morgan was silent at dinner. Dixie chattered, relieved he wasn't going to Chicago—that den of vipers, of money grabbers, of selfish, shallow people. Still, she couldn't shake her thoughts of Tony. His jacket was so thin. He ate as if he hadn't had decent food for days. What would become of him if Morgan dropped out of the diversion program? After dinner, the two of them sat before the TV. Dixie hesitated, then snapped off the set. "Tony needs much more than money."

Morgan said crossly, "You're right. It was a mistake to give him that sixty dollars. He certainly didn't get his hair cut or buy a new shirt."

"If you want to know what I think, Clay ignores him and his stepdad mistreats him—putting him in that wilderness camp just for borrowing his mom's car."

"He wrecked the car."

"It was a little harsh. He was in that camp for three months."

"It's good for him to learn some discipline." Morgan picked up the John Grisham book on the table beside him and started to read. "He needs to know there is a consequence for every act."

"The only other thing he'd done was to steal a tape recorder when he was 14. Do you know why he stole it? His parents—your Clay being one of them—were getting a divorce."

"What are you, a psychologist now?" Morgan looked at her over his book.

"While you were out, Tony told me things you should know." There, she got his attention. He looked off-kilter, like he really wanted to know but was afraid to show it. He looked almost cute, the way his eyebrow quirked. She wanted to go over and sit beside him, and take his hand.

"He was just buttering you up," Morgan said abruptly. "A kid like that, nothing's his fault. It's always someone else's fault."

"I wouldn't want my son, or grandson, in one of those places. Forced marches in the desert heat. He could have died." Morgan looked uncomfortable. Good!

"Well, he didn't die, did he?" Morgan murmured. "He came here, to torture us."

She picked up a magazine. Now was the time to tell him the rest. "Your son, Clay—"

"I'm thirsty. Are you?" Morgan asked suddenly. He headed for the kitchen.

Dixie raised her voice. "Clay forked over $40,000 to send Tony to that camp. No one came to his graduation."

"I can't hear you," Morgan called. "The water's running."

"Tony actually lived in a shelter here in Columbus." She realized she was yelling.

Morgan returned to the family room. "I should have known," he griped, "anyone who was soft on the hippies would be soft on Tony."

"He's not a hippie," she shot back. "He's a lost young man, trying to find himself. Like the young man in the movie we saw."

Morgan groaned. "Give me a break."

"You had a wife and kids for show. Now you want a grandson for show."

"How would you know how to handle teenagers?" Morgan asked irritably.

"I had a son, whom I cared for very much. Just because I didn't have the luxury of knowing him as a teenager doesn't mean I don't know about teenagers—" Her voice broke. She should end this conversation now. They both were tired and frazzled. Morgan was frowning, glaring into his book. "You can turn Tony's life around," she continued, a little louder and more officiously than she'd intended. "You let your own kids go down the drain. Clay was—is—a mess—"

"Who says Clay is a mess?" he demanded.

"Tony told me. Clay runs after every woman he sees." She added lamely, "Like you . . . used to."

"I'm tired of your criticizing, tired of being ordered around." He slammed his book shut. "You're the drill sergeant, I'm the recruit. The only reason you want me here"—he was red in the face, searching for words—"is for the security, the financial arrangement."

What did this have to do with Tony?

He spluttered to a stop, took a deep breath, and resumed, "You not only tell me what to do but how to do it. More likely than not, at the last minute you'll take the screwdriver or paintbrush away from me and finish the job yourself because I don't handle it the way you want me to."

She'd been feeling almost ready to take Morgan in her arms. *Who does he think he is? He has faults that rankle me too.*

Morgan wasn't through. "When we visit your friends or they come here, you shy away from my touch. You change the subject when I try to talk to you about my desire for an intimate future together." He lay his head back, eyes closed. "I daydream you're in my arms, then awake to disappointment." He turned to her abruptly. "I have one question: When will we start our lovemaking?"

She hurried to defend herself. "You're the one who isolates himself every time there's an opportunity for some intimate talk. You hide behind the newspaper at breakfast, in front of the television at night or," she pointed to the book he held, "hibernate in a good book."

She saw his mouth open and rushed to beat him to the draw. "You leave your room in a mess, with the bed unmade and dirty clothes on the floor. You're always pecking at my friends, trying to get me to write them off so you can be the only one in my life. You shout at me if I interrupt your train of thought to ask a question or make a comment. I hate like the devil to be shouted at." Her voice faded. "Don't get me wrong. You're an attractive man. I think I'm falling in love with you." Dixie's eyes filled up. She didn't want him to see her cry.

"You do your share of the housework, rake the leaves, and shovel snow," she continued, her voice breaking. "But why don't you brag on me for the caring way I look after you?" Her tears overflowed and ran down her cheeks. "I've heard you talking to your friends, using words like attractive, charming, unpredictable, and enthusiastic about every new experience. You never think to tell me these things when we're alone." She ran into the bathroom, collected a tissue, and came out blotting her eyes.

"If you promise to remember only the nice things I say about you," Morgan said in a low voice, "I'll mention one other thing that bothers me. You frequently ramble on about people I don't know and incidents I'm not interested in. You break in on conversations. You change the topic midsentence if a new thought enters your mind. The result is a mishmash of words that have lost their meaning."

Dixie gasped as if Morgan had struck her. Her chin quivered. "Why do you put up with me if I'm so irritating . . . and rude . . . and boring?" she spluttered. Then she erupted, "I guess the convenience of my home and cooking make up for all my faults!" Dixie turned on her heel, wiped away the tears gathering in her eyes, and stalked out to the kitchen. When she gained control, she challenged him. "Morgan, I think you owe me an apology." He wasn't answering. She peeked into the family room. He sat motionless, his back to her. "Morgan?"

She approached his chair. "We're both tired. It's my fault. I brought up Tony. We'll do whatever you think best." She came around to his side. He was staring straight ahead, pretending not to hear her. "I'm sorry I lost my temper." She patted his shoulder. He slid awkwardly off the chair. She stifled a scream. "Morgan, don't play games," she begged, panic-stricken at the sight of the silent figure on the floor.

He didn't move. Had he hurt his head when he tumbled from the chair? She knelt by his side, smoothing back his hair. She noticed white stubble on his jaw. He'd forgotten to shave. That wasn't like him.

His eyes were unfocused, as if trying to look back into a brain that had short-circuited.

Dixie wanted to scream and she wanted to weep, but she stumbled to the kitchen and called 911. "I have an emergency. My friend Morgan is unconscious on the floor. His eyes are open but he doesn't hear my voice."

"Ma'am, tell me where you are," said the voice at the other end of the phone.

She gave the address and hurried back to the family room. She slumped to her knees beside Morgan, holding him against her. "I love you, Morgan. Please wake up! Please, please."

BOOK IV

THE
HOSPITAL

22

Tests and More Tests

He can't be seriously ill, Dixie told herself. He'll open his eyes and be his usual cheery self, with a joke about the ravages of old age. "After all," he'll say, "I'm almost 90 and can't always be bouncing around like a teenager."

But Morgan wasn't talking. He lay still as death on the cot in the emergency room. His skin was grayish-white. A tube led from the wall to his nose, sending oxygen to his lungs. An IV line was attached to his left arm. She reached out a trembling hand to check the flow of blood through the artery in his neck.

"He's alive," assured a friendly voice. A nurse stepped into the curtained cubicle. She patted Dixie on the shoulder, then lifted Morgan's arm to slip on a blood-pressure cuff.

His eyelids fluttered briefly before they closed again.

"How is he?" Dixie croaked. It was all her fault.

The nurse removed the cuff from his arm and took his pulse. "Vital signs are stable. We just need to do a few more tests." She smiled briefly. "I think you need a chair." She filched an empty chair from in front of a computer and rolled it Dixie's way.

"Why, thank you," Dixie murmured, surprised she'd take the time when all about her was chaos, as the emergency room staff scurried from cot to cot to tend to the sick and comfort them. The nurse smiled again. "We don't want you in the hospital too," she said as she was leaving.

Dixie sank into the chair. She took off a shoe and massaged her instep. She should have kept her mouth shut. Blaming Morgan for Clay, blaming him for Tony. No matter Morgan had said terrible things to her.

A plump, dark woman wheeled in a machine. "What's that?" Dixie asked.

"EKG," the woman answered, undoing Morgan's hospital gown and attaching the electrodes.

The contraption noisily spit out results, spiky and ominous-looking. A heart attack, Dixie was sure. How bad? She clenched and unclenched her fists. Surely that screeching noise would wake him up. Morgan remained pale and still.

The technician left, clutching the printout. Another aide arrived to draw blood. Morgan moaned when the needle punctured his vein, but didn't open his eyes. Vial after vial of dark red blood flowed from his body. Dixie felt faint. Why did they need so much blood? She'd feed him lots of red meat when she got him home.

A tall young man, with bushy hair and deep-set eyes, burst through the curtain. "X-rays!" he announced, wheeling Morgan out.

As Dixie waited for his return, she fidgeted, bargained with the Lord, and berated herself, crying softly. She had a headache. She rubbed her eyes. Finally, the curtain parted. Morgan was back, accompanied by the nice nurse who'd given her the chair. "Did he break something?" Dixie asked. "His hip? Does he have bleeding inside his head?"

"The technician hasn't read the film yet." The nurse smiled sympathetically. "I'll let you know when we know something."

At last, a dark-haired man in a starched white coat stepped into the compartment. "I'm Dr. Musser, Cardiology."

Dixie stood, swaying. "It's his heart, isn't it?"

"We're still waiting for results of the blood tests. Are you his wife?" he asked.

"Yes." Maybe now she'd find out something.

"What happened?" the doctor asked.

Dixie took a deep breath. "Vandals broke into our home and wrecked the place. We later learned one of them was Morgan's grandson. We were," she swallowed, forcing herself to be honest, "fighting about what to do. About the grandson. Morgan had never met him. He'd left his family in Chicago years and years ago. Morgan, I mean, left. Not Tony. The grand—"

The doctor gently interrupted. "You were fighting. Then what happened? Did he cry out? Grab his chest? Fall on the floor?"

"He slid out of the chair onto the floor, unconscious." She whimpered.

The doctor gave her a kind look, then placed his stethoscope on Morgan's chest and listened.

"He's almost 90," Dixie whispered. "He has chronic asthma."

The doctor held up Morgan's eyelid and flashed a light into his eye.

"Did he have a stroke?" Dixie said to the doctor's back, as he was leaving.

She leaned over Morgan, patting his cheek. "Morgan? Can you talk?" she asked softly. "Please talk to me." She touched his hands. They were cold as ice. She rubbed them for several minutes. His eyes opened. He looked confused. But he was conscious. Thank you, thank you, she said silently. "You're in the hospital emergency room. They're doing tests."

He smiled wanly. His eyes closed.

The nurse popped in again. "Everything okay here?"

"He opened his eyes." Dixie felt elated.

"Did he recognize you?" the nurse asked.

"I don't know," she wailed.

The nurse turned to leave. "What about the X-rays?" Dixie asked quickly. "Anything broken?"

"Nothing broken."

"Well, that's good news." Dixie sighed.

"Sorry I didn't get back to you."

"It's a madhouse here. I don't know how you do it."

The nurse drew her hand across her brow. "We're almost ready to move Mr. Morgan to room 493. You can wait for him there if you wish."

"Thank you." In a daze, Dixie picked up the plastic sack filled with Morgan's clothes. She left the cubicle, dodging the harried emergency room personnel and the patient-filled cots that jammed the hallway. Dixie took the elevator to the fourth floor. If Morgan died, it would be her fault. Her eyes filled with tears. How could she go on without him?

Dixie hung up Morgan's shirt and pants and put away his shoes and socks. She paced the room. The light-green walls were attractive, she thought numbly. Two colorful but restful paintings hung on the wall.

The spacious room was for two people. The other bed, closest to the door, was empty. She hoped it would stay empty, at least until she and Morgan had a chance to talk. If he could talk.

Well, she'd talk. She'd tell him she was ready for a closer relationship. That she was looking forward to long evenings before the fireplace, to quiet discussions of their future plans. She'd welcome his hugs and laugh at his jokes. Dixie sat in the bedside chair, smiling to herself.

She was almost asleep when Morgan was wheeled through the door. Two hospital attendants transferred him and his IV from cot to bed. His eyes were at half-mast.

"He's so pale and tired-looking," Dixie said softly. "I'll take care of that when I get him home."

"I'm Bill Hanawalt," a tall, blonde, young man drawled as he attached Morgan to an oxygen supply. "I'll be his nurse tonight."

"Please take good care of him." Dixie crossed to Morgan's bedside, taking his cold hand in hers. He pulled away.

He hated her. He remembered all the awful things she'd said to him.

She leaned over and kissed him squarely on the mouth. "I love you. Hurry up and get well," she whispered.

Morgan opened his eyes, said "Wow!" and groggily reached out to pinch her left knee.

"He's going to live," Nurse Hanawalt predicted with a smile as he went out the door.

Dixie and Morgan held hands for a long time. "What happened?" he asked thickly, his voice slurred.

"You keeled over. I suddenly realized how vulnerable we are, and how little time may be left." She stroked his hand and looked into his eyes. He was asleep, snoring lightly.

"Good night, my love," she whispered in his ear. "We'll have time to talk things over tomorrow and all the days after that." She gathered up her purse and left.

⚬╬⚬

As soon as Dixie walked in the door at home, Jiggs ran to her, flinging himself against her legs. He stood on his hind feet and danced about. She threw off her coat and sank down on a kitchen chair. "Here, Jiggsy. Here, boy." He jumped in her lap and licked her face. She snuggled against his silky fur. "He'll be all right. He'll be home before we know it."

She fixed herself some hot chocolate. Absentmindedly, she fed Jiggs dog treats as she drank her cocoa. Tomorrow she would ask the doctors how serious Morgan's condition was, if he'd be in for a long period of nursing care and therapy. Could he recover at home where she could watch over him? Would he require a hospital bed in her living room, special equipment? If it was a stroke, what were his chances of complete recovery? What if he were a helpless invalid?

She felt suddenly angry. Morgan never should have been saddled with the responsibility of Tony. She'd call Pfeiffer Monday and tell him about the fight. Maybe she'd be calm by then and would know something about Morgan's prognosis.

When she climbed into bed, she knew sleep would be out of the question. She'd just close her eyes to rest them.

She opened them to the morning light and heard her favorite redbird at the window, calling to her to get up. Morgan was waiting for her at the hospital.

23

Prayers and Apologies

That morning, after Dixie showered, she peered into the bathroom mirror, shocked by her pasty, sagging face and her baggy eyes. Eye drops helped, as did mascara, blue eye shadow, and a dot of lipstick on each cheekbone. Still in her robe, she roamed the upstairs on automatic pilot, dropping items for Morgan into a shopping bag: toiletries, warm socks, clean handkerchiefs.

She poked through her closet, searching for something cheery but not too bright and busy. Nothing too jarring to Morgan in his weakened state. Ah, yes. Her turquoise jacket, the matching silk tee, her black skirt. She dabbed perfume behind each ear and carefully adjusted her blonde wig, ready for whatever was to come.

Downstairs, she collected his two pairs of glasses. What else? The *Reader's Digest*, the morning paper. She prayed he'd be able to read. Oh, yes, and his John Grisham book, which he'd slammed shut last night, a prelude to their blowup. What a dope she was. She should have said, "We're both frazzled. Let's talk later."

"Jiggs, I feel like such a failure," she sighed as she gave Jiggs food and water to last the day. She hugged the loyal animal that had been at her side for fourteen years. "While I'm gone, you're in charge."

What if Jiggs suddenly talked back to her? She laughed. She was losing it. Jingling her keys, shopping bag in hand, she climbed into her car and drove off.

Yesterday Morgan had been so listless, able to mutter only three words. How clearly was he thinking? Could he walk without help? She was in a fever to see him. Heading down the freeway toward the hospital, she suddenly exited, as if guided by an unseen hand, turned around, and zoomed back the opposite way. She pulled into the church parking lot just in time for the early-morning service. In the back pew, she murmured impassioned prayers for Morgan's full recovery. For herself, she asked for strength. And for willingness to change, to be more open to his wishes, and to tell him everything.

Afterward, Reverend Carmichael asked, "Where's Morgan?" Sobbing, she covered her face with her hands. "In the hospital," she squeaked out.

"Would you like me to visit?" he asked, touching her arm.

She shuddered, blotted her eyes. Morgan would be appalled by a visit from the minister—if he were himself. But he wasn't. She had to snatch the moment for his own good. "Room 493, St. Vincent's. He'd love to see you," she fibbed. She hurried to her car and sat inside, composing herself until she felt able to leave.

At the florist, she picked up a bouquet of sunflowers, lemon leaves, daisies, and pompoms, along with a vase. In the car, she worried the colors would be too shrill and tiring. Or worse, would he even notice? Dear God, she just remembered. What about his asthma? Well, if he sneezed, she'd dump the flowers. But at least he would have had a look.

At eleven o'clock she knocked on the partially-closed door of Morgan's room. No response. She pushed the door open. Morgan's bed was stripped. An attendant mopped the floor. "Where is he?" she managed to ask. The man shook his head slowly.

Dixie, heels clicking against the floor, ran out the door and down the hall, her shopping bag rattling against her legs like thunder, the vase of flowers crushed against her chest. She circled the hub of desks and computers and finally spotted a dark-haired woman with wire-framed glasses standing in the middle. "Morgan, room 493," she burst out. "He's not in his bed. It's stripped."

"Who's his nurse?" the woman asked another woman nearby.

"Carrie," the woman answered. "I'll see if I can find her."

Had he been moved to intensive care? Was he dying? Dixie waited, an empty feeling in the pit of her stomach.

A short while later, a small, chunky woman, in blue tunic and trousers, bustled down the hall toward her.

"Carrie, where's Mr. Morgan?" asked the dark-haired woman.

"Getting a heart reading."

Sweet relief flooded Dixie, promptly followed by anxiety. Why two heart readings in a row? "He had one yesterday in the emergency room. Did something happen during the night?"

Carrie shook her head, smiling kindly. "Yesterday was an EKG. Today it's an echo. Go back to his room. Make yourself comfortable."

Back in Morgan's room, Dixie filled the vase with water and placed the yellow and pink bouquet on his bedside tray, alongside his glasses, his book, and the *Reader's Digest*. She put away his socks and underwear. Now what? She plunked herself down in the chair and tried to read the paper, jumping up every time someone came through the door. First, an aide arrived to make up his bed. Next, a wisp of a girl, not more than 16, Dixie was sure, slid an orange-covered tray onto the bedside table. "Lunch," the girl said, sticking her nose into the bouquet of flowers and sniffing. "Smells wonderful," she flung back over her shoulder as she left. Finally, Carrie popped in to tell her she didn't know when Morgan would be back. "More tests," she said, adding, "don't worry."

How could she not worry? She didn't know where Morgan was, what they were doing to him, or why.

"I was scared to death," she cried when the orderly wheeled Morgan, sitting in a wheelchair, into the room. She rushed over and gave him an awkward but impassioned hug, maneuvering around a narrow, rectangular, black box that rested on his chest. "I didn't know where you were."

He smiled weakly. "Next time I'll leave you a note."

He wasn't walking, but he was making sense and speaking clearly without a slur. She could cross *stroke* off her list. Couldn't she?

The narrow, black rectangle on his chest had wires sticking out of it, but gave out not a beep or sputter. "What's that you're carrying around?" she asked.

"A heart monitor. The cardiologist determined I have a glitch that now and then interrupts the evenness of my heartbeat," Morgan explained grimly. "I'd like to get back in bed," he said to the orderly, who helped him stand and guided him into the bed.

After he lay back on the pillow, Dixie pulled the blanket up to his chin. She held his hand. "This glitch—would it have caused you to pass out?"

He smiled bravely. His eyes looked troubled. "They think I've had the abnormality for years. But I have to wear this thing until the doctor decides if it's dangerous."

Guilt swept over her. She'd made the glitch worse by fighting with him. "What else have they told you about your condition? What do they plan to do about it?"

He kissed her hand. "When the doctor arrives, we'll ask him."

"Your lunch is here." She moved the bedside tray in place.

His eyes lit up. "The flowers. Are they from you?"

She nodded. "I'm afraid you'll be allergic. I'd better move them." She put them on a shelf across the room where he could still see them.

He gave her a thoughtful smile. "And look at you, all dressed up today. For me?"

"Who else?" She grinned. She wouldn't say she went to church and prayed for him. She didn't want him to know how worried she was. She pushed the button on the bed frame to raise his head. "Now eat. You've got to do your share too."

He jabbed at the mystery meat, picking over the carrots, mashed potatoes, and gravy.

"Jiggs was looking for you this morning," she told him perkily. "He came out of your room so dejected."

"It's nice to know I'm missed." He gave her a searching look.

He must be thinking about their fight and the awful things she'd said. Her chin quivered. She put on a bright face. "I called Nate and Vera. They send their love and want an update from me tonight. Pauline phoned early this morning to say she'd seen the ambulance pull in, you carried out, and me wringing my hands behind you." She was chattering.

"Good old Pauline. Tell her to bring me some of her lasagna. This food tastes like cardboard." He let his fork fall to his plate. "You brought my book." He picked it up, glanced at it briefly and set it down again. "I'm sorry I yelled." His face was contrite. "I didn't mean to say all those things."

"I yelled back. I'm sorry too."

"I like a woman with spunk."

"It's my fault you're here." Tears came to her eyes.

He shook his head bleakly. "I brought it on myself."

She wanted to blurt out it was Tony's fault, as well. That damn kid should have shown up the day he was supposed to. He should have tried to get himself cleaned up, to look presentable for job interviews. If only he hadn't come into their lives! But she wouldn't say a word about him until Morgan was better. "Don't brood and get that glitch acting up," she said nervously.

Morgan sighed. "The boy was pleasant enough when he thought he could get some money from me."

Tony wasn't devious, she was sure. Rudderless was what he was. He would either straighten out or wind up in the mud. Maybe, just maybe, she'd try to reach him at the Y and tell him Morgan was in the hospital.

Morgan frowned, his face collapsing. "Maybe I deserve being hated." He leaned forward clumsily, steadying the black box with one hand, pushing the tray table away with the other.

She was speechless for a moment, hearing Morgan admit he might be at fault. "Hush, now. You're feeling low because you're sick." Later, when he was well, when he was ready to hear it, she'd tell him the family stuff Tony had told her. He'd see then that he played a part, but so did everybody else. "Can you eat some more?"

He shook his head. "I'll call Pfeiffer and fill him in."

"I'll call him," Dixie said. She'd discuss everything with Pfeiffer. She shouldn't barge ahead, contacting Tony on her own. Not without Morgan's permission. She'd ask Pfeiffer to keep them posted. She hoped the kid would get his act together; get a better job and his high school diploma. Stop it, she told herself. Her mind was babbling on. All she wanted was a moment's peace.

Morgan sank back into the pillow. "Oh, and Sara. I have to write Sara I'm not coming to Chicago."

"Later. Sleep now. No more talk about Tony, or any of them," she said, amazed she could sound so soothing when she felt as if a live electric wire were crackling through her body.

Morgan closed his eyes. His face was gray. She noticed for the first time he was no longer connected to the oxygen.

She squeezed his hand. "I have to find out what's going on." She left the room, in search of his nurse.

"Carrie's gone." A youthful-looking woman in blue looked up from the sheaf of papers spread across her desk. "The new shift is here."

"Morgan, room 493, his color's not good. He was on oxygen yesterday."

The young woman rose, selected a maroon binder from a nearby shelf, and thumped it down on the desk.

My goodness, Dixie thought as the nurse leafed through the pages, they'd found out an awful lot about Morgan. Why weren't they talking about it to him or to her? "He went out for tests this morning," Dixie said. "They forgot to reattach him." She sidled around the desk, craning her neck, trying to read the notes.

"Yes," the nurse said, closing the binder, trudging off toward Morgan's room. Dixie lingered, one eye on the nurse's slim back, the other on the binder.

The nurse whirled around, eyeing her suspiciously. "Are you coming?"

"Yes." She was itching to get a look at those notes.

Dixie stood by as the young woman hooked Morgan up to oxygen. She followed her into the hall. "What's wrong with him?"

The nurse's face was guarded. "You'll have to ask Dr. Musser."

"I've been here since nine-thirty this morning—five hours—hoping to ask him," Dixie said plaintively.

The nurse's face softened. "Sometimes Dr. Musser does rounds early, sometimes late. He hasn't been here yet today. Come with me."

Maybe, just maybe, Dixie thought, she'll take pity. Open up that binder and let me read.

But instead, when the nurse returned to her desk, she scribbled something on a small piece of paper. "If you don't see the doctor by tonight, call his office tomorrow."

"Thanks." Frustrated, Dixie put the slip of paper in her pocket. She'd never been able to talk to a doctor by calling his office. He was always guarded by his staff.

Hold on. An idea was cooking. She'd wait until the nurse's station was empty, sneak behind the desk, and steal a look at Morgan's binder. Would she have the guts? Darn right.

❧

Morgan woke up with a start. Someone dressed in black sat by his bed. Beside this person stood an apparition in turquoise blue.

Had he died? Was he at his own funeral?

"Morgan," said a deep voice.

Above the white clerical collar, he saw the scrubbed, pink face of the minister of Dixie's church. Well, he guessed it was his church too. But he only went with Dixie to avoid a fight. The sermon was always boring. It was just an excuse for people to wear their new clothes and try to impress the others.

"How are you feeling?" the minister asked.

"Okay," Morgan muttered. "I think."

The minister took his hand. "Let us pray," Morgan heard him rumble. The voice intoned, "The Lord is my shepherd, I shall not want . . .", and rambled on, smooth as a cello. Morgan drifted in and out of sleep. He woke up briefly at "Yea, though I walk through the valley of the shadow of death . . ." wanting to protest, but his eyes were so heavy.

The voice stopped. Morgan smelled perfume, felt a kiss on his forehead and heard Dixie whisper, "I love you." His eyes snapped open. The room was empty. Had the minister been here? Or had he dreamed it? Where was Dixie?

Whatever was wrong with him, it must be terrible. All these tests and no one telling him a thing. And now the minister was praying over him.

He felt a chill. Whispering Pines. He could see the trees there, their long limbs beckoning. Just when life was getting exciting. Wasn't that always the way?

One good thing. Whispering Pines still had his deposit.

24

Hospital Horror Stories

At nine-thirty AM, Dixie sneaked past the guard at the visitors' desk. When she reached the fourth floor, she made it by the nurses' desk without being challenged. Good, she thought as she scurried into Morgan's room, the other bed was empty. He still had no roommate who might complain about her arrival ninety minutes before official visiting hours.

"Why, hello." Morgan, smiling, took off his glasses.

"I hope I haven't missed the heart doctor!"

"I think he's forgotten me."

The box lay on his chest, black and silent, its data unexamined. "I called his office this morning and asked him to call me here. I also called your internist, Dr. Durning." She smiled brightly.

"Good," Morgan said hopefully.

And she'd left a message for Pfeiffer: I need to speak with you. It's important. I'll call again later.

"How are you?" she asked. He'd eaten nearly half his breakfast of cereal, egg, and toast. The open *Reader's Digest* lay facedown on the tray table. He'd been alert enough to read. He was off the oxygen again. His color looked normal, his eyes were clear, and the IV was gone.

"Better."

"Reverend Carmichael's prayers helped," Dixie blurted out, jubilant.

He gave her a wan smile. "So it wasn't a bad dream?"

"Patients who are prayed for make it out alive," Dixie answered.

245

Morgan's look was skeptical.

"I heard a doctor on *Good Morning America*. Her research, all scientific, showed that those who were not prayed for spent six-hundred-percent more days in the hospital."

Morgan whistled. "Well, thanks to you and the reverend, I should be leaving any hour now. That is, if they can figure out why I was admitted in the first place."

Sheepishly, she took a small tin from a plastic sack she held and handed it to him.

"What's this?" He put his glasses on again and read the label. "Testamints?"

"Peppermints with inspiring Bible verses printed on their wrappers. When you feel low, just take out a candy, read, and eat."

"Hmm," he grunted dubiously.

"I heard if you read a Bible passage with fervor, it releases a chemical in the brain. It gives you a natural high."

He opened the tin, selected a candy and read the message fervently, "Come to me all you who are weary, and I will give you rest. Matthew 11:28." He made a face. "Bad choice." He unwrapped the candy, popped it in his mouth, and smacked his lips. "Ahh, the high. It's coming. But I think it's a sugar high." He offered her a candy and, with a sigh, she took it. "Aren't you going into work?" he asked.

She shook her head. "I'm staying here until I get a doctor's report." She sat in the bedside chair and slid out of her coat. "Everyone at Whispering Pines sends their love. The gals in activities sent a care package." She dug through her purse, putting items on the bedside tray. "A book of crossword puzzles, a bag of chocolate money to help with the hospital bills, the latest copy of our newspaper, *Pine Scents*, which they've asked me to co-edit."

"Well, that's an honor." He leafed through the paper perfunctorily, sucking on his candy. "Why, here's a column entitled *Now You Know Everything* by Dixie Valentine!"

Morgan cleared his throat and proceeded to read aloud:

The liquid inside young coconuts can be used as a substitute for blood plasma.
No piece of paper can be folded in half more than seven times.
Donkeys kill more people annually than plane crashes.

He gave a hollow chuckle. He read on.

Apples, not caffeine, are more efficient at waking you up in the morning.
Most dust particles in your house are made from dead skin.
Pearls melt in vinegar.
A duck's quack doesn't echo, and no one knows why.
The first owner of the Marlboro Company died of lung cancer.
So did the first "Marlboro Man."

Morgan's voice faltered. He threw aside the paper and scrunched down into the pillow. "I'm checking myself out." He started to climb out of bed.

"Settle down," Dixie said, gently pushing him back in. "We'll get some answers from the black box. Meanwhile, laughter is the best medicine. Second only to prayer," she added.

"And testamints," Morgan said, taking another peppermint. He thought for a moment. "Okay, here's something funny." He smiled like the Morgan of old. "My little adventure with the condom catheter they put on me yesterday morning." He chuckled, getting red in the face. "The darn thing came loose and I drenched my hospital gown and the bed."

"Oh no."

"Two nurses answered my signal. One was that boy you met the night I arrived, Bill Hanawalt. Tall and blonde. Well, they debated whether they should reattach it. They called the doctor and he said no."

"See, there really is a doctor on your case." Dixie couldn't resist.

"So they joked as they stripped me and the bed. They left the urinal with me and went away chortling." He shifted to get a better look at her. "Well, about two hours later I soaked myself again."

"Again?" Now she was worried. Stroke, maybe a mild one? But he was still grinning.

"The problem was, I was hooked up to so many things, I had a time trying to get on my side and hold the container upright. I finally was able to let go. What a relief! The urine just poured out. My stomach and legs got warm. I realized too late that I'd pushed too far into the jug and had peed back on myself."

Dixie giggled.

"'It's you,' Hanawalt said when he answered my call. 'What happened?' 'My bed needs changing,' I said. When I told him what I'd done, he couldn't stop laughing. 'Ring for help the next time,' he suggested. 'We're running out of sheets.'"

"Nurses are the first line of public relations," Dixie observed. "When I was here, hooked up to a catheter and intravenous tubes, I had a sudden cramp and needed a bedpan right then." She couldn't believe she was talking about this. "I pressed the call button. The result, if you hold a perverted view, is almost as laughable as your battle with the urinal." Morgan's eyes were twinkling. "Two nurses rushed in, looked at the bedsheet to see if I had already soiled it, and carefully tilted me onto the bedpan. 'Stay there,' one said, 'while we look after a patient in the next room.'"

"I gazed serenely at the ceiling, shifted my position slightly, and slid off the bedpan, which overturned and dumped its contents all over my backside." Dixie expected to see a hint of sympathy from Morgan or a smile of enjoyment in her growing embarrassment. Instead he was gazing at her intently.

"When were you here?" he asked.

"About—let's see," she stammered, as if the date wasn't etched in her brain. "Uh, ten years ago." Go on, Dixie, tell him. They were feeling easy with each other. The setting was neutral. She cleared her throat. "For surgery." Her heart was beating so loudly in her ears she was sure Morgan could hear it.

"Hi, folks." Vera, tall and rangy, stood just inside the door.

Saved by Vera. Dixie felt dizzy with relief.

"How's the patient?" Vera asked.

"Ignorant and frustrated," Morgan fumed. "Dixie was just telling me about her hospital stay here." He looked at Vera expectantly.

Vera, eyebrows raised at Dixie, murmured, "Good for you."

She'd tell Morgan everything later. She gritted her teeth. She would. "My accident with the bedpan that tipped," she said quickly. "Remember?"

"Scintillating topic." Vera crackled the paper bag she held. "I hate to interrupt."

"We're cheering ourselves up with hospital horror tales. We've heard absolutely nothing from the doctors. Sit." Dixie plopped herself at the end of Morgan's bed. Vera threw off her coat and sank down in the chair Dixie vacated.

"The nurses now had bed and patient to clean." Dixie chattered on with her story, shooting meaningful glances at Vera so she'd understand that Morgan didn't know yet why she'd been in the hospital. "Was I mortified. But the nurses were so sweet, not blaming me but themselves for leaving me sitting there so long."

"Doctors could learn from nurses," Vera growled, "how to become more understanding of the patient's predicament."

Morgan held up the *Readers' Digest*, pointing to an article. "One New York doctor has been emphasizing that for years. According to him, most doctors listen briefly to the patient, then devote the rest of the session to telling him what he has and how he's going to try to cure it."

Good, Dixie thought, Morgan was getting wound up and wasn't asking more questions about her surgery.

"Then doctors wonder about the misunderstandings and the malpractice suits that follow." He thumped the *Reader's Digest*. "A course in doctor-patient communications should be mandatory in every medical college, this doctor says. What's his name?" Morgan looked at the cover. "Dr. Mack Lipkin."

"Can you really teach a bedside manner?" Vera asked.

Morgan nodded. "According to him, not only are these students who've taken the courses friendlier, they also listen more closely to the patients. And," he added grimly, "they order fewer unnecessary tests and are sued less often."

Dixie said to Vera, "You wouldn't believe the tests he's had."

"No wonder medicine is so expensive." Vera polished her horned-rimmed glasses on her blouse, slid them on her face, and tilted the open paper bag she carried toward Dixie and Morgan. "Bagels and cream cheese?"

Dixie took a bagel. "Vera, I do believe you're getting a belly on you."

Vera patted her stomach. "I may have to buy a new wardrobe if I don't go back to smoking." She glanced at Morgan appraisingly. "Any diet restrictions?"

"They haven't told me yet," he grunted, reaching in the sack, drawing out a bagel. "A course in communications is sorely needed."

For a few moments the three were silent, crunching and smacking their lips.

"My mother had hip surgery ten years ago." Vera took another mouthful and hurriedly swallowed. "The surgeon wore a scowl on his face and talked with us in monosyllables. After the surgery, he discharged her in five days. Two days later she was back with an infection. It took seven days to cure. She faced losing her leg or having the surgery all over again at age 84. The surgeon knew he was looking at a possible malpractice suit." She wiped her lips with a paper napkin, holding the remains of her bagel close to her mouth. "But we weren't the suing kind. All we wanted was an explanation. We got it, with a smile. We were told the infection occurred because my mother was too fat." She snapped up the last chunk of bagel between her fingers like a hungry frog gulping down a fly.

"Blame it on the patient," Morgan mumbled.

"I don't get it," Dixie said. "Too fat?"

Vera nodded, her brown hair bouncing. "The way he told it, the infection started deep down within the layers of fat, so it didn't surface until she left the hospital."

"Well, if they kept her another two days, it would have surfaced in the hospital," Dixie said.

"Exactly. Oh, yes, he assured us with a smile, there would be no additional medical costs for her treatment. That was the friendliest he'd been." She reached in the sack for another bagel.

"No additional medical costs, phooey. Who knows what Medicare got billed?" Dixie said.

"When you get old, doctors don't care. They think you're going to die soon anyway," Morgan sighed gloomily.

Dixie swallowed the lump in her throat. Morgan was almost 90. If the doctors didn't care, she did. She'd get some answers, one way or another.

"I overheard a nurse say later that obesity wasn't the problem," Vera said. "The surgeon hadn't sterilized his hands and his instruments as carefully as he should have."

"Your story reminds me of Emily." Dixie, all wound up now, hopped up from the end of the bed. "Six weeks ago she was having severe chest pain that moved from one side of her body to the other. She decided it must be pleurisy and treated it with pain killers. She missed church for four straight Sundays."

Morgan and Vera listened intently.

"Friends organized a prayer chain."

"Hey," complained Morgan, "how come I didn't rate a prayer chain?"

"You got the minister." Dixie went on, "Her doctor said she had a minor inflammation and prescribed pain killers and a muscle relaxant. She took the pills, vowing to go to church. The next Sunday she struggled into her clothes and managed to get to the chair in the hall to wait for her ride. When Fern pulled in the drive, Emily couldn't stand up. They had to call the emergency squad."

"The muscle relaxants!" Vera exclaimed.

Dixie nodded. "In the hospital, they decided she had polymyalgia rheumatica, told her it could be controlled with steroids, and sent her home. She had to wait two weeks for an appointment to hear her doctor's plan for treatment."

"You're kidding," Vera said.

"I better hear my treatment plan before two weeks are up," Morgan fretted.

"Friends who knew others with the disease told her she might have to take steroids for the rest of her life." Dixie halted her long diatribe. She felt better, telling these stories, venting. But Morgan was looking more and more perturbed.

"So," Vera clucked, "she learned more from her friends than from the doctors."

Morgan pushed the button on his bed frame and lowered his head, staring miserably at the ceiling.

Dixie, with a worried look at Vera, made a motion of zipping her lips shut.

A few moments later, a nurse entered. "I'm here to collect the Holter monitor." She untied Morgan's hospital gown.

"Maybe now we'll get some answers," Dixie murmured, taking Vera's arm. The two drifted to the other side of the room.

No sooner had the nurse left with the heart monitor than an aide in a vibrantly flowered jacket appeared. "Mr. Morgan," she asked pertly, "are you ready for your bath?"

"Darn right," Morgan said. "I haven't had one since they put that box on me."

Dixie nudged Vera. "Let's have coffee."

The aide pulled the curtain around his bed. As Dixie went out the door, she heard Morgan drawl, "You can wash down as far as possible and up as far as possible. I'll wash the possible."

Vera rolled her eyes. "That's a good sign," Dixie laughed.

&

"No one's there," Dixie muttered to Vera as they sauntered past the nurses' station on their way back from coffee. "They must be in a meeting." Dixie darted into the middle of the maze of desks, steel shelves, and computers.

"Dixie, what are you doing?" Vera exclaimed.

Dixie held her finger to her lips. "Stand over by the water cooler," she hissed, "and whistle when you see someone." Oh, God, now she was confused. Which shelf was it? This one was filled with forms, no patients' binders. Think, Dixie. At which of the four desks had she inquired about Morgan? Directly to the right of that desk was the shelf she wanted. Looking around nervously, she scurried to the desk nearest the hall that led to Morgan's room. To the right of it was a shelf of maroon binders. Eureka! She scanned them quickly. Where was his name? She was getting panicky. Ah, now she saw. No names on the binders. They were arranged by room number. And here he was! Room 493. Heart pounding in her ears, she lifted his binder from the shelf. Whatever it said she could deal with. Hands perspiring, she opened it on the desk. Scribblings she couldn't decipher, page after page. Wait, here was something she could read. "Well-nourished male suffering from dehydration. Possible multifocal atrial tachycardia. Elevated red blood cells." More unreadable scratchings.

Vera gave a whistle. Dixie shut the binder. A woman with long, gray hair, wearing a floor-length blue-gray jumper, walked into the hub of desks, gazing at her with a frown.

"I'm, uh, the new social worker," Dixie stuttered, her face growing hot. Shoulders back, head high, she swept out of the area, past Vera as if she didn't know her. When the two met up in Morgan's room, they sputtered into laughter.

Morgan, asleep, stirred.

"What did it say?" Vera whispered.

"Dehydration, for one thing and . . ." She'd tried to keep it in her head. "Something like atrium . . ."

"Atrium is some kind of big room," Vera said.

"Atrial!" Dixie said suddenly. "And something—cardia. Probably to do with his heart. And"—she frowned, motioning Vera out into the hall—"his red blood cells. They're elevated."

Vera's eyes grew wide. "Leukemia? It has to do with blood cells, I think."

Dixie shook her head in dismay. "I don't know."

Looking sympathetic, Vera hugged her. "You may be in for a siege."

"I love him." Dixie's eyes filled with tears. "I've prepared myself for the worst."

After Vera left, Dixie picked up a sandwich from the coffee shop and brought it back to eat with Morgan. Morgan pecked at his dinner. They watched the evening news in a suspended state of waiting. But no doctor arrived, no phone call came.

When she left at seven, she squeezed Morgan's hand. "Chin up, pal. They'll have results tomorrow from the heart monitor."

He smiled faintly. "I thought at least Dr. Durning would call. He's been my internist for a long time."

Knowledge is power, Dixie decided when she was in her car. She drove to the library and, with the librarian's help, looked up elevated red blood cells. She found out red blood cells are the carriers of oxygen in the body. That a high red-blood-cell count can occur in someone who lives at a high altitude, someone who's been exposed to carbon monoxide, or who suffers from dehydration. Okay, they'd said he was dehydrated. *A high rbc can also be caused by strenuous physical exercise.* The exercise bike. Had he been overdoing it? *Also the result of certain forms of congenital heart disease.* His glitch? That uneven heartbeat the monitor had been evaluating.

No mention of leukemia, but of other things just as bad: kidney disease, bone-marrow cancer. Her head ached with all the possibilities. How can doctors survive, she wondered. They had these decisions to make every day. She felt more kindly toward them.

If only they communicated better, even if it meant telling her and Morgan they hadn't been able to reach a diagnosis.

25

Uncertainty

"What's the matter, darlin'?" Dixie asked Jiggs as she was ready to leave for the hospital. He was stretched out beside his bowl of food. He hadn't eaten a bite. "You miss Morgan?" He stood up and shuffled toward her, every step an effort. "Oh, Jiggs," she cried, "you can't be sick too."

Jiggs lay down again, his face between his paws, eyes glazed. He barely responded when she scratched his ears.

She called the vet for an emergency appointment and put Jiggs on his leash. He didn't want to walk, so she carried him out to the car, wrapped in his blanket. He lay listlessly on the seat beside her. When she pulled up outside Dr. Kamel's office, he didn't whimper like he usually did. Ordinarily, she had to tug him into the office on his leash or carry his squirming little body through the door. Today, he lay limply in her arms. He was old for a dog, older than Morgan. "What would I do, Jiggs, if I lost you?" She nuzzled the top of his head. What if she lost both of them? She felt faint. *Stop it, Dixie.*

She hurried up the walkway with Jiggs, his nose peeping out of the blanket, pressed against her body. The wind was raw. It looked like more snow was on the way.

As soon as she stepped into the waiting room, a dog barked. Jiggs was too out of it to respond. Mandy, the receptionist, smiled kindly. "We'll squeeze you in between appointments."

The office was filled. A cat in a carrying case meowed frantically as the worried owner winced. A Pekinese with a splinted leg rested in his mistress' lap. He raised his head to growl at Jiggs. A collie with moist, brown eyes stared into space, his torn ear hanging limply. Dixie sat. She lowered Jiggs to the floor. Why oh why, did Jiggs have to get sick now? She'd be late getting to the hospital. She'd miss seeing the doctors who, she knew, would choose this very morning to appear at Morgan's bedside, his heart-monitor results in hand, and then would disappear forever. She wouldn't be there to ask questions about his heart problems and his high red-blood-cell count.

Jiggs made a little noise, halfway between a groan and sob. *Might as well say good-bye, Dixie.* Her eyes filled. *Don't be a doomster.* She picked him up and held him in her lap, stroking his head until he fell asleep.

She tried to lose herself in the pages of *Gourmet* magazine, searching for a festive dish to welcome Morgan home from the hospital. Nothing too complicated. Not too rich. Hearty chicken noodle soup. She'd leave out the sherry so Jiggs could eat it too. Putting the dozing Jiggs gently on the floor, she copied the recipe. She imagined Morgan and Jiggs, bursting with health, slurping it down and wanting more. She felt herself relaxing. She copied two more soup recipes before Mandy called out, "Jiggs and Dixie. The doctor will see you now."

Dixie lifted the bedraggled-looking little dog off the floor. Please, please, she said silently as she walked into Dr. Kamel's office, don't let it be serious. She wanted to take Jiggs home with her tonight.

⚘

"Hi, fella," a deep voice said.

Morgan, who was reading in a bedside chair, a blanket covering his knees, looked up. "Nate!" He perked up at the sight of his old friend, who was red-faced from the cold.

Nate tore off his earmuffs and nodded to Morgan's roommate, a bald man who'd been brought in in the middle of the night with chest pains. Nate strode over to Morgan. "So what's the story?"

"I wish I knew." Nate's sideburns were grayer than Morgan remembered.

Nate shed his coat and scarf and threw them across the bed. "Dixie said you've had quite a few tests."

"I'm beginning to think my disease is so exotic I'll go down in the annals of medicine as a freak."

Nate pulled a chair over and sat opposite Morgan. "Dixie at work?"

Nate probably wondered why she wasn't here, holding his hand. "What time is it?" Morgan asked.

"Eleven-thirty."

"Hmmm. By now she's usually fluttering around me like I'm made of glass. Hounding the nurses for answers." He pointed to the yellow and pink flowers. "Bringing me flowers." The sunflowers looked pretty droopy. "They're two days old," he apologized. "She didn't go to work Monday or Tuesday. She was with me all day. She even brought in the minister to pray over me."

Nate chuckled. "The minister? For an old reprobate like you?" His eyes grew concerned. "So what exactly happened?"

"Didn't she tell you? I just keeled over."

"Your ticker?"

"No one seems to know."

Nate nodded gravely. "The guys at the poker club and I—well, we wondered if Dixie might be putting too much pressure on you." He lowered his voice, glancing at the other bed. The man snored softly. "Nothing against her, but a new relationship puts a lot of stress on people. Even you, Morgan."

"Stress, yes. But not from Dixie," he hurried on to say. He didn't want to go into it all now, the Tony thing. He'd just get riled up all over again.

His friend nodded, his face skeptical.

Nate didn't seem convinced his being sick wasn't Dixie's fault. "Dixie and I—we've reached a new closeness in our relationship." She'd said she loved him. She'd kissed him on the lips. He fell asleep at night remembering the softness of her lips, the concern in her voice. He felt a silly grin spreading over his face.

"I'm glad for you."

"Don't worry," he dropped his voice, "we're not having wild sex. Not yet anyway." He threw a quick look at the sleeping patient in the other bed, and whispered, "I picked up some Viagra."

Nate ventured a smile, his expression part embarrassed, part amused. "If it's your heart, better check with your doctor first."

Might as well tell Nate how he wound up in here, so he could set the poker club straight. "My old life just started crowding me." He told him about the letter from his daughter Sara asking him to come to Chicago. "Barbara, my ex, is dying." Nate's eyes clouded over. *He must be thinking about his own wife.* "Did Dixie tell you about the uproar at the house?" Morgan asked.

Nate shook his head uncertainly.

Morgan told him about the break-in, the damages to furniture, drapes, and rugs. And the message on the wall, *you pig.* "I didn't know what to think. Run-of-the mill vandals? Or someone from my past looking to settle a score?"

"Someone from your past?" Nate asked incredulously.

Morgan gave a short laugh. "Well, we found out who it was."

"Yeah?"

"A grandson. From Chicago. He broke in while Dixie and I were at the movies." Nate listened, wide-eyed, as Morgan described being summoned to the police station and meeting 18-year-old Tony for the first time.

"Why'd he do it?" Nate broke in.

"He'd heard all the lies from my oldest, my son Clay."

"So you have a newfound grandson."

Morgan smiled wanly. *I did and I lost him.* He suddenly felt exhausted.

A young woman in a flowered jacket appeared, carrying two trays. "Lunchtime," she announced, setting a tray beside Morgan's new roommate softly snoring in the other bed. Bending toward him and raising her voice slightly, she asked, "Do you need any help?"

"Not hungry," he managed to mumble before he nodded off again.

The young woman put Morgan's tray on a table and wheeled it over to where he was sitting. "Molly with the beautiful blue eyes," Morgan said. "Now that's service."

"Relax, eat," Nate said. "I'll read the paper."

As Molly left, she grinned, murmuring to Nate, "He's so cute. He reminds me of my grandpa."

Morgan and Nate exchanged glances. "It's long story about Tony." Morgan was sorry he'd started it. "What's up with you?" he asked Nate, sliding his silverware out of the cellophane wrapper.

Nate wrinkled his nose, his mustache wiggling with a life of its own. "Same old stuff at the bank." His eyes sparkled. "But the Royal Flush— we were runners-up in a chapter barbershop contest two weeks ago. We're getting ready for the district competition. And we hope to be invited to the Buckeye Invitational in August."

⚜

"We'll have to do some tests," Dr. Kamel said heavily, after his examination of Jiggs. "We'll call you later today."

More tests. More waiting. Dixie gave Jiggs a hug. Both her loves were sick. She couldn't bear it. She felt as if she might explode through the ceiling. Except for the lead weight in her chest. What if Jiggs were dying too? *Too?* Why did she think *too?* Morgan was getting better every day. They just didn't know *what* he was getting better from.

When she left the vet's, it was twelve-thirty. She hurried straight to Morgan's bedside.

⚜

As Morgan finished his chocolate cake, Nate glanced up from his newspaper. "You said the house was pretty well torn up. How did Dixie take it? She loves that house. She's so particular about her things."

"You'll see a new Dixie when you come to poker club at our place."

Nate raised his brows. "A new Dixie." He laughed softly. "So it's *our* place now."

Morgan grinned, trying not to look too smug. He didn't want to lord it over Nate.

⚜

"Oh, Morgan." Dixie rushed into the room. "I'm late. Did I miss the doctor?" Her hand flew to her mouth. Someone was asleep in the other bed. Morgan had a roommate. "Sorry," she whispered. She crossed to Morgan, who sat in the chair, the remains of his lunch in front of him. "Jiggs is sick. I had to take him to the vet." She saw Nate then, sitting in the corner, and fluttered her fingers in his direction.

"Dixie!" he said heartily

She sensed they'd been talking about her.

"What's wrong with Jiggs?" Morgan asked.

"I don't know. The vet will call me this afternoon," Dixie groaned. "Any news from the doctor?"

Morgan sighed resignedly, "No doctors, no heart-monitor results."

"Everything in our lives is up in the air," she said to Nate.

Nate nodded slowly. "Heart monitor?" He shot Morgan a troubled glance.

Morgan shrugged. He turned to Dixie. "How sick is Jiggs?"

"He was dragging around. He could hardly put one paw in front of the other. I thought at first it was because he missed you." She gave Morgan a quick kiss on the cheek. "My two old codgers, you and Jiggs. Both in your nineties."

"Nonogenarians," Nate offered.

"On that note," Morgan said, "I think I'll crawl back into bed."

Dixie pushed the tray table away, removed the blanket spread across Morgan's lap, and waited nearby while he stood. Holding his hospital gown shut behind him, he took the few steps to his bed. "Did I ever tell you about the girl who put her hospital gown on backward?" he wise-cracked.

"No," Dixie said. "And don't tell us now. Get in bed."

Nate lifted his coat and scarf from the bed. Morgan climbed in. Dixie pulled up his blanket.

"Later, buddy," Nate said.

Morgan waved. His eyes closed.

Nate stood up to leave, motioning Dixie with his eyes. She went with him into the hall.

"What's this heart-monitor business?" Nate asked softly.

"The doctor found an irregular heartbeat he claims Morgan's had most of his life. The results of the heart tests—the monitor, the EKG, the echo—the experts haven't told us yet." She looked around to make sure no one was within earshot and said in a low voice, "I was so disgusted I sneaked behind the nurses' station and read his chart. His red-blood-cell count is high and he came in dehydrated. Three days here and that's all I know."

"So you sneaked a look at his chart? Good for you." Nate smiled down at her. He shifted from one leg to another, his eyes questioning. "He told me about the new grandson."

Dixie nodded glumly. "It's been quite a time." She wondered if Morgan had mentioned their fight, that he'd had his attack—whatever it was—because she never knew when to keep her mouth shut. She steered the conversation another way. "I've been thinking of having a surprise party for Morgan, if he's up to it. Next month. For his ninetieth. Maybe make it part of poker-club night?"

"Well, that sounds like a fine idea." He reached for her awkwardly and gave her a hug. "Morgan's a lucky guy."

Her eyes filled with tears.

"Give me a call when you hear something."

"I will." She waved after him as he loped down the hall. She noticed his socks were mismatched. *He's absentminded now that he's alone.*

⚙

"Thank you, Dr. Kamel." Dixie put down the bedside phone, squealing to Morgan, "It's his teeth! Just his teeth!" The one thing she hadn't thought of. She'd worried about heartworm, cancer, diabetes.

"That's all?" Morgan asked.

"He needed a booster shot and treatment for an oral infection. Gum disease, if not treated, can damage the heart and kidneys, the vet said. So he'll clean Jiggs' teeth and pull four molars. They'll keep him overnight, just because of his age." Maybe it was a sign that soon they'd know what ailed Morgan. Dixie had a sudden thought. "Let me see your gums."

Morgan opened his mouth.

She peered inside. "They look okay to me," she said uncertainly.

"You almost sound disappointed." Morgan gave her a wry smile. "Your vet sounds good. Quick answers, communicates well. Can you get me an appointment?"

⚙

That night, Dixie went to bed early. Outside, the wind whistled. The house creaked and groaned. Missing Morgan, without Jiggs, she felt almost sick from loneliness. She couldn't seem to get warm. She piled extra blankets on her. Just as she was going to sleep, she thought of Pfeiffer, and wondered if he'd tried to return her call. She wouldn't know, being out of the house all day for the past two days. Could Pfeiffer handle Tony alone? Would he feel she and Morgan let the boy down?

She imagined Tony cold and hungry, begging in the streets. Freezing to death in a gutter. Drunk in a bar. Murdered in a fight. He no longer had her and Morgan to bolster him up. Eddie was off limits. Tony wouldn't call home because his stepdad might answer.

Once she knew what was wrong with Morgan, she'd take some action. This waiting was driving her nuts. Maybe she'd stop by the police station and see Pfeiffer in person. Or go down to the Y and try to find Tony. Morgan wouldn't need to know.

Wide awake now, she turned on the bedside light. She took the photo from the nightstand and looked at her boy. He'd have grown up in a simpler time than Tony. After the usual sticky teenage years, he'd have gone on to college and become someone she'd look up to. What would he be today? A teacher? A minister? He'd be special, she knew, someone who did good.

Would he be tall? Or short like she was? He had her blue eyes, but her husband's big ears. The kids had laughed at his ears. He'd come home from first grade, crying. She wouldn't let herself think about that. But her heart squeezed like it always did and the thoughts kept coming. He might have grown into those big ears. Or he could have worn his hair long to cover them. It was the sixties. Long hair was allowed. She cried into her pillow.

Morgan didn't approve of Tony's long hair, but it was acceptable now—in most offices. The earring she wasn't so sure about.

She pulled herself together. She'd cried enough tears. Said enough *what ifs* and *if onlys*. She always told the residents at Whispering Pines, don't sit in a corner and wait to die. Do something. And do something she would. No more putting it off.

26

Doctors' Conference

Dixie stood for a moment in the doorway, watching Morgan, hunched in his chair, poring over the newspaper. A frown passed over his face, followed by a quick smile. He always became so involved. She trotted into the room, past the bald man, who was propped up in bed, eating his lunch. "How are you?" she asked Morgan.

"Better," he replied. "I was just about to call you." He folded up the paper and bunched it beside him in the chair.

"I know. Late again. I had to collect Jiggs."

"How is he?" Morgan asked.

"Very woozy. And I had to wait for his pain pills and antibiotics, and a special food for senior dogs with few teeth, prescribed by the vet." She'd charged the bill, the food, and the medicine on her credit card. If only there was Medicare for senior dogs! "He's in pain, poor little thing. I had to wait until he went to sleep. I left him lying on my bed."

"I'm glad you're here." Morgan reached up to catch her hand. "The doctors are meeting with me this afternoon. I'm afraid they'll tell me things I don't want to know."

She swallowed the lump in her throat, put on a smile, and gave his hand a squeeze.

At last a physician bustled in. He had a black mustache and thick, dark eyebrows. "I'm Dr. Charles Mathews," he said. "Your internist."

"Where's Dr. Durning?" Morgan demanded, looking ill at ease.

"I'm in charge of all hospitalized patients for the practice," he answered. "Durning sees patients only in the office."

"Something new?" Morgan asked.

"It increases our efficiency enormously," Dr. Mathews replied.

And your detachment, Dixie thought. No wonder Durning hadn't returned her call. He'd be invading Mathews' turf.

Dr. Mathews cleared his throat. "Dr. Musser, cardiology, and Dr. McCormick, a specialist in neurological disorders, are joining me. We'll tell you what we know." He held up his hand as if to stop their flurry of questions. "They'll be here shortly." He shuffled through a thick sheaf of papers.

The results, Dixie assumed, of the many tests performed on Morgan over the last four days. And now three doctors, two of them specialists, would be required to deliver Morgan's diagnosis. Her stomach was full of butterflies. She stole a look at Morgan whose face was set and tight.

Dr. Mathews muttered something about a missing report and swept out of the room.

"They're still ordering tests," Morgan said to Dixie. "I'm not sure if it's because my condition is hopeless or because they think they can turn me into a perfect specimen of a 90-year-old man." He laughed in disbelief. "This morning, a person I'd never seen came into the room and ordered me to lie on my side. He casually inserted his finger and gave me a prostate exam. 'It's not swollen much and seems to be in pretty good condition,' he reported before taking off."

"That's all he said?" Dixie asked.

Morgan nodded.

"He didn't even ask your name?"

"When he finished, he asked, 'You *are* Bryce Morgan?' I should have said, 'Hell, no, I'm just here visiting a friend.'"

"Hopefully, he was a doctor," Dixie said drily.

A chuckle came from the other bed. "I got the same treatment," the bald man said.

"He must pocket quite a lot of income by accosting patients in their rooms," Morgan grumbled, "using his educated finger, then billing Medicare."

"He should wear a ski mask instead of a prophylactic glove," Dixie started to say when three men in white jackets trooped into the room, looking a little like the Marx brothers. Dr. Mathews, with his thick eyebrows and wide black mustache, led the way. The doctor behind him had curly blondish hair. And the heart man, Dr. Musser, whom she'd met in the ER, wore his dark hair flattened across the top of his skull like a cap.

"We're ready to report our findings." Dr. Matthews looked at his two consultants for confirmation, then glanced at Dixie. "We've concluded that there's really not much the matter with him. One or two minor problems will be clarified this afternoon and then we'll think about sending him home."

Dixie, who remembered a stricken Morgan lying helpless on the floor, wasn't sure she'd heard correctly. This was a practical joke. Her friend was ill and the doctors were brushing him off. She'd made plans to nurse him back to health. She'd dreamed of dipping soft towels in cool water and gently wiping away the perspiration. She'd found recipes in *Gourmet* Magazine for three kinds of soup she planned to spoon into his fevered mouth as he struggled, with her help, to regain his strength. "What about his elevated red-blood cells?" she blurted out.

Dr. Mathews blinked rapidly as if he wondered how she knew about the elevated red-blood cells. Then he resumed his lecture, a little condescendingly, Dixie thought, and speaking as if Morgan weren't in the room. "Dehydration. Morgan's fainting spell was due to extreme dehydration."

So the high red-blood-cell count was from dehydration, not from any of those other awful things she'd read about.

"The Holter monitor," Dr. Musser spoke up, "revealed a strong heart, pumping steadily hour after hour. The glitch occurred regularly and has been traced to an abnormality he's had since early life."

"His blood pressure is a little high but can be controlled by pills, and the threat of a stroke or heart attack can be minimized by taking one baby aspirin a day," added the doctor with the curly hair. He was evidently the neurologist, Dixie decided, and so could speak authoritatively about the use of baby aspirin. The three men adjusted their white coats and prepared to leave.

Dixie had to scramble to find her voice. Her brain was wiped clean of further questions with this good news. "Well, that's wonderful. I guess he can go home?"

Dr. Mathews ruminated. "Tomorrow perhaps. Friday, at the latest. We have a couple of follow-up tests yet to do."

"Follow-up tests?" Dixie asked quickly.

"Blood tests." Mathews smiled. "Routine."

"Morgan's as strong as a horse," Dr. Musser asserted heartily. "He can keep himself healthy until he's past the century mark if he eats right and continues to exercise. He needs to drink more water every day, at least six glasses. Dehydration can be a serious problem for older people."

"Six glasses a day? I'll be peeing like a horse," Morgan grumbled as the doctors were going out the door.

"All those tests," Dixie clucked. "And now they say there's nothing wrong with you."

"They like to use those machines," Morgan said with a cynical smile. "They're so expensive they have to justify buying them. Besides, it covers them for possible malpractice."

"After you had that asthma attack last summer, didn't the doctor suggest you drink more water?"

"It seems to be a popular prescription." He scratched his jaw. "Did you notice? Not once did the doctors look at me as they gave out all that information. They looked at you. They must think I'm senile."

Dixie smiled in commiseration. "Maybe we should leave that article for them—the one you read about doctors communicating better with their patients."

Morgan gave a short laugh. "Well, you might as well stop hovering. Go back to work. Go home. Give Jiggs his pills."

"You won't be lonely?" She glanced at her watch. Jiggs was due for another pain pill soon. "I'll come back tonight and watch the evening news with you."

"Take a break from babysitting me. Didn't you hear the doctors? I'll be around past the century mark," he said, suddenly jovial.

☙

After Dixie left, Morgan walked slowly down the hall to the nurses' station. He felt wobbly but that could be because he had to hold his gown closed in back, while the other arm flailed. He felt like a chicken with a broken wing. He should have asked Dixie to bring in his robe. He returned to his room, cinched his gown together with the belt from his pants, and walked the same route a second time, both arms swinging, breathing deeply, making good time. Surprising what good news could do. And it was good news, even if he could scarcely believe it. For four days he'd thought he might not make it out of this place alive.

He was sitting in his bedside chair, on his second glass of water, when a young woman popped in. "Hey, you're good," he smiled, as she drew his blood with the almost-painless first puncture of the needle. His arms were covered with bruises from other less-skilled technicians.

He dozed and woke up to a see a young man with a scrubbed face and rosy cheeks standing over him. His starched, white coat barely creased as he bent to place his stethoscope on Morgan's chest. "Strong and even," he reported, smiling.

Morgan smiled back. "Are you a doctor or a nurse?"

"Cardiology fellow," the young man said. "Dr. Callahan."

Morgan hoped he hadn't insulted him. "Doctor, I want to run something by you." The young man seemed willing to listen. Being a fellow, he plainly didn't have to rush off right away to another patient. "How soon—" If only he didn't look so young. Morgan glanced over at his neighbor lying in the next bed. What the hell. Privacy was the last thing on Morgan's mind. "How soon can I have sex," he blurted out, "after I get out of here?"

The doctor's eyebrows shot up, then down they came. He thought for awhile. "Well, the general advice is, wait two weeks after a mild heart attack."

"Heart attack?" Morgan replied uneasily. "They told me I was dehydrated and my blood pressure was a little high—that was all."

"Let me take a look at your chart." The fellow left and returned shortly carrying Morgan's thick, maroon binder. He leafed through the pages. "You're right. I just assumed since you're on the heart floor—I didn't mean to frighten you." He read for a few minutes. "I see you're almost 90." His young face was earnest. He seemed to be thinking hard, choosing his words carefully. "If you can walk up a flight of stairs without panting and puffing too much, you can have sex."

"Any suggestions who with?" Morgan winked.

The young man grinned and blushed.

"Just kidding." Morgan cleared his throat. "Sounds like good advice." He walked upstairs at least once a day at Dixie's. He'd start using the exercise bike again. It shouldn't take him long to get in shape. "Another thing—"

Dr. Callahan nodded.

"It's been awhile since I've been in a relationship." How best to say it? "I don't want to disappoint my new lady friend."

The young man swallowed, looking wary. Then he nodded reassuringly.

"My internist, Dr. Durning, gave me some Viagra. But before I had a chance to try it, I wound up here." Morgan grinned. "He told me it would be like putting a new flagpole on an old building."

The doctor laughed. He leafed through more pages of the binder. "I see you aren't using nitrates. My advice is take one pill, one hour before intercourse. Because of your age, I recommend the lowest dose, twenty-five milligrams. Don't exceed one dose per day," he admonished. "If that doesn't work, call your doctor."

"Any side effects I should know about?" Morgan asked.

"Sildenafil citrate can cause headache. The face can turn bright red. Don't worry. It'll go away." Dr. Callahan hesitated, then confided gravely, "In rare instances there have been reports of erections lasting several hours. If that happens, go to the emergency room."

That was a startling image. "Thank you, doctor, I appreciate your time."

Callahan turned to leave.

Well, he turned out to be friendly, Morgan thought. He listened well and was full of good information. Maybe the younger doctors were getting some of those communications courses described in that *Reader's Digest* article.

Suddenly, Callahan was back in front of him, holding out his hand, grinning from ear to ear. "I'd just like to shake your hand. You're quite a guy, Mr. Morgan."

ॐ

First thing when Dixie arrived home, she called Vera and Nate to tell them the experts had found nothing seriously wrong with Morgan and he'd be home within two days. She was about to give Jiggs his afternoon pain pill when the phone rang.

"Dixie, Officer Pfeiffer."

Relief swept over her. "Did Tony—I guess he told you about the fight between him and Morgan—have you even seen him?" she wailed. It wouldn't surprise her if he'd done something drastic in the five days since he'd stormed out their front door.

"I've seen him and he told me."

"Is he okay?"

"Yeah."

She wanted to hear Tony's version of the fight. Pfeiffer was silent. "Morgan's in the hospital," she blurted out.

"What? When?"

"Last Saturday night."

"Oh, God," Pfeiffer said heavily, "because of—"

"He's doing fine. He'll be out tomorrow or Friday." She told him the doctors' diagnosis.

"I shouldn't have pushed him into this."

"It's not your fault. Tony showed up here looking terrible. We expected him Friday. He arrived on Saturday. Morgan was upset." That reminded her. She didn't want to sound accusing, but she needed to know. "He said he left you a message that he couldn't keep his Friday appointment with us?"

"That he did. He didn't remember your last name to look you up in the phone book."

She said a silent prayer of thanks. "He and Morgan, they're both hot-tempered. Like two gorillas beating their fists against their chests."

Pfeiffer cleared his throat. "Look, Tony asked us to find him a new community site."

Why did she feel let down? She was going to ask for just that. "He's not in any jeopardy because of us? Did he—"

"Dixie," Pfeiffer interrupted, "I blame myself. Send me an itemized bill. He'll be paying you back."

"The insurance will cover most of it." She hoped.

"Look, don't worry," he added gently. "He has family in Chicago. If he wants to finish out his contract up there, we can arrange it."

"Of course." But what about the stepdad? she almost asked. That situation could get nastier. Leave it, Dixie, she told herself. Tony said Morgan was as bad as his stepdad, giving orders and ultimatums.

"He's out of our lives, Jiggs," Dixie murmured after she'd hung up the phone. "Just as well." Still, she couldn't shake the feeling that she and Morgan hadn't held up their end. She wrapped Jiggs' pain pill in a piece of cheese and held it under the little dog's nose. He sniffed and opened wide. "Good boy." She held his mouth shut, rubbing his throat until he swallowed it. She spooned out his prescription senior food. He nosed it and took a small bite while she waited anxiously. Soon he was gobbling it down. Thank goodness; it had cost enough.

Hey, why was she moping around? Jiggs and Morgan were both on the mend. A celebration was called for! The new drapes were still in their plastic mailing bags. She'd put them up tonight. She'd have this place looking like a million dollars by the time Morgan came home. She called the rug cleaning company who said, yes, they could be there at nine the next morning to steam-clean the rugs. What the heck, she'd charge it!

She hung the new champagne-colored, crushed-chenille drapes over the sliding-glass door in the family room. Sunshine filtered though the drapes. The threads seemed laced with gold. The new TV set sparkled. Everything was bright and new, touched with a golden hue.

Now on to the dining room. She shook out the antique-satin cranberry drapes with the matching cascade valance and gave them a dubious look. She hadn't been sure when she'd ordered them. Too bulky? Wrong color? When they were up, she held her breath and stepped back for a critical look.

Yes! The drapes worked perfectly with the walnut table and Grandma Ruby's corner cupboard. The bridge-club group would be agog. She'd get out the linen tablecloth and the good china and silver when she served them dessert.

The living room was still a mess, left as it was when Morgan passed out. One wall was painted, the floor and furniture were covered in tarps, and paint cans and brushes were scattered about. But not for long. She rolled up her sleeves, opened the can of paint, and set to work. At ten o'clock, when she finished painting, she was moving in slow motion. Her arms and back were hurting. She transferred all the painting paraphernalia to the utility shed and went from room to room looking at her— *their*—home with fresh eyes. It was as if they were starting a new life.

She sank into a whirlpool bath, letting the pounding jets of water massage her aches away. In bed, she realized with a guilty start that she'd forgotten to call Morgan to wish him good night.

27

A Change of Attitude

"I don't think I'm ready to leave these cheerful surroundings," Morgan said when Dixie, heels clicking, pranced into his hospital room. "Where else can I get a sponge bath, shave, breakfast, and new bed linen before nine o'clock?"

"I can give you all that and more," she told him brazenly, stripping off her coat and throwing it into a chair. She wore her blonde wig, long earrings, and a shiny deep-maroon blouse that clung in all the right places.

He pushed the control on his bed. "Let me get a good look at you."

"Where's your neighbor?" she murmured as she hugged him.

"Out for tests." Her wig was slightly scratchy against his cheek. Her perfume filled his nostrils.

"We should ask the doctor how long before you can get back to a normal schedule." She added with a teasing grin, "I'm getting tired of doing all the dusting and cleaning by myself."

She was flirting with him. "As soon as I can walk upstairs without feeling out of breath," he flirted back, feeling slightly high, "I'll be ready for a normal schedule."

Her face lit up. "The doctor's been here? You're going home today?"

He shrugged. "The advice about the stairs came yesterday. After you left, a VERY helpful young cardiology fellow stopped by." He smiled, remembering their conversation.

She stole him a sidelong glance. "The evenings have been very boring since you left me for the pretty nurses."

270

"I'll have to get acquainted with the new Dixie," he answered quietly. "You've changed since I've been here."

She hesitated, then plunged ahead. "I realized I'd fallen in love with you over the past months. I knelt down and kissed you while we waited for the emergency squad. I prayed you'd recover. I promised things would be different between us if you came back to me."

Her eyes flicked to the door. She walked over and closed it. She drew the privacy curtain around his bed and stood squarely in front of him, resolute as a fighter. "Perhaps you won't care for me after you see what the cancer doctors did to my body." She began to unbutton her blouse.

"Dixie, you don't need to—"

"Almost ten years ago," she said matter-of-factly, "the surgeon removed my left breast and peeled away the underlying muscles and lymph nodes. It was one of the last radical mastectomies in our area. Skin was transplanted to cover it." She swept her hand down her chest from her collarbone and over to her armpit. "I was sent home with a mutilated body and a feeling that I was no longer a woman. I didn't want anyone ever to see."

So that was why she kept putting him off. He should have realized. What a numbskull he was. "I'll always love you, no matter what," Morgan said softly.

Her eyes, very blue and determined, bored into him. She opened her blouse, pulled down her bra strap, and showed him her flattened chest, like a boy's, with its slash of a scar.

Hardly knowing what he was doing, he threw off his bedclothes and tottered to his feet. He wrapped her in his arms, wanting to shield her from her pain, then and now. "You're so beautiful. I never would have guessed."

"I'm a cancer survivor," she said proudly. She pulled away and adjusted her clothing. "I learned then what it meant not to be in control. I learned to rely on my faith and my friends." She buttoned her blouse. Her hands were trembling.

He searched for something more to say. His mind was blank. "I'm sorry."

"If it hadn't been for Vera, I don't know how I'd have gotten through it. When my hair began to come out in clumps, I couldn't bear it. I looked like a plucked chicken. Vera gave a head-shaving party for me.

All the bridge-club gang was there. It took three razors and almost a can of shaving cream. Then my head was smooth as a cue ball."

She screwed up her face. Morgan didn't know if she was going to laugh or cry.

"I lost all my eyelashes, but only half my eyebrows. I looked like a Martian." She laughed unsteadily, her eyes glistening, her mascara running. "Vera bought me this wig." She patted her head. "My favorite to this day. We went out together to buy the chestnut wig and the strawberry blonde one."

"Good for Vera." He'd never say another unkind word about Vera. Or those wigs.

"I used to have wonderful hair, thick, naturally curly, auburn, streaked with gray. Now it's thin and brittle. Mousy-looking." She looked betrayed.

He sat on the bed and pulled her down beside him. "It's beautiful. You're beautiful." He confessed he'd searched her medicine cabinet after overhearing her conversation with Vera about tests and medical checkups. "I found some pills. I didn't know what they were for."

"They block estrogen. I take them twice a day." She dug into her skirt pocket, found a tissue, and blotted her eyes. "I learned a lot back then about myself and my friends."

His bare feet were getting cold, he dimly realized. Well, he wouldn't leave her side. "You must have gone through hell."

She crumpled the tissue and smoothed it out. "For almost six months my life consisted of doctors' visits, treatments, labs, nausea, fatigue, and an inability to plan anything around those things. I was working part-time at Whispering Pines. I didn't tell anyone what was happening. I kept on working, except for the times I was too sick or tired to stumble in."

He put his arm around her shoulders. "I wish I'd known you then," he said huskily.

Her face collapsed. She looked small and vulnerable. "There are times when I wake up in the night and wonder if this has really worked. Every time I go to the doctor for a checkup, or have a back pain or headache or cough, I worry that the cancer has metastasized. Can I go through it again?"

He gently touched her cheek, turning her face to his. "I'm here for you. Always."

They were seated on the bed, holding hands, when Dr. McCormick arrived, flinging the privacy curtain aside and uttering apologies for being so late. The morning was gone. "The last tests confirmed earlier findings, so you can go home tomorrow, Morgan," he announced.

He hurried away, leaving the two to contemplate a homecoming which Dixie envisioned as a sort of honeymoon and Morgan as the beginning of a long voyage that would touch every exotic port in the world.

28

Their First Rendezvous

The next day, as Morgan waited with Dixie for his discharge papers, he inspected every detail of the hospital room where, during the past week, he'd been made aware of his vulnerability, where Dixie had revealed her secret to him, and her love. He held out his hand to her, his eyes bright with tears. "I'm the luckiest guy in the world."

"We should both get down on our knees and give thanks," she told him. "You're getting your health back, and the free run of the house when you get home." Her eyes danced. "I may even let you take Jiggs' place." He put his arms around her and she hugged him back.

"Well, well," said a nurse, as she marched briskly into the room. "I'm sorry I have to break this up." She gave Morgan the doctors' instructions, his new prescriptions, and the good wishes of all the staff. "Get your things together. The volunteer with the wheelchair will be here soon to escort you to the lobby."

"I feel fine," he protested. "I can walk."

"It's our policy," she said firmly. She turned to leave.

"Nurse," Dixie said, stopping her at the door. "In your experience, have you ever heard of anyone fainting because of dehydration?"

The nurse frowned. "Being dehydrated is"—she smiled—"like driving a car that's low on oil."

Morgan and Dixie looked at one another.

"The car becomes more and more sluggish, and finally grinds to a halt."

"Interesting," Morgan murmured.

"The best explanation I've heard in this establishment," Dixie said. "Leave it to the nurses."

The nurse gave a little salute and left the room.

❦

Dixie drove home through the late January sunshine. "It looks as if God has painted the entire landscape." Her face was radiant. "During the night while we slept He tossed a handful of icicles and frost to cover every tree and shrub in sight."

Morgan, a wordless passenger at her side, took in the glistening snowdrifts, smoke curling lazily from chimneys, and the children, bundled up in bulky coats, frolicking. The trees stretched silently toward the sky all dressed in white, shivering white, laced with particles of crystal ice. White cumulus clouds floated overhead against the backdrop of light-blue sky. He felt the slight crunch of tires passing over icy snow.

He closed his eyes. When he opened them again, the sun had gone behind a cloud. The landscape had changed dramatically, as if a master painter had passed his brush across the heavens to shade the colors and soften the contrasts.

Dixie turned the car into the driveway.

"Stop," Morgan said. "It seems like I've been gone a year. I want to see the house and yard, what I need to do before spring."

Dixie idled the car at the bottom of the drive.

"I don't know what's happening to me." The pink stucco house he now called home looked like an illustration in some fancy magazine, its outline clean and sharp. The expanse of yard he'd once thought daunting to maintain now seemed welcoming. He was itching for the ground to thaw so he could prepare the flowerbeds and fertilize the elm tree and the shrubs. He turned to Dixie. "Colors are more vivid. Everything looks bright and new." He could almost believe there *was* a supreme power who threw this universe together.

She nodded, smiling. She tapped the garage-door opener. Tires spinning slightly, the car made its way up the icy driveway and slid noiselessly into the garage.

As soon as the two stepped into the house, Jiggs pounced on them, yipping, his whole rear end wagging along with his tail. "Hey, fella," Morgan said, ruffling his fur. Jiggs caught him on the cheek with a flick of his tongue. Their old game. "You don't act sick to me," Morgan joshed. He looked around the family room. "What's different in here?"

"Guess!"

"The room seems bigger. Brighter. Hey, wait a minute. You put up new drapes."

"Yes," she said, proudly. "Take off your shoes. The rugs are damp from the steam cleaning." They padded in stocking feet through the living room, where he praised the clean rugs and the paint job, and into the dining room, where he admired the antique cranberry drapes. "When did you do it? Running after me and Jiggs the way you did."

"After I heard you were coming home"—she snapped her fingers—"I did it in one night."

"The next time we need redecorating," he grinned, "just send me to the hospital."

❖

Home does look good, Dixie thought later, peeping into the family room. Morgan was asleep in a chair. Jiggs snoozed on the floor beside him. Her eyes were drawn to the spotless champagne-colored drapes, partly covering the sliding-glass door, and moved to the new, flat-screen television. Images flitted across the large screen. Music swelled. A salesman loudly pitched used cars. She walked into the room and fished out the remote wedged in the cushions of Morgan's chair. She turned off the TV. He didn't move a muscle. Worried, she looked closer and saw his chest was rising and falling.

He'd be good as new after a few days of nutritious meals, his new blood pressure medicine, and plenty of water. Funny, how certain she'd been he'd had a heart attack or stroke when he passed out so unexpectedly.

She'd never let either of them forget how important water was to the smooth running of the human being, like oil to a car motor. She shrugged off a momentary uneasiness and went to the refrigerator to pour a glass of cold water. She put a slice of lemon in it, took it out to Morgan, and set it on the TV tray beside him. He stirred and opened his eyes.

"Pauline brought over some lasagna as a welcome home. Will you be hungry in forty-five minutes?"

He nodded, his eyelids drooping.

She took the dish out of the refrigerator and slid it into the oven.

"As for you, Jiggs," she looked down at the little dog, who'd followed her into the kitchen, "you'll get your canned prescription dog food. But I just might top it off with some of Pauline's lasagna." Jiggs stood up, his furry paws against her legs, laughing into her face.

ॐ

"Smells delicious!" Morgan picked up his fork, eager to attack the thick wedge of lasagna. It oozed cheese, meat, and tomato sauce. He noticed Dixie was silent, her lips moving, saying the blessing as she usually did before meals. "Why don't you say it aloud?" he asked, surprising himself. "Make me a part of it too."

She looked at him as if she couldn't believe her ears. With a quirky smile that may have held a hint of triumph, she bowed her head, closed her eyes, and murmured, "We thank thee, Lord, for this food."

As she prayed, Morgan looked from under his fluttering lashes, watching Jiggs, who had no intention of being polite. He was hungry and was polishing off his supper.

Morgan, hungry too, hoped the prayer would end soon. Dixie seemed to be taking longer than usual.

"May this food strengthen our bodies, especially Morgan's." Dixie added, just as he was about to stab into his pasta, "Please let the doctors be right about Morgan's problems."

His throat constricted, then he relaxed. He felt so good. He knew the doctors were right.

"Amen," Dixie said softly.

"Amen," Morgan murmured. He took a big bite of lasagna. "Heavenly," he sighed.

"I thought you were agnostic," Dixie quipped.

Just because he'd joined her in the prayer didn't mean he was changing his views. "I'm getting soft in my old age," he said, not wanting to ruffle her feathers.

"You told me you never went to church before you came to live with me," she persisted, a mischievous glint in her eye. "You said you looked with suspicion on anyone who was too unctuous or went through the congregation glad-handing everyone like a politician."

He smiled. "True." Hypocrites were everywhere. But he wouldn't say that now. "Some people need God. Others need Prozac. Others, like me—" he shrugged.

"Are rascals," she laughed.

They ate silently, Morgan reveling in the delicious food, relieved Dixie had given up trying to convert him. "I'll have to send Pauline some flowers," he said. He took their two empty plates and put them in the sink. He poured himself another glass of water.

"Where's mine?" Dixie asked.

He smiled an apology, fetched another glass, put it in front of her, and sat down.

She reached for his hand. "I've had my son die in a freak medical accident. My husband was a womanizer and left me in terrible debt. I've survived breast cancer. I want to believe there is a God."

He was silent, mulling it over. "I never thought of it that way," he said finally. He pulled her onto his lap. He held her until the twilight deepened and Jiggs invaded their privacy to remind them that it was past his bedtime.

Hand in hand, they made their way up the stairway. He whispered in her ear that he loved her. "I'll try to make you the happiest woman alive. Just don't press your luck. You can make small changes in me, but essentially, for the rest of my life, I'll be the same contrary, opinionated, and obnoxious man with whom you made a live-in agreement less than six months ago." He pushed open her bedroom door. "You're different, and I am different. Thank God for that difference!"

Dixie, speechless, followed Morgan to their first rendezvous.

He watched as she placed the little dog on a blanket on the floor at foot of the bed. "At the first bark, out you go," he warned Jiggs.

⚬✛⚬

Sunlight streamed through the window. Morgan raised up on his elbow, looking down at Dixie's face on the pillow beside him, at her lips relaxed in sleep and the veined lids over her closed eyes. When he lay back, she stirred, reached for his hand, lifted it to her mouth, and kissed the back of it. He felt a thrill of pleasure. He must have pleased her. Or was she being kind? She turned away, her breathing regular. She'd fallen back to sleep.

Clothes were scattered over the floor. Jiggs was nowhere to be seen. Morgan quietly slipped out of bed. Naked and shivering, he picked up Dixie's blouse and skirt, arranging them over a chair. He took his clothes into his bedroom and dropped them on the bed, hurrying to his closet for robe and slippers. When he returned to Dixie's room, *their* room, she was awake, sitting up in bed, holding the sheet up to her chin. They grinned at each other.

"Leave," she ordered. He did, and waited in the hall. "I'm ready," she finally called.

When he walked in, he whistled appreciatively. She wore the black and maroon negligee he'd bought for her birthday. "You're as gorgeous as I imagined you'd be." She'd put on lipstick and her blonde wig. "Let's start the day by taking a bath together." He led her into the adjoining bathroom. He'd been in to inspect that whirlpool tub many times while Dixie was at work, noting it was built for two, wondering who might have shared it with her. Seats, side by side, each with a neck rest, had been sculpted into the tub. In the middle of the back of each seat was a water jet. "How does this thing work?"

She turned on the faucet, adjusting the hot and cold. "Water has to cover that small sensor above the jets before the whirlpool starts." Several jets dotted all sides of the tub. When the tub was filled, Dixie turned on the timer on the wall. "After you," she said with a smile.

He'd hoped she'd get in first. He had no waistline any more. His chest had dropped south. Last night in the dark he'd felt young and firm—well, almost firm—again. The bright lights of the bathroom would focus on his wrinkled, flabby, too-white flesh. Morgan took off his robe with what he hoped was panache and hung it on the back of the door.

Getting into the tub would be a challenge. What had he been thinking of? He held on to a wall bar and put one foot in the water. She grabbed his other arm. "Careful. We don't want you back in the hospital with a broken hip."

Not very romantic. He tried to be cool as he clumsily climbed in. He lowered his butt, hanging on for dear life to the back wall bar. She steadied him with both hands. He sat with a splash, straddling the two seats. "I think this thing was made for 20-year-olds." He slid over, making room for Dixie. "Your turn."

Dixie let her negligee fall off.

Morgan's instinct was to avert his eyes from her scar. But he made himself look and she saw him looking. "You're like those women," he said, "in the myth who cut off one breast so they could use their bow and arrow more efficiently. Strong and beautiful." She held her chin higher. He gave her a hand and she climbed in awkwardly beside him, almost losing her balance and her wig. She laughed as she slid into the water. "Not very graceful."

"Who wants grace? I like an experienced woman." Morgan gave her a meaningful look.

She pretended not to notice. He wondered again if he'd pleased her. As they'd walked up the stairs last night, when he realized he wasn't huffing and puffing, he'd made an impulsive decision. Not enough time to take Viagra.

If he had, he might have been more up to par. Well, he'd do a little experimenting with the stuff. Gradually. He smiled to himself.

"What so funny?" she asked.

"The way things work out."

She pressed the button on the corner of the tub. The jets spurted. The water boiled around them, over and under them.

"Worth the effort," Morgan said as the streams of water kneaded the muscles of his arms, legs, and back like a thousand tiny fingertips.

"Definitely worth the effort," Dixie said, leaning towards him.

By the look in her eye, he was sure she had a double meaning. He blurted out, "Last night was okay for you?" He'd never asked a woman that in his life.

"More than okay."

They sat side by side, shoulders touching, eyes closed as the water swirled around them. He felt so happy and relaxed he could go back to sleep.

After several minutes the timer went off. The water stopped spurting. Dixie slid down to the end of the tub and added more hot water. The two soaked in silence, perspiration running down their faces. Dixie took off her wig and threw it on the floor.

"You probably think this tub is a luxury," she finally said.

"A two-seater, at that," he answered with a twinkle.

"The salesman talked me into it. He said it would bring me inner peace. I bought it after my surgery, after I'd finished the chemo. As a reward. I charged it."

He knew how broke she was, paying off her husband's debts. "And it still gave you inner peace, knowing you had this bill to meet?"

"I took another job, besides working at Whispering Pines. Cashier in a restaurant. Week-ends. That was before I took the church job."

"Getting this tub was the most important thing?"

"Almost as good as prayer."

They each sudsed up. She washed his back, then he washed hers.

She stood up with the help of the bar and stepped out. He thrashed around, feeling like a hippopotamus, finally landed on his knees, and heaved himself up. "Made it!" he said, staggering out of the tub. She caught him. They embraced. Skin against skin, warm and wet. "Yesterday was perfect," she whispered in his ear. "Every minute."

ঌ✦ঌ

Breakfast was an adventure. Dixie cooked enough food for an army. "I'm starved," he said as he poured honey over the steaming biscuit on his plate. He ladled out heaping spoonfuls of scrambled eggs. She wavered between a buttermilk pancake and a sweet roll before taking both and splashing blueberry syrup over the pancake.

They stashed the dirty dishes in the sink and decided to take in a movie. First, Dixie popped the corn, putting real butter on it. "Just think how much money we could save," she said, "if we always took our own popcorn to the movies. The prices for movie popcorn are outrageous."

He chuckled to himself. This from a woman who'd paid thousands of dollars for a luxury item, the whirlpool tub. "What's on for tomorrow?" he asked.

"Church," she said.

Church it would be, without a frown.

ঌ✦ঌ

"Spare change?" an old guy with booze breath asked him on the front steps.

Tony jammed his numb fingers into his pocket, fished out a quarter, and dropped it into the outstretched hand. "God bless," the man said, smiling through rotted teeth.

Tony pulled open the heavy door. Inside, the air was hot and stale. But he was glad to be out of the cold. He rubbed his hands together, blowing on them. A familiar stairway loomed ahead. At the top was a locked glass door. Later, a man would stand behind it and buzz overnight guests into a small, shabby lobby. They'd get a bed for a night, not knowing if the guy next to them had lice, or was a crazy or a drunk. Tony felt like puking, remembering. One night, a guy fell backward down the stairs. His bottle of whiskey broke. The place reeked with the smell of alcohol. The man lay at the bottom of the steps, no more than a snoring pile of rags.

EVERYONE IS WELCOME read the sign on the wall. WE SERVE OVER 3,000 MEALS DURING AN AVERAGE WEEK. Under it was a second, smaller sign, *Showers, hygiene bags, winter coats*. A hand-drawn arrow pointed to the right. Did he have time to check out the coats? Maybe he could find some gloves too.

It was almost eleven. Lunchtime. He'd look for a coat after lunch. He walked over to the pay phone and dialed the operator. "I'd like to make a collect call," he told her. If that dickhead Fulkerson answered, he'd hang up.

After five rings, she said hello, her voice low and tentative, the way it always was, as if she couldn't believe anyone would want to call her.

"It's Tony." There was silence at the other end, and then a little sound. Was she crying? "Yeah, mom, it's me." His throat caught. "Just wanted to say hi."

"Hi," she said huskily.

Was she glad to hear from him? He couldn't tell. "I hitched a ride with my friend Eddie and his mom. From the place. The camp."

"I figured something like that," she said in a fakey voice. Fulkerson must have come into the room.

"You were too busy to come out."

Silence.

"No problem," he muttered. Not true. She needed to learn to stand up to that bully.

"Well, it's so nice of you to call."

"I'm looking for a place to live. I'll let you know where I end up." He ad-libbed to fill the silence. "I'm doing great. I have a job in a classy restaurant."

"Keep me—advised."

"I'm looking for something else, with better hours that pays more," he said in a rush. "I got a lot of things cooking. Gotta run now." He burst out, panic-stricken, "Mom?"

"Yes?"

"I'll call you later. Okay?"

"Please," she said. "And thanks, Sara."

He hung up the phone and gave his head shake. He'd been building up to making the call all week. Now he felt empty.

One day at a time, he told himself. He turned down the hallway to the left and turned left again. She'd been worried. Definitely worried. She just couldn't talk with Fulkerson breathing down her neck. *Sara*, she'd said, to let him know she was putting on an act. He was glad he got through to her.

They were lined up already, men, women and kids, bundled up in coats and scarves. The line started outside the door and snaked around through the room.

She didn't even ask where he was.

BOOK V

FAMILY BUSINESS

29

Apologies All Around

The following week, on Thursday, when Dixie came home from work, Morgan met her at the door. Without a word, he handed her two envelopes.

She pulled a sheet of paper from one. A ten-dollar bill fell out. Three sentences were scrawled in pencil across a yellow, lined page. *Dear Mr. Morgan and Miss Valentine, I'm sorry for what I did. Here's some money. Eddie Navotka.*

The second envelope also held a ten-dollar bill. The letter was typed on a sheet of white typing paper. *I'm sorry for the trouble. And for yelling back at you. I should have had more self-control. Here's a payment toward the damages. I'll send more. Just so you know, you'll also get back the sixty bucks you loaned me. Tony Morgan.*

Formal, a tad defiant, Dixie thought—*yelling back at you, I should have had more self-control.* He was insinuating that Morgan had started the fight, which he had, unless you wanted to count Tony, showing up the way he did, as starting it. Then he made things worse by parroting the family lies about Morgan's past, the scandal sheets, and the so-called hidden bank accounts. She looked at Morgan. He was glaring. If the boy were here right now, she could imagine another fight. Another 911 call. Dear God, no.

They'd both been careful not to mention Tony, ever since Morgan had been released from the hospital. She'd try to keep the discussion neutral. "Well, he doesn't waste words." She felt ambivalent about the money. It was so little that it couldn't begin to put a dent in what she'd put on her credit card to put the house to rights. Yet she worried about Tony going without clothing or food as he tried to send them money. But maybe he'd found a better-paying job, or was back in the bosom of his not-so-loving family, rent-free. She looked at the postmark. Columbus, not Chicago. He was still in town. She felt of two minds about that too. "Pfeiffer said they'd be sending money."

"You talked to Pfeiffer?" He was glaring at her as if she'd done something wrong.

"While you were in the hospital. We agreed I would. Remember?" Morgan still looked pained. Was he upset at the boy or at himself for pushing Tony away?

"I suppose Pfeiffer heard about the fight? Tony and me?"

She nodded. "He blamed himself for getting us into the mess."

Morgan pressed his lips together.

"We're free of that responsibility. It's a good thing," she said quietly.

"Yes," he said at last.

She felt compelled to add, "I want you to know, just for the record, then we can stop talking about it: Tony did leave a message with Pfeiffer asking to change his appointment with us because of a job interview."

"Job interview?" Morgan snorted. "No one would say two words to him looking the way he does."

"But he tried to reach us. Give him credit for that." Where was the regretful Morgan, who'd said in the hospital, *Maybe I deserve being hated*?

He looked at her quizzically. "You think I goofed!"

She told herself to keep her mouth shut. "What's done is done." She came over and ruffled his hair. "He has to grow up and learn to use some sense."

After dinner, as they sat at the table drinking their tea, Dixie said, trying to sound casual, "I don't see why he's sending money now." She didn't want to get into an emotional discussion. "We won't know what they owe us until we get the insurance check. Speaking of which, I hope we get it soon."

"Could be six months. By the way, what's the tab? The drapes, everything."

He must have seen her concern, though she tried to hide it. "Don't worry," she said, her throat catching, "I put it on my charge card."

"I'm going to write you a check. How much to pay it off?"

If he only knew. Perspiration erupted on her upper lip. The other day, in terror, she'd added up what she owed on her four credit cards: $21,359.63. The recent stuff for the house was just a fraction of it, but enough to freeze up all her cards.

"Most people don't realize it," he drawled in that smooth banker's tone he used from time to time, "but credit-card debt can pile up. If you pay the minimum, you're paying only interest and not putting a dent in the principal."

As well she knew. "The drapes were on sale. I got a special offer from the rug cleaning company." But they did charge extra to move the furniture. "Refinishing the table was pricey, but worth it. The plants were on special. If you can spare it," she said, "a check would be appreciated."

He grinned at her. "Spare it? I'll soon be a thousand dollars richer. I'm picking up my deposit at Whispering Pines tomorrow." He looked deeply into her eyes. "Now that you and I . . . are copacetic."

"A team," she said, smiling.

"I closed out my furniture storage too. So we don't have that monthly expense." He reached across the table and took her hand. "Maybe you can think about stopping work."

Panic-stricken, she pulled her hand away. "They can't get along without me." She took his plate and hers over to the sink and rinsed them. She could never stop work. The debt was a millstone around her neck, weighing her down until she sank beneath the waves.

"Maybe *I* can't get along without you," he said, coming up behind her, putting his arms around her waist.

"I mean, I have the newspaper to put out," she stammered, "and the Dixie Valentine Fund for the sight-impaired. Barry's expecting my progress report by next month's Kiwanis meeting." She turned to face him. "And I haven't even had time to recruit the readers."

He was frowning. "Good, old Barry," he said drily. "I rue the day we chaired a committee together in Kiwanis."

"Don't blame Barry. I asked him to check up on you. I worked for him for twenty-eight years . . ."

"And he wanted to please his former gal Friday."

She touched his face. "For all I knew, you could be a serial killer."

Morgan laughed feebly. "I just hope all that crap from Chicago—

embezzlement, suspicious death—isn't going to resurface here, thanks to Barry."

"He's not a gossip," she burst out. "I'm going to tell him, if he ever sees those people again from the Illinois Banking & Trust, to insist they stop spreading lies about you."

"Or we'll sue them," he said, leaning into her. "You look pretty when you get mad. Your cheeks get red and your eyes flash."

⚭

After the dishes were in the dishwasher, Morgan blurted out, "At least the kid's trying. Sending money, even just a little—that's a positive step, wouldn't you say?"

"You're right."

"Does he have to be perfect? I wasn't. Let's call him."

Her eyes widened in surprise. "Let's."

He found the number of the YMCA in the phone book and dialed it. "Tony Morgan, please," he said to the man who answered. There was a click, then silence. Finally, a monotone voice droned in his ear, "Please leave a message."

"Tony, it's," he paused, "me, Morgan, your grandpa. Give us a call." He left the phone number. "Voice mail," he grinned at Dixie, trying not to show his disappointment as he hung up the phone. "He must be out." He looked at his watch. Seven-thirty. Was he still at work? Probably, if he was still a busboy. He hoped he wasn't cruising the bars, getting into mischief.

"It's a cold night to be out," Dixie said, a frown creasing her forehead.

The two settled themselves in the family room, in front of the TV. Morgan couldn't have told you the name of the program they were watching. He was thinking what he would say to Tony. He'd ask him how things were going. He'd invite him over for a meal and apologize for yelling. Maybe Tony would do the same.

When the phone rang, Dixie looked expectant. Morgan rushed to answer. A salesman started to pitch a charity. "I can't talk," Morgan said gruffly, disconnecting. Thirty minutes later, the phone rang again. "I'll get it," he told Dixie. "Oh, Vera." He tried not to sound disappointed. "Yes, I'm feeling great. Never did thank you for those bagels. They made my day. Here she is." He handed the phone to Dixie, who'd followed him out to the kitchen. "I bet she's calling about bridge club to-morrow night," Dixie said, covering the mouthpiece with her hand. "Vera, hi!"

He could hear Vera's voice at the other end, high-pitched, slightly tinny. Dixie was silent, listening. He made a motion with his hands to speed it up.

"How about cheesecake?" Dixie broke into Vera's spiel. "Pumpkin bars? Millie is bringing brownies. The lemonade and ice cream, I'll furnish. Adele is down for nuts." Refreshments hashed out, talk drifted to prizes. Morgan paced from the family room into the kitchen and back, sighing and giving Dixie meaningful looks, trying to be as pleasant as possible after his vow never to be angry with or jealous of Vera again. Blah, blah. Endless chatter. He swore he'd get a second phone line. Finally, Dixie hung up. "Sorry," she said. It was almost nine o'clock.

Morgan kept his mouth shut.

Before they went up to bed, Dixie sighed, "I guess he doesn't want to talk to us."

Morgan tried to smile. "If he did, the line might have been busy."

"I was only on the phone for forty minutes. I was watching the clock," Dixie insisted.

Dixie was probably right. Tony didn't want to talk to them again. He'd not begun the letter with any sort of salutation. No *Hi grandpa. How are you? I heard you were sick. I'm sorry if I in any way caused it.* He'd signed it *Tony Morgan*, as if he were a stranger.

"Anyway, we didn't expect him to call tonight," Dixie said.

"He may not get the message until tomorrow," Morgan replied, hope rising again. "We don't know how efficient that voice-mail system is at the YMCA."

☙❧

As the two lay in bed that night, Dixie told Morgan her worries about Tony's stepdad. "I don't know if he's physically abusive, but he seems to be a control freak. And he doesn't give a damn about Tony. He called the cops on him and sent him away to boot camp for ninety days. And Clay, Tony's real dad"—she poked him—"your own son, is just as bad, putting up a small fortune to pay for the camp. No one came up to see him graduate after three months of forced marches in the desert, eating cheese three meals a day. What a family! No wonder he drifted to

Columbus with Eddie and his mom." Throughout her recitation, Morgan listened, murmuring and muttering, twitching and sighing, his arms wrapped around her. "I worry sometimes," she confessed, "that Tony's still drifting, cold and hungry, wandering the streets. Just like before."

"Before?"

"After Eddie's mom kicked him out, he lived at a homeless shelter."

"What?"

"He told me on his last visit. Before you returned with the paint."

"What a goddamned fool I've been," he cried out with such feeling that Jiggs jumped off the bed.

"Don't say that," Dixie said. "Who knows? Maybe he'll call us tomorrow." She was quiet for awhile, then murmured, "Now that you're sleeping with me, Tony could have your room. Morgan, are you awake?"

"I am now."

"Well, once we know for sure he's—"

"Not a serial killer," Morgan broke in.

"That he's okay. And he knows we're okay." With that, she grew quiet and soon was breathing evenly.

Morgan, on the other hand, was now wide awake, the evening meal burning his throat. He went to the bathroom and took a spoonful of antacid, then lay back in bed, trying not to think.

After awhile, he got up and went downstairs, took paper and a pen from a kitchen drawer, and sat at the table to answer his daughter Sara's letter. He'd been putting it off for two months. She'd probably given up on his ever answering. By now, Barbara could be dead.

The last time he'd seen Sara was the end of the summer after Barbara filed for divorce and he left the house for good. She'd be what? 56 or 57 now. But in his mind she was 14, tall and skinny, her straight, black hair down to her shoulders. She was his youngest and his favorite. She had a lisp, from her braces. She squinted when she wasn't wearing her glasses, which she hated. "Dad," she'd said, all smiles as she burst through the front door when he was coming down the stairs. "Dad, you're back." Then she saw the suitcase in his hand. She started to cry. When he walked out the door, she was screaming, "I hate you. I wish you were dead."

He wrote, *Dear Sara, I'm so sorry.* She was a real original. He smiled, remembering her chunky little baby's body, her crooked grin. She never crawled. She sat upright, rocking from one side to the other, and suddenly she'd be moving forward, walking on her bottom, swinging from cheek to cheek. Quicker than a minute she'd be there, grabbing on to something that had caught her eye.

After she learned to talk, she couldn't get a word in when the older kids were around. They drowned her out. She took it until she was four. One night at the dinner table, she yelled at the top of her lungs, "Shut up, I'm talking!" She had her say from that day on.

He wrote, *I'd hoped to come to Chicago, but I just got out of the hospital. I won't be there to say good-bye to Barbara, your mother. I hope you understand.*

He'd been there for Sara when she needed him only once that he could remember. In second grade, she'd burst into the house, crying, with an F in arithmetic. She didn't understand subtracting from a hundred, the whole borrowing thing. That night he was home for a change, wasn't impatient, took time, and explained it. She went on to major in accounting in college.

She loved to swim. She loved Elvis. His eyes stung. Tears trickled down his cheeks.

He felt Dixie's hands on his shoulders. When had she come downstairs into the kitchen? He turned, put his arms around her waist, and buried his face in her stomach.

⁕

The next day, while Dixie was at work, Morgan finished Sara's letter. *I'm sorry we lost touch. Let me know how you're doing.* He signed it, *Your dad*, his eyes misting as he sealed it. He put it in the mailbox for the mailman to pick up.

Then he dusted and ran the sweeper for the evening's bridge party. He washed the windows downstairs. He set up card tables in the living room, put Dixie's best dessert plates and goblets on the dining room table, wrapped the prizes she'd picked up for the winners, and made the lemonade. He had to smile. He was by now a well-broken-in house-husband. To relieve himself of this dubious honor, he'd work on coaxing Dixie into quitting her job.

"You're a sweetheart," Dixie said, with a kiss on his cheek, when she came home and saw all he'd done. "I can see I've trained you well," she teased. She opened the refrigerator to start fixing dinner. "Why, what's this?" she asked, drawing out a corsage. "It's beautiful. For me?"

"Don't be jealous. It's for Vera. I picked it up when I went to the grocery."

"Vera?"

He'd been touched by how she'd stood by Dixie during the bad times. "For being there when you needed her. I'll give it to her tonight, as a special prize for loyalty." That was something he'd not shown much of, in his former life.

Dixie threw her arms around Morgan. "Aren't you something! She'll be so pleased."

30

Deception

Dixie collapsed her umbrella, gave it a quick shake and threw it on the floor of the car. She stashed the large bag of party favors and decorations, the paper birthday tablecloth, and the birthday napkins on the seat beside her, glancing at her watch. Morgan's poker club started at seven. Did she have time? The sky was dark and nasty, spitting sleet. A depressing February day. But downtown Saturday traffic would be light at this time. *Go for it, Dixie.* It would be the best birthday present ever for Morgan.

She drove out of the shopping mall and headed for the freeway. She exited at Long Street, made a couple of wrong turns, and ended up on a one-way street that took her out of her way. Okay, back on course. In the next block, she spotted it, to her right, a large, square building. Institutional, impersonal.

What luck! A parking space, practically in front. She parked, snatched up her umbrella, and hurried inside, hardly feeling the icy water as it splashed her ankles. Heart thudding, she approached the uniformed gentleman at the front desk. "Tony Morgan, please." It had been three weeks since they'd received his ten dollars and Morgan had left a message for him to call. They'd heard nothing. But she'd fix that today.

"Not here," the man said brusquely, not even picking up the phone to see if Tony was in his room.

Her heart did a flip-flop. "Do you know where he might be?"

"Try the shelter."

"The shelter?" Dear God, he was homeless! "Where's the shelter?" Why had he sent the money? Ten dollars wasn't that much to her and Morgan but it was a lot if you had nothing.

The man gave her directions.

She trudged back to her car, shivering in her winter coat. It was after five. She still had to pick up the birthday cake for Morgan. She should do that now and go home. Tony would be upset if she found him living in the shelter.

She didn't care. She drove to the shelter, nosing the car into a parking space half a block away. It was not a very nice neighborhood. Soon it would be night. She slid out of the car, locked the doors, and hurried down the uneven sidewalk. Cold water dripped down her neck. She'd forgotten her umbrella. She wouldn't go back for it now. She walked faster, practically ran up the steps, and pulled open the heavy front door.

The entryway was dimly lighted. A sign on the wall in front of her proclaimed, EVERYONE IS WELCOME. But where was everyone? At the landing of the stairway to her right, a man stood inside a lighted glass booth. She was about to climb the stairs and ask him if he knew where Tony was. Then she saw another sign: DINNER IS SERVED MONDAY THROUGH SATURDAY, 4:00 TO 5:50. She smelled food and heard the clanking of utensils and the clatter of pans. Most likely, he'd be eating. She turned left, followed her nose around one corner, and then another. Suddenly she found herself in a huge room, filled with dark, hunched figures slouched at tables. The shadowy shapes looked so still, almost like a painting, except for hands lifting food mechanically to mouths. No one talked. Each ate steadily and silently, most with their coats on, hoods up over their heads. The room was stifling.

A tiny voice piped, "More corn?" Two pinched-faced children, a boy and a girl, sat at a nearby table beside a woman with stringy hair. How awful, Dixie thought. Children were starving. Entire families were homeless, needing food, warmth, and a place to sleep.

She went from table to table searching for Tony, dipping down now and then to peer under a hood. Most scarcely paid attention. Some turned blank faces to her, their heads swiveling in slow motion.

Beyond the tables was a queue of people, caught in a glare of lights from the ceiling. She walked over, searching the line. Then she spotted him, his face lit as if he were on stage. She found a gap between the bodies and pressed closer.

Tony was behind a steam table, not in the line of hungry people in front of it.

"End of the line, lady," muttered a smelly man in a tattered coat.

Tony held a dinner plate in his hand. He wore a stained, white apron. His face was clean-shaven, except for the mustache. He still had the earring, but his hair looked different. Ah, yes, a hairnet held it in a pageboy. "Tony," she called out.

He seemed confused, as if he wondered where the voice was coming from. He was still more confused when he saw her. Slowly, he forked a piece of meat and flipped it onto the plate he held, then flung on some mashed potatoes.

His face had filled out a little, as if he was getting three squares. A lock of hair hung over his forehead. Again, she was struck by how much he resembled Morgan, a taller, slimmer version. "Are you doing okay?" she asked. Was he a volunteer? Did those who lived in shelters have duties, like manning the steam table?

He dipped a ladle into a tub of gravy.

"C'mon, man, I'm starving," a man with a pitted face said.

Tony poured gravy over the meat and potatoes, added some corn, and handed the plate to the man. "I can't talk," he said to Dixie, looking trapped.

Dixie wavered, glancing at her watch. She had to pick up the cake for tonight and fix supper. She would send Morgan out on an errand. The poker club guys would be hidden when he returned to the house. Would Morgan ever be surprised when she walked out with the cake, nine candles blazing, the whole poker club behind her! But the biggest and best surprise would be tomorrow, if Tony showed up for Morgan's birthday dinner. A special dinner for just the three of them. They might even talk about Tony's moving in with them. "It won't take long."

Tony frowned, continuing to serve those who filed by, dodging Dixie as they did.

She stood her ground. "I can wait."

A young woman next to Tony, her blonde hair held in a net, pulled his head down to whisper in his ear. He nodded. The blonde gave Dixie a kind smile, then handed a plate of food to a woman in a hot-pink slicker.

Tony wiped his hands on his apron and made his way down the length of the steam table.

Dixie met him as he stepped out into the room. "The man at the Y told me you were here."

He looked down at her with troubled eyes. "This is my new community site."

The world turned right-side-up again. Why hadn't the man at the Y said that? *He's at the shelter, where he serves meals from time to time.*

"I shouldn't be taking time to talk."

"If you're free," she stammered, "to come for Sunday dinner tomorrow, around one, I'll pick you up and bring you back."

He lowered his eyes, seeming to think it over.

The line had thinned out at the steam table. The blonde girl was looking their way. Was the blonde his boss? Dixie wondered. She looked so young. Or was she, like Tony, in some sort of program with the juvenile authorities? "It's Morgan's ninetieth birthday. It's a surprise. It'll just be the three of us."

"How is Grandpa?" he asked. "Officer Pfeiffer said he was in the hospital."

So he knew that, but hadn't cared enough about his grandpa to return his phone call. She should walk away. No, she wouldn't let it daunt her. "Did you get the message Morgan called?" she asked innocently.

He nodded, shifting his weight from one leg to the other.

"He's feeling much better." She gave a nervous laugh. "He'd be so pleased to see you."

"I've been thinking," the words came out of his mouth slowly, "about a lot of things."

She braced herself for the turn down, the lame excuse.

He looked uncertain. "I talked to my mom. She wants me to come home."

The blonde came bouncing up to them, smiling expectantly.

"Uh," Tony said, nonplussed, "this is, uh, my grandma."

Dixie's jaw dropped.

"I'm Laura." The girl held out her hand. "Tony's told me all about you, how you and your husband are being so supportive with Tony's college and all."

Tony flushed. He glanced back toward the steam table. "Gotta get back to work." He waved at Dixie, mumbled something she couldn't hear, and turned and strode away. The blonde, after an apologetic look and a shrug, followed Tony.

What was going on? Telling the girl she was his grandmother, that she and Morgan were so supportive of his college, when he hadn't finished high school. Some kind of con game? Wishful thinking?

Behind the steam table, Tony and the blonde stood side by side. The girl was talking. He was looking down at her and smiling. Then they began to portion out food to a few stragglers who'd just walked in.

Dixie left, bewildered. Why string the girl along if he was going back to Chicago? Then she understood. Going to Chicago was his lame excuse to get out of coming to Morgan's birthday dinner. He just couldn't say no outright.

Once inside her car, she realized her hair was soaking wet. She was shaking. It was dark now. She locked all the doors, started the motor, turned on the heater, and sat. Tony seemed to be up to his old tricks, making bad choices.

Two ragged-looking individuals, bathed in pale light from a nearby streetlight, mounted the stairs to the shelter. Before they disappeared inside, a tall figure emerged, galloped down the steps, and came her way. He held a newspaper over his head.

He passed under the streetlight. It was Tony. He wore a bulky two-breasted tan overcoat, too large across the shoulders. A button was missing. Still, he looked presentable, almost elegant. She shot out of the car.

He stopped, his eyes wide, and put up a hand protectively, clamping the newspaper to his head with the other.

"What's going on?" she demanded.

"What do you mean?" he glared.

"Telling Laura you were in college. That I was your grandma. That Morgan and I have been so encouraging. You won't even return our telephone calls."

He raised his shoulders, scrunching his head down as if he was a turtle.

Whether it was from guilt or the cold water rolling off the newspaper down his neck, she wasn't sure. "Do you really believe those lies your family told you about Morgan?" she snapped out. "He's not rich. He was forced out of his job, mid-career, and had to start over." Water trickled into her eyes. Impatiently, she wiped it away. "But he took care of his kids. He put them all—your dad Clay included—through college. He's not perfect, but it's about time he got some respect from you people."

Tony moved his mouth, but no words came out. He let out a stran-gled howl, turned, and ran back the way he'd come. "You can't always run away," she yelled. She watched him round the corner beyond the shelter and disappear.

⚭

"Your hair is soaked," Morgan exclaimed when she burst into the family room from the garage. "You'll catch pneumonia."

"I got caught in the rain," she said, "but it's letting up now."

"I made you a sandwich. I already ate." He took it out of the refrig-erator. "I was worried."

"I should have called on the cell phone." She needed to put on a party face for Morgan. She grinned. "The traffic was murder." She handed him a paper sack. "Why don't you fix up the table while I get my hair dried?"

"Sure."

"I decided we should have a President's Day theme since it's the holiday weekend. We'll give everyone a paper hat. Aren't they festive? They're decorated like the American flag." She felt a twinge of guilt re-membering those poor souls at the shelter, denied the bare necessities, while she squandered money on frivolity. "I also bought these small paper plates, with the silhouettes of Washington and Lincoln."

She dried her hair while she ate her sandwich, standing up. It was twenty of seven. "Pauline made a special dip for the guys," she called out to Morgan, who was in the dining room decorating the table. "Can you go over and get it while I change out of these wet clothes? Take your umbrella, just in case."

"She'll keep me talking forever," Morgan groaned as he walked out the front door. She'd better, Dixie thought, at least for twenty minutes.

She whisked the cake and the bag of birthday decorations from the car where they'd been hidden. She redid the table, putting down the paper birthday tablecloth and placing birthday napkins beside her best dessert dishes. She'd save the presidential paper plates for chips and dip.

One by one, the seven poker-club cronies trailed in. Dixie hid them in the kitchen. Then she clicked the back porch light twice to signal Pauline to release Morgan.

Morgan, covered dish in hand, exploded through the front door. "I thought she'd keep me there all night. Hey, why is it so dark in here?"

Everyone cried out, "Surprise!" Nate snapped the lights on. The guys sang "Happy Birthday" as Dixie came forward with the cake, nine candles lit.

"Well, what do you know!" Morgan looked absolutely beatific with surprise.

"We carried it off," Nate said with a grin at Dixie, rescuing the covered dish clutched in Morgan's hands.

Not quite, Dixie thought. She'd hoped to write on Morgan's birthday card, which he'd open tonight, *Surprise guest for tomorrow's birthday dinner. Guess who?*

She couldn't believe she'd been thinking of asking Tony to move in. He'd have them crazy. They'd be sick with not trusting him.

"You're a wily one." Morgan kissed Dixie on the lips as the guys whistled and stamped their feet. Nate opened the bottle of champagne he'd brought and poured them each a small glass. "To Morgan and Dixie!" he toasted, as did the others.

They gravitated to the dining room for ice cream and cake. Then Morgan, wearing an American-flag hat, opened cards and funny little gifts from the guys. Finally, they helped Dixie clear the table and settled down for a not-so-serious evening of poker. Dixie outdid herself, waiting on them hand and foot, serving beer, making sure the chips bowl was always filled and Pauline's dip replenished. She wouldn't let herself think about Tony and his treachery. The beer flowed. She laughed at the jokes and had a couple of glasses of beer herself. She realized she was having fun. "More cake anyone?" she asked.

A few of the fellas said yes. She served them as they played. Crumbs would be all over the floor when they left. Scads of beer bottles would have to be gathered up. She prayed there'd be no rings on the table. She'd provided coasters, but her good dishes and silver would have to be washed by hand. Well, she didn't care. Morgan seemed so happy, engrossed in his game, with small stacks of nickels, dimes, and quarters in front of him. It looked as if he was on a winning streak.

❦

Tony hung up the coats, peeking over the rack at Laura. She sat at the table, smiling, kind of dancing in her chair to the background music, her hair like gold against her black turtleneck. Every guy who passed her gave her a second look. He couldn't believe his luck.

"Neat shirt," Laura said when Tony returned to the table. "Ralph Lauren?"

"Yeah." He'd picked it up for a buck at the thrift shop. "What do you want on your pizza?" He scanned the menu. He hoped he could relax. Mrs. Valentine had spooked him, jumping out at him the way she did on the street. Telling him off. She'd looked right through him.

"Veggie, with broccoli, peppers, and onions?" She made a face and her dimple showed.

He looked around. Every table was occupied. Colorful murals, filled with sunny vineyards, blue water, and laughing people, covered the walls. Prices were reasonable. "I like this place."

"Yeah. It's my favorite of all the campus hangouts."

She was looking at him funny, like, why didn't he know it was a campus hangout? "Yeah," he said, leaning back in his chair, trying to look at ease. "My favorite too."

"What do you want?" she asked.

"Veggie is fine." He wanted the sausage.

"We could get half and half."

Might as well tell her, so he wouldn't go hungry all night. "I like sausage."

"Let's get half sausage, half veggie." She smiled again, a mischievous look in her eye. "I might even sneak a piece of yours, though I shouldn't."

"Why not?"

"You guys can eat anything. I'm always on a diet."

She looked too thin to him. "Something to drink?" he asked.

"Diet Coke. Your grandma's cute."

Grandma? Oh, Mrs. Valentine. He nearly said it aloud. "I'll tell her you said that." God, his tongue felt stuck to the top of his mouth. He put on his coolest look and smiled into her eyes.

"It's great you have them in your corner since, I mean, you know, since your parents have passed away."

Why had he said that? He put his head in his hand, rubbed his face.

"What's the matter?"

He flashed her a smile. His upper lip caught on his teeth. "Busy day. At—at the library, before I came over to the shelter."

"Paper due?"

"Yeah. Let me put our order in." He was getting in deeper and deeper. He went up to the counter and ordered the pizza and drinks. "Make that one water, instead of a Coke," he said when he checked his wallet. "Yeah, I still want the Diet Coke." He didn't want to run short if they decided to go to a movie.

When he came back with the drinks, Laura said, "You're having water?" She opened her purse.

"I drink too many sodas. They give me a headache."

"Let me pay half."

"No way. I asked you out."

With an uncertain smile, she closed her purse. "You said your major is accounting?"

"Yeah. I think I'll probably end up in banking." Her face lit up, so he expanded. "Maybe something on an international scale."

"International banker." She looked pleased. "You must be good in math. I'm not."

"Lots of money to be made in banking," he said. He didn't know what he was talking about.

"You can help people," Laura said earnestly. "Help the global economy."

"Yeah." What exactly did she mean? Best to play it cool and not ask too many questions.

"Half sausage, half veggie?" a young man asked, holding a pizza aloft.

"Right here," Tony said.

"Careful. The tin is hot." The waiter put the pie, which rested on a wooden block, between them.

"Go ahead," Tony said to Laura. "Have some of mine, if you dare."

"I'm starving." With a cocky smile, she lifted a sausage slice to her mouth and took a bite. "Yikes," she said, holding her mouth, reaching for her coke.

"I'm hungry too." To be polite, he took a veggie slice and pepped it up with hot pepper flakes and garlic.

"When do you graduate?" she asked. She blew on her pizza and took another bite.

"It'll be awhile." Yeah, quite awhile. "So you're a sophomore?"

She nodded.

An older woman. He didn't want her to know he'd just turned 18. He felt stressed, having to guard everything he said. She must see right through him.

Better set her straight. "I'm just taking night classes now." Well, he planned to enroll in college night school, after he passed the GED. "If my grades are good, Grandpa hinted he'd help me out, support me all the way. Probably."

"Financially?"

He nodded. Pie in the sky. Who was he kidding? "I have a day job." She nodded slowly.

Was she disappointed he wasn't in college fulltime?

"Where do you work?" she asked.

"An accounting firm." Another fib. But he had an interview next week at a couple of places. If he said he was a busboy, she'd walk out on him. "My grandpa was an accountant. Went into banking."

"A chip off the old block," she smiled. "I hope you don't think I'm too nosy. But losing your dad and mom, it must be hard. I lost my dad a couple years ago. I still miss him." Her eyes filled up. "When did they die?"

What a fuckup he was. He'd just been blabbering that day, the first day he and Laura met. He'd felt down. He'd just got off the phone with his mom, and she hadn't asked where he was, what city or what state he was in.

"I'm sorry. I can see you don't want to talk about it," she said.

He made a noncommittal sound. He was beginning to sweat. He wasn't a good liar.

"You live on campus?" she asked.

"Not yet." He couldn't say he lived at the Y. Squaresville. "I live near downtown. I'm looking for a place near campus. Like you. Want dessert?"

She shook her head. She giggled. "I can't believe it," she said, looking at the empty pizza tray between them. "I ate all your sausage pizza."

He gave her a gallant smile. "And I ate all your veggie."

They took in a movie, some foreign film she wanted to see, with subtitles. He was having fun for the first time in a long time.

He'd never seen a foreign film. This one was pretty hot. He kept stealing looks at her from under his eyes. She seemed to be enjoying the sex scenes. She didn't seem embarrassed, anyway.

He walked her to her apartment and hesitated outside. She leaned into him. They were nose to nose. "Wanna come in?" she asked.

"Sure."

Three girls were watching TV. "My roommates," Laura said, making the introductions. They waved, but their eyes kept darting back to the TV.

Tony followed Laura to the kitchen. "So four of you share this place?"

"Yeah, it's the only way we can afford it. Want a beer?"

"Sure," he said. She clicked on a radio that sat on top of the refrigerator. Side by side at the cluttered table, the two drank their beers from cans. Jazz played softly in the background.

"You said you were interested in international banking," she said. "You plan to get your MBA? Major in international studies as well as banking?"

"Uh." He had to think a minute. What was an MBA? "Probably."

"Me too. A master's is a must for social work."

"Yeah, I wanted to ask—" He wanted to get the focus off himself. "Do you plan to do something, I mean, like help out at places like the shelter?"

"I'm not sure yet. I'm investigating all sorts of venues."

Venues? He'd have to remember it and look it up. "What kinds of things would you do if you were a social worker, say, at the shelter?"

"Counsel people, help them to find a job, teach them to do a resume." She smiled. "Be their cheerleader."

"Okay." The woman at the shelter, after he was kicked out of Eddie's, she must have been a social worker. She'd helped him find a job as a busboy, so he could get a paycheck and move to the Y. She'd even given him a few lessons on the computer at the shelter. "Must be depressing, working all the time with losers." Like me, he thought.

"They aren't losers, most of them. Most have just plain bad luck. Or their parents don't set good standards. They get hooked on drugs or alcohol. They lose their job through no fault of their own. They don't know the value of an education. You have to get a college degree these days, even for a clerical job."

She was so lively. He loved watching her face as she talked.

"And if you have gumption—even if you don't get a scholarship or your parents can't afford to send you—you can get a degree. It just may take longer." She laughed. "You know all this. I don't need to tell you."

He felt ready to dissolve with guilt, drop to his knees, and cry out a confession. He took a couple of swallows of beer. "Makes sense to me."

Then she told him she'd dropped out of college after her freshman year to work for a year so she could afford to continue. Her mom couldn't help out much with finances. "And I'll have to get a part-time job in the summer. Right now I'm taking extra credit hours and don't have the time for a part-time job." She laughed. "I'm going on and on. What about you? You work at the shelter too. You must want to help people who need another chance."

"Yeah, I guess you could say that." He didn't want her to know he'd been in trouble with the law. That's why he was working at the shelter. She was there as a part of her college studies and assumed he was too. That's how it started, one lie leading to another. "You said your mom, she couldn't help you much financially?" he asked.

"She works at a department store. She never got a college degree. When Dad died, she had to go out and find a job for the first time in her life. She's my cheerleader. She wants me to be a professional. I guess that's how your grandpa and grandma feel about you."

"Yeah." He felt like sinking through the floor. He saw her looking at a clock on the wall. Nearly two AM. "I guess I'd better be going." It was quiet in the other room; the TV was off. Her roommates must have gone to bed. "Can I see you again?"

She looked at him long and hard. "I'd like that. You're not like the other college guys."

"Oh?"

"You're shy, a little mysterious," she teased.

Mysterious! No one had ever called him that.

"The other guys mostly—they have a line."

If she only knew.

"They try to push themselves on you."

She was looking at him like she wanted him to do just that. He got up his courage, leaned down, and kissed her. Her arms went around his neck. He stood and pulled her up against him. Her hair smelled so good. She felt so warm, so fragile. He could crush her if he squeezed just a little harder. But he wanted to protect her.

"You still have stuff to do at the library?" she asked as he started to leave.

He nodded.

"We could study together tomorrow, if you want."

"Yeah. That'd be cool." Oh, boy, he'd have to come up with something to study. Think up the name of the college course he was taking. Would it never end? Well, he'd worry about it tomorrow.

31

The Confession

Morgan felt Dixie prod him with her toe. "Wake up, sleepyhead," she murmured, stretching luxuriously. "You're about to witness the most exciting performance of your life. But it has nothing to do with you and me," she added as Morgan reached for her.

"Why not?" he murmured. Her eyes were blue and sparkling; her skin clear and shiny. He pulled her close. She smelled like peaches.

They snuggled and watched from the comfort of their bed while bluebirds and cardinals pecked through the grains Dixie had sprinkled on the windowsill the night before. Robins wheeled in circles singing their morning song, and smaller birds like sparrows and finches waited offstage for their chance to eat.

Then the loudmouthed jays arrived, not to join the party but to disrupt it. They scattered the grain and tried to chase away the other, more peaceful birds. Morgan cheered in approval when some mousy-colored mockingbirds took charge.

"I never knew the mockingbirds could make the jays eat crow," he joked. "I always thought of them as an outlaw bird because they steal the beautiful lyrics of redbirds, robins, and meadowlarks."

He looked out the window again. The birds were nowhere to be seen.

"They'll be back tomorrow," Dixie said. "Spring is just ten days away."

While Dixie was downstairs rustling up breakfast, Morgan donned his warm-up suit and migrated to the spare room for a spin on the exercise bike. He opened the window, took a deep breath of the crisp air, and gazed at the sunny skies. Slowly, the window slid shut. What was happening? He raised the window next to it. It slid shut too. "What's the matter with these damn things?" he complained to Dixie, who'd just walked in with a glass of orange juice.

"Use the stick in the windowsill." Dixie handed him his juice and propped open the window with a stick. "Fatigue," Dixie said. "Haven't you noticed? Almost every window in the house is just like these."

"How long has this been going on?" he asked.

She shrugged. "Ten years."

"Can't they be fixed?"

"Only replaced," she said with a rueful look. "Thirteen windows. It would cost thousands of dollars!"

He shook his head, grinning. "So you opted to buy the whirlpool bath instead of windows?"

She nodded sheepishly. "Only three or four were bad then. The rest went, one by one."

Morgan finished his juice and handed her his empty glass. "Thanks, sweetie." He climbed on the bike. New windows would only make the house more valuable. But he'd been after Dixie to quit her job. Which was more important? New windows or Dixie staying home with him?

"Don't overdo," she warned before she left the room.

"I feel great," he insisted, pedaling away. He'd been out of the hospital two months, slowly upping his workouts on the bike. No pain, no gain.

Jiggs, his head on his paws, watched him intently. As soon as Morgan had a good speed going, Jiggs growled and sprang, grabbing hold of his pants leg, gnawing on it with the few teeth he had left. It was a game they played every day. He laughed, stopped pedaling, dragged Jiggs out of the room, and shut the door. He climbed back on the bike. He'd take it easy today. His legs felt heavy.

⚜

Morgan tore open the envelope and fished out the clipping enclosed with Sara's letter. He read the headline, surprised by the wave of sadness. "She died ten days ago." He passed the clipping on to Dixie. He imagined how his ex-wife must have changed, her long hair white and thin instead of thick and blonde, her slim figure wasted, loose flesh over bone. Her eyes vacant from the strokes—or terror-filled.

He hoped she was peaceful at the end.

He unfolded Sara's letter, absurdly pleased to see she'd written two full pages. *Hi*, she'd written, not *Hi, Dad*. He felt disappointed. But could he blame her?

He read aloud to Dixie:

Thanks for writing. I'm sorry you were in the hospital. I hope you're better. Since you asked, I'm married to a good man, a banker (surprise!). My three boys are grown. I'm back at work now as an auditor, tired of rattling around an empty house (empty until the grandkids arrive).

Thought you'd like to get caught up with the rest of the gang. Your middle daughter, Evelyn, is married to a local politician, who's planning to run for the state senate. Her son has his own catering company.

Your son, Clay, is a highly-paid clothing executive. He divorced his wife four years ago. Or maybe she divorced him. It should have happened sooner. He wasn't a very good husband or father. His kids suffered, especially his youngest, who had some run-ins with the police up here. Clay paid to send him to a private boot camp, an awful thing to do to a 17-year-old. Then the kid disappeared. They don't know where he is.

Morgan looked at Dixie, concerned. "What's Tony trying to prove?"

"He told me he called his mom," Dixie blurted out, "and that she asked him to come back to Chicago."

What was she talking about? "Who told you?"

"Tony." Dixie looked guilty. "Don't get mad. I was going to tell you. I went down to the Y to invite him to your birthday dinner." She threw up her hands. "Anyway, they steered me to the shelter . . ."

"He was living in a shelter?" Morgan broke in.

"Calm down. It was his new community site. He looked fine, thriving even." She pursed her lips. "You suppose he was telling the truth about talking to his mom?"

Morgan rubbed his face. More trouble because of that damn kid.

"Should we tell them we think he's here? In Columbus?"

"Well, we don't know, do we? We only had that one letter, back in January, when he sent the money. You saw him, when?"

"The afternoon of your poker party."

"They're probably worried sick." He had to admit he'd been fretting too, hearing nothing from the kid for a month and a half, not even a polite return of his phone call. Now Dixie tells him she saw him just three weeks ago. Exasperating! "Why didn't you—"

"I didn't want to upset you. Especially the way things turned out."

She could be maddening, giving him these bits and pieces. "Now what does that mean?"

"Don't get your blood pressure up." Dixie then told Morgan the troubling conversation with the blonde girl who worked beside Tony at the shelter. "He told her he was in college. That we, his grandpa and his grandma"—she jabbed her thumb toward her chest—"were supporting him. No, supportive of his college." She gave him a meaningful look. "Whatever that means."

Morgan was stunned. "I thought he didn't want anything to do with us." He didn't know what to think. "This girl? What was she like?" Was she cheap and tough? "Do you think she was there because she was in trouble with the law?" She might be as bad an influence on Tony as Eddie was.

"I don't know. She looked decent enough. I felt sorry for her. I waited in the car. As soon as Tony stepped through the door of the shelter, I was out on the sidewalk, blocking his way. I told him exactly what I thought of him, leading that girl on." She took a deep breath, pressing her lips together, holding her shoulders high.

"So what did he have to say to that?" he asked, trying not to sound as impatient as he felt. She sure knew how to string out a story.

"I told him it was about time he and the rest of your family stopped bad-mouthing you. That you'd put them all through college, including his dad Clay. They're a bunch of spoiled brats. I was damn mad because he wouldn't come to your birthday dinner. I planned it to be a big surprise and . . ." Her voice trailed off. She was running out of steam.

"Dixie, Dixie, my little firebrand." He chuckled. "Good for you. Did he get a word in edgewise?"

"He stared at me, let out a yell, and ran away."

Morgan rubbed his chin. He finally walked over to the phone. "Where's Pfeiffer's number? He'll know what's up."

Where was Tony? Still at the YMCA? He hoped Dixie's verbal

trouncing hadn't sent him off on a tangent. He knew what a hothead he'd been at 18. "I hope to God the kid's not out on the road somewhere, hitchhiking."

⚛

"Where are your roommates?" Tony asked when he stepped into Laura's apartment.

"Library." She wore jeans and a baggy, green-plaid shirt. Her long hair was tied back with a ribbon. She made a face. "Term papers."

"We're alone, for once." He wanted to kiss her. Instead he handed her a bottle of red wine, feeling pretty darn smooth that he'd managed to buy it. The clerk hadn't asked to see his ID.

She opened the closet, clearing a space. He hung up his coat. "I like your perfume," he said, smiling down at her.

"You smell good too."

Okay! She noticed his musk aftershave.

"You stir the spaghetti sauce while I boil the pasta." She headed into the kitchen.

He followed her. The thick sauce was bubbling on the stove. "So how do I do this?"

She gave him a skeptical look.

"I'm a klutz in the kitchen."

She handed him the spoon resting on the stovetop and closed his fingers around the handle.

"Your hand's soft," he grinned.

She guided his hand as the two of them stirred the sauce. Chunks of beef, tomatoes, and mushrooms surfaced. Her closeness and the aroma of the sauce were overpowering. He was starving. He could hardly wait.

"I think you can manage now." She raised an eyebrow. Her dimple showed. "Don't let it stick to the pan." She opened the box of spaghetti, broke the strands in two, and dropped them into boiling water.

"Should I open the wine?" he asked when they were ready to eat.

"I'll have half a glass. We can save the rest as a reward for after we study."

"Good idea." He hoped it might lead to other rewards. About time. It was their fourth date!

"I have five exams." She rolled her eyes.

"Yeah."

"You said you have two?" She dished out the spaghetti and poured the sauce over it. His plate was heaped high. Hers was a third the size.

"Yeah." He poured them each a couple of swallows of wine, then sat down across from her at the table. "Hey, this is great," he said after his first bite.

"Homemade. My mom's recipe." She passed him a basket of Italian bread.

"How's the job going?" she asked halfway through the meal.

"Okay." Not okay. None of his interviews had panned out. He was still at his dead-end job, bussing.

"Did I tell you? This is my last week at the shelter. Next quarter, I have to choose a new location."

"Yeah, I'm finished too." And that was the truth. He'd put in the sixteen hours he'd agreed to in the contract.

She talked about her courses and her instructors. All he could do was nod and feel like a first-class creep. "What about you?" she asked. "Do you like your professors?"

"They're okay."

"My mother is coming to Columbus for a weekend soon. She wants to meet you."

His bite of spaghetti stuck in his throat. "I'd like to meet her too." Someone else to try to keep his stories straight with.

"How's your grandma? I'd love to meet your grandpa."

"Yeah," he squirmed. "He'd like to meet you too." He pushed his plate away. "Whew, I'm full. Great meal."

"Is something wrong?"

"Nah, just a busy week."

After dinner they cleared the table and settled down across from each other to study. He kept looking up from his notebook. She had a pile of books in front of her. One was open. She ran her hand through her hair, frowning, making notes. The ribbon came loose. She shook out her hair. It spread over her shoulders.

He forced his eyes back to the work in front of him. He needed to ace the GED test and get into college soon. He felt relaxed thinking about it. One less lie to keep up. He became so involved in his algebra problem he was surprised to find her suddenly behind him, her hands on his shoulders. "My brain is numb," she said. "I need a break. Want a Coke?"

He quickly closed his notebook. If she copped a look at what he was poring over, sample tests in high-school math and science, she'd know he wasn't studying college courses.

"You're so secretive."

"What do you mean?"

"You won't give me your phone number. You won't let me see what you're studying." She darted in a hand and, with a giggle, snatched up the notebook. He grabbed for it and they struggled. She was so close, laughing up at him. "I don't want you to see my dirty pictures," he grinned, finally wresting it away.

He put an arm around her and let the notebook fall to the table. She hugged him back. Umm, she felt good. He kissed her. Her lips were soft; they tasted like garlic and wine. Soon they were glued to each other, breathing hard, swaying back and forth. She broke away, her face flushed. "You're strong," she said, feeling his upper arm. "You've been working out."

Yeah, he wanted to say, the boot camp made me strong. He liked her a lot. He didn't want to fuck this up. He was tired of conning her. "Laura," he said vehemently, "I have something to tell you."

She looked startled.

"I'm a busboy. I've interviewed for jobs at two accounting firms since we met. I hoped the lie I told you would finally be the truth. They turned me down." He picked up his notebook, ready to hand it to her for a look at the sample high-school tests, and spill all.

She frowned thoughtfully. "What do you wear when you job hunt?"

That threw him. He pointed to his outfit. Jeans and his faded blue designer shirt.

"Well, accountants are pretty conservative."

"Yeah?"

"You need a suit and tie. Or maybe a blazer and pants." She hesitated. "Some firms don't allow their male employees any sort of body piercing. The earring may have to be scratched." She ran her hands through his hair, smoothing it back against his head, nodding. "You'll definitely need a haircut." She grinned. "You may have to look a little more nerdy."

"Neither place said anything about it." But his grandpa had.

"They don't always tell you why they turn you down. And," she sighed, making a humming sound, "you might think about shaving off your mustache."

She was asking him to change his whole style.

She giggled suddenly. "Just for me. I don't like the way it tickles when you kiss me."

Whew! Round one over. He was still standing. He handed her his notebook. "Take a look."

She opened it and leafed through the pages. "What does it mean? Sample GED tests?"

"I'm studying to get my high-school diploma. I'm not in college." He couldn't look at her. He didn't want to see how her face would change. "I live at the YMCA. I buy my clothes at thrift shops. And," he took a deep breath. This was the hardest. "I was helping at the shelter because I had to do community service. I got in trouble with the law."

She turned away from him. That did it. It was over. Maybe not. She was bringing over what was left of the wine and a couple of glasses. She poured them each a drink. They sat across from each other.

"What kind of trouble?"

He took a swallow. He couldn't tell her everything, could he? That he'd served time in a boot camp? That he wrecked his grandpa's place? And now he was in a diversion program for delinquents. It was that or go to jail.

He did. He told her everything.

"So your parents aren't dead?" was her only comment. Her eyes were troubled.

"They might as well be. They don't give a damn. I know your dad dying—it was for real. I know you were torn up about it."

"What about your grandpa and grandma?"

"Well, she isn't my grandma. They're not married. They just live together."

She nodded, a dazed look on her face.

"I blew it with them. They aren't offering to help me with college, like I said." He forced himself to go on. "I wrecked their house. I was supposed to help them clean it and fix it up. I screwed that up too. I said awful things to my grandpa and sent him to the hospital. The day you saw her—Mrs. Valentine—at the shelter? She came to invite me to Grandpa's ninetieth birthday party. I blew her off."

"Why?"

"I don't know. Stupidity. I can't face them again, not until I have a plan that works."

"What would that be?"

He shook his head. "Get a real job, pass the GED, get into college. The only thing new I have to report to Grandpa is that I met you. I don't think that's what he wants to hear." He hurried to explain. "Not that it's not great I met you. You're the best thing that's happened to me. Ever."

Laura was quiet. Her eyes were sad.

He felt free of the burden he'd been carrying around. He felt depressed knowing how he'd changed in her eyes. He picked up his notebook, went to the closet, and took out his coat. She didn't try to stop him.

He left her sitting at the table, holding her wineglass, still as a statue. Outside, he cursed himself, "You fuckin' idiot," and started running. What a fool he'd been to tell her. He stopped off at a bar, ordered a beer, staring at the bartender, daring him to ask for his ID. The guy didn't. He was breaking the law and the terms of his contract with Pfeiffer. He felt victorious!

He chugged down half a glass, intending to drown his sorrows. The place was too depressing: the gabby bores, the sad sacks, the angry—all the losers. He walked out, not finishing the beer.

The next day, he decided he'd been a fool not to tell her sooner.

Three days later, he called and left her a message. "Hi. I miss you." He stopped by the campus hangout for pizza, hoping he'd run into her. He didn't. He sent her flowers. By the end of the week, he knew he'd never see her again.

32

The Unexpected Guest

Morgan stepped out of the garage and took a deep breath, sucking in the cool air. Invigorating! Across the street, the forsythia was already in bloom, and the red and silver magnolia. Spring was here at last! Should he wear a sweater under his jacket? Nah, he'd soon warm up.

First, he'd get the lawn ready for the fertilizer. Too soon to plant new annuals, since a hard frost was possible even into mid-May. But he could get the roses ready for summer. He'd promised Dixie he wouldn't overdo. But, heck, he needed the exercise. He was getting a bit of a paunch again, even though he used the bike every day.

He was raking at the side of the house when he glanced up to see someone gliding down the street toward him on a scooter. Looked like a kick scooter, something his kids had when they were little. The rider was very tall, not a child. An engine sputtered. The thing had a motor. What do you know?

The guy turned into his drive. He wore an official-looking dark-blue dress suit. Maybe he was the insurance rep come to settle up about the house. On a scooter? Wearing a helmet, and knee- and elbow pads? A little informal, but hey, these days anything was possible.

Morgan walked over to ask him his business.

"I followed your advice," the young man said, flipping a switch on the handlebar. The motor sputtered to a halt. He stepped off the scooter. "I went out and got myself a job with an accounting firm." He took off his helmet, smiling anxiously.

"Why, hello." Morgan hardly recognized him. His hair was trimmed short, all one color, dark brown. No earring. No mustache and no five-o'clock shadow.

"I'm learning the business from the ground up. I sweep out, I act as mailman." He spoke rapid fire, almost a monotone, as if the speech were memorized. "I even answer the phone sometimes. And I'm getting first-hand instruction from one of the partners in the firm. I'm only working four days a week right now."

Morgan, stunned by his new look, was silent. He felt a growing wave of pleasure, then stifled it. He didn't want to be disappointed again.

"I thought I'd come over, sort of to," Tony faltered, mumbling, "make up for not helping when I was supposed to."

"Well," Morgan said drily, "that's very kind of you. And if you will, we can do something right now."

Tony seemed taken aback.

"We'll prune some rose bushes and put down fertilizer in the back yard."

"I don't have any work clothes with me."

Oh, no, Morgan chuckled to himself, you can't wiggle out now. "How about wearing some of mine? They may be big around the waist, but we can fix them up. And we'll get better acquainted. When I spoke to Officer Pfeiffer a few weeks ago," Morgan put on his sternest look, "he didn't have much to say, except that you were keeping to a schedule, as agreed." That should be a pretty good hint that he and Dixie were upset not to hear from him all these weeks. He'd had more than a few sleepless nights worrying about the kid.

"Yeah," he said. "I'm doing okay."

"Glad to hear it," Morgan said. "Put your wheels up on the porch here. Let's go inside to find you some work clothes."

⚬⟊⚬

Dixie heard the front door open. "Finished already?" she called from the family room.

"Come on out. See who's here," Morgan said.

She stopped in her tracks as she came around the corner into the hallway. She looked Tony up and down. He didn't look so scruffy any more. "I don't think I'd recognize you if I ran into you on the street." Why was he wearing those pads on his knees and elbows?

"Take off your gear," Morgan said to Tony. "He has wheels now. Look out on the porch."

Dixie did and saw what looked like an oversize child's scooter, except it had a seat.

"It has a gasoline motor. Goes twenty-two miles an hour," Tony said proudly.

It seemed so flimsy, with skinny handlebars and a skinny pole holding up the seat. "I hope you aren't riding that in downtown traffic."

His face fell.

She should have kept her mouth shut. It was no concern of hers. She supposed scooters were the rage now with kids. Cheaper than a car certainly. Where had he got the money for it? He hadn't sent them any more installments toward the damages. Not that she wanted any. But it would have been a way to keep in touch, so they'd know he was still alive. Tears sprang to her eyes. She turned away so he wouldn't see them.

Tony unbuckled his knee pads and elbow pads.

"Put them over there, on the landing to the stairs," Dixie said.

With a questioning look, Tony put them where she'd said.

"In the corner so no one will trip," she added, pleased he did her bidding so meekly. After all, it was her house. Hers and Morgan's. They could ask him to leave if he didn't watch his step. *Cool it, Dixie*. She realized she was still upset over the way he'd treated her, yelling at her, running away. Now showing up without notice.

He drew an envelope from an inside pocket of his suit jacket and handed it to her, pasting a grin on his face. "I missed a couple of payments."

Dixie opened the envelope. It had two twenties inside. *New clothes, the scooter, now a payment of forty dollars*. Dixie worried about that girl, Laura, and prayed he wasn't borrowing from her. "Thank you."

"He has a job," Morgan said, "with an accounting firm."

"I bought the scooter second-hand from a guy I work with."

"That's nice," Dixie said, determined to keep her voice neutral. She was shaking from all the feelings running through her. She hoped to God he wasn't putting on an act. She had to admit she'd been worried sick he'd never want to see them again after the way she'd talked to him outside the shelter.

"I also work weekends bussing tables," Tony said. "For extra." Jiggs suddenly appeared, sniffing at his pant leg. "Hi, Jiggs." He reached down to pet him. The little dog lingered for a moment, walked away, returned, and sniffed again. Even Jiggs wasn't sure who he was, Dixie thought, and what his intentions were.

"Tony's here to help me in the yard," Morgan said.

He was actually here to help? "Good."

Morgan started up the stairs. "Come on up. I'll find something for you to wear."

◌╬◌

Tony tore off his suit jacket and threw it on the bed. He felt like leaving. He'd purposely worn his new thrift-shop clothes to show his grandpa he'd got his act together. Shot down! He'd given Mrs. Valentine money toward repairs. She'd stared at him like he'd stolen it. He caught a look at his face in the mirror on the back of the door. Red and ugly-looking, like his dad Clay when he got mad. He did some deep breathing, saying to himself, *you promised Pfeiffer. You promised the class. Get it over with.*

He took off his pants and climbed into his grandpa's baggy slacks. Too short, too big around the waist. He squeezed into a faded green and brown flannel shirt and replaced his worn dress shoes with an old pair of sneakers. He emerged from the spare room, sneakers flapping against the floor, feeling like a circus clown. Morgan, who'd been waiting in the hall, solemnly handed him a belt and a pair of work gloves.

He wasn't making it easy. Neither was Mrs. Valentine. They were adults, after all, supposed to be above getting even. Tony threaded the belt through the loops as he followed his grandpa downstairs.

"The rose bushes are in the back," Morgan said. The two walked into the kitchen past Dixie, who frowned as she rolled out pie dough on the table. Tony slunk through the family room, his eyes taking in the new TV. The drapes looked new too. They'd have to be. The others had been pretty well torn up.

He felt sick to his stomach remembering that awful night, the headlights in the drive, the pure terror. He'd scrambled to get the exercise bike into the yard, then left it to help Eddie drag the bag of food over the snow to the car. He'd been wet with sweat.

"Close the door behind you," his grandpa said, startling him. He slid the glass door shut with a bang.

"Sorry," he apologized.

"Come around with me to the garage."

Tony followed Morgan around the house and into the garage.

Morgan gathered a shovel and some pruning tools hanging on the wall and put them in the wheelbarrow. "I'll let you take charge of the wheelbarrow," he said with a raised eyebrow.

His stomach tight, Tony wheeled it around to the backyard, seeing in his mind the TV spilling out of it, Eddie ripping down the drapes, and the plant stand falling. Everything had crashed down around him, while he worried that the little dog had been crushed.

"Have you ever worked with roses?" Morgan asked.

"No."

"First, we have to dig up this dead bush. It's diseased. We don't want the other two bushes to go bad." He handed Tony the shovel. "Have you ever used a shovel before?"

"At the boot camp," Tony mumbled. Backbreaking, monotonous work. He hated it.

As he shoveled, he tried not to show his misery. He glanced up once to see Mrs. Valentine watching him through the kitchen window. Morgan stood nearby, watching too, nodding. It looked like he was going to have to pass inspection.

"Be careful not to cut the roots of the other bush," Morgan said.

After that, the only sounds came from the shovel chinking against the hard earth. Tony stopped once to wipe the sweat from his eyes. His hands were getting blisters, despite the gloves.

"The roots go deep. Want me to spell you?"

"No," Tony grunted. He wouldn't give in and look like a wimp. He dug until his hands felt ready to fall off.

Finally, his grandpa said, "Okay, you've got it. Yank it out with your hands. Throw it in the wheelbarrow. Be careful of the thorns."

Tony took hold and heaved. The bush broke free. "Ouch." He slammed it into the wheelbarrow. He pulled off his glove and examined the tiny wound made by a thorn.

"Good work." Morgan gave him a little smile. "You need a bandage?"

Tony shook his head, sucking away the blood.

"What's new?" Morgan asked. "Besides the job?"

Had he heard right? Was he really interested in what was happening in his life? "I finished my community site work at the shelter." He wished he hadn't mentioned the shelter. His grandpa was looking like he'd heard the full story from Mrs. Valentine, about the way Tony had treated her. "I guess she told you—" He glanced up, saw her framed in the window. She quickly walked out of view. "Did she tell you she saw me there?"

"Yes."

His face felt red hot. Should he say, I'm sorry I yelled at her? I'm sorry I didn't come to your birthday party? He was making a mess of this whole thing. "I'm studying hard for the GED test," he finally said. He wouldn't mention his hopes for college. "At the end of June, I'll be finished with Officer Pfeiffer and the, you know, the program." His grandpa seemed distant, unbelieving maybe. Tony blurted out angrily, "I realize it was my own fault that got me where I was. I have a temper."

"Well, so do I," Morgan acknowledged.

"I was bored. I got mixed up with the wrong friends." He looked away, embarrassed. Go on, tell him, he said to himself. You told the class you would. "I'm in a class for anger management. Pfeiffer made me go. I didn't like it much, but everyone's in the same boat. I'm learning," he sighed heavily, the words an effort, parroting the class chant, "I can change my life and my luck."

Morgan nodded gravely. "That's progress."

That's all he had to say? "One of my first assignments was to write that letter of apology to you." It had been damn hard to do.

Morgan chortled. "Pretty piss-poor effort."

He tried to stoke up his anger, but he felt his mouth twitch. The next thing he knew he was laughing. "Yeah, it was."

"Okay, next step," Morgan said. "Push off some of the protective mulch that's beneath the other rose bushes. Just half. The weather's iffy yet. Use the shovel." His grandpa seemed to be thinking something over. Then he asked, "Can you come by again in a week or so and finish the job? Help me fertilize the lawn?"

Tony stammered and stuttered around. "I guess—" What was he getting into here? Yard man? "I guess I could."

His grandpa pretended he hadn't heard him. He could at least grunt out a thank you, Tony thought.

"Next, we have to remove old stems of roses. See, do it from the center, like this." Morgan showed him how. "So the plant will have a better airflow."

"Why does it need it?" He'd never thought of flowers needing airflow.

"To keep the fungus down. What do you hear from your folks?"

He shrugged.

"I had a letter from your Aunt Sara. She said no one knew if you were alive or dead."

He gave Morgan an anxious look. "Did you tell them I was here?" He didn't want Fulkerson sticking his nose in. As if he'd give a damn. Anyway, he was 18 now, out of that creep's reach.

Morgan shook his head. "I didn't know where you were until I talked with Pfeiffer. You told Dixie you were going back to Chicago."

"Yeah." Then he met Laura and everything turned upside down. "Mom knew I was okay," he mumbled. "I called her."

"When?"

"A couple months ago. She didn't ask where I was."

"And you didn't tell her?"

"I didn't have time." He bit off the words. "Fulkerson walked in the room. She didn't want him to know she was on the phone with me."

"Call her again. Tell her you're in Columbus. She'd rather hear it from you than me."

Tony heard a noise and looked up. Mrs. Valentine was standing in full view at the window, nodding. She'd propped the window open with a stick. She wasn't even pretending not to listen.

"Yeah, okay. I'll call her." Tony looked from one to the other. They both were smiling. He began to relax.

"We need to cut back the bush to four or five of the healthiest stems." Morgan demonstrated how. "Cut away from the center of the plant, to lead new growth in that direction. Cut close now." Morgan took his hand and guided it. "Just above the bud, but be careful you don't hurt it. Tell me about this stepdad of yours. You call him by his last name? Fulkerson?"

"Yeah." Tony scowled. "My mom does everything he wants and he always wants it his way. I never liked him. I know the way I acted made things worse." Should he say what he was thinking? Yeah, he would. "He was glad to get rid of me, to hustle me into that boot camp."

Morgan frowned. "Clay, your dad—I guess he's not much help?"

Tony gave a bitter laugh. "He paid the money for the camp."

Morgan bent to clean up the clippings.

Tony bent down too, gingerly picking up the thorny stems and putting them in the barrow. "I looked up to my dad when I was little. Then I got to know he wasn't interested in us kids." They were eye to eye, the wheelbarrow between them. "I don't believe what he said about you," Tony stammered. "You know, about the money. It was one of those family stories. You heard it so much you believed it without thinking."

His grandpa's face screwed up. Tony thought he was going to cry.

"I understand," Morgan said, his eyes so sad that Tony wanted to touch him, or at least pat him on the arm.

Morgan cleared his throat. "Someday your parents will be gone for good. My advice is to get to know them while you have the chance." He disappeared into the nearby shed. "I wish I'd gotten to know my kids." His voice sounded hollow. He emerged with a jug. "Now we fertilize." He grinned. "You'll want to come back, see the roses in bloom. See what you helped do."

ᐧᐧᐧ

Dixie, glued in front of the window watching the unfolding scene, sighed, dabbing at her eyes with her apron.

She heard Pauline call out, "Looks like you've got yourself some good help." She was waving from the other yard.

"My grandson." A proud smile lit Morgan's face.

Pauline, jolly and round, bounced through the gate in the fence. "I didn't know you had a grandson here." Her eyes were bright with curiosity. She looked up at Dixie, standing by the open window, and waved.

"I do now," Morgan said heartily. "Tony, meet Pauline. Great neighbor, great cook."

She shook Tony's hand. "My, you're the spitting image of your grandpa. Are you from Chicago? Do you have a job here? Are you in school?"

Tony uncertainly opened his mouth to speak.

"Pauline," Dixie called out, "you were telling me about your azaleas. How are they doing?"

"Better," her neighbor said, looking surprised.

"That's a relief." The last thing she wanted was Pauline finding out Tony was one of the kids who broke into the house. Just a little slip and Pauline would put two and two together, and the whole neighborhood would know. Pauline still stood her ground, and looked ready to resume her grilling. Dixie noticed car keys in her hand, so she took a chance. "We're just about to have dessert and coffee. Join us?"

"I'm on my way to visit a friend." Pauline jingled her keys. "But I just had to meet this handsome stranger working in your yard." With a wave, she turned and hurried through the gate in the fence.

"Finish up, you two." Dixie breathed a sigh. Pauline was a nice sort, if only she weren't so nosy. "I don't want you overdoing, Morgan, and winding up in the hospital again."

Tony looked up at her, his eyes clouded. She guessed he was remembering the part he played in that drama. She heard him ask, "How are you feeling now, Gran—?" He still can't say the word *grandpa*, she thought. She listened closely for Morgan's reply and was relieved to hear him answer, "Great." Some days, when she walked in after work, he'd be snoozing in the chair. He blamed it on his blood-pressure medicine.

She had to face it. He was in his ninety-first year. Every year, every month from now on would be a milestone.

When the two came inside, Dixie cut the butterscotch pie and dished it up, while Jiggs looked on hungrily. "Coffee or tea?"

"Milk?" Tony asked timidly. "Hey, Jiggs." He bent down and scratched the little dog under the chin. Jiggs rolled over and let him rub his stomach. Soon Tony was on his knees, slapping his work glove on the kitchen floor, bouncing it from left to right. Jiggs growled and pounced. As soon as Jiggs caught hold of the glove, Tony laughed and pulled it out of his mouth, and the game began again.

One thing, Tony certainly livened up things around here. "Sit down, everyone," Dixie said.

"Good pie," Tony said, his mouth full.

"How's your friend at the shelter?" Dixie asked. "What's her name, the blonde girl?"

"Oh, you mean Laura?" A smile wobbled onto his face. He shrugged. "I'm finished up at the shelter."

"Yep," Morgan said. "He fulfilled his contract."

"Congratulations."

"I want you to know, Mrs. Valentine," Tony blurted out, "it was her idea. I mean, she jumped to the conclusion that I was in college, like she was."

"Oh, she's a college girl?" Dixie asked.

He nodded. He looked down at the table and sighed heavily. "I didn't want her to think I was a loser. So I let her think it. I straightened it out with her."

"Good." Hmm. Something was going on. He looked pretty dismal.
They finished their pie. "More?" Dixie asked Tony.

"Yeah." Tony ate his second piece. Morgan, across the table, smiled
kindly. Dixie rose to feed Jiggs, who'd been begging under the table.

"I guess I'd better get changed and go." Tony stood. He shifted awkwardly from one foot to the other. "I'm taking the GED next month."

"Good luck," Morgan said. "If you pass, you going ahead with college?"

Tony nodded. "Night school." He grinned at Dixie. "Accounting
from the ground up."

"Maybe you can be a banker," Dixie smiled, "like your grandpa."

"International banking," he said. "I'm thinking of doing a double
major."

"A double major?" Dixie exclaimed, on the brink of adding, "That'll
take forever in night school," but Morgan loudly cleared his throat.

"Mind if I gave you some advice?" Morgan leaned back in his chair.
"About what an employer expects of a young man? How you can play
the game to get ahead as rapidly as possible?"

Tony nodded. He sat back down

Apparently, Dixie thought, he was eager to hear his grandpa's suggestions. She cleared the table.

"Working overtime will endear you to your boss," Morgan went on.
"Do more than you're paid for."

Tony nodded again.

Dixie lingered in the kitchen, cleaning up.

"I see you've conformed to your employer's dress code," Morgan
said.

Tony grinned crookedly. "Accounting firms are pretty conservative.
Laura—" He stopped abruptly, then nodded toward his grandpa. "You
were right."

Morgan beamed. "If you decide to take a new job, keep the one you
have until you get another one. And give your employer plenty of notice.
That way you have the good will of both."

She drifted into the family room and sat in the chair nearest the
kitchen, ears perked, pretending to read the paper. He seemed under
the spell of Morgan's voice. He was probably just being polite. But she
wouldn't doubt that Morgan was the first adult male to take an interest
in him.

"You have youth on your side," Morgan continued. "Don't waste it. You can do anything you set your mind to."

Dixie hoped Morgan didn't pontificate too long. She twisted around to see what was going on. Morgan was leaning forward, hands clasped on the table in front of him. Tony was frowning, nodding slowly. "Sometimes I worry if I'll, you know, be able to—" Tony sighed.

"Usually the things you worry about never come to pass." Morgan smiled wearily. "The real problems, more often than not, are something you never thought about until they knock you sideways when you least expect it."

The silence crackled. Dixie turned away, fearful of seeming to intrude. She heard Tony say, "I'm sorry I didn't come to your birthday party."

That pleased her more than anything he'd said all day.

"Forget it. Who wants to remember birthdays at my age?"

"I wanted to have something positive to tell you before I saw you again," Tony mumbled. "I knew you expected that, Grandpa."

Morgan replied gruffly, "Well, son, I'm pleased with what you've accomplished since we last were face-to-face. What's it been now? Three months?"

"Yeah." Silence. The kitchen chair scraped across the linoleum. Tony stood. "Well, thanks for everything. I better go."

Morgan laughed. "No, you don't. You aren't leaving with my clothes. Better take a shower before you change into those nice duds of yours."

While Tony was showering, Morgan said to Dixie with a twinkle in his eyes, "He's like the young man who kept criticizing his folks for not knowing anything. Then he became more educated and discovered his elders had acquired a wonderful education while he was away. They knew so much more than he ever gave them credit for."

Just as Tony was ready to step out the door, Morgan gave him an awkward hug. "It was good to see you, Grandpa," Tony said in a strangled voice.

Morgan stepped back and said heartily, "Well, we have a lot of work to do yet. Mulch under the shrubs, balance and sharpen the blades on the mower, edge the flower beds, front and back."

Enough work to keep him coming back and busy for the next two months, Dixie thought. She prayed he would. It would mean so much to Morgan. Well, she'd believe it when she saw it.

"Next time, bring this girl Laura with you," Morgan said with a shrewd look at Tony. "I'd like to meet her."

"Yes, bring her," Dixie echoed. She'd like to see her up close, find out what she was studying in college, and make sure she was a good influence.

Tony looked uncomfortable. "She's kinda busy," he mumbled.

Before she could stop herself, Dixie found herself moving forward, wrapping her arms around him. "Come back now." She broke away, embarrassed.

Tony clutched his helmet with both hands, his face red, looking pleased. He gave a half wave, put his helmet on, and stepped out onto the porch.

Dixie cracked the storm door. "Be careful," she yelled as the gasoline motor fired. "See you soon." He waved.

The two stood by the door, listening to the motor's whine grow faint.

Morgan closed the door. "He worked hard. We had a nice talk while we worked."

Dixie slipped her arm around Morgan's waist.

Morgan cleared his throat. "Good news that he's still thinking of going on to college."

Dixie raised her brows.

"I know what you're thinking." He gave her a rueful smile. "We'll take it one step at a time."

⊛⊛

After Tony left, he headed over to the university district. He picked up a pizza, half veggie, half sausage, at the campus hangout, struggling to hold it upright with one arm while he guided the scooter with the other. He stopped in front of Laura's apartment, sprinted up the steps, and rang her bell.

Her roommate Millie opened the door. At first she didn't recognize him, all dressed up. When she did, her face fell.

"Is Laura in?" he asked. He wouldn't get his hopes up. He wouldn't beg.

"I don't know." Millie closed the door. He was about to leave when it opened again. "Hi," Laura said huskily.

Tony's heart lurched. The words came pouring out. "I wanted to say thanks for your advice about the suit, and the hair, and the earring. I got the accounting job. I made things up with my grandpa. He's invited me back to help in the yard. He wants to meet you. I picked up a pizza. Want to go to a movie?"—all said in one breath. "I've missed you. "

She held the door open wider. "Come in." Her face was very serious.

He handed her the pizza, then lugged his scooter up onto the porch and stepped inside the door, feeling like it was the biggest step of his life.

33

Leave It to a Banker

Dixie hurried along the hall, almost colliding with the frail woman who tottered out of the Whispering Pines dining room. She swayed. Dixie steadied her. "Why, Ruth, what's the matter?" The woman's eyes were filled with tears.

"I can't find my husband. He said he'd meet me here."

Dixie took her by the hand. "Let's you and I look together." They twisted through the labyrinth of tables, filled with diners for the noon meal. "I see him." Dixie waved. "See. He's waiting for you." Ruth's husband, his pale face worried, rose. He walked over to his wife and put his arm around her shoulders.

"I thought I'd lost you," Ruth sighed.

Dixie watched him lead her to the table they shared. Poor dear. The maze of tables, which she usually navigated, had overwhelmed her today.

On her way out of the dining room, Dixie heard Wally joking with his tablemate Ed. "Did you hear the one about the 97-year-old man who goes into his doctor's office and says, 'Doc, I want my sex drive lowered?'" Ed said that he hadn't.

Dixie lingered to catch the punch line. "'Sir,' replied the doctor, 'You're 97. Don't you think your sex drive is all in your head?' 'You're damned right it is! That's why I want it lowered!'" Both men chuckled.

Black humor. It helped. In the fourteen years, she'd worked here,

329

something always happened to inspire her or make her smile just when she thought she couldn't take the heartache any more.

She rode the elevator to the second floor and hurried to the auditorium. The gal who usually helped her with the programs was out sick today. Dixie plopped down at the back of the room, glad to stop for a few minutes. She slipped off her high heels and rubbed her feet as the maintenance staff set up chairs for the afternoon show. "Dixie Valentine," an urgent voice announced over the loudspeaker, "please come to the front desk immediately." She stuffed her feet back into shoes. Had something happened to Morgan?

Heart racing, she hurried downstairs. Behind the desk, Florence was making a face. "Dixie, thank goodness. I thought you might be at lunch," she wailed. "Today's program can't make it. The piano player— he's been rushed to the hospital."

Dixie scurried back upstairs to the activities office, pawing through papers, files, videotapes, and packages of all sizes that cluttered the desk and the table beside it. Ah, here was what she was looking for. Next Wednesday's program. She snatched up a DVD.

By 2:30 the hall was filled. Dixie told the crowd of expectant residents and aides, "Jazz Seniors had a sudden emergency. In their place," she paused dramatically, "*Swan Lake*, performed by the New York City Ballet." There were a few groans. Most residents preferred the live programs. "We'll reschedule as soon as possible." Dixie pulled down the large screen at the front of the auditorium. The lights went down. The audience grew quiet. As the music swelled, a few conducted the orchestra from where they sat. Janet, in a shapeless dress, danced in a corner by herself, arms fluttering above her head. Janet rarely spoke, or smiled, except when music played.

Volunteers fanned through the gathered crowd, serving containers of ice cream, feeding those who couldn't manage by themselves.

Dixie took an offered cup of chocolate ice cream, spooning the soft dessert contentedly into her mouth, swept away by the music and the dancing. She had a lot to do, but she stayed to the end.

By three-forty, she was back in the Activities office, cursing herself for taking the time. She had a big article to write for the newsletter, which she'd been putting off.

She lifted a folder from the file drawer. In the last issue of *Pine*

Scents, she'd asked, Which twentieth century development was the most effective in promoting social or economic welfare?

It had stirred up conversation among the residents beyond the usual grumbling about the food, but no one put words on paper. So she'd gone from room to room, gathering answers. She shuffled through the sheaf of papers. Everyone had a different opinion, from transportation to new medications to World War II. How best to honor the beliefs of all and make it an interesting article?

Morgan would be worried if she stayed later. She'd take it home with her. It was only right that he should help her, since the article was his idea—undoubtedly, she smiled to herself, generated by her insistence when he first moved in that the two of them discuss the highlights of each decade. That reminded her. They were only up to the 1950s. Time to revive that project!

She left the office, folder in hand, and doubled back. She almost forgot. She scribbled a note to herself: Try to book the dancing dogs for next Wednesday (to replace *Swan Lake*).

What a beautiful day, she thought when she stepped outside, clear and sunny. The trees were beginning to bud.

There was one more thing to do before she left—visit Effie. Dixie took the walkway to the convalescent/rehab center.

In Effie's room the blinds were drawn. Her bed was draped in shadows. Dixie drew closer. Effie's little elfin face was pinched. She huddled in the bed, her eyes squeezed shut, as if to ward off an attack of wind or rain. "Please stay away," she whispered, her eyes fluttering open.

"Oh, Effie," Dixie sighed.

"I thought you were the nurse." Silence. "I want to die." More silence. "Dixie, please help me."

Dixie took her hand. If only, when the time came, you could just push a button and the lights would go out.

Dixie searched for the nurse in charge of the wing, who sighed, "Effie came back from the hospital Monday with a feeding tube inserted."

"Why?" Dixie raged. "She's a hundred years old. She can't see, can't hear, can't walk."

The nurse grimaced. "The doctor talked her family into it."

Should she call the family and ask them to honor Effie's wishes? They'd probably tell her to mind her own business. In a turmoil, Dixie returned to the room. Effie's eyes were shut tight again as if she wanted no sensation to reach her, nothing to break her resolve to die. She was willing herself down that long, dark road. With the feeding tube inside her, the journey could be hellishly long. "I'll be back, Effie," Dixie whispered.

๑๑๑

Morgan heard the garage doors rumble and the car enter the garage. Dixie was home. Boy, did he have a surprise for her! As soon as she stepped into the family room, he thrust a brochure in her hands. "Take a look," he said excitedly. "Our new windows."

"Morgan," she cried, "you haven't gone ahead and done this without asking me?" Not looking at the brochure, she put it down on the end table.

"A very nice young man stopped by and said he noticed our windows," Morgan stammered, caught by surprise. This was not the response he expected! "The very windows we were talking about just the other day. In fact, he took me around outside the house and pointed out the rotting wood and peeling paint on the frames. I brought him inside, showed him how the darn things won't stay open."

Dixie sat down heavily on the couch, flinging off her coat and kicking off her shoes. Tears rolled down her cheeks.

He sat down beside her and rushed to explain. "I thought it was a sign we ought to invest, seeing as how the fellow magically appeared in our neighborhood. He's doing the neighbor's house, three doors down."

She began to sob. "I had an awful day."

He hugged her, patting her on the back. "You need a pick-me-up," he soothed, handing her his handkerchief. "Dry your eyes. I'll be right back."

He went out to the kitchen and put the teakettle on. Darn. He should have gauged her mood before he sprang it on her. He hurried back to the family room.

Dixie wiped her eyes. "Remember Effie?"

"I have a soft spot for Effie." He sat at her side and pulled her close. "I might not have met you," he said softly, "if you hadn't run into me with her birthday cake." He tried to coax a smile out of her. "With all those gooey red and yellow roses that stuck to my best pants."

"She's in a terrible way." Dixie spoke in a monotone, twisting a tissue in her lap. "She came back from the hospital with a feeding tube. They're keeping her alive against her wishes. She kept asking, 'Dixie, please help me.' I feel so helpless. All I can do is pray for her." She sobbed into Morgan's chest. "Effie loved the readers' program," Dixie hiccupped. "Every day she'd ask to hear her horoscope, Today in History, Ann Landers' advice."

The teakettle whistled feebly. He patted Dixie's back until she murmured, "You better get that." He made two cups of tea and, setting up a tray table in front of the couch, put down the cups and eased himself down beside her.

She touched his shoulder. "I'm so glad I have you. You're so understanding and upbeat."

They drank their tea in silence for a few minutes.

"It drains you," he said, "working there."

"It's not all sad." She managed a watery smile. "A couple of days ago two policemen stopped by. Did the rumors fly!" She spoke in a hushed voice. "Maybe someone in their midst was a bank robber!"

"Yeah," Morgan grinned. "One of the residents hobbling around on a walker."

"Someone else remembered a woman in a wheelchair, last seen taking a young man into her room."

"Debauchery."

"Then there was the ninety-year-old man who couldn't be found when his family came to visit."

"Hmmm. Familiar pattern."

She giggled. "The one that caused the most laughs was the resident who'd come back from a poker game to find a strange woman in his bed. She insisted he was her husband. He denied it and called the guard."

Morgan chuckled. Now she looked better; the worry lines were smoothed out.

"By the end of the day, things returned to normal. The wheelchair-bound woman had been showing her grandson around the place. The 'missing' 90-year-old had eaten dinner with a friend. And the 'strange' woman in the bed was an Alzheimer's patient who'd wandered into the wrong room."

"So why were the police there?" Morgan asked.

"To clarify information about the death of a resident." Her mouth drooped.

"More tea?"

She nodded.

He prepared the tea in the kitchen. When he returned to the family room, Dixie was staring into space, frowning.

"The young man gave me an estimate," he said lightly, to change the subject to a more cheerful one.

She looked blank.

"On the windows." He picked up the brochure. "They aren't brand names, but are double hung, vinyl triple pane. Both sections fold in for easy washing."

"We can't afford them."

"Hey, we received the insurance check. We could use that as a down payment and pay the rest off on time."

Tears rolled down her cheeks again.

"You've been wanting new windows for ten years," Morgan said. "It would be fun to have something new, and it would add to the value of the house."

She stood up, disappeared into the bathroom, and came out with a handful of tissues. "Morgan," she said at last, wiping her eyes. "I have a confession."

Oh, no. He thought they'd both confessed everything.

She went to the corner cupboard in the dining room and took out a Bible. "I hide them here." She pulled out a sheaf of papers and handed them to him.

Credit-card statements. Each was in the thousands. Her name was at the top of each. The dates were current. Stunned, he did a quick tally in his head. "You owe over $20,000 on your credit cards?" he asked. "How did this happen?"

"It built up over the years." She sniffled.

"You only pay the minimum payment each month?" He swallowed hard.

"It's all I can afford," she squeaked. She blew her nose. "Plus the ducts need cleaning. Plus we have another year to pay on the mortgage. And there's Tony. I know you want to help him. We can't possibly afford new windows." She started bawling again. He put his arms around her. He could cash in his CD, use the money to pay off the debt, and buy the new windows too. Gulp. Well, he'd think about it.

☙❧

All through dinner Morgan brooded about what Dixie owed and what could be done. The high interest on her credit card debt just wasn't cost effective. As far as cashing in his CD, it was the only asset they had, besides the house.

After they'd cleared the dinner dishes, Dixie took a file folder from her purse and said with a meek smile, "I brought work home with me tonight. I have to write an article for *Pine Scents*. I thought you might help me."

Well, it might get his mind off the state of their finances.

"After all, it was your bright idea."

"My idea?"

"What was the greatest achievement of the twentieth century? Remember?" She handed him the folder.

"So you used it after all?" He felt a glow as he leafed through the pages.

She placed a pad and pen in front of him. "The deadline is day after tomorrow."

She brought out her old portable electric typewriter, set it on the table across from him, and plugged it in.

"Well," he said, after he'd read through the collected material, "we have votes for transportation, from the horseless carriage to spaceships. Communications—the telephone, television, computers. Medications that lengthen people's lives." He frowned. "I think your retired union worker hit the nail on the head. The two most important developments of the century were World War II because it liberated women from the kitchen and the civil rights movement of the 1960s."

Dixie nodded. "Sounds good to me. Any suggestions for a catchy opening sentence?"

Referring to one of the papers in the folder, he scratched his pen against the pad for a few moments and handed it to Dixie.

"Alice Stokes," she read aloud, "a resident of Whispering Pines Retirement Center, spoke proudly of how she became the first white Rosa Parks. Rosa herself had defied law enforcement officials in 1955 when she refused to leave the white section of an Alabama bus." Dixie nodded eagerly.

He lifted his pen again. A few minutes later, he read. "The seventy-four-year-old resident explained, 'I was so inspired by Rosa Parks, I decided to do something about it. With my eight-year-old at my side, I refused to leave the black section of a New Orleans bus. I told the driver and the policeman he'd summoned that a black woman prepared my family's meals and cared for my children when I was not able to. The officer ordered the bus driver to continue his route. We rode quietly, with the driver glaring back at us, his first white passengers in a black person's seat.'"

Dixie gave him a quick kiss on the top of his head. Then she sat down behind the typewriter. By ten o'clock she'd hammered out, with Morgan's help, the first draft of the article, entitled *The Twentieth Century Bows Out*. And by then he'd figured out a solution to their financial problems.

⚛

That night as they lay in bed, Dixie asked, "What's the cost for the windows?"

He smiled, delighted she'd brought it up. "A little over $7,000 for thirteen windows."

"Did you sign anything?"

"No. I said I'd have to confer with the lady of the house."

She sighed deeply, as if she really ached for those windows.

"I've been thinking," he ventured. "If we take out a home equity loan, we can absorb your credit card debt and"—he paused for effect—"pay for the windows."

"Take out a loan on the house?" she asked, sounding panicked.

"Just listen. The interest rate on the loan will be lower than on your credit cards. And it'll be tax deductible."

"But I'm not making enough to pay taxes," Dixie said.

"Well, over time, those airtight triple panes will save us the cost of the windows in what we pay for heating and air conditioning," he argued.

"Leave it to a banker," she said finally.

"If you want, I'll call tomorrow and set up some appointments for the two of us."

"You're very persuasive." She kissed him. The kiss lingered.

"Hmmm, so are you." He felt her hands on his back. He moved his fingertips over her, stroking lightly. "I love you," he said. "Me too," she murmured. He was learning to please her. She was learning to please him.

They fell asleep, their arms wrapped around each other.

Morgan woke up at two. He thought about his stormy relationships in the past. The athleticism, the thrashing about, the exultant cries. There'd been too much to drink, and flirting and jealousy were required to fuel the fires.

He'd never have the ardor he had in his younger days. Now it was about tenderness. Love with Dixie was deeper, quieter, and a little more generous than it had been with his ex-wife Barbara. Or the others.

A romantic evening with Barbara had been to go to an expensive restaurant where she could be seen in her gowns and jewels. For Dixie and him it was having popcorn and a black Russian while they watched reruns of Lawrence Welk.

Dixie always wanted him to dance with her when the people on the screen danced to Welk's champagne music. He always poo-pooed her. Next time she asked, he decided, he *would* get up and dance.

He laughed to himself. Who'd ever believe the best things that ever happened to him happened at age 90?

34

A Very Special Day

Morgan sat on the bed watching Dixie skitter around the room. She snatched her dress from the closet, a bright green and gold outfit bought especially for today. "What if she hates us?" she moaned.

"You mean the way all our friends hate us?" Morgan laughed.

She wriggled into the dress, smoothing it down with fluttering hands, sighing as if she was going to a funeral instead of hosting a festive meal. Another trip to the closet produced a pair of shiny brown high heels, which she shoehorned on. Her feet would be killing her before the day was over, but he didn't dare say a word.

Her hand hovered over her array of wigs. She plucked up the blonde wig and jammed it on, fussing with it for several minutes before she tore it off and donned the auburn one, then the brown one.

"You'd look good with a wet dishcloth on your head," he murmured, trying to sound amiable. She was making him as nervous as she was. He came up behind her, nuzzling her behind her ear, hoping to calm her down.

She squirmed out of his arms. "I hope Tony's told her the whole truth." She shot him a meaningful look as if to say, *even though you didn't level with me at first*. She adjusted the brown wig, then brushed the hair into soft waves that framed her face. She tried on earrings, pair after pair, settling at last on large gold circles. "What if she's a fly-by-night?"

"Well, you met her. You said she seemed decent, that it was Tony who was leading *her* down the garden path."

"The more I think about it . . ." Dixie pulled a long face. The door-bell rang. Morgan left the bedroom and hurried down the hall, Dixie's voice floating after him down the stairs, ". . . the more I think Laura may have worn too much lipstick. Her hair might have been too brassy."

Why did she always get so dramatic? He peeked through the long panel of glass beside the front door, half expecting, after Dixie's out-burst, to see a blowsy barmaid. The girl caught him peeking and gave him a mischievous smile. She looked pretty normal to him. He flung open the door and pushed the storm door wide.

"Hi, Grandpa." Tony's face was a mask of studied nonchalance. "Laura Winters."

Laura held out her hand.

Morgan shook it. "A real pleasure." She's a little thing, he thought, hardly comes up to his shoulder. Her eyes were dazzlingly blue, her complexion creamy. "Where's the scooter?" he asked Tony.

"At Laura's. We caught the bus."

Just as the two stepped inside, Dixie, dressed to the nines, made up to the gills, arrived breathless at the bottom of the stairs. Jiggs followed, his tail wagging happily.

"Hi, Mrs. Valentine, you remember Laura?" Tony smiled cautiously.

No wonder he seemed guarded, Morgan thought. Dixie looked ready to hit the warpath. She'd added more rouge after he left the bed-room. She'd fixed up her eyes so they looked almost as vibrant as Laura's. He felt sloppy in his paint-smeared work clothes, but he and Tony had unfinished work in the yard.

"I certainly do. I understand you're in college," Dixie said, with a big smile.

Morgan tensed, waiting for the answer.

Laura nodded. "Social work."

Dixie's eyes shone. Okay, off to a good start. He was about to say, "Sensible choice. Always be a demand for social workers," when Dixie rat-a-tat-tatted without taking a breath, "Your folks live around here? When will you graduate? Do you have brothers and sisters?"

"Why don't we sit down?" Morgan slid in when Dixie paused for breath.

"Thanks for inviting me, Mrs. Valentine." Laura sprang forward and kissed Dixie on the cheek.

Dixie was startled momentarily into silence.

Laura pressed a small, wrapped package into Dixie's hands. "I hope you like fudge. It's homemade."

"Hi, Jiggs." Tony bent down to scratch Jiggs' ears.

"What a darling little dog," Laura said.

"Let me hang up your jackets," Dixie said, regaining her momentum. "This weather, up one day and down the next. Hardly seems like May. Iced tea? Cookies?" she asked after everyone was seated in the family room.

Morgan admired Laura's tiny waist as she followed Dixie into the kitchen. He bet he could reach around it with both hands.

Tony perched himself on the couch, about to burst the buttons on that white shirt of his. He grinned conspiratorially. "What do you think, Grandpa?"

"Quite an eyeful," he winked. "How's the job?"

"I start working five days a week in June." He made a face. "Sitting at a desk all day."

"My first job, I dug ditches. I was grateful for the work. And I had a college degree." Watch it, don't get preachy, Morgan told himself. "Don't worry. You'll settle in."

Dixie swayed in with a tray of iced tea. Laura followed with a plate of butterscotch cookies.

Before the snack was finished, Dixie and Laura had admired each other's outfits, Dixie had told Laura and Tony to call her Dixie, and Morgan was beginning to relax. "Well, should we get started?" Morgan asked Tony, who'd grabbed up the last cookie. "Your work clothes are in the spare-room closet." He smiled at Laura. "He brought his own duds after slopping around in mine."

Munching on his cookie, Tony headed toward the stairs. Morgan waited for Dixie to tell him not to drop crumbs all over the house, but when he glanced her way she was looking fondly at Tony's retreating figure.

"Come on outside and take a look?" Morgan motioned Laura.

She followed him through the sliding-glass door. "What a beautiful yard. It's so big."

Morgan, grinning, nodded. "Last time Tony mowed it, back and front.

Looks like it's ready to be mowed again." He pointed. "See those rose bushes—all pruned and ready to bloom? They were our first project."

Dixie, standing in the doorway, ventured outside. "We'll have azaleas, hollyhocks, and rhododenrons up here by the house," she said. "Come back when the yard is in its full glory."

"I'd love to," Laura said.

Dixie shivered, hugging herself. "Looks like we lost our sun."

Morgan smiled to himself. Dixie looked like a filly at the start gate, barely able to contain herself, eager to get Laura to herself to resume the questioning. "Tell Tony to meet me in the garage." Morgan headed around to the front of the house.

"Dinner's at four," Dixie called out.

᎒Ꮭᎆ

As soon as Tony was out the front door, Dixie leaned forward in her chair, uncertain how to proceed. She didn't want to seem nosy, but she needed to be sure that Laura knew everything she needed to know about Tony.

"I feel very honored you asked me here," Laura said haltingly. "Tony's told me how much he likes to work outside with his grandpa . . . to come here for dinner."

Well, Tony had only been by twice. Once she served butterscotch pie. Two weeks ago she baked a ham. She and Morgan weren't letting themselves count on him, just because he had his work clothes hanging in the spare-room closet. "He seems to be settling down," Dixie said carefully. "He's had quite a time these last months." She raised her brows, leaving space for Laura to fill in whatever she wanted.

Laura pressed her lips together and sighed. "He told me." She looked as if she wanted to say more but didn't want to be disloyal.

"You know I'm not his grandmother, I suppose?"

Laura gave her a rueful smile. "And that he's not in college. Yet. And that I'm two years older than he is." She rolled her eyes.

Dixie smiled briefly, acknowledging her little jest, holding her glance.

Laura looked away, swallowed hard. "He told me about his scrapes with the law. Ever since he was 14. That he and his friend Eddie wrecked your place." She shook her head slowly. "It must have been a terrible time for everyone."

"It was," Dixie said. The girl seemed sensible—just what Tony needed.

"Truthfully," Laura spoke softly, almost to herself, "I wasn't sure I'd see him again. For a month I thought it over. Then he came by." Her eyes grew warm. "All dressed up in a suit. I'd never seen him in a suit. He told me about his new job, and that he'd set things straight with you two." Now her eyes were questioning.

"That he did."

Laura wrinkled her nose, gave a shrug.

She was attractive, Dixie thought. She wouldn't have trouble getting college boys her own age. A lot of girls would have decided Tony's future was too uncertain.

The girl's face was stern. "I told him he couldn't let me down again." She blushed. "My dad was the same way, my mom told me, kind of a screw—a goof-up when he was a kid. He turned out to be a wonderful, responsible man. I loved him very much. So did my mom." Her eyes filled. "He's dead now."

"I'm sorry." Dixie patted her shoulder. "It's been forty years since I lost my son, but I miss him every day. What happened to your dad?"

"Cancer. He only lived six months." Her lower lip trembled. "What about your son?"

"He went in for minor surgery. His ears were too big and the kids laughed at him. He died on the operating table. He was seven," she wailed, no longer able to control herself.

"Oh, Dixie." Tears rolled down Laura's cheeks.

Dixie disappeared into the bathroom, emerged with a box of tissues. As the two blotted their eyes, Dixie sniffled, "Would you like to see the rest of the house?"

"I'd love it." Laura blew her nose.

Dixie gave her the grand tour, starting upstairs. "This is my room. And Morgan's." She stole a look at the girl, wondering if she was shocked that Morgan and she, unmarried, shared the bedroom. Laura's face was inscrutable.

Dixie picked up the photo of Ronnie. "My son."

"He's—he was adorable." Laura's eyes swam with sympathy.

"Don't let's get started again," Dixie said with a mournful laugh. She led Laura into the master bath.

"Is that a whirlpool tub?"

Dixie nodded, on the brink of saying, *built for two.* But she didn't need to.

"Cool," Laura said with a merry smile.

When they reached the spare room, Dixie burst out, "I almost forgot. My new windows! I have to brag. They were just put in this week." She worked the locks. "And they open like a dream." She pushed the window open. Below, Tony mowed the grass while Morgan, off to the side, pruned shrubs. A feeling of contentment spread over her.

Dixie turned back to Laura, her hand on her chest. "You must think I'm a numbskull, going on about windows. I've only wanted them for ten years!"

"Your home is beautiful. You're proud of it, and you should be."

Dixie glowed.

Downstairs in the dining room, after admiring Grandma Ruby's corner cupboard, Laura squealed, "What a beautiful collection of dolls!"

Dixie opened the glass-paneled door. "Go ahead. Pick them up if you want."

Laura did, one by one, exclaiming over each as Dixie related its history.

She seemed interested, not just pretending, so Dixie showed her the pigs and the pincushions, saving the Bibles for last. Was she religious? It would be almost too much to ask for.

"Awesome." Laura thumbed reverently through the pages of the Bibles.

Dixie took a chance. "Maybe you and Tony would like to go to church with us tomorrow."

"Oh," Laura stammered, "that's very nice of you." She sighed heavily, as if disappointed. "We've been studying in the library on Sundays."

Maybe Laura wasn't Protestant. "It's a Presbyterian church. We could go to the early service."

Laura chewed her lip. "I guess we could study after. Let me ask Tony."

Dixie told herself not to push it. The oven timer rang. She looked at her watch. "Almost four," she said, surprised. She hurried into the kitchen, lifted the beef roast out of the oven and checked the meat thermometer. "Why don't you dish up the salad? It's in the fridge." She took down the salad bowls from the cupboard. "I'll tell the boys."

She looked out the kitchen window. No sign of Morgan and Tony. She went to the front door and opened it. The two were working up by the porch, Tony rearranging the bricks that lined the flowerbed, Morgan mixing fertilizer. The sun had totally disappeared. The sky looked dark and menacing. The temperature must have dropped twenty degrees. "You'll catch cold in those thin sweaters." The two glanced up briefly and went back to work. "Dinner's almost on the table," she said. Morgan looked tired. She was glad Tony was helping. She just hoped Morgan didn't try to keep up with him. "Get in here, you two, and get your hands washed."

৵৵

As Dixie murmured the blessing, Morgan peeked from under his lids. Across the table, Tony stared into space, waiting out the prayer. Laura's head was bowed. Her eyes fluttered open. She nudged Tony with her elbow, signaling him to bow his head. His eyes, mischievous, tender, locked into hers.

Guess that's what's known as a smoldering glance, Morgan chuckled to himself.

The two kids' eyes snapped shut just in time for Dixie's *Amen*, echoed by all.

Morgan carved the roast and put a slice of beef on everyone's plate. The food was passed and plates piled high, Tony's mound of mashed potatoes three times the size of anyone else's.

When Dixie left the dining room to take the garlic bread from the oven, Morgan sneaked a tender morsel of meat down to Jiggs and felt his furry tongue lick his fingers. Tony, grinning, caught Morgan in the act, and with a furtive glance toward the kitchen, started to feed Jiggs too.

Morgan whispered, "Keep the pieces small. He only has four teeth," just as Dixie returned with the steaming hot bread and set it on the table.

Jiggs had a grand time scurrying back and forth between the two, begging, until one or the other gave in.

Dixie would hit the ceiling if Jiggs upchucked all over the floor. Morgan was about to signal the boy to cool it when Dixie suddenly peered under the table. "Jiggs, you little beggar," she exploded. "Get out from under there." Jiggs scampered out, toenails clicking, and ran into the family room.

Morgan and Tony exchanged guilty smiles.

As they finished second helpings, Dixie asked Laura what she planned to do with her social-work degree.

As Laura expounded on all the possibilities, Dixie clucked and murmured. Morgan thought she looked a little envious of the limitless potential for women these days, so when there was opening, he offered, "Dixie works at a retirement center. She even has a program named after her."

"Really?" Laura looked impressed.

"The Dixie Valentine fund," Morgan said proudly. "For the sight-impaired."

"Is it hard, working there?" Laura's eyes were concerned. "I mean, you get so attached, and then people die."

"Or people live longer than they're meant to," Dixie said somberly.

Uh-oh, Morgan thought, Dixie's thinking of Effie. She looks about to cry. He switched the topic. "Where are you from, Laura?"

She shook her head. Her dimple flickered. "Toledo now. I was born in Kenton. Bet you never heard of it. A small farming town, about nine thousand population."

"I've not only heard of Kenton. I visited. In 1936." Morgan pushed back in his chair, grinning broadly. "I had some business to transact with the loan officer in our bank branch there. You see, the Kenton Hardware Company, which employed half the town at that time, was moving toward bankruptcy. You kids ever hear of Gene Autry? America's favorite singing cowboy?"

"No," Laura said.

"Movies about cowboys were really popular back in the thirties and Gene Autry was a big Hollywood star." Good. The kids now looked properly impressed. "He stopped at the Kenton Hardware Company, almost accidentally, with plans for a cowboy outfit, replete with lariat, gun, and holster in his pocket. A deal was made and the firm started producing the Autry six-shooter." He chuckled. "It turned out to be the most popular toy gun in the nation's history. Autry not only saved the company, he saved the town of Kenton, and the loan we'd made to the Kenton Hardware was paid back in full."

"I never heard the story. I'll have to remember to tell it to Mom."

"The company was so grateful that when Autry died in 1998, employees stopped their machines to pay silent tribute. He was 91. Just a year older than me."

"You're 90?" Laura asked. "You don't look it."

"I was born in 1910."

Tony whistled. Morgan looked at him askance.

"You've seen a lot of changes," Laura ventured.

"You kids today really have it soft." Morgan smiled. "Growing up, we had no television or computers."

"But we had radio," Dixie piped in. "We always knew when Bob Hope started his radio program. Our dog Shep, lying outside by the chimney, would bark, get up, and wag his tail!"

"Bob Hope," Tony nodded. "I've heard of him."

"Remember those old shows?" Dixie asked Morgan. "'Jack Benny,' 'Fibber McGee and Molly.' Nowadays, no one knows what you're talking about when you apologize for a 'Fibber McGee's closet.'"

Laura and Tony shook their heads.

We should stop this right now, Morgan thought. The kids would soon get bored. But Dixie was having so much fun remembering.

"When Fibber McGee's closet door was opened, the crash of the junk falling out was hilarious," Dixie chortled, her head thrown back, her face wreathed in smiles. "Every program we waited to hear that crash."

The kids smiled politely.

"We loved 'Burns & Allen,' 'The Shadow' . . ." Dixie's voice trailed away as if she realized she was losing her audience.

"Who knows what evil lurks in the hearts of men?" Morgan gave a sinister laugh. "The Shadow knows." Laura giggled. Tony looked astounded.

Dixie, revived, squeaked in a high-pitched voice, "Whatcha doin,' Mister?"

"Baby Snooks?" Morgan asked.

Dixie shook her head. "I think she was a character on 'The Great Gildersleeve.'"

"I love the old movies," Laura chimed in, "*Random Harvest, Gaslight, The Maltese Falcon* . . ."

"Me too," Dixie agreed. "I just hate all the violence and sex in the movies now."

"I like shows with action," Tony complained.

"Anything goes today," Dixie said. "When my mom met my dad at Painter Creek Grange, they played drop the handkerchief, can you believe it? Now kids of 17 have cars and do things we never heard of."

Morgan looked over at Tony and saw him blush. "Everything looked better in black and white, and everything turned out right." Morgan stood, clearing plates from the table. Laura and Tony started to help.

"Sit, sit," Dixie said. "We'll leave the dishes. Let's have dessert and coffee, and a piece of Laura's fudge in the family room. Let me feed Jiggs first."

At the mention of his name, Jiggs bounded eagerly into the kitchen and danced around under Dixie's feet as she added bits of meat and gravy to his dog food. She put his bowl on the floor, but he sniffed contemptuously and walked away. She threw a withering glance at Morgan and Tony. "I hope he doesn't get sick."

After dessert, Tony and Laura rose to leave. They were in their coats, standing by the front door, when Dixie asked, "Are we going to see you two tomorrow morning?"

Tony did a double take. "Tomorrow morning?"

Surely Dixie hadn't—Before Morgan could finish the thought, Laura finished it for him. "Dixie's invited us to church." She smiled brightly at Tony.

Fast work. Morgan struggled to keep a straight face.

"Oh," Tony gulped, "I thought we were going to study."

"We could study after. I mean, what do you think?"

"If you want to," he said slowly, "it's okay with me."

"We'll pick you up in the car," Dixie offered, throwing Morgan a triumphant look. "About eight-thirty." She asked for Laura's address and phone number. "And then we can swing by the Y for Tony."

"In that case," Morgan said, "we'd better be at Laura's at eight-fifteen."

"Look, it'll be simpler," Tony said, offhand, "pick us both up at Laura's," adding quickly, "I'll come over to her place on the scooter tomorrow morning."

"You'll have to get up awfully early," Laura frowned.

Tony shrugged, his face turning pink.

Morgan suppressed a smile. He could almost read Tony's thoughts.

ණ

"Thanks for coming," Tony said as he and Laura stepped off the front porch.

"It was fun."

He turned her around to face him and kissed her. She started to pull away. He held her tighter, slipping his hands under her jacket. "You feel good."

"So do you," she murmured, kissing him back. She took his hand

and pulled him along the sidewalk. "Do you mind about church? Getting up so early?" They turned up the street toward the shopping center.

"Nah." Could he hope? No, it was too much to hope she'd let him stay the night. He knew Millie, who shared Laura's bedroom, was away for the weekend.

She took his arm. "We always went to church when I was younger."

"I'll try to stay awake," he grinned. "You really liked them?"

"They're adorable. She's feisty. She says what she thinks. Your grandpa sits there, taking everything in, his eyes twinkling. And Jiggs, he's the lord of the manor." She giggled. "Dixie took me on a tour of the house. They sleep in the same bed. They have a whirlpool tub built for two. They rock, they really do."

"Yeah." He laughed, feeling as if he could conquer the world.

She shivered. "That wind is cold." They reached the bus stop.

"You can see your breath tonight." He put his arm around her and held her close until the bus came.

⚜

Morgan paused from loading the dishwasher. He patted himself on the stomach, letting out a discreet belch. "Wonderful dinner," he said to Dixie, who stood beside him in her stocking feet rinsing off the dinner dishes. "The only thing that would have made it better," he pronounced, "would have been a cold bottle of beer." He thought about chiding Dixie for the oversight and changed his mind. "I wish I'd remembered to put it on our grocery list." He smiled at his diplomacy.

Dixie smiled back. "You're starting to operate a little more smoothly."

"So's Tony," Morgan chuckled. "You pulled a fast one."

Dixie looked innocent. "I don't know what you mean."

"Trapping them into church."

"Laura wanted to come," Dixie said indignantly. "If you could have seen the way she looked at my Bibles."

Not something to joke about, he decided. "Nice girl."

She filled a pan with sudsy water and put in her good silver to wash by hand. "Did we monopolize the conversation?" she worried.

"Well, their eyes glazed over when you went into all those old radio shows." Morgan took down a dishtowel.

"You were no help. With your rendition of The Shadow!" She giggled.

He picked up spoons from the rinse water, drying off each one, and placing it carefully in the silver chest. "So, you and Laura have a good talk?"

"I feel like I've known her all my life." As they finished up the dishes, she told him the ups and downs of Laura's relationship with Tony.

☙

The place was dark. There was no TV on for a change. "Where are Carla and Kate?" Tony asked.

"On dates."

Hope fluttered in his chest. "Nice to have the place to ourselves." When an invitation to stay didn't come, he sighed, "I guess I better go."

"Tomorrow will be an early day." She was facing him. A field of electricity danced between them. Should he make a move? His lips brushed hers, then lingered. Was she wavering? No such luck. He broke away and sauntered over to his scooter, parked in her entry hall, every nerve in his body tingling. As he grabbed the handlebars, she blurted out, "Want to stay? You can have the couch. It's lumpy. Carla and Kate may wake you up when they come in."

He slipped out of his jacket, trying to hide his exultation. "Better than schlepping to the Y tonight and getting back here at the crack of dawn tomorrow." He said a silent thanks to Dixie for inviting them to early church.

They settled on the couch in front of the TV, each with a beer. Laura did some channel surfing. "*Gilda*," she said. "Want to watch?"

"Sure." Tony took a slug of beer, sliding an arm around Laura. "Sexy lady." The TV screen flickered. Rita Hayworth belted out, "Put the Blame on Mame." He set his bottle on the coffee table and nuzzled Laura's ear, blowing in it softly.

With a shiver, she turned to him and kissed him. He felt her breasts against his chest. Before he knew it, he was touching them. She didn't pull away. She must like it as much as he did. He unbuttoned her blouse. She slid out of it and helped him unfasten her bra. Her skin was silky and smooth.

☙

"Should have had decaf," Dixie said when she and Morgan went upstairs, hand in hand, after watching the late news. "Let go of me," she warned, as Morgan followed her into the bathroom, "or I'll never be able to get my teeth cleaned."

He kissed her on the cheek. "We're getting to act like an old married couple," he remarked as she removed her partial denture and placed it in a glass of water. She smiled slightly and took off her wig. He used the commode. She cold-creamed her face and with a tissue removed the coloring from her eyes.

In bed, they snuggled together. He realized the room had turned quite cool and reached down to pull another blanket over them. "Your feet are freezing," he said. "What's with this weather? It's May, for heaven's sake." He padded into the hall to see if he could coax the gas furnace to send some heat their way. "Hold your hand in front of the register and tell me if it's sending out cold air."

"It's warm as toast."

He felt a cold draft coming from the spare room. "Hey," he called, "this window is wide open."

"I forgot. I was showing Laura . . ."

Morgan closed the window, admiring the way it slid down so smoothly, settling in with a firm click. He locked it.

"Get in here," Dixie called, "and wrap yourself around my back."

He scrambled into bed and warmed his feet against hers. The couple said "good night, sleep tight, don't let the bedbugs bite," and went to sleep curled against each other.

Morgan roused himself when he heard Jiggs climb onto the bed and flung him a knitted throw to burrow under.

Morgan tossed and turned. Was it the coffee? he wondered at one point. Sheets were torn from under the mattress as he—or was it Dixie?—fought unknown demons. Morgan thought he heard Dixie cry out and slap him sharply on the shoulder. "Wake up," she commanded.

"Just call me when it's time to dress for church," he heard himself say.

He never heard the church bells ring. He didn't hear the noisy birds. He didn't hear the phone, the doorbell, or the crash of breaking glass.

BOOK VI

THE
ACCIDENT

35

Panic

Tony woke up happy and then remembered why. He raised up on his elbow, looking at her. He touched her soft cheek and trailed his fingers down to the hollow of her throat. She stirred and opened her eyes.

Her blonde hair fanned out over the pillow. "You look like sunshine, the way your hair is all spread out."

Laura stretched and gave him a dreamy smile. "Standing on end, you mean." She turned into him, her face against his chest. "I've never gone all the way before," she murmured.

He wanted her to think he was worldly, but he let it slip, "Me neither." He slid his arms around her.

After awhile, she asked, "What time is it?"

He searched for a clock on the stand beside him, then thought of his watch. Yep, still on his wrist. Somehow it survived all the acrobatics of last night. Yikes, they'd overslept. "Eight o'clock."

She sat up as if electrified, holding a sheet over her breasts. "They'll be here in thirty minutes. Want to take a shower first?"

He sprang out of bed. "Right." Suddenly he felt shy, standing bare-assed in the middle of her bedroom, her mischievous eyes looking him over. He pulled the blanket off the bed and wrapped it around his waist.

She held her finger to her lips.

"Yeah," he whispered. He picked up his shirt, pants, and underwear strewn over the floor. He opened the bedroom door and peeked out. No sign of Kate or Carla. He tiptoed into the bathroom.

He showered and dressed, and gargled with the mouthwash he found in the cabinet.

He met Laura in her bathrobe, just as he stepped out the door. He hugged her.

"You smell good," she said, wriggling free. "We have ten minutes."

At eight-thirty on the dot, they sat in her living room, grinning at each other, waiting for Morgan and Dixie. At eight-forty, Laura said, "That's funny. Dixie was so insistent we go with them. They must be running late." At eight-forty-five, Tony rang their house. "No answer. Maybe—you think they're on the way?" he asked.

"I think maybe something's wrong."

Kate ambled out of the bedroom she shared with Carla, rubbing her eyes. "Oh, hi," she said sleepily. "What's up?"

"Grandpa and Dixie—" Tony struggled into his coat.

Laura yelled back to Kate as they ran out the door, "If they call, tell them we're on the way to their place."

They managed to grab a cab. When they arrived at the house, it was after nine-thirty. "Ring the bell," Tony said to Laura. He looked in the garage. "Both cars are here." He opened the storm door, tried the inside door. Locked. He pounded on it. He peered through the narrow window alongside the door. A shape lay on the floor. It looked like—it was. "Jiggs." He tapped the window loudly with his knuckle. He rapped again, harder. "He isn't moving."

Tony felt ready to jump out of his skin. Laura yelped, "Does someone, a neighbor, have a key?"

He suddenly spotted the bricks that edged the flowerbed, snatched one up, and shattered the glass panel. Jiggs didn't stir. Tony reached through, unlocked the door, and burst in, bellowing, "Grandpa, Dixie!"

He ran into the kitchen. "Grandpa." He quickly checked the family room and the dining room—empty. He wheeled around and came back down the hall toward the front door, where Laura was kneeling beside Jiggs.

Tony dashed up the stairs, screaming, "Morgan! Dixie!" He found them in their bed, looking as if they were asleep. The room smelled sour. Vomit stained his grandpa's pillow. "Call 911," he yelled down to Laura. It was hot as hell up there. He opened all the windows.

☙

Dixie heard herself mumble, "It's all a blur." Her head hurt too much to talk. Who was that, standing over her? It looked like Tony. What would he be doing in their bedroom? She fell asleep and woke up to hear Morgan yell out, "Why am I here? Did the bull throw me?"

He thinks he's a rodeo cowboy. Her head felt stuffed with cotton. "That's the first time you ever had a question about who was throwing the bull," she joked. Or thought she did. Her voice sounded so far away. Where was Morgan? She reached for him. He wasn't in his usual place, next to her in bed. She raised up to look. She felt a wave of dizziness. Her head was splitting.

Why, there he was, on a cot beside her. She was on a cot too. This wasn't their bedroom.

Morgan looked like an alien, his angry eyes peering at her over a mask that fit so tightly over his nose and mouth it made a deep crease in his cheeks. He worried with the mask, snapping the elastic band that held it in place. He finally managed to pull it off.

"Did you do it intentionally or was it an accident?" she asked. What a silly thing to say.

"What?" he answered.

"That we wound up here." Why did her voice sound so faint? She put her hand to her face. She too wore a mask.

"What did I do?" he demanded. "Why are we—wherever we are?"

Dixie felt nauseated. She lowered her head and found herself thinking about the little dog. Was it possible? Of course it wasn't! "What happened to Jiggs?" she cried out. The fog in her brain cleared a little. She remembered all the people crowded into their bedroom. The emergency squad, the police. Firemen too. Who else? Pauline. Tony and Laura. What did they say about Jiggs? Something bad had happened. She needed to get up and find out about Jiggs. Her head was so heavy. Her eyes too. She couldn't hold them open.

She'd rather sleep than think.

❦

On the cot beside her, Morgan grumbled, "My head hurts! I have the right to know what happened to me." He looked over at Dixie. Her eyes were closed. She wasn't listening. "Where am I?" he yelled at the ceiling.

"Well, young man," a female voice said, "I see you've pulled off your oxygen."

"It hurts my head," he complained.

She clamped the mask back on. "It's time for you to go to bed." She wheeled him down a hall.

He pried up a corner of the mask. "Hold on," he ordered. "I want to sleep in the same room with Dixie. She needs me."

"Oh, are you two married?" she asked, maneuvering him into an elevator.

"No." The doors closed.

"Our rules forbid us placing persons of the opposite sex in the same room," she said.

The next thing he knew, he was bouncing up and down. Was he in a wheelbarrow? Where were they taking him?

"We'll arrange for you two to talk from adjoining cots tomorrow, if you wish."

He tried to raise up. He'd find Dixie somehow. Hands were on his chest, pushing him down. Morgan felt a prickly stab in the fleshy part of his shoulder. "I want Dixie." His voiced sounded as if it came from deep inside a well. Hands tucked him under the covers. He couldn't argue anymore.

36

The Heroes

Needles pierced his eyes. Morgan opened them, squinting. It was too bright in here. Where was she? "Dixie!" he tried to yell. His mouth was full of mush. *This damn thing covering his face!* He tore it off and threw it on the floor. "Why are we here?" he demanded. Tiny men with hatchets seemed to be chop, chop, chopping inside his head. "Have we been thrown out of our home? Have our doctors been called? Should we contact the police? Our congressmen? The mayor?" No one knew anything, or refused to talk if they did. He fell asleep.

⚭

Dixie felt a gentle shake. She opened her eyes. A nurse was bending over her, slipping off the tight-fitting mask. "Am I better?" Dixie croaked. Her voice was rough as sandpaper.

Something niggled at the edge of her brain, something she wanted to remember.

The woman's eyes crinkled. She nodded. "I'll just need to take your blood pressure." She wound the cuff around Dixie's arm and squeezed the bulb. "Good," she purred. "Almost normal."

Dixie became aware of angry voices in the hall. "What's all the ruckus?" she asked the nurse, who peeked out the door. "Whatever it is, it's heading this way," she said as she left the room.

The voices grew nearer. "You aren't to get out of bed without help, you understand?"

"All I wanted to do," another voice replied meekly, "was to see my friend."

Why, it was Morgan, Dixie realized.

"I want her to tell me why we're in the hospital."

"You already know that," the woman said. "The doctor told you."

"I forgot," Morgan replied timidly. The voices were in the room now.

A short, stocky woman in a blue uniform roughly moved the chair and bedside table aside and pushed a wheelchair containing Morgan up to the edge of Dixie's bed. "Here we are," the woman announced, putting her hands on her hips. "You ask her yourself," she ordered Morgan.

A smile lurched onto Morgan's face. Dixie reached over and touched his arm. He wasn't wearing a mask either. He must be better too.

"Why are we in the hospital?" he asked.

She cleared her throat to get rid of the frog. "Don't you remember?" She felt irritated that he didn't. "We were overcome in our sleep by carbon monoxide."

"How could that happen?" he demanded truculently. "The last thing I remember was snuggling up to you in bed."

Was he saying it was her fault? He'd been the one to turn up the furnace. "I wish you'd not accuse me of things for which I'm not to blame," she flared.

"You always jump to conclusions."

"You're not so perfect yourself, you know."

"That's news to me," he retorted. "I thought I did everything right."

"Well, you don't," Dixie shot back. "You always read the newspaper at the table. You leave the bathroom in a mess. You never put your clothes away." She was babbling about old resentments. What was wrong with her? Her brain felt short-circuited.

"You have faults too," he replied sullenly. "You order me around like I'm your servant. You never ask me what I want. You treat me like I'll break, like I'm some kind of . . ." He mumbled incoherently.

What was that? Did he really say, *you treat me like I'm some kind of banana*? The nurse was looking at them as if they were both bananas.

Morgan was still muttering when a man in a white coat appeared. "Oh, here you are, Mr. Morgan," he said. "I couldn't find you in your room." He fixed his face in a smile, glancing from one to the other. "We need to keep you both for another day or so for observation. You've responded nicely to the humidified oxygen. We plan to keep you on oxygen awhile longer, Mr. Morgan. We'll use the nasal cannula, since you say the mask hurts your head." He peered at Morgan, then Dixie, his eyes concerned. "You do know why you're here?"

"Of course," Morgan replied. "Carbon monoxide."

Well, Dixie thought, it had finally sunk in.

She suddenly remembered what she'd been trying to think of. "What happened to Jiggs?" she blurted out. How could she have forgotten about Jiggs?

The doctor, who was leaving, threw her a confused look, as if he thought Jiggs was Morgan's name.

"We need to get you hooked up again," the nurse said, wheeling her patient out of the room.

Morgan twisted around to look at Dixie.

"Is Jiggs alive or dead?" Dixie wailed.

"I don't know." Morgan's voice, mournful, echoed from the hall.

She had to call someone and find out.

Vera. Vera would know everything. She always did.

She lifted up the phone to dial. She couldn't remember Vera's number. What was the matter with her? That number was etched in her brain.

⊙╪⊙

Morgan looked askance at the young man in the light-blue shirt. Why was he here?

"Hi, Grandpa," Tony said. "I've been worrying about you. I called the hospital but they didn't tell me very much. Laura's with Dixie."

"She is? Where *is* Dixie?" He pulled out the tubes stuck in his nose. They stuffed him up and made his voice sound funny.

"Dixie's down the hall." Tony gave him a curious look. "Grandpa, should you be taking out your oxygen?"

"It's easier to talk."

"We wanted to tell you the good news. Jiggs is doing fine. He's still at the vet but better."

"I'm glad to hear it," Morgan said. "What exactly happened at our house?"

"You were supposed to pick us up for church. Remember?"

Morgan thought hard and finally nodded.

"When you didn't come by, we rushed over to your place and found Jiggs stretched out by the front door as if he'd been trying to get out to find help. I broke the glass and ran in. Laura called 911."

"You broke the window?" Now that made him upset.

"We got it fixed."

"Do I owe you some money?"

"Pauline, your neighbor. She took care of it."

"Well, that's nice."

"She came over when she saw the emergency squad, the police, and the firemen pull up in your drive." He gave Morgan a worried look. "That reminds me. The fire department said you should have the furnace checked."

He wasn't following all these details very well.

"They think that's what caused it," Tony said.

Morgan nodded uncertainly. Now he'd lost track of what they'd been talking about.

"The build-up of carbon monoxide."

Strands of information seemed to hang at the edge of his brain, but bobbled out of reach when he tried to grab hold. He frowned, concentrating. "You saved our lives," he said. "Thank you."

Tony replied fervently, "We were lucky we got there in time. You couldn't have lasted much longer."

Morgan rubbed his forehead and complained, "Everything is so fuzzy. How it happened keeps slipping away."

"Well," Tony said, "you were upstairs. The fumes were probably denser than on the ground floor where Jiggs was found. He was getting some air from under the door. And," he stumbled, "you both looked pretty bad when I saw you, very pale and all. The EMT men slapped you to get you awake. Dixie woke up on her own from all the noise. Everyone was clomping around in the room."

"Sounds like a TV show."

Tony nodded, his eyes troubled. "It was intense. I rode along with you and Dixie to the emergency room. Laura took Jiggs to the animal hospital."

"I seem to remember in bits and pieces, and then forget again." If his head would stop hurting, it would help.

"Maybe you better put your oxygen on again." He tried to help him.

"I'll do it," Morgan said irritably, his fingers fumbling with the plastic tubing.

Tony patted him gingerly on the shoulder. "I have to go, Grandpa. I have to get back to work. Laura has classes this afternoon."

"Where did you say Laura was?"

"With Dixie. In Dixie's room. We'll see you later." He smiled an uneasy smile. "I'm glad you're better."

☙❧

When Tony's gangly figure appeared in the doorway, his face so serious, his dark hair drooping over his forehead, he looked like family to Dixie. She sat up straighter in the bed. "Laura just told me everything." She held her hands out to him. "You saved our lives. You're a hero." She turned to Laura. "Both of you are heroes."

Tony shyly took Dixie's outstretched hands. She pulled him down to her level and hugged him. "You saved Jiggs too."

"No problem," he mumbled into her shoulder.

She released him, wiping her eyes with a hand. "How's Morgan?" she asked in a teary voice. "I haven't seen him since this morning."

Laura handed Dixie a tissue.

"Pretty good," Tony hedged.

"Does he remember what happened?"

"Not at first, but it came to him, kind of."

"That'll pass, the doctor says. The memory problems." She hoped so. She was having them too.

"I asked Dixie, is there anything she needs?" Laura said. "Anything we can do?"

Their lives were so busy. "You've done enough." She wanted her wig and some clothes to wear home. Morgan needed clothes too.

"We better be going," Tony said to Laura, "so you can get to your class. See you later, Dixie." Such a handsome couple, Dixie thought as they walked out the door, he so tall and dark, she so small and blonde.

She closed her eyes, feeling almost serene, knowing that Jiggs was alive and well, just waiting for her and Morgan to pick him up. She dozed and woke up refreshed. Suddenly, Vera's number popped into her brain. She dialed. Vera answered. "Vera, you won't believe this. We're both in the hospital. Tony saved our lives." Dixie told her everything about the furnace and the carbon monoxide.

In shock, Vera exclaimed over and over, "How lucky you are!! Just think what might have happened . . ."

Dixie interrupted her emotional friend. "Can I ask a favor? You still have the spare key?"

"I do."

"We came in our nightclothes. I look a fright. Bring me a wig, the blonde one. And makeup. Clothes for us both." What was she thinking of? "You can't go in," she groaned. "The house is a death trap."

"Calm down," Vera said at the other end. "I'll call the furnace company and let them in to take a look."

Dear Vera, Dixie thought drowsily after she hung up. What would she do without a friend like Vera?

37

The Unknown

The car glided down the driveway at the shady side of the hospital and slid smoothly into the street. Dixie felt giddy, dressed in street clothes, thanks to Vera. Her wig was firmly in place. The world sped by past the window. She was free at last of the confinement of her hospital room, happy to have her senses back—well, almost back. The doctor said she might have lapses for awhile; headaches, memory problems, some confusion. "What a beautiful spring morning!"

Vera, in the front seat at the wheel, agreed. "That it is."

"Ungodly hour to get us out of bed," Morgan, seated beside Dixie, grumped. A cane rested on the seat between them.

Nine o'clock in the morning was not ungodly, but whatever he wanted to believe, Dixie wouldn't argue. "I, for one, can't wait to be home," she sang out, hoping to infuse Morgan with her joy.

"Be patient," the neurologist had advised her privately. "He'll get better less quickly than you. He had higher levels of monoxide in his blood."

"Why was that?" she'd asked.

He'd held his chin, thought for a moment. "His existing lung disease, most likely. And it didn't help that he pulled off his oxygen over and over again."

The car burst out into sunlight, revealing the most astounding sight she'd ever seen. "Morgan, you don't know what you're missing." She grabbed him by the shoulder, shaking him awake. "It's a miracle."

He grudgingly opened one eye, leaned forward, and tumbled back, as if exhausted. "There's no miracle here," he said testily. "During the night, the clouds were close to the ground. When they lifted, they left this dew over the trees and shrubs and all the landscape. I've seen it before, maybe two or three times." He closed his eyes.

Dixie continued to gaze out the window. The sun would soon melt the dew but it would be beautiful until then.

"Turn left at the stoplight," she said to Vera. "We're picking up Jiggs, Morgan. It'll be like old times." Morgan snored quietly in the corner. In the rearview mirror, Dixie saw Vera's worried eyes looking at her.

Vera pulled up in front of the animal hospital. Dixie hurried in. She glanced at the bill, pulse quickening, the vet's charges plus board for two extra days. Oh, well, it would be worth it, even at three times the cost. "I'll send you a check," she told the billing department. "I just got out of the hospital."

Her spirits lifted when Jiggs, with a glad yip, scrambled into her arms. She rubbed her nose against his. He slathered her face with kisses.

She carried him out to the car. "Morgan, open the door." She held Jiggs high so the two could see each other through the window. Morgan's eyes were closed. "Morgan!" He stirred. Vera stretched over the seat from the front and opened the back door. Dixie lowered the little dog onto his lap. Jiggs bounced around in a circle, put his paws on Morgan's shoulders, and licked his face. Dixie entered the car from the other side, dismayed to see Morgan turn his face away and push Jiggs off his lap.

Vera started the car. The little dog jumped and leaped around the back seat.

"Hard to believe, Jiggs was 98 years old just three days ago!" Dixie exclaimed, catching him up in her arms. "He acts like a two-year-old."

Morgan came to life then and couldn't be silenced. "Why, he's no 98 years old!"

"You're right, he's only 14 in man years," Dixie placated him.

"Who would believe he was 98 years old," he scoffed.

"In dog years he's 98," she explained, holding back her irritation at the sluggish Morgan. "But he's spry as a two-year-old. Why aren't you as happy as Jiggs?" she burst out. "This is a happy time. We're so lucky! We're getting better and going home to our lives."

He grunted.

Vera drove on silently.

"Remember when you gave Jiggs to me, Vera?" Dixie asked, determined to be cheerful.

"Yep," Vera answered. "You'd just retired from Barry's agency."

They turned the corner. The house, the green lawn, the flowering shrubs and trees appeared. She gasped. The beauty of it overwhelmed her.

Vera drove the car up the drive.

"Morgan," Dixie said, waking him up. "We're home."

He fumbled at the car door and opened it.

"Wait. Let me help," Dixie urged. His balance was off. *It'll come back, the doctor said. In time.*

"I don't need help." He climbed out and fell back against the car.

"Please use the cane." Dixie handed it over to him.

"I've never used a cane." Morgan walked unsteadily toward the house.

She threw an exasperated look at Vera, telling herself to be patient. She scrambled out of the car. "Morgan," she ordered sharply. The weaving figure stopped where he was. "Stay where you are." Her headache was back. She pulled the plastic bag filled with their clothes out of the car, put his cane under her arm, and hurried to his side. "Hold on to me." He must have felt as shaky as he looked. He took her arm.

They trudged toward the porch. I feel like I'm a hundred years old, Dixie thought. Jiggs skipped jauntily beside them. Vera brought up the rear, holding a crockpot in her hands. "I hope you like beef stew."

"Love it," Dixie answered.

Once inside, Morgan sank into the easy chair in the family room.

"By the way," Vera called from the kitchen, where she was plugging in the crockpot, "when the furnace men were here, they put up monoxide alarms, upstairs and down."

"What would we do without you?" Her brain still felt fogged over. So many details. Some would just have to wait. That wouldn't be one of them, thanks to Vera.

Morgan roused himself. "What caused it? Did they say?"

"I told you yesterday," Dixie said, "after Vera called me to report. Don't you remember?"

He looked confused. She'd have to stop saying, *Don't you remember.*

Vera walked into the family room and stood by his chair. "The flue on your furnace chimney was partially stopped up." She spoke loudly as if he was hard of hearing. "Some birds had built their nest. Carbon monoxide spilled back into the house."

"Not very thoughtful." A smile flickered across his face.

Vera crossed her arms and threw a look at Dixie. "The new windows were too efficient, they said, so air-tight they made things worse."

"I'd been wanting those windows for years." Dixie barked out a laugh.

"Be careful what you wish for," Vera grimaced. "Oh, yes, the guys also swept out the chimney. It should be done every year."

Dixie squeezed Vera's hand. "You did all my work. How can I thank you?"

Vera glanced at Morgan, already snoozing. "I think your work is cut out for you," she said in a low voice. "Hungry?"

"I could eat." Dixie shook Morgan gently. "Want some beef stew?"

He mumbled, "No," eyes closed.

Vera spooned the stew from the crockpot onto two plates while Dixie put on a kettle for tea and fixed a bowl of senior dog food for Jiggs. "Put some gravy over it?" she asked Vera. "Maybe a couple of chunks of beef?" Dixie cut the beef into small bites.

Vera grinned. "That dog is spoiled rotten."

The two sat at the kitchen table. Dixie hadn't realized how hungry she was. "This tastes so good."

"I think he should have stayed in the hospital longer," Vera said in a whisper.

"The doctor told me it'll just go more slowly with Morgan, being older and all."

"They should have given you an aide."

Dixie smiled tiredly. "I'm the aide."

"What about work?"

She couldn't meet Vera's glance. "I'll take the rest of the week off. The doctor said we both should take it easy for a few more days."

Vera shook her head slowly.

Before she left, she helped Dixie get Morgan upstairs to bed. As she stood at the front door, ready to leave, she asked, "You really think you'll feel like going in to work next week?"

"I'm sure," Dixie answered brightly. The doctor hadn't set a timeline. He didn't know she had a job—*had* to have a job, as a matter of fact. She owed the vet. She owed the furnace men. She owed for the replacement of the windowpane Tony broke. And then there were the payments on the $30,000 home-equity loan, which had allowed them to buy the new windows . . . that almost killed them.

"You have dark circles under your eyes, kiddo. Get some sleep." Vera gave her a hug. "I'm going to phone and stop by every day," she warned.

In bed that night, Morgan lay beside her, out like a light. Jiggs snuggled at their feet, just like always. They were alive. Life was going on.

Dixie had a sudden revelation. If she hadn't asked Laura and Tony to go with them to church, no one would have found them in time. Her religion, her devotion to God, had saved their lives. It was a miracle. She'd tell Morgan when he was better.

38

You Used To Be So Full of Life

Dixie slipped quietly out of bed. She didn't want to wake him. Best take a shower now, while he was asleep. He seemed more confused and more unsteady now than when they'd left the hospital four days ago. Where was the gradual improvement the doctor had promised?

She was exhausted, plagued by headaches. But she always had to think ahead to what pickle he might get himself into. He was like having a child. He forgot to turn off the lights when he left the bathroom, forgot to tie his shoes and missed large patches of whiskers when he shaved. He even started to eat a second breakfast yesterday, forgetting he'd just had cereal, toast, and coffee. But most terrifying was the way he lurched through the house, reeling up and downstairs without his cane, she with her heart in her throat, nagging at him to use it.

He hadn't yet processed that a dramatic change had taken place in his brain.

After her shower, when she returned to the bedroom, Morgan had his shirt on and was standing on one leg, trying to get into his pants. "Sit. Sit," she cried out, exasperated. At her feet, Jiggs looked up, confused, and sniffed her hand. "Not you, Jiggs, Morgan." She only asked Jiggs to sit when she had a dog biscuit in her hand. Jiggs was smarter than Morgan. She put an arm around Morgan, steadying him. "Honey, I'm sorry. But you'll fall." She led him to the bed, gently pushed him down, and helped him pull on his pants.

She unbuttoned his shirt—he hadn't matched up the buttons with the holes—and rebuttoned it, and helped him into his shoes and socks. Finally, he was dressed.

Where was his cane? She constantly had to run all over the house looking for it. His glasses, too. As soon as she found them, he'd fall asleep, spectacles half on, half off, the paper spread across his lap.

Now she held onto him as they walked downstairs. It seemed to take forever, but at least he paid attention to her and held tightly to the railing. She got him seated at the kitchen table and searched for his cane. She found it in the dining room, of all places. They hardly ever used the dining room. She was ready to cry tears of desperation, anger, and confusion. She hooked the cane over a kitchen chair, right in front of him.

She dialed her office at Whispering Pines. "Beth, look, I can't make it today. Last week I thought I'd be up to it. Yeah, I still feel pretty shaky." She felt half sick to her stomach from her constant headaches. "I just want to give you a heads-up. I may be out all week." If she took another week, she'd be out of sick leave and getting into her vacation time. If she used that up, she'd be off without pay.

She made tea, put a bowl of cereal in front of him, sugared it, and poured milk over it. He ignored it and drank his tea, staring over the rim of his cup as if mesmerized by an exotic scene never before viewed by humankind.

She had to snap him out of it. She had to snap out of it herself. Her impatience was destructive to them both. "I think this would be a good time to discuss some of the major problems in our country," she suggested with forced gaiety.

He smiled, looking not at her, but over her shoulder.

She stood up, planting herself in front of him, demanding his attention. "You were always rabid about keeping Social Security solvent." His eyes glazed over. She traipsed back and forth across his line of vision, hoping the movement and color would jolt his senses. "Should old folks be taxed on part of their Social Security earnings? Should people work longer before they can collect?"

Morgan gazed at her as if this was something he'd never considered. Or if he had, he wasn't going to commit himself.

"What about Medicare? And the high cost of prescription drugs?" A favorite complaint of his.

"Let the people who are paid for it make those decisions," he mumbled.

She circled him, feeling like a street-corner radical. "Well, then, what about gun control? The environment? Remember, this is a world that Tony will inherit." Even Tony's name didn't light a fire. "Don't you care anymore?" Tears sprang to her eyes. "For awhile there, I thought you could solve any problem in the world."

"Something will happen one way or another," Morgan sighed. And he lapsed into a sort of semi-comatose condition.

At least it seemed that way to her. "Can you think of anything you want to talk about?" she cried out in desperation.

"I'd just like to sit here, have my tea, and look at the house, the colorful way it's decorated," he muttered irritably.

"What can I do with a man like you?" He was almost a stranger. "You don't pat me on the shoulder when you go by. You don't smile. You go to bed with me but you're like a zombie. You have no emotions at all." She hoped she'd made him angry so she'd see a spark of something in his eyes.

He looked apologetic, almost ready to cry.

She knelt down at his feet and flung her arms around his knees. "I want you close, snuggling close to me," she said raggedly. "I want to feel the touch of your hands and your soft kiss on my lips."

He slowly raised his tea to his lips.

Her eyes stung. She heaved herself up. "I have to do some dusting upstairs."

He waved his hand in a desultory fashion.

She started to leave the kitchen, then turned back. Where was the man who used to accost her in the hall, who had all those teasing suggestions, who insisted she be a part of his every waking moment? She'd lost him entirely. At last, she said briskly, "Why don't you snap out of it? Come upstairs with me and clean up the shower in the bathroom."

"In a minute."

She didn't see him the rest of the morning. When she came downstairs, he was still sitting there staring.

She went back upstairs, lay on her bed, cried a little bit, and fell asleep.

❦

Morgan made himself half a cheese sandwich and another cup of tea. As he ate, he gazed at the wallpaper on the opposite wall, noticing the floral pattern. That reminded him, he should get out and do some work outside. He stood and walked out the front door. He'd weed the flowers by the porch. He pulled the door shut behind him. He noticed two things. It was hot outside, and the door had automatically locked. He shambled around to the back and tried the sliding-glass door. It was locked too. His legs felt so heavy he could hardly lift them. He returned to the front and rang the bell.

"Morgan?" A voice was coming from somewhere. He looked around. The neighbor was on her porch, taking in the mail. "Where's Dixie?" Pauline asked.

"I guess she went out." Panicked, he pushed the doorbell again and again. "She didn't tell me she was going out. I can't get back in."

Pauline was heading his way. "Where's your cane?"

"I don't use a cane."

"You were using one yesterday when you were out here with Dixie." She took him by the arm. "Come over and have some cookies with me."

"That sounds like a good idea." Morgan let her lead him over to her house.

☙❧

Dixie woke up. How long had she been asleep? "Morgan," she called. Jiggs, on the end of the bed, twitched his ears. She hurried down the stairs. "Morgan?" She searched the house, Jiggs trotting along beside her. She looked in the backyard and the front yard. "Where is he, Jiggs?" Her head throbbed.

Just then the phone rang. "It's Pauline," the voice said. "I called to see if you were home yet."

"I've been here all day."

"I found Morgan outside. He said the door was locked. We're having cookies."

Thank goodness he was safe. Where would she have begun to look for him? "Dixie's home," she heard Pauline say, as if she was talking to a child. "She's been there all the time."

Dixie waited on the front porch as Pauline escorted a rather shame-faced Morgan home. Of course he didn't have his cane. He was walking like a duck.

After Pauline left, Dixie exploded. "I was worried sick."

"I went out to work in the yard but it was too hot," he apologized. "I locked myself out. I rang the bell." He gave her a reproachful look. "You didn't answer."

She'd left him alone. It was her fault.

He sank into the kitchen chair, his hands clasped in front of him.

"I'm sorry I didn't hear the bell." She went over and kissed him on the top of his head. "I was so worried and so relieved you were inside with Pauline." She put on a bright smile. "Are you up for a little conversation?"

"Sure. Let's talk."

For a split second, he seemed so much like the old Morgan she was dumbfounded. "Well," she spluttered, her brain nearly blank, "let's talk about the international situation."

He stared.

"How about the China trade bill? The evolution debate in high schools?"

He stood, shuffled by her into the family room. She followed. He turned on the television. His eyes closed.

"What's your feeling about going upstairs to bed?"

"It's early. I'm not sleepy."

But he was asleep in five minutes.

She went back to the kitchen, flummoxed. She had the man she wanted. She had him to herself. But he was out and probably would be out until suppertime. She'd never felt so alone. She took two aspirin and prayed for strength.

She'd make something special for dinner tonight. She looked in the freezer. She had a pork roast. Morgan loved pork, mashed potatoes, and sauerkraut.

She'd soon start feeling herself again. The headaches would go away. She wouldn't be so impatient.

39

Almost Like Old Times

Dixie dried her hands on her apron and opened the front door. Tony, helmet in hand, looking like a gladiator, grinned from ear to ear. "I passed the test."

She was overjoyed to see him. "That's wonderful!" She threw her arms around him as he stepped inside.

Jiggs leaped up against him. Tony knelt, scratching his ears. Jiggs rolled over. Tony rubbed his stomach while the little dog thrashed about with delight.

Tony unfastened his knee- and elbow pads and stashed them in the corner by the stair. "How's Grandpa?"

"He's in the family room. He'll be so glad to see you. Go tell him your good news. I'll finish making the salad. I hope you'll stay for dinner. We have stuffed shells, thanks to Pauline."

"Sounds good."

She took him by the arm and whispered, "Ask your grandpa what his plans are for you and him. There's so much more to be done in the yard."

"Grandpa," she heard Tony declare, when he walked into the family room, "I passed the GED test."

"Test?" Morgan asked in a thick voice. He'd been asleep.

"Isn't that wonderful, Morgan?" she called from the kitchen.

Tony talked a while longer about the test and how tricky it had been. Dixie dished out the salad and set the table for three. Then she

373

heard Morgan going on and on. She felt elated. He was carrying on a conversation. The murmuring between the two continued for several minutes.

Tony burst into the kitchen, upset. "What's the matter with Grandpa? He's like an old car that needs a new battery and spark plugs, the motivation to get going."

It sounded to her as if they'd been conversing like normal, intelligent human beings. "What did he have to say about your news?"

Tony looked flabbergasted. "He went on and on about his bank job and how he was negotiating a three-million-dollar loan for some client. But he didn't know where this client lived, or what bank the loan was coming from."

"When he wakes up from a sound sleep, he's disoriented sometimes." She tried to keep a smooth face, hoping her frazzled soul didn't show through. He'd never been in a time warp before, thinking he was back in his previous life.

"I asked him to come out to the yard," Tony went on, "so we could talk about what to do next. I couldn't budge him from the chair. He said you were figuring out a work schedule for him, but he couldn't understand what was it was yet and had no interest in knowing." Tony shook his head in disbelief.

"Yesterday he was better. The doctor told me to be patient." She had to go back to work next week. She couldn't lose her job. Sometimes she felt life would be this way always, a colorless monotone. She opened the oven and pulled the stuffed shells out. "I've been thinking . . . I'll take him in next week, have some tests run. We're ready to eat. Go get your grandpa."

Tony, with a long face, brought Morgan to the table.

As the three ate, Tony talked about his job. "Like you said, Grandpa, I offered to work overtime. They dug it. I'm learning a lot. I like it there. They like me." He looked at Morgan eagerly as if he expected to see the animated face of old, but Morgan was just nodding blankly.

"We're both so proud of you," Dixie said. She knew Tony was disappointed. He had plans and liked having his grandpa cheering for him.

Tony brightened. "Tomorrow I'm going over to the university to register for evening classes."

"My goodness. So soon?" Oh, dear. She hoped he wasn't counting on them to help with fees. Morgan's condition . . . the uncertain future . . . she pushed a smile on her face.

He held up crossed fingers. "I hope I get accepted in time for summer school."

Morgan looked up from his food, seeming interested for the first time.

"My boss said if I keep my grades up, they have a tuition plan at work."

"Why, that's wonderful!" Dixie exclaimed. One less worry—how Tony was going to get through college.

Morgan nodded, a smile forming on his face.

"I'll be moving out of the Y, so I'll be closer to my job and school. And," he grinned, looking from one to the other, "closer to Laura, and to you and Grandpa."

"What's the matter?" Morgan asked gruffly. "Your wheels give out?"

"What do you mean?" Tony looked uncertain.

Dixie gave a nervous laugh. What was his logic?

"I thought you liked all that gallivanting around on your scooter." His eyes almost twinkled. He was trying to be funny.

Tony smiled like it was a good joke. "I do, but it burns a lot of gas. Laura says I pollute the air. And I don't make good time—twenty miles an hour, if I'm lucky."

"Why don't you take my car?" Morgan inclined his head toward the garage. "I'll give it to you for a dollar. You take care of the transfer fees."

So this was where he was heading. Was he serious?

"You have a driver's license, I presume?" Morgan asked.

Tony looked bowled over. "Yeah. From Illinois."

"Well," Dixie hedged, "it's something to think about." Morgan still used the car for errands. "It's kind of a rattle trap."

"It's a perfectly good car," Morgan said indignantly.

"But you use it while I'm at work," Dixie reminded him. Did this mean he was giving up?

Morgan's face was blank, as if he'd forgotten she worked. Maybe it was because she'd been with him all day, every day, for the past week. Only a week? It felt like a year.

Tony seemed at a loss. He finally asked, "Can I help with the dishes?"

"You're rushing off?" She didn't want him to leave.

"I'm taking Laura to dinner."

Dixie laughed. He'd just eaten two helpings of shells, a salad, three pieces of garlic bread, and a dish of ice cream.

Tony blushed. "I'll just have soup and maybe a sandwich." He grinned. "We're going to celebrate."

"Celebrate?" Morgan asked.

"I passed the GED, Grandpa. I can go to college."

Morgan took his hand and pumped it effusively.

"Go on to Laura, right now," Dixie said.

Tony rose from the table, went over to his grandpa, shyly gave him a hug, and came back to Dixie and did the same.

"Bring that beautiful girl next time you come," Morgan said.

"I will, Grandpa. I will."

Smiling, Morgan watched him as he put on his elbow- and knee-pads and his helmet, murmuring something about *getting into his armor*. Tony stepped out the door.

Dixie followed, saying in a soft voice, "Can you come back next week? Let's get Morgan working in the yard."

Nodding, he gave her a surreptitious thumbs-up.

She closed the door, more hopeful than she'd been since the accident. Tony's visit had perked them both up. Her spirits fell again when Morgan retreated to the family room and slept in the chair until bed-time, as if the effort to visit had been terribly tiring. One step forward, two steps back.

The next day, Morgan smiled as she rambled on about her ideas for redecorating their bedroom and for landscaping the yard. She patted his shoulder and gently tweaked his cheek to show affection. It almost seemed like old times.

Morgan seemed to improve daily right through the weekend, not sleeping as much, really listening to the TV, and using his cane more and more. Maybe, just maybe, the doctors had been right.

40

The Wanderer

Dixie backed her car out of the garage. She couldn't wait to get in to work, to have her time scheduled again, to have life, complexity, give and take. She wasn't deserting him. He was better. And they needed her desperately at Whispering Pines, what with being short-staffed because of summer vacations. She turned up the radio, letting the music wash over her.

That first day back, she hurried home every hour to check up on him. "Why, hello," he greeted her with a big smile each time she walked in the door, looking surprised and pleased as punch to see her, as if she'd been gone for days. She fixed him lunch and he ate hungrily.

At lunchtime Tuesday, he pushed away the homemade chicken soup Vera had brought over, saying he'd already eaten. For the life of her she couldn't see he'd eaten anything. When she asked, he didn't seem to remember what it was he'd had. "I'm just not hungry," he finally said, getting up and going back to his chair in the family room. As she zoomed back to Whispering Pines for an afternoon meeting, she wondered if he was paying her back for leaving him alone all day.

Wednesday went smoothly. He slurped up the soup, had two helpings, in fact. He didn't seem to miss her. At any rate, he seemed to understand she'd be away for a period of time and then return. She'd won her freedom. She was truly back at work! And he was getting along fine without her.

Early Thursday morning, before she left, she made his favorite butterscotch cookies, while Morgan watched. She added segments of English walnuts to the batter, formed the dough into long rolls, cut off wafer-thin slices, one at a time, and put them on a cookie pan. They came out of the oven crisp and delicious.

For breakfast, they ate fresh-baked cookies, along with cereal and hot tea. "Thank you," he smiled, "for the cookies. How are things at work?"

She almost fell off her chair. She told him about the busy day she expected, with the final tweaking of the current issue of the newspaper, *Pine Scents*. "And," she added, "I'm in charge of the afternoon program. We have a young singer who's majoring in music at the university."

"How's Effie?" he asked.

He remembered. She felt tears spring to her eyes. "Still hooked up to the feeding tube."

He took her hand.

"'It's just a matter of time,' the nurse said when I visited on Monday."

He nodded. He had that funny, spacey smile on his face again.

"Thanks." She squeezed his hand, hoping to bring him back.

"For what?"

"For being you. For being here."

He kept the funny smile.

"I'm not sure I'll make it home for lunch today." She hurriedly fixed him a tuna sandwich and left it in the fridge. "And there's milk and cookies."

"I won't forget those cookies," he grinned, kissing her on the cheek. *He was back.*

When she went into work, she told everyone who asked, "I'm very optimistic."

She called at noon to remind him to eat the sandwich. The rest of the day passed in a blur, with no time to phone. At three-thirty she hurried home, bursting through the door. "I'm here." Jiggs sleepily rose to greet her. The house seemed empty. With a sinking feeling, she scurried from room to room, calling his name. She checked the backyard. She telephoned Pauline. He wasn't there and she hadn't seen him.

She looked out the front door. The neighbor was mowing his lawn. "Have you seen Morgan?" she asked as she crossed the street, walking toward him.

"I glanced out the window a couple hours ago and saw him leave the house. He was headed that way." He pointed toward the playground.

Growing more panicky by the minute, she climbed into her car. Two hours was quite a head start. She prayed he'd stopped at the playground to watch the children play ball. She searched the bleachers. No sign of him.

In the next block she met Tony, on his scooter. She rolled down her window. "I was just going to stop by," he grinned.

"Your grandpa's missing. Leave your scooter at our place. Let's look for him in the car."

She followed him to the house and waited while he lifted his wheels onto the front porch. Then she drove back to the playground, slowly circling the block, the two of them scanning the landscape for Morgan. If they didn't find him, she'd have to call the police. What if he were hit by a car? She wove around the streets, one square block after the next, more frantic by the minute, ready to jump out of her skin.

"Is that him?" Tony asked when they were about two miles from home.

He was wobbling down the sidewalk, leaning on his cane, his gray raincoat flapping against his legs. He must be burning up in that coat, Dixie thought. Well, he'd used some sense. He'd remembered his cane. That must be how he'd made it this far.

"Hello," he said, waving as if it was natural they should meet this way.

"Where are you going?" Dixie asked.

"Well," he said, licking his lips, turning to his left. He frowned, turned to his right. "I was looking for you."

"You mean you were coming to find me at work?"

He hesitated, then nodded.

"But this isn't the right way."

Tony asked him if he wanted a ride.

"Oh, I'd just as leave walk."

"You must be tired," Dixie said.

"Nah, there's places to sit."

"Where?" Dixie asked, curious.

He waved distractedly toward the houses.

They finally convinced him to get into the car. He squeezed in beside Tony in the front seat. "Can we drop you anywhere?" he asked the boy.

"I'm going with you back to the house, Grandpa," Tony said, giving Dixie a look.

Dixie drove on, only half listening as Tony talked about his college plans, rather feverishly, it seemed to her, but maybe that was just her state of mind.

"I still have to take the entrance exam," Tony announced, "and write a personal statement. Laura's helping me with that." He then delivered a blow-by-blow description of a movie Laura and he'd seen. "Laura's mother came down from Toledo especially to meet me." He looked at Dixie, who made encouraging sounds. He turned to his grandpa. "I spoke with Mom. I told her all about Laura."

Morgan nodded his head now and then. He didn't seem to understand what was being said or why he was there. He didn't seem to realize he was in the car going back to his house.

When he stepped out on the driveway, he mumbled, "Now where am I supposed to be?" He asked Dixie to take him to his room.

"Come in the kitchen with Tony and me," Dixie said. "We'll have cookies and tea. Those butterscotch cookies you like so well."

He shook his head.

"Why?"

"I never liked butterscotch cookies."

"But they're his favorite," she wailed to Tony.

She coaxed him to sit down at the kitchen table while she made the tea. She persuaded him to taste a cookie and finally convinced him to dip a piece of it into the tea. He ate only one. "That's all I want." He stood and walked down the hall, Dixie following. He pulled himself up the stairs. She stayed right behind him until he got to the top landing.

Dixie came back to the kitchen. "He's going to bed."

Tony sighed in a dismal voice, "I thought he was getting better."

"He was. But now he seems worse."

"I'd like to help, if I can." He patted her shoulder.

She had to use every ounce of self-control not to collapse in his arms. She straightened up, walked over to the sink and looked out the window. "The grass is getting high again."

"Why don't I mow it right now?"

While he mowed, Dixie sat in front of the television, staring. She should do a washing. She should run the sweeper. Her head ached dully. She felt empty, as if the life had been sucked out of her.

When Tony came through the sliding-glass door saying he was finished, she looked at the clock, amazed to see two hours had passed. She switched off the TV. "I bet you're hungry."

Tony nodded.

"Why don't you take Morgan's car?" It needed charging. And the way Tony's eyes were lighting up, she knew it would give him a lift to drive it. "Go out and get us some Big Macs." She gave him money and the car keys. "You may have trouble starting it."

She heard the car motor grinding. Finally, it turned over. She stepped into the garage, watching him back out. "Be careful," she called, remembering how he'd totaled his mom's car. Well, he was more mature now. She watched the car glide smoothly down the driveway into the street.

Then she sat down at the kitchen table and ate another butterscotch cookie. Tony was such a comfort. It had crossed her mind, more than once, Tony moving in with them. They weren't too far from the university. He could have free room and board. And he could help out when he was needed. But he'd be gone all day at work. Evenings too, at school. Maybe it wasn't such a good idea.

She liked seeing his scooter on the porch, his helmet and shin guards piled at the bottom of the stairs.

She'd planned so desperately for her future, which was now. She put her head down on the table and cried, big bawling sobs.

⚛

Dixie didn't go in to work on Friday. That morning, she decided on a final test. She donned the black and maroon negligee he'd given her, and nothing else. "Morgan," she called from the living room, "come here for a minute, would you?" The kitchen chair scraped across the floor. He appeared in the hallway. She stood in front of the window. Bright sunlight streamed through. "Stop right in front of me and look at the scenery," she said.

He held onto the wall, then onto a chair and made it into the living room. He stopped and tried to look through the window but she was blocking his way. "I could see better if you'd step aside."

"That isn't what I want you to see. Look at me!"

Morgan looked at her.

She knew her slender, straight form was outlined by the sunlight, barely hidden by the filmy, clinging negligee. "What do you think?"

"Well," he answered, "I think it would be nice if we'd have breakfast pretty soon."

"I mean, look at me and tell me what you think of the way I look with the sunshine coming in."

"Well, you might need to go and get some clothes on." He turned his back.

He's hopeless, she said to herself. He used to be so alert, so full of jokes, flirting and kidding about me being afraid to let him pat me on the bottom.

She marched upstairs to her closet and took out her heaviest, most unflattering outfit, an old navy blue suit a size too big. She put it on and left the jacket unbuttoned over a red, polka-dot, ruffled blouse. She wore flat shoes with white anklets. She went downstairs, made pancakes with sausage for him, along with a cup of steaming coffee, and heard him compliment her on what a nice breakfast she'd prepared for him.

She sniffed and turned away. She could be wearing a sack and he wouldn't notice.

They didn't speak the rest of the morning as they trudged around the house. Later when he went outside, she followed him to make sure he didn't wander away.

Maybe it was more than monoxide poisoning. A stroke? Senility? What if he got so he couldn't take care of himself at all? What if she had to care for him the rest of his life?

41

Bring Him Back

As Dixie sat beside Morgan in the doctor's office, she ran a hand over her eyes. Her headache was back. She'd rarely had headaches before. Now at least once a day they sprang on her ferociously. When the doctor bustled through the door, she stood. "Dr. Durning, I'm a good friend of Morgan. In fact, we share a home. I pray you'll be able to help us."

He nodded. "Morgan, how are you?" he asked heartily, leaning down to shake his hand.

"Just fine," Morgan grinned. The cane rested by his side.

Oh, yes, just fine, Dixie sighed to herself. She sat down again, perching on the edge of her seat.

"What's the trouble?" the doctor asked.

"Trouble?" Morgan thought for a moment, shook his head. "No trouble . . ."

"I can't leave him alone. Before I know it, he's two miles away and lost." She hadn't planned to do this, tell him Morgan's deficiencies while Morgan listened. "He roams around the house in a trance," she rattled on. "He forgets to eat or eats twice. He's been out of the hospital three weeks. The neurologist said to be patient. He started to get better. Now he's getting worse. I'm worried sick."

Morgan seemed shocked by the outburst, then gave Dixie a look as if to say, *You're crazy*.

Dr. Durning opened the file folder on his desk. "Morgan, can you tell me why you were in the hospital?"

Morgan frowned. He turned to Dixie.

"Carbon—" Dixie blurted out before Dr. Durning held up his hand.

"What was the problem, Morgan?"

"Carbon . . . something." He thought and thought. "Fumes . . ." He shrugged apologetically.

"How are you feeling now?"

"My head hurts."

"Anything else?"

"I'm tired."

Dr. Durning did a physical exam. He asked Morgan to walk in the hall, with the cane and then without.

Morgan concentrated on walking and, with the cane, did better than he did at home. But at home he usually refused to use it, instead grabbing onto pieces of furniture.

Dr. Durning asked him to name the current president of the United States.

Morgan answered, "Ronald Reagan."

A few years off, Dixie thought, her heart sinking.

"What's the date today?" the doctor asked.

Morgan leaned forward to try to read the calendar on the desk. The doctor shifted in his chair to block his view.

"May," Morgan said. He shook his head when the doctor asked what day of the month.

"The year?" Dr. Durning asked.

"1999? No, 2000!" Morgan replied.

The doctor smiled and nodded. Then he asked him to count backwards from one hundred, in units of seven. "One hundred, ninety-three," he prodded.

"One hundred, ninety-three," Morgan echoed. He frowned, he winced, he rubbed his forehead. "That's a little harder." He looked at the doctor, abject. "I don't know what's the matter with me."

"That's all right," the doctor said gently. He silently read through Morgan's file. Dixie, her heart in her throat, prayed he'd come up with a solution that would bring Morgan back to her.

"Monoxide poisoning can be tricky," the doctor said at last, with a glance at Dixie. "After treatment, you can start to get better and then later can have a relapse." He turned to Morgan, his voice louder. "I think that may be what's happening to you, Morgan."

Morgan nodded cautiously.

The doctor leafed through the pages in the folder. "You weren't sent to a hyperbaric chamber, I see."

Dixie shrugged. "I remember masks. It was humidified oxygen, they said."

"What caused the fumes?"

"A bird's nest partly covered the flue. It was a cold day so we turned the furnace up. We'd just got new windows." If only they'd kept the old ones, loose and rattling. The cold air blowing through would have diluted the poison. She was beginning to hate those windows.

Durning dropped his eyes to read again. "You were hospitalized earlier this year, Morgan?"

When Morgan didn't reply, Dixie answered for him, ignoring Dr. Durning's frown. "He passed out at home in January. They said it was from dehydration."

"I see he had a high red-blood-cell count then," the doctor murmured.

She knew it. It had been important. "What about it?"

"It can be a symptom of monoxide poisoning, among other things."

Dixie slapped her forehead. Of course, it had been right in front of her, when she looked it up in the library, hidden among all the other reasons for a high red-blood-cell count. "So he—we—could have been exposed to the fumes for the past few months?"

He pushed up his glasses on the bridge of his nose. "Small doses of monoxide poisoning are hard to diagnose. Symptoms are confusing and can sometimes be mistaken for the flu or other ailments."

"But why am I better and he's not?"

"Do you sleep in different rooms?" he asked.

She shook her head. Realization trickled in. "But I'm out of the house at work. He stays home."

"We'll do some tests. Morgan, I'm going to readmit you to the hospital for a few days. Would you mind waiting in reception while I make arrangements?" Dixie lingered as Morgan shuffled out of the room, leaning on his cane.

She had to know. "I'm hoping Morgan and I, we can be a team for the rest of our lives."

He nodded sorrowfully. "Chronic poisoning can cause permanent neurological damage."

She suddenly feared she'd be the keeper of a man who for the rest of his life couldn't make a decision of his own.

"We won't leap to conclusions. We don't know how long the bird's nest covered the flue." He smiled kindly. "The high red-blood-cell count in January might indeed have been due to other factors." He patted her shoulder. "The neurological problems might just go away after a few weeks. Or months."

Months? She wanted to scream. "How can I go on this way for months?" she cried. "Not knowing if I can leave the house and trust him not to wander off? I work. I have to work."

"You might have to consider other arrangements," the doctor said carefully.

BOOK VII

OTHER ARRANGEMENTS

42

Get My Suitcase

Light from the hall dappled the floor and threw shadows on the wall. Her eyes darted to the bed, with the still figure lying on it. She hoped Morgan was asleep.

This afternoon, when she'd brought him through the front doors, he'd asked, upset, "Why am I here?" Earlier, when the doctor told him he'd be going from the hospital to a nursing home, he hadn't flinched. He'd worn the pleasant look he sometimes wore when he wasn't listening.

When she'd wheeled him down the hall into the small cubicle he'd be calling home, he'd clutched her sleeve. "Are you leaving me here?"

It was the last place on earth he wanted to be.

She heard him stir. Pushing off her blanket, she rose from the chair and crossed to his bed. His eyes were open. She touched his face, whispering, "You know where you are?"

"Whispering Pines," he said in a dull voice.

He sounded betrayed. She was the traitor. She deserved to die. No, she was saving him. He'd get back his spark. "You're in rehab. You'll be home before you know it," she insisted.

He closed his eyes. They opened again, concerned. Would she have to repeat it?

"What I want to know," he asked crankily, "is who's paying for this?"

He was so much like himself that she laughed, bent down, and folded him up in her arms.

"Did you hear me?" he demanded, twisting away.

"You old tightwad. Medicare pays." For twenty days. After that? She didn't want to think about it.

The doctors seemed to agree he was suffering the effects of the monoxide poisoning. No stroke had occurred to compound the damage. They also agreed that he might, or might not, recover one hundred percent. She stood beside him until his eyes closed. When he was breathing evenly, she returned to her chair and pulled the blanket up over her. She wedged the pillow between the wooden arm and the hard plastic back, rummaging for the most comfortable position. One lucky thing—she'd managed to get him a single room, one of three on the rehab floor.

She woke up often, stood and stretched out the kinks in her back and neck, and tiptoed over to Morgan's side. Each time, his eyes were closed, his breathing even. Maybe he was coming to terms with this decision.

The next morning, her neck felt sprained. She had to turn her whole upper body to look at people. Her legs ached. Her head was throbbing.

She ate breakfast with Morgan. After the rehab staff arrived to do their evaluation of him, she kissed him on the cheek. "See you later, darlin'." He held onto her wrist. Then he opened his hand, as if she were a bird he was setting free. She had to force herself to leave. But for her it was a workday.

"Dixie, go home," a colleague urged when she stumbled into the activities office. "You look awful."

She ducked into the staff bathroom to see for herself. Her hair, mousy and gray, stood on end. She had no lipstick on. Her face was washed out, all but her eyes, which were puffy and bloodshot. "I think I will go home," she said to her vacant face in the mirror.

She went home and slept, woke in the afternoon, her heart pounding like a sledgehammer, and hurried back to Whispering Pines. When she arrived breathless in Morgan's room, he was dressed, sitting in a chair, looking—suspended? As if he'd been plucked up mid-motion, set down here, and wasn't quite sure why. She kissed the top of his head. "Here's a big bag of candy kisses. For after meals, not before," she admonished. "The latest *Reader's Digest*. A funny get well card from Tony and Laura." She spread out the items on the table beside him. He didn't even look. "How did it go?" she asked with a bright smile.

"What?"

"The therapy? What did you do?"

He waved a hand at her as if it was too boring to mention.

"They said you walked the entire length of the hall." He was slow, therapy told her when she'd stopped by their office on her way to Morgan's room; he grew tired very quickly. He'd been irate at having to use a walker. But that's what they were starting him with. "Don't worry, Dixie. We'll make him into a new man!" She'd warned them to keep an eye on him, that he might walk right out the door and end up miles away.

Morgan's eyes roamed the room, found the open closet, and saw his suitcase sitting on the shelf. He pointed. "Get my suitcase, take me home."

She wanted nothing more. It broke her heart. "When you're better," she said crisply, taking his chin and turning his face to her. "You're here to work, my friend."

He shook her off, glaring into space.

"Medicare will NOT pay the tab here unless you show improvement every day." That made him take notice. His jaw jutted out. His spine became stiffer.

He picked up the card from Tony and Laura and opened it. He made no comment. Did he even read it? He set it down and tore open the bag of candy kisses. He offered her one, took one himself, and chewed it solemnly.

She realized she was sitting there with as long a face as his. It wasn't the end of the world. It was a chance, a gamble. Three weeks, paid for by Medicare, to wake up his sluggish brain. And she'd do her damndest to make it work.

๏๘๑

One day merged with the next. She stopped by her office early every morning to organize her day. Then it was down the elevator, through the lobby, past the dining hall, and into the other building. She always ducked first into Effie's room in the convalescent wing to say hello. Each time, Effie's eyes were shut tight, her cheeks sunken. She looked like a wax figure. Dixie said a silent prayer it would soon be over for Effie.

From there, Dixie hopped on the elevator to the fourth-floor rehab wing to visit Morgan. His eyes were open—usually—and for that she was grateful. She cajoled him to eat his breakfast, then hurried back to her office, returned for Morgan's lunch, then rushed home to feed Jiggs and take him for a short walk. Then it was back to work and then to Morgan's room to share dinner with him. And so the routine continued. Some days she brought in food from Pauline or Vera to tempt him, or a favorite dish of his she'd fixed herself. Finally, she went home, Jiggs gaping at her, looking as stunned as she felt, had a hot bath, and fell into bed.

She gathered progress reports from therapy every day and reports from the nurses on his state of mind. One day, as someone shuffled toward her in the hall, using his walker, his baggy pants held up by suspenders, she found herself wondering who that old geezer was. With a shock, she realized it was Morgan.

She cheered him on at occupational therapy, where he placed cones, one by one, on top of other cones, matching the colors, muttering, "This is stupid."

Every day he asked her to get his suitcase down and take him home. She tried to keep the closet door shut so he wouldn't see the suitcase. But someone, an aide, maybe Morgan himself, would open the door, so he remembered to ask her, sometimes as many as three times a day. It killed her every time

That first Friday, after work, Tony stopped by to mow the lawn. Laura was with him, a bag of groceries in her arms. "I'm making dinner," she told Dixie firmly. "You relax."

"I can't," Dixie protested. She let Laura lead her outside to the back patio, where she set up a lawn chair, and all but pushed Dixie into it.

Dixie watched Tony mow the grass, hypnotized by the fluid movements of his angular body, the precision and grace with which he rounded the end of one swath and began the next.

When he finished the backyard, she followed him around to the front, sinking into the porch swing, idly rocking, letting her mind drift, letting herself smile, as the motor hummed and the green grass sprayed off to the sides. She inhaled the fresh, clean smell. She felt normal for the first time in days. Just as Tony was on his last lap, Laura called out the front door, "Dinner's ready."

The kitchen table was set, a green salad beside each plate. Laura poured sauce over the pasta. "My mom's spaghetti recipe," she smiled.

"It's terrific," Tony said, popping out of the downstairs bathroom, drying his hands.

"I feel absolutely pampered." Dixie hugged Laura. They sat down at the table. Dixie said grace, adding, "Dear Lord, you gave us one miracle. You brought Tony and Laura to us and they saved our lives. Now I'm asking you to make Morgan well enough to come home again."

She heard an intake of breath. Her eyes fluttered open. Tony and Laura were looking at her with alarm.

Time to be more upbeat. "Make him well enough to come home soon," she corrected herself. "Amen."

She took a bite of spaghetti and rolled it around in her mouth. She was sure it was good. But she couldn't taste anything right now. "Laura, this is so lovely of you." She pasted a smile on her face. "What's happening with you two?"

Taking Dixie's cue, Laura chattered gaily about the part-time job she'd taken for the summer, and about her two classes. Tony chimed in, "If I get accepted for summer school, I'm taking beginning accounting. Grandpa can give me some tips."

"He'd love that," Dixie said with an empty smile. At this point, she thought, he can't even count backwards from one hundred by sevens.

"Tell Dixie about last weekend," Laura nudged Tony. "Mom came down from Toledo," she said to Dixie.

Tony grinned. "We went to the zoo. You know, it's one of the best in the country." He launched into a lively description of the tropical birds, the feeding of the penguins, and the playfulness of the polar bears.

Scarcely listening, Dixie smiled and watched his face. Hard to believe he was the same sullen boy she'd met at the police station less than six months ago.

"Mom fell in love with Tony," Laura said.

Tony squirmed and grinned.

"Is it okay to visit Grandpa tomorrow?" Tony asked when Dixie was ready to return to Whispering Pines to say goodnight to Morgan.

"Wait another week," she answered. "I think you'll see a big improvement." He had to get better. Otherwise, she'd what? Yell and curse at him for slacking off? Shake him till his teeth rattled to get his attention? Curl up and die?

⚘

When Dixie arrived in rehab that night, Bridget, the nurse, was delivering medications to the patients. "You might as well move in," she joshed, adding in a low voice, "The doctor thinks he's depressed. He's put him on antidepressants. He's also changed his blood pressure meds. He thinks they might be contributing to his unsteadiness and confusion."

If she hadn't been home enjoying herself with the kids, Dixie thought guiltily, she could have talked with the doctor herself.

She said goodnight to Morgan and left, hopeful. Maybe he was going to get out of Whispering Pines alive.

ॐ

On Saturday, she toured the neighborhood with a get-well card, collecting signatures and messages for Morgan, explaining to all about his setback and asking each one to say a prayer.

It had been quite an effort, so she was later than usual getting over to see him. She handed him the card, hoping he'd perk up when he saw that so many people—strangers even—cared. He nodded, smiled, and put the card down. She picked it up, read the messages aloud, describing each person and where they lived. "That's very nice," he said vaguely, before going on to complain about the food and a therapist who'd made him work too hard.

Sunday, when she returned home from church, Jiggs' peaked little face looked up at her. "Poor Jiggs. You're an orphan. You and I are going visiting!" She gave herself the once-over in the living room mirror, adjusting her wide-brimmed blue hat, a favorite of Morgan's. So was the deep blue dress with the scoop neck she wore. He always said it showed off her stunning figure.

She led Jiggs out to the car on his leash and had to coax him to climb inside. The only time he rode in the car was when he saw the vet. "You're going to visit Morgan," she told him. His tail wagged warily.

When she pulled up in the parking lot of Whispering Pines, Jiggs' nose was pressed against the window. Satisfied she hadn't tricked him, he hopped out and trotted happily through the front door of the rehab and convalescent wing.

He bounded, yipping, into the room. Morgan's face lit up. Jiggs put his paws on his knees. Smiling, Morgan scratched his ears as Jiggs scrambled up in his lap, and, licking and snuggling, settled into his arms.

Morgan laughed silently, his chest shaking, until his eyes became slits. Dixie was pleased to see him laugh. But it made her uneasy too. It seemed to go on so long. Tears rolled down his cheeks. Was he laughing or crying? "You're really glad to see him?"

He nodded, wiping his eyes with the back of his hand.

She felt a flicker of hope. One week was up of Medicare's twenty paid days. Two more to go. She'd bring Jiggs in to visit as often as possible.

Some days, when she popped into his room on her way from bingo or a program in the auditorium, Morgan was asleep in his chair, the newspaper dangling from his lap.

She read aloud to him as often as she could. He seemed to listen for awhile. But if she quizzed him on what he'd just heard, he stumbled and stuttered. He did have the grace to look embarrassed. Maybe that was a good sign.

She was always peering into his face and his eyes, watching for good signs.

She arranged for readers for the blind to stop by and read to him. It wasn't exactly fair, but she was in charge. She could do what she liked. The readers came daily, like a drill team, and reported back to her.

By the end of the second week, with adjustments in his meds, rigorous physical therapy, the daily readers, and visits from Jiggs, he seemed more alert and interested. Once, only once, had he managed to escape, and that was the Saturday after Tony's and Laura's visit. It had been a fun visit, one Morgan enjoyed. Laura had given him a snapshot that her mom took during her stay. "Morgan," Dixie exclaimed, "isn't it adorable? Of both? Tony looks so much like you! He could be your son."

Then she'd gone out with the kids for a bite to eat. When she returned to Morgan's room, he was sitting in his chair with a chastened look. The nurse out front told her he'd managed to sneak past the desk and get outside as far as the front sidewalk. "He said he was going home. Back to Chicago. When I told him, 'You're in Columbus,' he said with a little smile, he knew that."

It crushed her. *Going home to Chicago*. If only he'd said he was going home to Dixie's. "Was he using his walker?"

The nurse nodded.

Dixie swallowed the lump in her throat. "Good." That surely counted for something.

Vera, dear Vera, who'd been calling every day, said Sunday, in an ominous voice, "I had a dream about you last night." She wouldn't tell Dixie what it was. She only sighed, "I'm afraid you're going to crack in two if things don't work out the way you want."

One bright spot shone like a beacon that weekend. Tony told her he'd been accepted for summer session and was taking an evening class in beginning accounting. His company was paying all fees.

43

Do You Want to Dance?

At the beginning of the third week, Dixie wheeled Morgan over to the other building for an afternoon program. He'd said he'd rather sleep. He'd had a tiring morning in therapy. He agreed only when she said he didn't have to walk.

She found a spot for his wheelchair at the back of the crowded auditorium and sank wearily into a seat beside him.

On stage, Jazz Seniors, clad in cheery red and crisp white, tuned up their instruments. The female singer, plump and dark, stepped up to the mike, crooning introductions in a smoky voice, "John on bass, Al on guitar, Freddie on trumpet, Eli on the drums, Teddy on soprano sax, and Mike, our fabulous pianist. My name is Frances and I'll be singing some of your favorite songs today. If they're not your favorites now, they will be when I finish."

Laughter and scattered cheers rose up from the collected crowd. Jazz Seniors, a sprightly gang, none under 70, were a favorite. They came back every three months.

Their first song, "Mary Ann," was a calypso. The audience clapped. Staff danced with residents who wanted to and could. Maria, a short, dark, curvy young woman, her full hips undulating, danced exuberantly with a graceful, weaving, gray-haired lady who wore a rapturous smile and seemed to be dreaming of another time, another place.

A blonde volunteer in a bright-orange jacket and black pants clapped her hands and did a half-dance step up and down the aisles, pausing in front of a wispy woman in a wheelchair, her crooked body slumped to one side. The volunteer took her hands, gently swinging them back and forth. The woman smiled, moving her head and shoulders, the movements almost too tiny to register on the human eye.

By the third song, "New York, New York," aides were dancing with wheelchair patients, swinging them around to the beat of the band. Morgan smiled and tapped his feet.

The female singer began crooning "All of Me." "Do you want to dance?" Dixie asked, meaning she'd roll him around in the wheelchair.

He pushed himself up and, fumbling, threw his arms around her. The two of them swayed in place. The next song, they shuffled. By "Night and Day," they were slowly moving around a small section of the floor, the only real couple. Other dancers stopped to look. "Is she his wife?" Dixie heard someone ask.

She smiled up at the man in her arms. "Did you hear that?"

"Hear what?"

"Someone asked if I were your wife."

"Well." Morgan smiled back.

"Remember the Elks dinner dance?"

"Our first big date."

She was elated. He remembered. "Our first kiss." She felt a thrill. It surprised her.

"I stepped all over you, like now."

"You're doing fine." She glanced around. "And look at all these women giving you looks, jealous of me."

He smiled an inscrutable smile. His chest puffed out. They danced to "Begin the Beguine." His step became more confident. He was filling out, becoming a person again.

If he had to remain here, she decided, she'd take him to all the dances and every one of the music programs. Two dances later, Dixie murmured, "I'm getting tired," so Morgan would sit down. She didn't want to wear him out. "Did you have fun?" she asked when the program ended.

He nodded, his face one big smile.

She wheeled him back to his room. When she was ready to leave, he stood up to kiss her goodbye and held her with a viselike grip. "This is what I miss." He pulled her down to sit beside him on the bed. "Just lying together at night." He buried his face in her neck, his arms still wrapped around her.

"I miss you too," she murmured. She heard footsteps in the hall and pulled away. She didn't want anyone to look in and see them like this. He looked hurt. Silly of her. She kissed him on the cheek and took his hands in hers.

"I feel like I'm coming back." His eyes were hopeful. "I'm sixty-forty."

She squeezed his hands.

The next morning, as she rounded the corner into his room, he commanded sternly, "Dixie, come here."

"I'm here." She stood in front of him.

"Go home and get a pistol."

Her heart stopped. Why would he say that when he's feeling better?

"Get a pistol." He grinned raggedly. "And get me out of here."

She laughed, relieved and nervous at the same time. "I don't think we'll have to shoot our way out," she said lightly.

His grin, ferocious, stayed glued to his face. He was getting better. Wasn't he?

The next afternoon, a few days before Medicare's one hundred percent pay ended, the assessment team—therapy, the head nurse, the doctor, the social worker, the dietician—conferred with Dixie. They felt he wasn't ready to leave and be left at home alone. The social worker advised, "See financial counseling."

☙

In all her years at Whispering Pines, Dixie had never been down this corridor. She tapped on the door that bore the sign, ANGIE WHEELER, MEDICAID.

"What happens next? Medicare's twenty free days are almost used up," Dixie asked the plump woman whose hips sagged over her office chair. At the outer limits of Angie's black dress, creamy, unblemished flesh gleamed on her round face, thick neck, and plump arms and hands. At the ends of stubby fingers were blood-red nails.

"If he stays on, he'll have to co-pay, at $110 a day," the woman said. Her chubby face, cut in two by severe-looking, dark-rimmed glasses, broke into a smile. "He gets up to eighty more days at that rate, as long as he improves with the therapy."

$110 a day for eighty days! Cold sweat trickled down her armpits. How could the woman look so complacent?

"When he stops getting better, or after eighty days, Medicare will pay nothing toward the daily costs. He'll be considered custodial care."

Dixie clamped her lips together. Morgan was several cuts above custodial care.

But, she had to admit, someone might need to keep an eye on him to make sure he didn't roam.

"My advice is prepare for the worst. Have him start to spend down his assets so he can apply for Medicaid." The woman peered at Dixie, a hard glint in her eye, as if she were a dealer at a blackjack table in Vegas.

What were Morgan's assets? Not much. Whatever he had in his checking account plus his CD.

"Once he's approved, his Social Security and pension will be signed over to Whispering Pines. Now what about property? Are you two married? Home owners? The remaining spouse can stay in the home. But if you sell it, half the money may be claimed by Medicaid."

"Well, thank you." Dixie stood up, feeling lightheaded.

The woman started to enumerate all the documents Dixie would need for Medicaid. Dixie threw up her hands. She didn't want to know. Finally, Angie reached into a drawer and handed her a sheet of paper. "It's all in here." She looked at her kindly. "It's overwhelming at first."

Oh, dear, how should she proceed? Well, she had her debt-free credit cards, just waiting to be filled up again, thanks to Morgan's home-equity loan. Should she charge the co-pay and wait to cash in Morgan's CD until she was sure he'd be here for awhile? He'd have to pay a penalty if she cashed in his CD now.

Dear God, she hoped he wouldn't have to spend it all and sign over his pension and Social Security checks to Whispering Pines.

She gulped. She could be paying off the $30,000 loan by herself. Another month here at $110 a day and they'd owe a few more thousand.

Maybe she should bring him home. She could quit her job and be his keeper for—how long? She wasn't getting any younger. What was in store for her? she wondered.

He might never return to the way he was. That was always at the very back of her mind. She didn't want to deal with it.

Don't do anything hasty, she told herself.

44

Where Have You Been?

The day started as the most dismal of her life, almost. Dixie became Morgan's power of attorney, cashed in his CD, and began to worry about the black spots. She'd noticed something was wrong a few days ago when she was watching TV. On that big, beautiful television Morgan had purchased, the picture seemed fuzzy—anyway, not quite right. Then, as she and Morgan sat with the social worker at Whispering Pines, going over the power of attorney forms, the letters seemed to jump around.

Now, in the bank, as she waited for the money from Morgan's CD to be transferred to his checking account, the stack of papers on the desk beside her seemed to be dotted with black spots. She'd never had so many floaters. She closed one eye, then the other. The spots were in her right eye. She rubbed it. They didn't disappear.

She was cracking, she decided, her body disintegrating from the stress.

She arrived at work late, rushing to catch up. At one-thirty she was in the residents' dining room, helping Beth with bingo.

As Beth called out the numbers, Dixie drifted among the players. "You have B-2," she pointed out to Lois, placing a chip on the oversize number on Lois's oversize card, noticing as she did that part of the number seemed to be missing. Was it her eyes? Or a misprinted bingo card? She was about to try to sort it out when a movement outside the window distracted her.

Was that Morgan on the sidewalk, leaning on his cane? Holding out his hand as if he was begging? She had to corral him before he wandered away.

"I'll be right back," she told Beth. "It's Morgan." She pointed. "He's gotten out." Beth grimaced. Dixie scurried from the dining room and was through the front door like a shot.

Dear Lord, he seemed to be talking to himself as a little bird circled him. No, he was talking to the bird. Did he think he was St. Francis of Assisi? Things had gone from manageable to downright dismal.

She rounded the hedge, surprised to see Billie, one of the nurses, several feet beyond Morgan, standing under a tree near the feeder. A white-breasted bird lit on her forearm, daintily stepped into her hand, and ate from it.

Dixie glanced back at Morgan. The bird had stopped flying around his head and had landed in his hand. She looked at Billie, who grinned and gave Dixie a wave. Morgan didn't seem to notice. With a soft smile on his face, he watched the bird eat from his hand.

Dixie walked back inside to finish bingo. He was with someone, doing something. Hope glimmered in her breast.

Don't jump to conclusions, she told herself.

⊙✿⊚

Morgan felt the prickle of the tiny claws as the little bird pecked away at the chopped nuts in the palm of his hand. "That's right," he said. "These are for you." When the bird finished eating and flew away, Morgan walked over to the nurse. "Thanks, Billie," he said. "That was fun." Why was she looking at him so funny?

"So you had a good time?" she asked.

"Why, yes. Why shouldn't I?"

"Well, you haven't been yourself for awhile. Dixie will be pleased to see you so alert. Poor thing, it's been a long siege for her."

Morgan waved goodbye to Billie and trudged over the lawn, steadying himself with his cane. He heard a redbird singing gaily. It was summer, he noticed. The trees were thick with leaves. The flowers were in bloom. Why, that looked like Dixie, through the window of the dining room. He walked closer. He'd been wondering where she was. Awkwardly, he stepped through the flowerbed and tapped on the window. She didn't notice.

He cut across the lawn to the cement walkway, strolled through the automatic doors of the independent living wing, and headed toward the dining room.

"Dixie, Dixie?" He waltzed into bingo, shouting, "Hi there, lovey dovey! Where have you been? Boy, am I glad to see you."

❦

She felt like dancing on the ceiling. Please, please, don't let me be disappointed, Dixie prayed. She excused herself from bingo and shepherded Morgan into the hall, where they huddled beside the entrance to the dining room. She touched his face, peered into his eyes, rubbing his sandpapery jaw. "It's not where I've been, it's where you've been."

"What's been happening? What day is today?"

"I thought you'd left me." Her smile grew bigger and bigger.

"What do you mean? I'll always be with you." He gave her a quick hug.

He didn't seem to realize he'd been in another world. She was quiet, tears trickling down her cheeks, welcoming him back with a pat on the shoulder and a tender squeeze. Finally, she said, "I thought you never were going to be yourself again. Why don't you give me a real hug?"

He swooped her up and crushed her hard right up against him.

She held him just as tight and kissed him on his bristly cheek.

"I was outside with Billie, when all at once it came to me that I was thinking straighter," he told her with his familiar cockeyed grin. "I knew what I was doing, feeding the little bird. Billie acted so pleased I was talking with her. She said I'd been kind of confused and that you were worried. I was so happy to see you, with the bingo, still taking care of business here at Whispering Pines."

She asked him if he remembered what had happened.

"I think so."

She walked him through it anyway, step by step. Tony and Laura saving their lives, Jiggs' life too; his wandering away while at home; coming here for rehab. "You've not been yourself," she stammered, "for two months, over a month of it here at Whispering Pines."

He shook his head, amazed. "I remember," he said, frowning. "We went to bed and were overcome by furnace fumes."

She nodded. He'd got it right. "I'd about given up." Dixie burst into tears again. "Tony's been taking care of the yard."

"I can't wait to see it. I can't wait to get home." He gently wiped away her tears with his hand.

She dimly realized that a small crowd, residents and staff alike, had stopped to watch, and they were grinning. The bingo players too had gathered, looking on with melting eyes and tender smiles. Beth came up to them, giving her and Morgan each a hug, whispering in Dixie's ear, "A lucky day. A day to remember."

Dixie glanced at the calendar that hung on the wall outside the dining room. Only then did it dawn on her the date was doubly lucky. "Do you know what day it is?" she almost shrieked.

Morgan gave her a quizzical look.

"July seventh. Our first anniversary. The day you bumped into me."

"Oh, no," his eyes twinkled, "you bumped into me."

"I thought you were an oaf," she grinned.

"I thought you were a witch." They were nose-to-nose.

"So much for first impressions." She kissed him, and soon they were in another clinch, oblivious to walkers and dawdlers, sightseers and well-wishers, the bored, the restless, the prurient.

That night, Dixie, still on cloud nine, called Tony, Vera, and Nate. She was on the phone for hours.

She came down to earth hard just before bed, when she picked up the paper to read the front page. Whole letters as well as parts of letters were missing in some words. She realized with growing dread that the black spots weren't floaters. She remembered residents at Whispering Pines with these exact symptoms.

Her double-lucky day flipped back to a single, her bad luck wiping out one of the good ones.

She'd gotten what she wanted, Morgan restored. Morgan, the love of her life. It looked like she'd have to give something back as an offering.

45

We Can't Put It Off

"You're a terrifyingly handsome sight," Dixie smiled as Morgan joined her at the breakfast table. He wore a dark-green knitted shirt tucked into his tan pants, the belt drawn tight, bunching the material into a loose bulge at the front. His cheekbones were more prominent. He'd lost weight. A few home-cooked meals would remedy that. Impulsively, she went to him, rubbing her cheek against his. "Smooth." He'd been back home a day, and she was still pinching herself.

"I feel better than I've felt for weeks." His eyes were clear and lively. "I got up this morning, took a shower, cleaned my teeth and shaved—got fixed up as if I was going to see my best girl. Then I came down here for breakfast with you." He winked. "Maybe we can get together later."

"Sounds good to me," she smiled. They ate breakfast, flirting blatantly. After the dishes were cleared, Dixie said, "How about a walk? Since you've been gone, the flowers have bloomed all over the neighborhood. The trees are green and leafy. Let's enjoy the morning before it gets too hot." She had several things on her mind. "Don't forget your cane!"

He gave her a rueful smile and unhooked it from the banister.

They strolled down the driveway arm in arm. Dixie was pleased to note that Morgan walked at a sprightly pace. He picked up his feet instead of shuffling like he did before. The therapy team had kept him another week after that awful and wonderful day, July seventh, when he had his breakthrough, when the synapses in his brain ignited. Rehab had done memory tests and word games, had walked him through the halls till he was ready to drop, and finally concluded, though not yet one hundred percent, he was well enough to come home. "How do you like the way Tony's kept the yard up for us?"

He stopped and looked around. "The grass is perfect. Not too short, not too long. I see he dug out the weeds from the flowers along the drive. Let me take a peek at the back." They went around the side of the house, through the gate, and into the yard.

He carefully examined the rose bushes, the flowerbeds, and the shrubs. "Almost as good as I could have done myself," he finally nodded, breaking into a smile.

They returned to the front and started their tour of the neighborhood. A half-block away, the mailman passed them, pushing his cart. "Good to have you back," he smiled at Morgan.

"Thanks." Morgan whispered to Dixie, "How did he know I was away?"

"I told him." She'd told everyone who would listen. "He signed your get-well card." She almost said, "Remember?" but stopped herself in time.

They strolled along, admiring the beautiful lawns. Red, white, pink, and purple impatiens bordered the porch of one home. At another, a trellis of deep-red roses added splashes of color. The day was so beautiful, the mood so tranquil, she hated to spoil it. "Look at that basket with the cascading petunias," Dixie cried. "I'd love one just like it, hanging on our porch." In the next breath, she blurted out, "We can't put it off any longer."

"Put what off?"

"How we're going to handle our future. We both could have been disabled for good. It's given me quite a scare." She was still coming to terms with her own news from the eye doctor. "When you're ill, it's hard for me to take care of you. And if I get ill—" she paused. Should she tell him now? "You won't be able to do everything," she stumbled.

"Well, I don't see the reason for any rush," Morgan frowned.

It was as if he'd forgotten the trauma of the last two months. Well, she hadn't.

When they reached the playground, they sat on a bench, watching the children climb and swing and slide, their gleeful cries filling the air.

"Should we think about moving into a smaller home?" Dixie ventured, hurrying on before she lost her courage. "Maybe even independent living at a retirement center? I know this was something we vowed to avoid."

He looked at her aghast.

"So we wait for another emergency?" Her voice sounded sharper than she'd meant it to.

"Why would we move?" he blustered. "The mortgage is almost paid off, we have our joint funds—"

She'd remind him. "I had to cash in your CD while you were sick."

His eyes were horrified. He'd forgotten he'd given her permission.

"I only had to use a little of it, thank the Lord. For about three weeks. What Medicare didn't cover."

"Okay, we have most of our funds," he said, off-stride, looking perplexed, as if he'd lost the thread. "We get along together. I love you and I think," his worried eyes latched onto hers, "you like me well enough."

She gave his arm a shake. He thought she was giving him the bum's rush.

"What do you mean?" she looked deep into his eyes, their noses almost touching. "I love you."

"I want to be at your side the rest of our lives," Morgan said passionately. "I want to be your helpmate, your friend, your lover."

"We'd still be together if we moved."

Morgan stared straight ahead, his jaw set.

"What if you have another event? You're still having problems." And she'd have problems sooner than she wanted.

"I use my cane, but I'm walking almost as well as I used to," he flared.

And the memory lapses? Well, she wouldn't go into that. "If we stay here, we're going to have to get some help sooner or later." Why was it so hard to tell him? Probably because she couldn't believe it herself. She took the plunge. "I have macular degeneration, the wet kind, in my right eye. It can be slowed by laser surgery." She knew from the residents at Whispering Pines that sight could go quickly, despite laser treatments. "In my left eye, I have dry macular degeneration. It's slower, but it can turn into the wet kind, just like that." She snapped her fingers. "I could be blind in a year."

"Oh, my God," he sighed. "My sweet Dixie. How awful." He put his arm around her. "Why didn't you tell me?"

"I just found out three days ago." She swallowed hard and put on a stoic face for Morgan.

He took her hand. "Maybe you should quit your job. We could take some trips, while we're able to. I've heard Hawaii's beautiful."

She gave a short laugh. "As if we need more debt. I like to work, to feel I'm making a difference." She watched three boys—they looked to be seven or eight—shooting baskets. They were yelling and hopping around, arguing and laughing. They made her smile. Neither Morgan nor she wanted to move from their lovely home. She had another card up her sleeve. "Tony's offered to help us."

"That's great. I like the work he does in the yard—"

"It might be a godsend to have Tony to move in with us," she said in a rush. "For him and us both. He'd be close to his work, close to campus, close to Laura."

Morgan was silent.

"He saved our lives."

Morgan nodded bleakly.

"When you were roaming the neighborhood, out of your mind, I was worried sick you'd be hit by a car and no one would know who you were. Tony helped me find you. He's growing up. He's accepting his role in life," Dixie said softly.

Morgan nodded and was quiet for awhile. "Let's ask him," he said at last, "what he thinks when he comes over this afternoon."

They left the playground, crossed the street, and rounded the corner, passing larger, more expensive homes, all beautifully landscaped. In the middle of a footbridge, they stopped to gaze down into a small ravine. A thin, clear stream of water trickled over rocks. Dixie closed her eyes, soothed by the sound.

"I hoped we'd both stay healthy and independent right up to the last and then we'd just depart—for other realms. But it doesn't work that way, does it?" Morgan asked with a crooked grin. They backtracked to their street and, hand in hand, returned the way they'd come. "Welcome back," said a man who dug weeds beside his driveway. A woman who watered the lawn waved. "Looking good, Morgan."

He turned to Dixie, amazed. "I don't know these people. They don't even live on our block, but they seem to know me."

"You're famous! Look, Morgan!" Dixie pointed to a home whose porch was enclosed with honeysuckle. "Don't you just love the smell?"

She breathed in deeply. "Why don't we plant some in the backyard for next year?"

"Why not?" He cracked a grin. "Tony could help." They ambled on without talking. "If Tony did move in," he mused, as they reached the corner of their block, "he'd have a base of operations, and a chance to prepare for a home of his own. He'd learn about maintenance and how to do household chores."

Dixie nodded. It would be a learning experience for them all.

Morgan chuckled. "You might even bring the job jar out of retirement."

When they reached their driveway, Pauline waved from her front porch and headed their way. "You're looking bright as a button." She gave Morgan a hug. The man across the street called out, "Hi, neighbors."

"Before I forget," Dixie announced when they were back inside the house, "we need to plan on going to church tomorrow."

"Oh, no, my first Sunday back?" he groaned.

"We have a few miracles to give thanks for. We're alive, Tony and Laura came into our lives, and you're out of Whispering Pines."

"Miracles?" He laughed good-naturedly. "Or luck?"

She gave him a mock stern look. "I'm not in the mood to argue."

"Neither am I." He held her close. "When's Tony coming?" he murmured.

"Not till three."

"I think we have a date in the upstairs bedroom."

She took his arm. "Me and my favorite infidel."

⚶

Tony couldn't wait to share his news. He parked his scooter on the porch and jabbed at the bell. Morgan opened the door, Dixie at his side. Tony burst out, "I know how much you both like Laura. I want you to know we're very serious about getting married."

Morgan and Dixie turned to each other. "When?"

They looked so solemn, Tony thought. Weren't they pleased? "A few months, maybe a year. I'm saving for an engagement ring." He tore off his helmet, his elbow- and knee/pads and threw them into the corner of the stairwell.

"Come into the kitchen," Dixie said. "Have some iced tea. We have some news too."

Tony followed Dixie, wriggling out of his backpack. He sat down at the table, stashing his bag on the floor beside him. He searched his grandpa's face. Was he sick again?

Morgan, across from him, cleared his throat. "We've just been talking about what a help you've been to Dixie while I was out of commission."

Tony smiled. Hey, it was cool to be appreciated. "No problem."

Dixie poured him a glass of tea and dropped in ice cubes.

His grandpa frowned and took a deep breath. "We know you're looking to move out of the Y, closer to school. What would you think about moving in with us?"

Dixie, standing beside him, nodded.

Tony was speechless.

"Whatever's best for you is fine with us," his grandpa added awkwardly.

"Wow! I mean I don't know what to say." Places near campus were expensive. He'd have to share digs with guys he didn't know. "You mean move in—like now?"

"Room and board free," Dixie said. "You'd have to help Morgan with the yard and help keep the place up."

Room and board free! Was he dreaming?

"Take your time. Think it over," Morgan mumbled, looking embarrassed. "But if you're planning to get married, you'll need that extra cash."

Free room and board could save him a bundle. He could buy a fancy engagement ring for Laura. A wedding ring too. He was getting excited about the idea.

"Why don't you and Laura come over tomorrow for dinner, about five?" Dixie suggested. "We can talk more about it."

"Okay," Tony said, still feeling dazed. How would they all get along together? Well, it was a big house. He liked working in the yard. He liked being here. It felt comfortable, like family. He pulled a textbook and a sheaf of papers out of his backpack. "Hey, Grandpa. I'm kind of stuck. Can you help me out with my homework?"

Morgan took the book from him, his face lighting up. "Beginning accounting. Well, well. Come over here and sit beside me."

๑๖๑

"Did Tony tell you?" Dixie asked Laura over dinner the following day. She'd hoped Morgan or Tony would bring it up, but they both seemed tongue-tied. It was up to her. "We asked him if he'd like to move in with us."

Laura turned to Tony, her dimple flickering in her cheek. "He told me."

"Yeah," Tony said thoughtfully. He scratched his head and opened his mouth to speak.

What had he decided? Dixie held her breath and said a silent prayer.

He grinned. "I think it'll work out just fine."

"Well," Morgan said, glowing, "that's great."

"Maybe I'll bring my stuff over at the end of summer term, if that's okay. About two weeks?"

Dixie felt like jumping up and down. "Sounds good." Two weeks would give her time to look for new drapes for the spare room, and clean out the closet and the chest of drawers.

The others talked on about this and that. Dixie was silent, her mind racing. As Tony and Morgan sat finishing their iced tea, she and Laura cleared the table. "I hope you don't think I'm butting in," Dixie purred. "Tony told us he's saving for an engagement ring."

Laura nodded, her cheeks pink. "We haven't set a date. Mom wants us to wait until after we graduate." She made a face. "But we want to be together now."

"Your mother has a point," Dixie murmured. They were just children. "It's a hard life, working and studying, making ends meet." Kids were so starry-eyed. Just as well, or they wouldn't have the nerve to do anything. "If you got married now, where would you live? How would you make it?"

Tony finished his iced tea and stood. "We can find a place near campus."

"I'll graduate in three years. I can support Tony while he finishes," Laura said.

Tony carried his empty plate over to the sink. "We could just shack up together." He slung his arm over Laura's shoulder. "But her mom doesn't buy that."

"I don't blame her," Morgan said sternly.

Laura played with Tony's hand. "We hashed out all the pros and cons."

"What about you two?" Tony teased.

"What about us?" Morgan took a cookie from the platter on the table.

"Have you ever thought of getting hitched?"

Dixie's eyes lit up. She smiled at Morgan to show him she thought the idea was well worth discussing.

Morgan put the cookie down and hemmed and hawed. "You're both starting a journey through life." He pulled at his chin. "We're at the end of ours. It's appropriate that you get married and assume legal responsibilities."

Tony and Laura looked secretly amused. Dixie had the feeling they were thinking, 'hypocritical adults.'

After the two left, Dixie drifted over to sit on Morgan's lap. "What about it?"

Morgan growled, "What about what?"

"Maybe it's time you made an honest woman of me."

"Are you proposing to me?" Morgan chuckled. He kissed her. Then he gave her a long, hard look. "There'll be financial implications."

"I know."

"I vowed I'd never marry again."

"I'm sure." He looked bemused, Dixie thought, but he hadn't said no.

Later, in bed, she sighed, "You know, there's really room here for them both."

"What are you talking about?"

"After they get married. Our home is surely better than a cramped, overpriced apartment near the campus."

"Now hold your horses. They'd want their privacy. So would we."

She continued smoothly. "The spare room has a double bed, big enough for two. They could have the free run of the kitchen and the yard. You offered your car to Tony for a dollar."

"You're kidding!"

"Well, the offer was made when you weren't yourself."

Morgan grunted. He twisted and flopped around for awhile. Then he was quiet. She thought he'd fallen asleep when he murmured, "If they moved in with us," he paused, "essentially they'd be starting out with what their parents had after several years of work. I hope they'll appreciate that fact."

"If they don't," Dixie said, laughing, "we'll remind them." Then she continued, "Your old bedroom, the middle room, would be perfect for a child. And there's the playground nearby. We could put up a swing set in the backyard."

"Dixie," Morgan asked in a muffled voice, "are you sure we're up to this?"

"Oh, yes." She'd be a terrific great-grandmother. Her heart was singing.

EPILOGUE

Five Months Later
Christmas Joy

Dixie raised her face to the church ceiling and said a silent thank you. She felt like doing handsprings down the aisle. She almost laughed out loud at the thought of her in her blue gown, flopping like a fish, everyone thinking she'd lost it, Morgan understanding perfectly. "Oh, Dixie," he'd say, grinning, "You're so unpredictable."

He did look handsome in his light-gray tux, holding his silver-knobbed cane, a gift from her. The Reverend Carmichael from her church was presiding. Morgan had been sure he'd expect favors from them in return, like showing up at services every Sunday from now on. Tony, on Reverend Carmichael's left, was movie-star handsome in his gray-blue tux, but looked as if he might pass out. Behind them, a beautiful Christmas tree adorned the sanctuary. Tiny white Christmas lights and white tulle decorated each pew, a glittering of stars showing the way.

The organist began a joyous "Wedding March," the chords bouncing off the ceiling. Dixie felt the goose bumps rise. In front of her, Vera and Millie, matron and maid of honor, took their first steps. Dixie clutched Nate's left arm. Laura was on his right. The three, bunched together, were poised to launch themselves forward. She felt Nate's arm tense. The march began. Laura's and her full skirts made it a tight fit, but they squeezed through the aisle fine until Dixie's streaming veil snagged on a

413

Christmas light halfway down. She hardly faltered as she freed it. She thanked the Lord she'd secured her wig with extra bobby pins.

The church was packed. Dixie tried to look straight ahead, but she needed to know who was here. She closed her right eye—it was so exasperating to look through the black spots—and glanced discreetly to her left and to her right. Every one of the bridge club was here with their spouses. The poker club, yes, they were all here too. Why, there was Officer Pfeiffer! He sat very straight, a proud smile on his face. She spotted a small group of colleagues, even a few residents from Whispering Pines. Two members of the therapy staff were here. They'd grown to know Morgan over the course of his rehab and had gotten a kick out of him. There was Mr. Miller, the postman. She'd invited him but she didn't think he'd come. She spotted Paul's bald head, and Barry with his wife. A few neighbors. Good! She'd gone door-to-door inviting them. Pauline, of course. And Dr. Durning, Morgan's doctor. Wasn't that nice?

The unfamiliar faces belonged to Laura's friends and Tony's coworkers at the accounting firm. Oh, there was Dorothy, Laura's mom. Dixie almost waved. She'd met her at the rehearsal dinner. She was almost as petite as Laura, and pretty too, with her ash-blonde bob. Probably her real hair.

What do you know? Now she was beside Morgan, facing the minister. She'd made it without stumbling over her long gown, losing her wig, or ripping her veil on a Christmas decoration. In fact, she'd felt as if she were flying, her feet about four inches off the ground.

Nate scrambled to his place beside Morgan. He'd be giving both brides away and doubling as best man for Morgan.

"We are gathered here to witness the marriages of Dixie Valentine and Bryce Morgan, of Laura Winters and Anthony Morgan." The minister turned to Dixie and Morgan. "You both bring passion, history, life, and love to this relationship." And to Tony and Laura, he said, "You both bring passion, youth, love, and promise to this relationship."

After the two couples exchanged vows, the minister blessed the rings. Morgan's eyes were darker than she'd ever seen them as he slid the ring on her finger. Then Dixie took his hand and slid a matching ring on his finger. His hand was almost as shaky as hers. The rings were gold, inscribed to each other, with the word *Always*.

The minister said, "I now pronounce you man and wife—Morgan

and Dixie, Tony and Laura. What God has joined together let no man put asunder. You may kiss your brides."

Morgan's lips were pressing against hers. She felt a sliver of regret. Why hadn't they met years ago? The children they might have had! She peeked around Morgan's shoulder. Tony and Laura were kissing, their arms wound tightly around each other. She hoped the kids would have a baby while Morgan was still around. She yearned for all the good things the future promised. She wanted to gulp it all down in chunks. She hoped there'd be time.

A triumphal "Hallelujah Chorus" shook the rafters. She and Morgan turned to leave. In the front pew sat Morgan's daughter Sara and Tony's mom Annabelle, surprise visitors from Chicago, here at her invitation. They were weeping. So were almost all the other guests. Come to think of it, she was too. She gave a quick look behind her. Laura, pale and beautiful, had tears shimmering in her blue eyes. Tony was leaning over her, whispering in her ear. Or maybe he was kissing her. Dixie looked up at Morgan, whose eyes were bright. He said in a stage whisper, "Congratulations, Mrs. Morgan!"

ॐ

He was determined to get rid of his cane, although Dixie said he looked quite dashing with it. Everyone commented on the silver eagle handle. Dixie had said the look in the eagle's eye reminded her of him, of his determination to get better once he'd been released from Whispering Pines.

At any rate, he was glad to lean on the cane now, as he stood in the reception line for who knew how long. Dixie, beside him, still clutching her bouquet, asked, "Do you know why brides carry a bouquet when they get married?"

Her eyes glittered deep blue. Her cheeks were flushed. Her veil streamed out behind her. She looked like a million in her blonde wig and blue gown. "I have no idea," Morgan said.

"It started in the 1500s when people took a bath only once a year. Brides carried flowers to hide the smell."

Morgan chuckled. Dixie and her trivia! "Some things have changed for the best."

Flashbulbs popped. He felt like a celebrity. He shook hands with well-wishers as they streamed by. From across the room, a woman headed his way determinedly, as if she knew him. She wore a very expensive-looking cream suit. Tight grayish curls framed her intelligent face. She had dark-brown eyes and full lips. She was smiling at him. "Hello," he said uncertainly.

She threw her arms around him. "Congratulations." She pulled away, the smile still on her face, her eyes shining. "Dad."

Could it be? "Sara?"

She nodded. "Dixie picked us up at the airport this morning."

"Our big secret," Dixie chortled.

"Why," Morgan stared at his daughter, trying to reconcile his memory of her at 14 with the woman standing in front of him, "you've turned gray."

"So have you," Sara laughed.

She nudged another woman forward. "This is Annabelle, Tony's mom. I talked her into coming."

"Well, hello." Morgan shook the hand of a faded, rather pretty woman. Had the years with Clay, his son, washed her out? Or her life now with Tony's stepdad? "You have a fine boy, Annabelle. First in his class. A rarity."

"He is," she answered, as if she only just now realized it.

"Mom." Tony suddenly appeared, crushing her in a hug. "I couldn't believe my eyes when I saw you and Aunt Sara in the church." The smile faded. "Where's Fulkerson?"

She shook her head. "Not here."

"Is everything okay?" His eyes were troubled.

She nodded.

"Come meet Laura." He grabbed her hand.

"Don't want to cause a traffic jam," Sara said to Morgan. "We'll get caught up later."

"I hope you brought pictures," Morgan called as the two women walked toward Laura.

"Most certainly," Sara answered.

Dixie gave him a smug look, obviously crowing to herself that she'd put one over on him. "Terrific wedding present," Morgan said. He had a surprise for her too, a two-week trip to Hawaii with a cruise around the islands. He'd talked Vera and Paul into going with them. They'd take the trip next May, a more elaborate honeymoon—delayed. He'd use some of the remaining money from his CD and reinvest the rest.

He felt tense about spending it, but he felt the cold breath of time on his neck. The laser treatments on Dixie's right eye were working for now. He'd been getting stronger every day. Life was to live. As far as money, well, there'd be something extra for Dixie from his life-insurance policy.

Nate and his barbershop group, the Royal Flush, had changed into Dickens' costumes, with ascot ties and Victorian top hats, and sang a stirring rendition of "Anniversary Waltz." The two couples gathered at the cake, a three-tiered coconut butter-cream decorated with fresh holly leaves. Dixie cut the first slice and stuffed it, sticky and gooey, into Morgan's open mouth. He looked into her eyes and knew she was remembering their first meeting and the one-hundredth-year birthday cake that had changed their lives.

The Royal Flush followed with "Love is a Many-Splendored Thing," "To Each His Own," and finished up with "We Wish you a Merry Christmas," doffing their hats at their finale. Then the boyfriend of Laura's roommate Millie stepped in as DJ, with recorded music for the younger set. "'It's Your Love,'" he announced, "sung by Tim McGraw."

When it was time to toss the bouquets, jolly sounds of "Girls Just Want to Have Fun" rang out. The brides stood side by side. With both hands, Dixie held her bouquet over her head like a victorious prize fighter. Laura wound up, ready to pitch her roses, white with red-tipped petals. The skirt of her gown, a white, lacy, three-tiered affair, swung and rippled.

Women residents from Whispering Pines—they looked to be in their eighties—jockeyed for a good position, determined to catch a bouquet. With a squeal, Kate, another of Laura's roommates, caught Laura's roses. Laura's mom jumped into the air and snagged Dixie's grape hyacinths and white sweet peas, tied with a blue satin ribbon.

Laura rushed over to her blushing mother and hugged her.

Cute lady, Morgan thought, lively and small, just like Laura. Morgan took Nate by the arm, dragging him over to meet her. "Dorothy, meet Nate." As Morgan walked away, pretending to be needed elsewhere, he heard Dorothy compliment Nate on his singing. Oh, boy, Morgan chuckled to himself, was she going to get an earful.

❦

"Hello, beautiful," Tony said softly, coming up behind Laura, slipping his arms over her bare ones. "Don't I know you?" He nuzzled the nape of her neck. Her wedding gown lay across the bed in the spare room, formerly his room, now theirs to share as long as they wanted. He zipped up her dress, she straightened his collar and tie, and, holding hands, they hurried down the stairs.

They headed toward the sounds of laughter and chatter in the dining room. Tony nudged Laura and pointed. Christmas stockings, one for each, Laura, Tony, Dixie, and Morgan, lettered in red sequins, hung from a living-room table that also held a manger scene. Laura smiled her beautiful smile. "Leave it to Dixie!"

Something brushed his leg. Tony looked down. "Hi, old buddy!" The little dog wore a big green Christmas bow around his neck. "Jiggs looks bummed out," he whispered to Laura. With a shh, he bent down and removed the bow. Like a jack-in-the-box, Jiggs sprang up happily against them, his tail wagging.

They entered the dining room, passing under mistletoe sprigs and silver, white, and gold balloons. "So beautiful," Laura cried. A wreath centerpiece, entwined with small, sparkling Christmas lights decorated the center of the table, with tall lighted candles in silver holders on either side.

Tony and Laura squeezed in at the table, between his mom and Laura's mom.

After the catered dinner of shrimp scampi and wild rice, after the champagne toasts with Dixie's best crystal goblets, the speeches came from everyone, including Tony's mom, who stood shyly, and said in her soft voice, "I love you, Tony. I couldn't be happier for you." Tony felt blown away. As he finished dessert, he caught the eye of Laura's mom, seated next to the tall singer with the floppy mustache. She looked like she was having fun.

His aunt Sara was showing his grandpa photographs of the family. "Clay, Evelyn," he heard Sara say. "And this is Mom, just before she got sick."

"Still a handsome woman," Morgan murmured, passing the pictures on to Dixie. Across the table, Millie and her boyfriend were jabbering to each other, not looking left out at all.

Then it was time to leave. After hugs and kisses, Tony shepherded Laura out the front door, through a shower of snowflake confetti and cries of "have fun" and "be careful." The couple hurried down the drive to the car, which Tony had bought from Morgan for a dollar. "Oh, no," Laura laughed. Old shoes hung from the handle of the rear door, JUST MARRIED painted on the window above.

Tony started the motor. "I've never skied before." Laura's mom had given them a ski trip to northern Ohio.

"Me either," Laura answered.

"I don't think we'll be outdoors all that much," Tony said with a mischievous grin.

⁂

Morgan watched them back down the drive. The motor sounded smooth. He was glad he'd paid for a tune-up.

Then Vera ordered, "You two. It's time," even though the guests were still milling about. Dixie and Morgan brought their overnight bags down from the bedroom. "Don't you worry," Vera said, with a nod at Paul. "We'll take care of everything, including Jiggs."

Dixie swooped the little dog up and gave him a snuggle. "We'll be back in two days, darling." Amid a flurry of hugs, kisses, and promises to the out-of-towners for future get-togethers, Morgan and Dixie were swept out the door in a cloud of snowflake confetti too. A limousine whisked them to their hotel.

In their honeymoon suite, they made a quick tour, holding hands and laughing at the heart-shaped bathtub. Morgan turned the lights off and the radio on. "Come over here, Dixie," he said. They stood side by side at the tall window. As far as they could see, downtown Columbus was lit up with Christmas lights that glittered like jewels, red and green, yellow, white, and blue.

"It Was a Very Good Year" by Frank Sinatra played softly in the background.

Morgan took Dixie's hand. "May I have this dance?" He pulled her close and slowly they turned, circling the room.

Reading Group Guide

1. Here in an aging America—unlike so many other cultures—we have a love affair with youth. Our television commercials, magazine ads, and even most television shows are geared to the younger, beautiful people. Instead of being overlooked, how could the contributions of our older generations be acknowledged and used to benefit society?

2. In the novel, Dixie is 79 and Morgan is 89. How realistic is it to expect to fall in love at that age? Discuss the complications of romance and marriage at this stage in life. Also talk about the advantages.

3. Dixie would possibly like a relationship but does not want to turn into a caregiver. Do you think she is selfish? Would you take the kind of risk she takes by inviting Morgan into her life? Discuss your thoughts about whether women manage being alone better than men do.

4. Although the novel explores problems related to aging, it also explores relationships, motivations, and needs of human beings at every age. How does your view of Tony change as the novel progresses?

5. Dixie has concerns regarding Morgan's past. Is she right to be worried? Tony has been led to believe that Morgan is wealthy. Had Morgan been treated fairly by his family? Did he create some of his own problems?

6. Dixie is afraid Morgan will be repulsed by her body and Morgan is afraid he might not be able to perform. Discuss the nature—and truth—in these fears. Do we all have young minds in aging bodies? Discuss your thoughts on sexuality as life progresses into the later years.

7. There are many new challenges that surface as we age. In the story, Dixie struggles to keep her house up and is considering taking in a

boarder. For retirees, finances can be a huge issue even with the best of planning. The thought of not being able to drive and losing independence is painful. The decision to consider a move to a retirement home means giving up privacy and independence for the rest of life. The novel also touches on end-of-life choices. How do we prepare to face these difficult decisions? Discuss others you know who have helped determine what you'd do—and what you wouldn't do.

8. What does the novel suggest about the importance of stability in family life? How has lack of it affected Dixie? Morgan? Tony?

9. How important are the following people to Tony and how do they influence his outlook and attitude? His father, his stepfather, Eddie, Officer Pfeiffer, Dixie, Morgan, Laura. How important is Tony to Dixie? to Morgan?

10. As the novel progresses, the reader sees change and growth occurring in Morgan, Dixie, and Tony. What events seem to most influence growth and change in Morgan? Dixie? Tony?

11. After the accident, Morgan's recovery is slow—in part due to his age. Dixie ends up being the caregiver after all and cannot go to her job even though she has bills to pay and needs the money. Morgan ends up in Whispering Pines Nursing Home and Dixie must face the cold hard facts of Medicare and Medicaid and the sad cost of being old and sick in America. Are there solutions to these problems? Do you have hope that they'll be implemented for your benefit?

12. Morgan thinks to himself, "Who would ever believe the best thing that ever happened to me happened at age 90!" Do you think the same is possible in your own life?

13. The author, Mardo Williams, wrote his first novel at age 92. He suggests we live life every minute and always be in search of new experiences regardless of age. Discuss the title of the book and how it fits the story. How did the novel influence your thoughts and expectations for the future?

DATE DUE

NOV 2 1 2007			

#47-0108 Peel Off Pressure Sensitive